P9-CCY-584

Dark Encounter

"I am *not* a leopard," he said into her ear, and the sound was so rough she wondered if he'd come back fully from the animal.

"Oh." Her mistake was no surprise—she knew less than nothing about the reality of changelings. Her world had never been one where they intruded. "I apologize for offending you."

"Aren't you curious what I am?"

"Yes." She was also curious about his human face. "Can I turn around?"

His soft chuckle vibrated along her body and demanded her complete attention. "It's not that dark, Red— I didn't have any clothes with me."

It took a few moments for her brain to work through that statement. The second she did, she became hyperconscious of the sheer heat of the body aligned so closely to her own. The part of her that craved new experiences wanted to turn, but she knew that would be sheer foolishness. This man was hardly likely to indulge her intellectual curiosity about his body. He'd almost bitten off her head for daring to call him the wrong species.

"Please let go."

"No."

The flat no took her by surprise. Nobody said no to her, not like that. They always tried to couch it in more polite terms. That treatment may have kept her cooperative and rational, but it had also left her no tools with which to deal with the hard reality of a world where people didn't follow the accepted rules of behavior. "Why?"

"Why not?"

Berkley Sensation Titles by Nalini Singh

SLAVE TO SENSATION
VISIONS OF HEAT
CARESSED BY ICE
MINE TO POSSESS

Visions of Heat

NALINI SINGH

BERKLEY SENSATION, NEW YORK

THE BERKLEY PUBLISHING GROUP
Published by the Penguin Group
Penguin Group (USA) Inc.
375 Hudson Street, New York, New York 10014, USA
Penguin Group (Canada), 90 Eglinton Avenue East, Suite 700, Toronto, Ontario M4P 2Y3, Canada
(a division of Pearson Penguin Canada Inc.)
Penguin Books Ltd., 80 Strand, London WC2R 0RL, England
Penguin Group Ireland, 25 St. Stephen's Green, Dublin 2, Ireland (a division of Penguin Books Ltd.)
Penguin Group (Australia), 250 Camberwell Road, Camberwell, Victoria 3124, Australia
(a division of Pearson Australia Group Pty. Ltd.)
Penguin Books India Pvt. Ltd., 11 Community Centre, Panchsheel Park, New Delhi—110 017, India
Penguin Group (NZ), 67 Apollo Drive, Mairangi Bay, Auckland 1311, New Zealand
(a division of Pearson New Zealand Ltd.)
Penguin Books (South Africa) (Pty.) Ltd., 24 Sturdee Avenue, Rosebank, Johannesburg 2196,
South Africa

Penguin Books Ltd., Registered Offices: 80 Strand, London WC2R 0RL, England

This is a work of fiction. Names, characters, places, and incidents either are the product of the author's imagination or are used fictitiously, and any resemblance to actual persons, living or dead, business establishments, events, or locales is entirely coincidental. The publisher does not have any control over and does not assume any responsibility for author or third-party websites or their content.

VISIONS OF HEAT

A Berkley Sensation Book / published by arrangement with the author

PRINTING HISTORY
Berkley Sensation mass-market edition / March 2007

Copyright © 2007 by Nalini Singh.
Excerpt from *Caressed by Ice* copyright © 2007 by Nalini Singh.
Cover art by Phil Heffernan.
Cover design by George Long.
Hand lettering by Ron Zinn.
Interior text design by Stacy Irwin.

All rights reserved.
No part of this book may be reproduced, scanned, or distributed in any printed or electronic form without permission. Please do not participate in or encourage piracy of copyrighted materials in violation of the author's rights. Purchase only authorized editions.
For information, address: The Berkley Publishing Group,
a division of Penguin Group (USA) Inc.,
375 Hudson Street, New York, New York 10014.

ISBN: 978-0-425-21575-3

BERKLEY SENSATION®
Berkley Sensation Books are published by The Berkley Publishing Group,
a division of Penguin Group (USA) Inc.,
375 Hudson Street, New York, New York 10014.
BERKLEY SENSATION is a registered trademark of Penguin Group (USA) Inc.
The "B" design is a trademark belonging to Penguin Group (USA) Inc.

PRINTED IN THE UNITED STATES OF AMERICA

10 9 8 7 6 5

If you purchased this book without a cover, you should be aware that this book is stolen property. It was reported as "unsold and destroyed" to the publisher, and neither the author nor the publisher has received any payment for this "stripped book."

This one's for my Mum, Usha,
the most extraordinary woman I know.
With love.

MADNESS

Clinical insanity.

The number one cause of death for F-Psy before Silence.

Death by insanity? For the F-Psy, it was very much a harsh reality. They became lost in the visions of the future their minds created—so lost that they forgot to eat, forgot to drink, and, in extreme cases, forgot to make their hearts beat. The Psy are their minds, and once those minds are lost, their bodies can no longer function.

But the dead were the fortunate ones. Those who broke under the pressure of the visions and yet survived were no longer sentient, no longer anything close to sentient, their minds locked in a world where the past, present, and future clashed and splintered over and over. As time fractured, so did they.

Surprisingly, the F-Psy were divided about the implementation of the Silence Protocol. Some thought it would be a precious gift to feel no emotion, for then they'd be safe from the threat of insanity, safe from the hideous illusions of their minds . . . *safe*. But there were others who saw Silence as an act of betrayal against their very gifts. The F-Psy had stopped countless massacres, saved countless lives, done endless good, but they had done it all with emotion. Without emotion, their abilities would be controllable, but crippled.

It took ten years, but the proponents of Silence won the mental battle raged across the millions of minds in the PsyNet. As a result, the F-Psy stopped foreseeing the human darkness of the future and withdrew into the sheltered walls of the business world. Instead of the saviors of innocents, they became the most powerful tools of many a Psy enterprise. The Psy Council declared their services too valuable to share with the other races and gradually, the F-Psy disappeared from public view.

It is said they prefer to remain out of the limelight.

What very few know, what the Council has hidden for over a century, is that though they are wealthy and cosseted, the once-resilient F-Psy have become the most fragile of beings. Something about their ability to foresee the tangled threads of what could be leaves them unable to function fully in the real world, necessitating constant surveillance and care.

The F-Psy rarely travel, rarely mingle, rarely function on any level aside from the mental. Some of them are close to mute, able to communicate their visions and only their visions, by scattered bursts of sound or, in severe cases, through diagram and gesture. The rest of the time, they remain locked in their Silent world.

Yet the Council says this is what they were meant to be.

CHAPTER 1

Faith NightStar of the PsyClan NightStar was aware she was considered the most powerful F-Psy of her generation. At only twenty-four years of age, she'd already made more money than most Psy did in their entire lifetimes. But then again, she'd been working since she was three years old, since she'd found her voice. It had taken her longer than most children, but that was to be expected—she was a cardinal F-Psy of extraordinary ability.

It would have surprised no one if she'd never spoken.

That was why the F-Psy belonged to PsyClans, which took care of everything the foreseers couldn't, from investing their millions to checking their medical status to ensuring they didn't starve. The F-Psy weren't very good at practical things like that. They forgot. Even after more than a century of forecasting business trends rather than murders and accidents, disasters and wars, they forgot.

Faith had been forgetting a lot of things lately. For example, she'd forgotten to eat three days in a row. That was when NightStar employees had intervened, alerted by the sophisticated Tec 3 computer that ran the house. Three days was the allowable window—sometimes F-Psy went into trances. If that had been the case, they would've put her on a drip and left her to it. "Thank you," she said, directing her words to the head M-Psy. "I'll be fine now."

Xi Yun nodded. "Finish the entire meal. It contains the exact number of calories you need."

"Of course." She watched him leave, preceded by his staff. In his hand was a small medical kit that she knew contained both chemicals designed to shock her awake out of a catatonic trance and ones to knock her down from a manic state. Neither had been required today. She'd simply forgotten to eat.

After consuming all the nutritional bars and energy drinks he'd left behind, she sat back down in the large reclining chair where she usually spent the majority of her time. Designed to double as a bed, it was uplinked to the Tec 3 and fed it a constant stream of data about her vital functions. An M-Psy stood on alert should she need medical attention any time of day or night. That wasn't normal procedure even for the F designation, but Faith was no ordinary F-Psy.

She was the best.

Every prediction Faith ever made, if not purposefully circumvented, came true. That was why she was worth untold millions. Possibly even billions. NightStar considered her its most prized asset. Like any asset, she was kept in the best condition for optimum functionality. And like any asset, should she prove defective, she'd be overhauled and used for parts.

Faith's eyes blinked open at that furtive thought. She stared up at the pale green of the ceiling and fought to bring her heart rate down. If she didn't, the M-Psy might decide to pay her a return visit and she didn't want anyone to see her right now. She wasn't sure what her eyes would reveal. Sometimes, even the night-sky eyes of a cardinal Psy told secrets that were better kept within.

"Parts," she whispered out loud. Her statement was being

recorded, of course. The F-Psy occasionally made predictions during trance states. No one wanted to miss a word. Perhaps that was why those of her designation preferred to keep their silence when they could.

Used for parts.

It seemed an illogical statement, but the more she thought about it, the more she realized that once again her abilities had told her of a future she could never have imagined. Most defective Psy were rehabilitated, their minds swept clean by a psychic brainwipe that left them functioning on the level of menial laborers, but not the F-Psy. They were too rare, too valuable, too unique.

If she went insane beyond acceptable levels, the levels where she could still make predictions, the M-Psy would see to it that she met with an accident that left her brain unharmed. And then they'd use that flawed brain for scientific experimentation, subject it to analysis. Everyone wanted to know what made the F-Psy tick. Of all the Psy designations, they were the least explored, the most shadowed—it was difficult to find experimental subjects when their occurrence in the population was barely above one percent.

Faith dug her hands into the thick red fabric of the chair, hyperaware of her breath beginning to grow jagged. The reaction hadn't yet proceeded to a point where M-Psy intervention would be deemed necessary, as F-Psy displayed some unusual behavior during visions, but she couldn't chance her overload turning into a mental cascade.

Even as she attempted to temper her physical body, her mind flashed with images of her brain on a set of scientific scales while cold Psy eyes examined it from every angle. She knew the images were nonsensical. Nothing like that would ever happen in a lab. Her consciousness was simply trying to make sense of something that made no sense. Just like the dreams that had been plaguing her sleep for the past two weeks.

At first, it had been nothing more than a vague foreshadowing, a darkness that pushed at her mind. She'd thought it might herald an oncoming vision—a market crash or a sudden business failure—but day after day, that darkness had grown to crushing proportions without showing her anything concrete. And she'd *felt*. Though she'd never before felt anything, in those dreams she'd been drenched in fear, suffocated by the weight of terror.

It was as well that she'd long ago demanded her bedroom be free of any and all monitoring devices. Something in her had known what was coming. Something in her always knew. But this time, she hadn't been able to make sense of the raw ugliness of a rage that had almost cut off her breath. The first dreams had felt like someone was choking her, choking her until terror was all she was.

Last night had been different. Last night, she hadn't woken as the hands closed about her throat. No matter how hard she'd tried, she hadn't been able to break free of the horror, hadn't been able to anchor herself in reality.

Last night, she had died.

Vaughn D'Angelo jumped down from the branch he'd been padding along and landed gracefully on the forest floor. In the silvery light that had turned darkness into twilight, his orange-black coat should've shone like a spotlight, but he was invisible, a jaguar who knew how to use the shadows of the night to hide and conceal. No one ever saw Vaughn when he didn't want to be seen.

Above him the moon hung, a bright disk in the sky, visible even through the thick canopy. For long moments, he stood and watched it through the dark filigree of reaching branches. Both man and beast were drawn to the glimmering beauty, though neither could've said why. It didn't matter.

Tonight the jaguar was in charge and it simply accepted what the man would have been tempted to think about.

A whisper of scent in the breeze had him lifting his nose into the air. *Pack*. A second later, he identified the scent as that of Clay, one of the other sentinels. Then it was gone, as if the leopard male had realized Vaughn's prior claim to this range. Opening his mouth, Vaughn let out a soft growl and stretched his powerful feline body. His lethally sharp canines gleamed in the moonlight, but tonight he wasn't out to hunt and capture prey, to deliver merciful death with a single crushing bite.

Tonight, he wanted to run.

His loping gait could cover vast distances, and usually he preferred to run deep into the forests that sprawled over most of California. But today he found himself heading toward the populated lake city of Tahoe. It wasn't hard to walk among the humans and Psy even in his cat form. He wasn't a sentinel for show—he could infiltrate even the most well-guarded of citadels without giving himself away.

However, this time he didn't actually enter the city proper, drawn to something unexpected on the fringe of it. Set back only a few meters from the dark green spread of the forest, the small compound was protected by electrified fences and motion-sensor cameras, among other things. The house within was hidden behind several layers of vegetation and possibly another fence, but he knew it lay inside. What surprised him was that he smelled the metallic stink of the Psy around the entire compound.

Interesting.

The Psy preferred to live surrounded by skyscrapers and city, each adult in his or her own personal box. Yet deep within that compound was a Psy, and whoever that person was, he or she was being protected by others of their kind. Rarely did a non-Council Psy qualify for such a privilege.

Curiosity aroused, he prowled around the entire perimeter, out of range of the monitoring devices. It took him less than ten minutes to discover a way in—the Psy race's sense of arrogance had led them, once again, to disregard the animals with whom they shared the Earth.

Or perhaps, the man thought within the beast, the Psy just didn't understand the capabilities of the other races. To them, changelings and humans were nothing because they couldn't do the things the Psy could with their minds. They'd forgotten that it was the mind that moved the body, and animals were very, very good at using their bodies.

Climbing onto a tree branch that would lead him over the first fence and into the compound, the cat's heart beat in anticipation. But even the jaguar knew he couldn't do this. He had no reason to go in there and put himself in danger. Danger didn't bother either man or beast, but the cat's curiosity was held back by a deeper emotion—loyalty.

Vaughn was a DarkRiver sentinel and that duty overcame every other emotion, every other need. Later tonight, he was supposed to be guarding Sascha Duncan, his alpha's mate, while Lucas attended a meeting at the SnowDancer den. Vaughn knew Sascha had agreed to stay behind reluctantly and only because she'd known Lucas could travel faster without her. And Lucas had only gone because he trusted his sentinels to keep her safe.

With a last lingering look into the guarded compound, Vaughn backed down the branch, leaped to the ground, and started to head toward Lucas's lair. He hadn't forgotten and he hadn't given up. The mystery of a Psy living so close to changeling territory would be solved. No one escaped the jaguar once he was on their trail.

Faith stared out the kitchen window, and though only darkness looked back at her, she couldn't shake the feeling of being stalked. *Something very dangerous circled the fences that kept her isolated from the outside world.* Shivering, she wrapped her arms around herself. And froze. She was Psy—why was she reacting like this? Was it the dark visions? Were they affecting her mental shields? Dropping her arms through sheer strength of will, she went to turn from the window.

And found she couldn't.

Instead, she pressed forward, lifting one hand to press against the glass, as if to reach outside. *Outside.* It was a world she hardly knew. She'd always lived inside walls, had had to live inside them. On the outside, the threat of psychic disintegration was a continuous drumbeat in her head, a pounding echo she couldn't block. On the outside, emotions hit at her from every angle and she saw things that were inhuman and vicious and painful. On the outside, she was breakable. It was far safer to live behind walls.

But now the walls were cracking. Now things were getting in and she couldn't escape them. She knew that as certainly as she knew she couldn't escape whatever it was that prowled the edges of her property. The predator hunting her wouldn't rest until he had her in his claws. She should've been afraid. But she was Psy—she felt no fear. Except when she slept. That was when she felt so much, she worried that her PsyNet shields would crack, revealing her to the Council. It had gotten to the point where she didn't want to fall asleep. What if she died again, and this time it was for real?

The communication console chimed into the endless silence that was her life. This late at night, it was an unexpected interruption—the M-Psy had prescribed certain hours of sleep for her.

She looked away from the window at last. As she walked, a sense of impending disaster seemed to cloak her, a sinister knowing that lay somewhere in the shadowlands between a true foretelling and the merest inkling of what might be.

This, too, was new, this heavy awareness of something hovering maliciously in the wings, just waiting for her guard to slip.

Schooling her face to show nothing of her internal confusion, she pressed the answer key on the touch pad. The face that appeared on-screen was not one she'd anticipated. "Father."

Anthony Kyriakus was the head of her family. Until she'd officially reached adulthood at twenty, he'd shared custody of her with Zanna Liskowski, with whom he'd formed a fertilization contract twenty-five years ago. They'd both had a say in her upbringing, though her childhood had been nothing anyone would ever label as such. At three years after birth, she'd been removed from their care, with their full cooperation, and placed in a controlled environment where her ability could be fully trained and utilized.

And where the encroaching tendrils of madness could be kept at bay.

"Faith, I have some unfortunate news concerning our family."

"Yes?" Her heart was suddenly a sledgehammer. She pushed all her strength toward containing the reaction. Not only was it unusual, it was the harbinger of a potential vision. And she couldn't have a vision right now. Not the kind of vision she'd been having lately.

"Your sibling, Marine, is deceased."

Her mind went blank. "Marine?" Marine was her younger sister, a sister she'd never really known, but had kept an eye on from afar. A cardinal telepath, Marine had already climbed high in the family's interests. "How? Was it a physical abnormality?"

"Fortunately not."

Fortunately, because it meant Faith was in no danger. Though having two of the rare cardinals had made NightStar a line of considerable power, it was indisputable that Faith was the biggest NightStar asset. She was the one who brought in enough income and work to place the entire PsyClan above the masses. Only Faith's health was truly important— Marine's death was a mere inconvenience. So cold, so brutally cold, Faith thought, though she knew she was as cold. It was a matter of survival. "An accident?"

"She was murdered."

The blank that had been her mind buzzed with white noise, but she refused to listen. "Murder? A human or a changeling?" she asked, because the Psy had no killers, hadn't had them for a hundred years, ever since the implementation of the Silence Protocol. Silence had wiped violence, hate, rage, anger, jealousy, and envy from the Psy. The side effect had been the loss of all their other emotions.

"Of course, though we don't know which. Enforcement is investigating. Get some rest." He nodded in a sharp physical period.

"Wait."

"Yes?"

She forced herself to ask. "What was the mode of murder?"

Anthony didn't even blink as he said, "Manual strangulation."

CHAPTER 2

Vaughn jumped up onto the outer platform of the aerie Sascha shared with Lucas, having passed Mercy on her way down. He wasn't pleased to see Sascha outside—the platform might be high off the ground, but it was well past midnight and the Psy Council would like nothing better than to see this particular cardinal dead.

"Hello, Vaughn. Why don't you shift and keep me company?"

He let her know what he thought of that idea with a coughing roar unique to his species.

"Yes, I'm aware that I should be sleeping, but I can't." She leaned back in the chair she'd apparently dragged outside. "Mercy played chess with me." In the darkness, her night-sky eyes were lit with white pinpricks. Her fingers tapped constantly on the wooden arm of the chair.

Responding with a growl, Vaughn walked into the house. He shifted in the bedroom, then grabbed a pair of jeans and an old black T-shirt from the trunk where all the sentinels kept a change of clothes. When he walked back out, Sascha waved at the empty chair across the small folding table from her. He raised an eyebrow and perched instead on the railing that ringed the platform, hooking his legs around the posts.

"I'll never get used to the way you cats do that." Sascha shook her head and rubbed her bare feet on the wooden floor. "Do you realize you could fall and break every bone in your body?"

"Cats always land on their feet." Vaughn sniffed the night air and found everything as expected, but did a visual scan to confirm. Even in human form, his keen eyesight remained undiminished. "Are you always like this when Lucas is gone?" She seemed jumpy, agitated, though she was usually a calm pool in the midst of the predatory turbulence that was DarkRiver.

"Yes." She continued tapping her finger. "Were you running?"

"Yes." He looked at his alpha's mate, able to understand Lucas's fascination. Sascha was beautiful and utterly unique. It wasn't the night-sky eyes or the face, but the essence of her. She glowed from the inside out and that was to be expected. After all, she was an E-Psy—an empath, able to sense and heal the most damaging of emotional wounds.

But though he understood Lucas's fascination, Vaughn couldn't imagine feeling the same. Sascha was Pack. As a sentinel, he'd lay down his life for her, but he'd never have mated with her—because the concept of mating was alien to him. He didn't understand how the leopards could tie themselves to one person for the rest of their lives. It wasn't that he was promiscuous. He was very choosy about his lovers. But he liked his freedom, liked knowing that no one else was emotionally reliant on him.

His death wouldn't tear the soul out of anyone.

"I never know what you're thinking." Sascha stared at

him, tilting her head slightly to the side. "I'm not even sure you like me."

The cat enjoyed being seen as inscrutable. "You're Lucas's mate." And therefore had his loyalty.

"But what about me as an individual?" she persisted.

"Trust takes time." Though she'd earned a good chunk of it the day she'd almost died trying to save Lucas's life. The other male was the closest thing Vaughn had to true family, a blood brother in the most brutal sense.

"There's something about you—you're less . . . civilized than the others."

"Yes." There was no reason to deny it. He was far more animal than most predatory changelings, had had to become so to survive. As Sascha had had to become Pack. "Do you ever miss others like you?"

"Of course." She looked away and out into the forest, a lone Psy in a pack of leopards. "How can you not miss the world you lived in for twenty-six years?" Her eyes returned to him. "Do you?"

"I only lived in another world for ten." More than enough time to have the scars of betrayal burned into him. "Tell me something. Why would a Psy live alone, apart from the crowd?"

Sascha didn't berate him for his lack of a real answer. "Well, she could mate with a panther who prefers to live in the middle of nowhere on top of a tree." She made a face, but her smile gave her away. "It's uncommon but some Psy do prefer to live in isolated surroundings—they're usually on the weaker end of the Gradient. Maybe because their gifts don't threaten to overwhelm them like they do the rest of us."

"No." He shook his head. "This one was guarded like she was the president." *She.* Of that, the beast was suddenly certain.

"Are you sure?"

"Fences. Hidden cameras. Live guards. Motion sensors."

Sascha's eyebrows rose. "Of course. It must be one of the F-Psy."

"Foresight?" It helped to have a Psy in the pack. Before Sascha, they'd been close to blind about the intricacies of the Psy world. "I thought they were extremely rare. Wouldn't the Council want them locked up tight somewhere closer to where they could keep an eye on them?"

She shook her head. "I've heard it said that the most powerful of them need space even from other Psy. So though you saw live guards, it's likely no one actually lives in the home except for the F-Psy herself. I don't know that much more about them—foreseers are close to a subrace within the Psy and they belong to PsyClans, which represent them in public. Meeting one face-to-face is almost unheard of. Rumor has it that some of them never leave their homes. Ever."

Vaughn understood the need for aloneness, but there was a pathology to what Sascha was describing. "Are they prisoners?"

"No, I don't think so. They're too important to be made unhappy," she said, then seemed to catch herself. "You know what I mean—Psy don't feel happiness or unhappiness, but if the F designation decided to cease forecasting, the economic consequences would devastate the Psy.

"So no, I don't think they're prisoners, just that they prefer to live in a shell where they don't have to face the dark side of light." Her voice dropped to a whisper. "Maybe if they stepped out occasionally, they'd remember the world they'd forsaken and wake up to the reality of their gift."

He watched her and knew she was remembering the vicious torture her mate had undergone as a child and his resulting vengeance—vengeance that had cemented the bond between Vaughn and Lucas. Perhaps if the F-Psy hadn't retreated into Silence, if they hadn't stopped forecasting disaster and murder, Lucas might've been spared that horror.

And perhaps Vaughn could've grown up jaguar, instead

of being abandoned to the most savage kind of death by his own parents. Perhaps.

Manual strangulation.

Faith stared at the ceiling of her darkened bedroom, the two words slamming around and around her skull in an unstoppable loop. It was tempting to call the whole thing a coincidence and shove it to the back of her mind. Part of her wanted to do precisely that. It would be so much easier, so much more bearable. But it would be a lie.

Marine was dead.

And Faith had foreseen her murder.

If only she'd known how to interpret the visions, her younger sister might still be alive. If only. She'd been taught since childhood that it did no good to cry over the past, that it did no good to cry at all, and so now she didn't cry. She didn't even think she needed to, but deep inside herself, a caged and almost irretrievably broken part of her screamed in torment.

Faith was deaf to those agonized screams from her disintegrating psyche. All she knew was that she couldn't turn back from this. This wasn't some misjudged market trend, but the matter of a life. She couldn't choose to look away . . . not when she continued to feel the weight of the darkness pressing against her eyelids, violent and ugly.

The killer wasn't finished.

A discreet chime split the heavy silence. Glad that the bedroom hookup was vocal, not visual, she answered without turning on the lights. "Yes?"

"We've received no readings since yesterday." It was Xi Yun himself.

"I'm tired." And she hadn't wanted to sit in that red chair and possibly give away the tumult in her mind. "I need to catch up on my sleep as you suggested."

"Understood."

"I won't be back online for a few days."

"How many?" The question was supposed to be a precaution against her kind's tendency to forget, but Faith had begun to resent the intrusion of late, begun to see it as yet one more way to chain her, to ensure her talents were never out of reach.

"Three days." It was the longest they'd allow her, the longest they'd "trust" her capacity to care for herself. She'd often thought it was as well that NightStar and the Council were wary of damaging her abilities. Otherwise, they'd probably shove aside her PsyNet shields and monitor her on the most intensely private level—through mind control. All for her own good, of course.

She shivered and told herself it was because the room temperature was low. It had nothing to do with fear. She felt no fear. She felt nothing. She was Psy. More than that, she was an F-Psy. Her conditioning had been harsher than that of even other cardinals—she'd been taught to *never* allow even the faintest tendril of emotion to filter through to her conscious mind, because to do so would equal the utter destruction of her psyche. That, she believed. Her PsyClan had a history of producing F-Psy and in the days prior to Silence, one in every four had ended up in a mental institution before they'd completed their second decade of life.

Three days.

Why had she asked for that? Regardless of what Xi Yun thought, she wasn't tired. She slept less than most Psy, satisfied with four hours at most. But she hadn't asked for those three days in order to do nothing. Her mind had a purpose, a destination, albeit one she wasn't consciously aware of at that point. Despite that, she suddenly got out of bed and began packing a small backpack with enough clothing and toiletries for a few days.

She'd asked a member of her PsyClan to buy the backpack for her a month ago, for no reason that she could fathom. No one had questioned her demand, assuming it had to do with using a physical trigger for a vision. She hadn't disabused them of that notion because she hadn't been sure it wasn't in fact the truth. But now she saw that once again, her ability had led her to act in preparation for something that was yet to be.

Even as Faith packed for a journey she didn't know she was about to take, a psychic door slammed shut on the PsyNet, enclosing the six minds within it in a seemingly impenetrable vault. The Psy Council was in session.

"It's becoming imperative that we find a replacement for Santano Enrique." Nikita glanced at the minds surrounding hers—each appearing as a cold white star against the blackness of the Net—and wondered who was, at this moment, plotting to knife her in the back. Someone always was. The fact that their physical bodies were scattered across the world was no guarantee against attack.

"Maybe it's not just Enrique we need a replacement for." The silky suggestion came from Shoshanna Scott. "Are you sure you weren't the one who passed on your daughter's genetic deficiency?"

"We all know Sascha wasn't deficient," Marshall answered. "Nikita produced a cardinal—how many cardinals in your family tree, Shoshanna?"

Nikita was surprised by Marshall's support. As the most senior member of the Council and its tacit leader, he tended to remain neutral. "We can't afford to be divided at this stage," she pointed out. "DarkRiver and SnowDancer will take advantage of any weakness."

"How sure are we that they'll follow through on their threat?" This came from Tatiana Rika-Smythe, the youngest mind in the vault.

"We all got pieces of Enrique after they executed him. I think we know exactly how the leopards and wolves will react if we attempt to harm Sascha." Henry Scott's mind wasn't the star of a born cardinal, but it was extremely powerful nonetheless. Added to Shoshanna's razor-sharp political skills, the pair had the potential to rise to the leadership of the Council. Perhaps that was why Marshall was suddenly so willing to support Nikita.

"We need another cardinal to replace Enrique," Ming LeBon asserted, his mental voice as coolly lethal as his physical presence would've been in a meeting on the physical plane. An expert at mental combat, he was also a master in the human disciplines of karate and jujitsu. "No other Gradient will do—he was an anchor and did the most to keep the NetMind in check."

No one disagreed. Facts were facts. The NetMind, the policeman and librarian of the PsyNet, had a tendency toward unpredictable breaks of erratic behavior. For the past six generations it had been such that the Councilors took turns keeping an eye on it. Two particular Psy talents seemed to have an affinity for the task.

"Enrique's access to the NetMind also allowed him to hide his defective mind from us," Henry pointed out.

Ming's star remained absolutely calm. "That's unavoidable. Despite all our research, we can't predict the ones for whom conditioning will fail."

"Most of the cardinals in the Net are unsuitable for Council ranks," Nikita said. They were too cerebral, having little to no idea of the ruthless practicality needed to keep the Psy at the top of the food chain.

"Did you have anyone in mind, Ming?" Marshall asked.

"Faith NightStar."

Nikita took a few moments to locate the basic information files on the cardinal. "An F-Psy? I understand that the F and Tk designations are best able to control the NetMind, but the F-Psy are . . . unstable."

"Over ninety-five percent of them are in institutions by

the time they're in their fifth decade," Shoshanna added. "She's not a viable choice."

"I disagree. Faith NightStar has a mind as powerful as Enrique's and she's been giving us highly accurate predictions since she was three years old. No other foreseer has been as productive or as accurate. During her entire lifespan, she's shown no symptoms of mental deterioration and as an F-designation cardinal, she's been under extremely close observation."

"Ming makes a good point," Marshall broke in. "It may be that Faith is the safest choice after Enrique. At least we know she's not psychotic at this stage, and the monitoring she'll continue to need while doing forecasts as a Councilor will ensure any changes are immediately picked up."

"Whoever we choose, we need to confirm a successor soon." Ming's psychic voice was resolute. "I've prepared a comprehensive report on Faith NightStar." He showed them the mental storage shelf within the Council chambers.

"Does anyone else want to suggest a candidate?"

"Another possibility is Kaleb Krychek," Shoshanna responded. "He's a cardinal Tk and part of the Council ranks. I'm placing the files on him beside the ones on Faith. You'll note that his control over his telekenetic abilities is reputed to be superb."

"Kaleb is younger than I am," Tatiana pointed out, "and he's already nearly at the top. I'd say that makes him a better choice than Faith—aside from being incredibly young even compared to Kaleb and myself, she's been isolated. She won't have the capacity to survive being Council."

"I disagree." Nikita wasn't convinced of Faith's suitability either, but she *was* certain of the threat presented by Krychek. "Kaleb's risen to the top despite his youth. That displays a single-minded determination that might make him susceptible to the same kind of sociopathy as Enrique."

"We're all power hungry to some extent," Tatiana retorted.

"However, you may be correct in this instance—we may need a less aggressive Councilor to soothe the populace."

"The chosen candidate also needs to have the power to last." Shoshanna again. "If we go through two Councilors in a short time frame, it may undermine everything."

"Shoshanna's correct." There was no longer anything in Marshall's tone that hinted of partisanship. "Look over the files. We'll meet tomorrow and set up a timetable for evaluation meetings with both candidates. Unless any of you have a third suggestion?"

"Not so much a suggestion as something we need to keep in mind." Shoshanna's mind blazed with power. "There have been no M-Psy on the Council for the last two generations. Perhaps we need to remedy that. It might serve to keep us from unknowingly taking another Enrique into our midst."

For once, Nikita agreed with the rival Councilor. "The other option is to mandate M-Psy checkups for the entire Council."

"It would be much more confidential if the medic were one of us." Henry.

"But it would also give that Councilor too much power in comparison to the rest of us." Nikita didn't like the idea of any of her fellow Councilors being privy to her body or her mind.

"I concur." Tatiana Rika-Smythe. "An M-Psy should be considered for inclusion, but as a representative of that designation, not our caretaker."

"What about the NetMind? F and Tk are the two specialties that control it best," Henry pointed out.

"That's something we can consider in the final stages of evaluation." Ming, the most Silent of the six and the one Nikita knew the least about. "Does anyone else have a suggestion?"

It was Marshall who answered, but not directly on topic. "It's a pity we lost Sienna Lauren. She showed great potential."

"That *was* unfortunate," Ming agreed. "I had my eye on her as a possible protégée."

Which could only mean, Nikita surmised, that Sienna Lauren had been born with the mental combat abilities that made Ming so deadly. "Given the Lauren family's tendency to break conditioning, rehabilitation was the logical response. They would still be alive if they hadn't attempted to circumvent our judgment."

"Of course," Ming said.

"In terms of M-Psy," Nikita continued, "Gia Khan on the Indian subcontinent has proven very useful in undertaking Council matters."

A small pause as the others scanned the basic files on Khan.

"She looks like a possibility. Let's add her to the candidate list along with Kaleb and Faith." Marshall.

"What about the aspirants? Anyone we need to take seriously?" Shoshanna.

"No. There are a few who think they're powerful enough, but if they were, one of us would be dead by now." Tatiana knew what she was talking about—she'd ascended to the Council when the Councilor who'd held her place, Michael Bonneau, had had an unfortunate "accident" while alone in his home with his most senior aide, Tatiana.

"Then we're agreed. Kaleb Krychek, Gia Khan, or Faith NightStar."

CHAPTER 3

Faith had never left the compound on her own. They'd put her inside twenty-one years ago, telling her that her mind couldn't survive in the outside world, that the visions would come too thick and fast if she lived closely with others. She'd had no reason to disbelieve them and over the years, her home had become her chosen prison, a place she rarely left.

But today, she was going to go out into the unknown. Her conscious mind had finally understood what it was that her subconscious had spent months preparing her for—a search for answers. It was clear to her that to find those answers, she had to speak to someone who had nothing to do with either the Psy Council or NightStar. Both her PsyClan and the Council had vested interests. They wouldn't tell her what she most needed to know—whether these dark visions were the first stirrings of an inevitable madness, or whether they indicated something far more treacherous: the awakening of a facet of her ability she had no desire to face.

Though she lived in almost complete isolation, she knew everything she needed to know for this journey. There was no way to block the highways of the PsyNet from flowing with information that buzzed in the real world. Gossip had a way of infiltrating even the strongest defenses. That gossip had brought her news of a Psy who'd dropped out of the Net.

Sascha Duncan.

The Council had made it known that Sascha was a fundamentally flawed cardinal too weak to hold the Net link, a link that provided biofeedback no Psy could live without. And yet Sascha had survived.

The renegade Psy was the only person Faith could come up with who'd have nothing to gain by lying, nothing to lose by telling the complete truth. Everyone else was linked to the PsyNet. Therefore everyone else could betray her, whether it was by choice or by accident. Sascha was the one. It was logical.

She preferred not to remember the dream she'd had a few weeks ago in which she'd seen the face of a leopard staring back at her with feral hunger, preferred not to try to understand what her ability was attempting to tell her. Because sometimes, too much foreknowledge was a curse.

Leaving the compound was going to be difficult, but not impossible. The PsyClan guards were interested in keeping people out. No one had ever thought that Faith would attempt an escape. Taking a deep breath, she slung on the small backpack then calmly opened her back door and walked out into the night.

She knew precisely where she was going. There was a very small section of the outer fence that fell into a blind spot of the motion sensors and wasn't quite covered by the sweeping cameras. It had probably not even seemed like a weakness to NightStar Security. No criminal would ever be able to work out the exact location, and the live guards ensured that that part was under near constant surveillance, es-

pecially since many of the guards also had the ability to telepathically scan the area.

Faith had figured out how to deflect the scanners years
ago, boredom and isolation proving fertile ground for invention. More importantly, she was certain she could climb the
fence in the short window of time after one guard went
around the corner and before the other started to turn. She
knew that because two months ago, she'd suddenly started
coming out here at night and doing exactly that, going over
the fence and then back into the compound without alerting
anyone.

She'd thought she was doing it because she needed a
challenge. Of course, with an F-Psy of her capabilities, nothing was ever that easy. Tonight, it took her ten minutes to
walk the distance from the back door to the part of the outer
fence she was aiming for—the inner fence had never presented her with any real problems. Her eyes picked up the
form of a guard turning the corner on her right. A second
guard would appear ten seconds later with Psy precision.
She started climbing, silent and careful.

Vaughn crouched on a large branch overhanging the
compound that continued to fascinate him. He'd intended to
infiltrate it tonight and find out what lay behind the computronic and Psy security. But that was no longer necessary—
his prey was coming to him.

Her hair was a red flame despite the darkness and part of
him wanted to growl at her for being stupid enough not to
cover or contain the waist-length mass, but another part of
him was impressed by the quick, almost catlike way she
scaled the fence. She didn't hesitate, didn't look around. It
was as if she'd done it a hundred times.

Landing on the forest side, she walked in a straight line
from the fence and into the surrounding trees until she was

hidden from the sight of the guard now turning the corner. Vaughn padded along the treetops and came to rest almost on top of her as she paused to pull something from her pack.

A small light from her watch soon illuminated what appeared to be a computer printout of the surrounding area—a crude map that showed nothing of changeling routes or territorial markers. After a minute, she folded it up and put it back in her pack. Then she started walking. If he'd been in human form, he would've frowned. She was heading deeper into DarkRiver territory rather than toward Tahoe.

She wouldn't get very far on foot, but there was something about her that made the fur on the back of his neck rise. As a sentinel, he was used to trusting his instincts and this time they said that this woman had to be watched. Carefully. Very, very carefully.

Faith felt as if she were being stalked. An irrational reaction—she was alone in the forest. But if all went well, it wouldn't be for long. She didn't know the location of Sascha Duncan's home; however, she'd reasoned that if she ventured deep enough into leopard territory, one of them would find her and take her where she needed to go. A tenuous plan, but based on what she'd researched about the territorial nature of predatory changelings, it had a good chance of success. Heading to DarkRiver's business headquarters in San Francisco would've been far easier but she couldn't chance exposure.

After dropping out of the Net, Sascha Duncan had been labeled off-limits to all Psy. Going near her without Council authorization equaled automatic rehabilitation—a euphemistic label for the complete psychic brainwipe that destroyed the punished Psy's personality and higher mental skills. Faith knew enough of her own worth to understand she'd escape that fate, but she didn't want anyone becoming aware of her actions. The same part of her that *knew* this had to be kept a secret also knew she'd find an unlocked car on a nearby forest road.

And there it was. The car. She opened the door and slid in. Bending forward, she pulled open the control panel in order to bypass the computronic security. This wasn't something her ability had told her she'd need—it was a hobby, something that kept her mind occupied in the hours she spent alone. As a result, she could bypass most computronic hardware in seconds.

This time it took five and then the car was hers. Taking her mind back to the driving lessons she'd received in case of emergency, she turned it in the direction she wanted to go and pushed the accelerator. She had less than three days to find her answers. If she wasn't back in the compound before that deadline, they'd launch a full-scale manhunt. They might even use the excuse to try to smash through her PsyNet shields.

After all, she was a billion-dollar asset.

The man in Vaughn wanted to swear, but the animal simply acted, racing parallel to the car for almost a hundred meters before taking off in another direction. Lucas's lair was still over an hour away by car, but Vaughn wasn't taking any chances. Why the hell would one of the Psy venture this far into DarkRiver territory if she wasn't out to reach Sascha? And he knew the redhead was Psy—he'd seen her eyes.

Night-sky. Pinpricks of white against a pure black background.

His powerful heart was thumping hard by the time he made it to where he needed to be. Walking out to the center of the road, he stood in wait. Not only was he way too quick to be run over, most Psy would be so rattled at seeing a live jaguar that they wouldn't be able to do anything other than stop. They might have tried to kill their emotions, but some reactions came from the most primal core and those could not be controlled. No matter what the Psy believed.

She turned the corner, lights on low beam. They had little effect on his night vision. He watched her. Watched and waited.

Predatory eyes glowed out of the darkness. With no time to think, Faith slammed on the brakes and brought the car to a rocking halt. The huge hunting cat in front of her didn't move, didn't react like an animal should have. Unprepared, despite all her planning, for the dangerous reality of coming face-to-face with a live leopard, she sat in the car, hands clenched around the steering wheel.

The leopard seemed to get impatient when she didn't make any further moves. Prowling up to the car, it jumped onto the hood and she had to force herself not to react. It was big. And heavy. The hood of the car was slowly buckling under those powerful claws. Then it snapped its teeth at her through the windscreen.

It wanted her to get out.

Faith knew without a doubt that there was no way it was going to let her go any farther down the road. Though she'd never before met a changeling, every part of her said she was in the very real presence of one. And if she was wrong?

Not seeing any other logical course of action, she turned off the engine, picked up her backpack, and opened the door. The cat landed in front of her as she stood frozen beside the vehicle, belatedly conscious of her ignorance about the protocol governing interspecies contact. Nobody had ever taught her how to speak to the changelings. She didn't even know if they communicated like other sentient races.

"Hello?" she tried.

The cat pressed against her leg, nudging her away from the car until she stood alone in the pitch black of the road, a very large, very dangerous creature padding around her.

Hello, she tried again. It was a cautious and extremely polite mental page, something considered acceptable in exigent circumstances.

He lifted his head and growled at her, teeth gleaming even in the heavy darkness that cloaked the world. She withdrew immediately. The cat didn't like her mind attempting to touch his, recognized what she'd been doing. Someone had taught him shielding beyond natural barriers. And there was only one person who could've done that.

"Do you know Sascha?"

This time the teeth that were bared at her made her want to take a step backward but she stopped herself. She was Psy—she felt no fear. But all sentient beings had a survival instinct and hers was now asking what she'd do if the cats didn't want anyone near their personal Psy. The answer was that she had no real choice but to continue.

"I need to speak to Sascha," she said. "I have very little time. Please take me to her."

The cat growled again and the tiny hairs on the back of her neck stood up in a reaction her body would usually have controlled. There was something very territorial, very aggressive about the sound. Then it walked away a short distance and looked back at her. Surprised at the easy acquiescence, she followed. Instead of heading up the road, it led her into the forest, deep enough that they were hidden from the road. Then it marked a tree with its claw.

She didn't understand until the cat nudged at her legs hard enough to collapse them under her. "Okay, I get it. I'll wait here." That was when strong jaws closed around her wrist. She froze. It wasn't hurting her but she could feel the power of those teeth. One press and she'd lose her hand. "What? What do you want?" She fought her need to reach out with her mind and speak to it on a level that was normal and familiar. Teeth scraped over her watch.

"Okay." She waited for him to release her and he took his time doing so—the cat was very definitely male. Her eyes met his and she saw the sharp intelligence, the power and the fury. Dangerous and wild, he was also the most exotic thing she'd ever seen in her life. The urge to stroke her hands through the fur so close was almost impossible to resist. Except she knew this was one cat who'd never allow such an experimental touch.

Finally, he let go. She removed her watch and he took it in his teeth. Then he was gone, a blur so fast she barely caught the movement. Alone again, she shivered in the chill of the night and wrapped her arms around her pack. Would he come back? What if someone else found her here? The possibility of being surrounded by more of those cats made her reconsider the logic of what she was doing. They were unquestionably *not* Psy; therefore the rules she'd based her preparations on didn't apply.

Pressing hard against the tree, Faith waited. She had no other option.

Vaughn walked out of the bedroom and into the living room of the aerie wearing only a faded pair of jeans. He held *her* watch in his hand. "It doesn't have a tracker."

Lucas frowned and reached out to take it. Vaughn felt the irrational urge to keep the slim metallic band for himself, a surge of possessiveness so unusual that it startled him. He handed it over.

"Let me see." Sascha peered at it from beside her mate. "It's relatively ordinary as far as Psy timepieces are concerned." She took it from Lucas and looked at the back. "Not engraved with any family designation."

"I thought you might be able to pick up something from it."

Sascha shook her head. "My psychometric skills are growing but this is too cold. I don't think your Psy places much emotional importance on it."

The oddness of the statement wasn't lost on any of the three. The Psy placed no emotional importance on anything.

"You said she came out of that compound in Tahoe you were asking about?"

"Scaled the fence like she didn't want anyone to see." He retrieved the watch, hiding it away in his pocket. Where no one else could touch it.

"I didn't think you Psy were much into the physical," Lucas said, and there was a vein of sensual teasing in the words that Vaughn felt as sharply as a knife blade, though he'd never before been affected by the open sexuality of the pack's mated pairs.

"Why don't we discuss it tonight, hmm?" Sascha leaned her back against Lucas's chest. "But that is unusual—did she do it with any skill?"

"Smooth as a cat." It was the highest compliment Vaughn knew how to give. "Like she'd done it before."

"Odd. And she said she wanted to see me?"

"Yes." There was no way Vaughn was going to take Sascha out there and he knew Lucas wouldn't allow it either. Psy couldn't be trusted. Not even pretty redheaded Psy with skin as soft as cream.

Sascha's night-sky eyes unfocused for an eerie second. "What did she look like?"

"Red hair." He'd never seen hair that deeply red, that luxuriously silky. The cat had wanted to play with it while the man had wanted to do much, much more intimate things. "Cardinal eyes."

Sascha stood up ruler-straight. "It can't be. Impossible."

Both men watched as she started to pace around the aerie.

Vaughn felt Lucas's possessiveness as if it were a physical being between them and for the first time, he saw a glimmer of where that emotion might spring from.

"What is it, Sascha?" Lucas caught her around the waist as she passed.

She leaned into the embrace. "I could be wrong, but red hair is common in one particular family in this area of the Psy. The NightStar line has an unusually high incidence of the recessive gene." Sascha sounded utterly Psy at that moment. That was to be expected. She hadn't been cat for much more than a few months. It would take time.

"NightStar line?" Lucas played his fingers through her hair.

"They're a group of related families who operate under the PsyClan NightStar."

"You said PsyClans were utilized by F-Psy." Vaughn crossed his arms, his fingers tingling with the urge to know what it would be like to comb through the flame-red silk of a woman who climbed as well as any she-cat he knew.

She nodded. "The NightStar family has a history of producing F-Psy. They're rare, but NightStar has always had at least one in every generation. Some weak, some powerful. The only cardinal I know of in this entire region is Faith NightStar."

Faith.

He tested the name on his tongue and it fit, felt right. "Her name is the same as her PsyClan?"

"Yes. I'm not sure why, but that's how it works for them. They align themselves to the PsyClan as a whole rather than to their individual families." She bit her lip. "Cardinal eyes and red hair plus an isolated location—it could be Faith, but I don't know every Psy in the area."

"You've never met her?" It was Lucas who asked.

"No. The F-Psy are like shadows. People rarely see them.

Even lower Gradients are considered too important to be left unprotected."

"Why would an F-Psy want to see you?" Lucas looked at Vaughn. "She say anything else?"

"No. But she's been waiting for over an hour and a half now if she's where I left her." And for some reason, that made Vaughn edgy. "We need to take care of this."

"I want to speak to her," Sascha said.

"Absolutely not."

"No."

Both men spoke simultaneously, Lucas with the protective instincts of a mate and Vaughn with those of a sentinel. Sascha rolled her eyes and shook her head. "You two still haven't figured it out, have you? I'm never going to turn tame."

Lucas scowled.

"Neither of you knows how to deal with her, how to ask the questions that need to be asked. Vaughn probably terrified her into silence anyway." She turned those night-sky eyes on him.

"Psy don't feel fear." But her wrist had been very delicate under his teeth. "She's much smaller than you." And despite her height, Sascha was already fragile in comparison to the changelings.

Sascha nodded. "That would fit if she really is one of the F-Psy. Let's go. And don't even argue about it."

The low growl came from Lucas. Vaughn wisely left the room and went out onto the platform, using the chance to get out of his jeans—leaving the watch tucked safety inside—and shift. He was waiting there when Lucas and Sascha exited.

"Head out and scout the area. Sascha and I will be behind you in the car." Lucas didn't sound pleased and Vaughn couldn't blame him. "If you scent *anything*, let Sascha know."

Vaughn nodded. Sascha was now connected to the sentinels

through the Web of Stars, a mental network that Vaughn wasn't completely comfortable with, but which did have its uses. Though they couldn't communicate telepathically, they could send each other emotions, feelings. That in itself made it different enough from the PsyNet to calm his more aggressive instincts.

With a further nod, he jumped off the aerie and onto the ground. The night air rushed past him in a cool caress and then the earth was soft under the pads of his paws. He began to run.

CHAPTER 4

Faith had no concrete idea of how much time had passed since the cat had taken her watch. But she estimated that it had been two hours at least, maybe three. What if he had no intention of coming back? She took a deep breath and told herself to focus. If he didn't return, she'd get back in the car and drive on. Then it struck her that if the cat was intelligent enough to have stopped the vehicle, he was probably smart enough to have put it out of commission.

Something rustled to her right and she hunched closer over her bag, but when nothing happened, she allowed herself to relax. Strangely enough, though this was an unfamiliar place and situation, she was far more comfortable here than she would've been in a city. The rare times that she'd visited cities, she'd come away feeling bruised on the mental plane—as if she'd been under constant attack. Those experiences had always made her home seem more haven than prison.

She turned her head to scan the area again and felt every muscle in her body lock tight. Feral eyes looked calmly into hers. If she'd been human, she might've fainted. As it was, containing her reaction took every ounce of her control. "You're very quiet," she said, blindingly aware of the lethal danger scant inches away. "I guess it's one of the benefits of being a leopard."

A low, deep growl.

"I don't understand." What had she said to provoke that aggressive reaction?

Suddenly, the leopard loped off and she was left alone again. "Wait!" But he was gone. Logic stated she should get up and start walking. Sooner or later, she'd run into another member of DarkRiver. Leaving her pack on the ground, she stood and took a couple of steps in the same direction as the cat, hoping to see a path.

A hand closed around her neck and a hard male body pressed against her back, a line of living fire. She went completely motionless. He might be human now, but she knew with every ounce of her being that this was the same predator who'd growled at her a second before. The hand around her neck wasn't the least bit painful, but she felt the power in it, understood that he could crush her windpipe without effort.

"I am *not* a leopard," he said into her ear, and the sound was so rough she wondered if he'd come back fully from the animal.

"Oh." Her mistake was no surprise—she knew less than nothing about the reality of changelings. Her world had never been one where they intruded. "I apologize for offending you."

"Aren't you curious what I am?"

"Yes." She was also curious about his human face. "Can I turn around?"

His soft chuckle vibrated along her body and demanded her complete attention. "It's not that dark, Red—I didn't have any clothes with me."

It took a few moments for her brain to work through that statement. The second she did, she became hyperconscious of the sheer heat of the body aligned so closely to her own. The part of her that craved new experiences wanted to turn, but she knew that would be sheer foolishness. This man was hardly likely to indulge her intellectual curiosity about his body. He'd almost bitten off her head for daring to call him the wrong species.

"Please let go."

"No."

The flat no took her by surprise. Nobody said no to her, not like that. They always tried to couch it in more polite terms. That treatment may have kept her cooperative and rational, but it had also left her no tools with which to deal with the hard reality of a world where people didn't follow the accepted rules of behavior. "Why?"

"Why not?"

She raised her own hand to the one he had around her neck and tugged. No movement. The message was clear. He wasn't going to hurt her, but neither was he going to budge. "If you're not a leopard," she said, deciding to attempt a civilized conversation, "then what are you? You're in DarkRiver territory and according to my information, it's a leopard pack."

"It is." His thumb stroked absently over her skin. She cut off the physical reaction before it began. If her body felt, then soon her mind would want to experience emotion and that was unacceptable.

"You're not with DarkRiver?" Had she been fooled into trusting the wrong cat?

"I didn't say that."

"Why are you refusing to tell me anything?"

"For all I know, you're a spy or an assassin."

The logic of his statement couldn't be refuted. "I only want to speak to Sascha and leave. The Council would mete out severe punishment if they knew."

"So you say."

She became aware that he smelled of the earth and the

forest, of a kind of animal energy that was alien to her. Alien, but not unpleasant. If she'd felt things like that, she might even have admitted that she . . . appreciated the scent of him. "Jaguar," she said almost before the thought fired through her neurons. *"Panthera onca."*

His hand stroked her neck. "Very good."

"I read a book approximately two months ago about different cat species." At the time she'd thought it a strange choice, but had been compelled to finish it nonetheless. "You can't blame me for not knowing immediately. Leopards and jaguars have very similar markings."

"I can blame you for whatever I like."

She was starting to feel like cornered prey. "Let me go."

"No."

Almost at the point where she was considering doing something psychic, no matter that she'd never been trained in offensive maneuvers, she heard the whisper of a vehicle. "Sascha?"

"Maybe."

"Thank you."

"Don't thank me. If you so much as breathe wrong, I'll kill you."

She believed him. "Maybe you should release me now and change back to your jaguar form."

"Why?"

"You're naked."

"They'll have brought me clothes. If not, who cares?"

"Oh." Her eyes went to the trees in front of her. Another male stepped out. He was dressed ordinarily enough in blue jeans and a white T-shirt, but his face bore some savagely primitive markings—as if he'd been mauled by some great beast and come out the winner. Now she was trapped between two predators, both primed to kill.

Then a slender female form moved out from behind the new male. Cardinal eyes met hers. "Hello."

"Sascha Duncan." She would've moved, but the jaguar continued to hold her by the throat. "Can you make him let go?"

The other woman tilted her head to the side. "Nobody can make Vaughn do anything he doesn't want, but I can ask. Vaughn?" Lifting a hand, she threw a pair of jeans in their direction.

A muscular arm shot out from beside Faith's head. The jaguar named Vaughn caught the material at the same instant that he released her. She knew better than to move.

"My name is Faith NightStar," she said, able to hear Vaughn pulling on the jeans.

Sascha tried to step closer, but the male with her used his back to keep her in place. His eyes never stopped tracking Faith.

"Why are you here?" Sascha asked.

"I need to speak to you."

"So speak." This time, it was the marked male who responded. Faith knew he had to be the DarkRiver alpha, the man Sascha Duncan had emotionally partnered with. Faith couldn't imagine how—there was nothing human in the eyes looking back at her.

"And be careful what you say," Vaughn whispered in her ear, his arm coming in front and around her shoulders to pull her against him.

This time, she struggled. "I can't process that much touch." It was a blunt statement. "You should let go unless you want me to have a seizure." Touch set off her senses and she couldn't handle the overload. It was something the M-Psy had warned her about repeatedly. After seeing images of other F-Psy going through the same thing, she had no desire to do so herself.

"Vaughn, she can hardly attack me with both you and Lucas here." Sascha Duncan looked at the man who was threatening Faith on a level she'd never before experienced, and had no idea how to deal with. "I'll let you know if she makes any moves on the psychic plane."

Vaughn's arm slid away after a slight hesitation. But she could still feel him at her back. The urge to turn around and see his face was so powerful it shook the foundations of her confidence in her ability to survive the outside world. Already, it was influencing her, making her act in ways that she couldn't afford to, not if she were to remain sane.

"What did you want to talk to me about?"

Faith noticed the way Sascha placed her hand on the shoulder of the DarkRiver male called Lucas. It was shocking to her. Her skin tingled from where Vaughn had held her—she couldn't understand how Sascha bore the overwhelming influx of sensory input. But that thought was hardly relevant to her situation.

"I heard that you were no longer part of the PsyNet," she began.

"That's correct."

"I need some information."

"What kind of information?"

Faith glanced at the man in front of her, but suddenly realized it was Vaughn who was the more dangerous. Sascha was connected to Lucas so the alpha had to have some sense of civility. But the jaguar whose human face remained a mystery? He was nothing but pure wild animal. "Could we discuss this alone?" She sent out a telepathic feeler, a polite request for mental contact.

"Stop." Even as Lucas moved to block Faith's view of Sascha, Vaughn stepped close enough that the heat of him threatened to sear her through her clothing. "You don't have mind privileges with Sascha."

She held herself immobile. How had the changeling known what she was doing? "I'm sorry. I didn't mean any rudeness." Telepathic communication was de rigueur among her race. And living as she did, she'd already conversed aloud more tonight than she had in the past week.

"Anything you have to say can be said in front of us or not at all," Lucas stated.

Sascha managed to get the alpha to move enough that she could look at Faith. "He's my mate and Vaughn is Pack."

The renegade cardinal's loyalties couldn't have been clearer. Nothing Faith had learned on the PsyNet had prepared her for this . . . or for the considerable power in Sascha Duncan. Whatever she was, she was no flawed cardinal who couldn't hold on to the Net link. Faith would bet her life on that and perhaps she was going to have to. "If this gets back to the Council, they'll imprison me completely." And then they'd use her. Use her until she was empty of everything but madness.

"Not sentence you to rehabilitation?" A silky whisper against her ear.

"No. I'm too valuable."

Vaughn was startled by the complete lack of conceit or pride in that pronouncement. Faith spoke of herself as if she were talking about a machine or an investment. He looked down at the top of her head and wondered at the mind within. Was she as inhuman as she sounded, as cold? His instincts said otherwise—they saw her as something more, something intriguing.

"We don't tattle to the Council," Lucas spit out. "Now talk or leave."

"I think my ability is mutating." Cool, clear, haunting, her voice wasn't quite right. Wasn't quite . . . complete. "I'm seeing things. Disturbing, violent things."

"Are the visions about specific events?" Sascha leaned against Lucas.

"Until two days ago, I thought not." Faith shifted a subtle inch.

Vaughn knew she was attempting to increase the distance separating them, but he didn't want that. He moved with her and felt her spine stiffen. But she didn't say anything to him, concentrating on answering Sascha's question.

"The relevant dreams and visions have a recurring motif of suffocation until death." Her voice remained unshaken by the horror of what it was she was describing. "Then two nights ago, I was told that my sibling, Marine, had become a victim of murder by manual strangulation."

Vaughn felt Sascha's empathy reach out to Faith but it seemed to have no effect. It was as if Faith NightStar were encased in a shell so hard, nothing could get in . . . or out.

"Why come to me?" Sascha finally pushed around her unhappy mate to stand face-to-face with Vaughn's Psy.

Faith shifted her feet, but her voice remained steady. "You're the only Psy I know who won't immediately turn me in to the Council."

Vaughn's beast reacted strongly to the utter isolation implied by Faith's confession—it couldn't comprehend that kind of aloneness. Though he was a loner by nature, he knew his packmates would lay down their lives for him. Lucas wouldn't blink. Neither would Clay or any of the other sentinels. Even the damn wolves would defend him against anyone but another wolf.

Sascha shook her head. "What I have to tell you might not be what you want to hear."

"If I'd wanted lies, I would've gone to the Council or to my PsyClan."

Vaughn felt an unexpected stroke of pride. She was small, but there was strength in the female in front of him.

"How long before someone misses you?"

"I said yesterday that I'd be out of commission for three days, but I don't think their patience will last that long. I need to be back inside the compound sometime tomorrow night at the latest."

Sascha looked over her shoulder. Lucas scowled at the silent question, but jerked his head at Vaughn. "You got any ideas?"

"The old cabin." It was both far from any of their vulnerable people and hidden enough to provide privacy. "We have to blindfold her. Sascha can make sure she doesn't pull any Psy tricks."

"Don't talk about me as if I'm not standing right in front of you." A cool comment, but Vaughn wondered what had driven her to make it. Psy weren't known to take offense, because to take offense, they'd have to feel.

"Any objections to being blindfolded?"

"No. So long as it's Sascha who leads me."

"Why?"

"Leave her be, Vaughn." Sascha frowned. "She can't handle your energy."

"No way she gets to put a hand on you." He glanced at Lucas.

"Vaughn's right. We don't know anything about her."

Sascha turned to argue, but Vaughn knew Lucas wouldn't budge on this point.

The other man gripped his mate's wrist and said to Faith, "Let Vaughn lead you or leave."

Sascha seemed to realize this was one battle she wasn't going to win. "He won't touch you any more than necessary," she told Faith.

"Fine." She gave a short nod that sent her hair sliding everywhere. Standing so close, Vaughn couldn't fight the urge to run his fingers over the fire that shimmered even in the darkness. She went immobile, though she shouldn't have felt his featherlight touch.

"Here." Sascha pulled off her scarf and threw it to him.

Catching the makeshift blindfold, Vaughn enclosed Faith in the circle of his arms. She didn't move as he placed the soft material over her eyes, despite the fact that his front was pressed against her back. He was being deliberately provocative, taunting her. He'd never have done it if he'd thought her weak and easily bullied. No, this woman, despite her apparent fragility, was more than tough enough to take him on.

But as he finished fastening the knot, he felt a different kind of stillness steal over her. He imagined what it must be like—darkness, complete darkness, and she was having to trust people she'd only met minutes ago to do her no harm. It was to her credit that she did nothing but stand there in an appearance of utter calm. Deciding not to push her any more than he had already, he came around, took her hand, and hooked two of her fingers through a belt loop on his jeans.

A slight tug as she curled her fingers. "Thank you."

"Let's go."

As they followed Lucas and Sascha more slowly to the car, Faith spoke to him. "You think I'm making it up. I'm not."

"What?"

"About the seizures. I've seen recorded instances of F-Psy collapsing after too much sensory input."

He scowled. "Are you telling me you're never touched?"

"Once every six months they do a medical checkup that involves some unavoidable touching. And of course, I sometimes need other medical attention." She tripped and pressed a hand against his back to steady herself, a fleeting imprint of feminine softness that was gone as soon as it had come. "I apologize."

"Only medics touch you? You've never been held?"

"Perhaps when I was an infant, I might have been cradled by nursing staff."

Even after all that he'd learned from Sascha about her race, he couldn't imagine the inhuman coldness of such an existence. "We're at the car."

She let him nudge her into the vehicle. Taking the seat next to her, he pulled the door shut. They started moving almost immediately. Faith was like a statue next to him. If he hadn't been able to see the rise and fall of her breath, hadn't been able to smell the soft woman scent of her, he would've thought her made of—

Soft woman scent.

His beast went into a hunting crouch. Because unlike the guards who had blanketed the area around her home in their distinctive scent, Faith didn't smell Psy. Just like Sascha. Most of the psychic race gave off a metallic stink that repelled changelings, but nothing about Faith repelled him, though neither man nor cat liked her coldness. The lack of the distinctive smell could be coincidence. On the other hand, it could be an indicator of those Psy who hadn't given in completely to the inhumanity that was Silence.

Curious, he found himself leaning over to take another sniff. She went even more stiff and Sascha looked around to glare at him. He smiled. Shaking her head, she turned back. Sascha was learning that sometimes, cats would do what they'd do.

"Why do you think your gift is mutating?" he asked Faith, shifting to sit closer than he knew she would've liked.

"I forecast for business. That's what I'm trained for and what my ability has always manifested itself as."

"Always?"

She turned her head, though she couldn't see him. "Why do you sound unconvinced?"

"The Psy have a way of training away powers they don't like." The cat in him was fascinated by the beauty of her skin. It was so rich and luscious he almost thought it might taste of cream.

"You can't train away foresight."

"No, but maybe you can channel it." This came from Sascha. "Tell a child something often enough and she starts to believe it."

Lucas stroked his fingers over his mate's cheek and Vaughn wanted to do the same with Faith. Delicate, icy, she was hardly the type of woman who usually attracted him, but there was something fascinating about her, something compelling.

"How old were you when they started training you?" he asked his Psy. He'd found her first. Therefore, she was his. It was the cat talking and Vaughn didn't feel like arguing.

"I was placed in the care of the PsyClan at three years of age."

"What does that mean?"

"Most children are raised by a parent or parents. I was raised by the PsyClan's nurses and medics. It was for my own good—F-Psy need isolation or they go clinically insane."

His beast clawed at the walls of his mind. "Three years old and you were *isolated*?" This time he did reach out and slide strands of her hair through his fingers. She didn't react in any obvious way, but he could feel her tension. Good. He wanted her disturbed—that damn shell she had around herself irritated the hell out of him.

"Yes." She moved, causing her hair to slip out of his fingers. "I had the necessary teachers and trainers, but they all came to me. I rarely left the compound as a child."

"I didn't know they did that," Sascha whispered from the front. "How did you survive?"

"It was for my own good." There was something almost childlike in the staccato rhythm of Faith's voice, as if she was repeating something that had been pounded into her.

It made Vaughn want to hold her.

His thoughts slammed to a halt at the alien urge. Drawing back to his side of the car, he armed every one of his protections and reminded himself that, blindfolded or not, Faith was a cardinal. And cardinals didn't need to raise a hand to incapacitate their prey.

They could manipulate or kill with a single thought.

CHAPTER 5

Faith felt Vaughn move away and breathed a soft sigh of what some might have called relief. He was too big, too intimidating, though she'd never admit that out loud. Without having seen him, she already knew what he was built like, all lean muscle and fury. Part of her, the same part that had walked into a dark forest without stopping and then stepped out in front of a huge hunting cat, was fascinated by him.

Of course the fascination was purely intellectual, but that made it no less unwelcome. Apparently there was a streak of idiocy in her mental makeup that had survived conditioning, a streak that delighted in sticking its hand into the fire and waiting to see how badly it burned.

Added to the stress of their questions about her childhood, it was too much. She could feel herself reaching her mental limits. She'd rarely interacted this much with anyone and never with people who hid nothing of what they felt, who touched and spoke with the most unacceptable degree of emotion.

What if her shields cracked? Going into a seizure could cause major damage to her brain and leave her exposed in the most intimate sense. In the recording she'd seen, the F-Psy in question had almost bitten off her tongue. She'd also lost control of her mental processes for the duration of the seizure—even her shields against the vast public spaces of the PsyNet had come down. Faith couldn't imagine anything worse. Every day of her life, the visions forced their way into her mind. She needed some sense of control, some sense of safety, some sense of being alone within the walls of her psyche, if nowhere else.

"Why did your parents let them take you away?" Sascha's voice cut through the silence.

Faith didn't want to talk about her past anymore. But that was irrational and she wasn't an irrational individual. "Night-Star has a long history of producing F-Psy. They knew I wouldn't survive in a normal environment."

"Or maybe that's what it was useful for them to tell you." Vaughn's voice was a rough scrape over her skin. Impossible. Such an effect had no basis in the physiological responses of humanoid species.

"My family had, and still has, nothing to gain by lying to me."

"Tell me, Faith, how much do you earn for the PsyClan?" Sascha's voice was somehow different from every other Psy voice Faith had ever heard. It seemed to effect calm without the application of any discernible psychic pressure.

"I don't keep records." But she knew. "My family ensures I have everything I need."

"I have some idea," Sascha said. "You're worth millions. And you've been worth millions since the first day they started training you to give them what they needed—forecasts in the lucrative field of commerce."

"The visions can't be halted."

"No. But like Vaughn said, maybe they can be channeled."

Faith didn't answer and nobody said another word, but she heard their silence. No matter how hard she tried not to hear anything.

Vaughn felt irritable, as if his fur were being rubbed the wrong way. He glanced at the blindfolded woman less than an arm's length away and knew she was to blame. But having checked his mind for possible traps—a trick Sascha had taught all the sentinels—he was sure that Faith wasn't using any Psy powers on him.

The cat figured that made it okay to indulge.

He raised his hand to finger a strand of her hair where it lay against the back of the seat. Once again, he felt her go infinitesimally quiet. He frowned. Psy weren't known for being that sensitive to physical stimuli, which only made Faith more interesting.

The car slowed.

Moving with catlike speed, he was out almost before it stopped moving. "We're here." Though he opened her door, he let her exit on her own.

Her movements were hesitant, but she was soon standing beside the door, back held in the poker-stiff posture patented by her race.

"Don't," he ordered when she began to raise her hands. Reaching around, he undid the scarf himself. The cat took the chance to roll in the rich sweetness of her scent, but the man remained on guard.

She blinked against the light coming off the porch—Lucas had turned on the single bulb—and he saw her eyes for the first time with the sight of a man and not that of the beast. They were just as unearthly, just as beautiful. Two pieces of captured night sky.

Faith looked up. And up. As she'd guessed from the feel of him at her back, the jaguar was tall in human form. His hair was a thick amber-gold, long enough to brush his shoulders, and his eyes . . . they were an odd almost-gold, the eyes of a cat made human. There was nothing soft about him, nothing tame. Yet she, a woman who'd never before understood the concept, found him beautiful. It was an inexplicable reaction, one her brain couldn't accept, going as it did against every rule of Silence.

Her breath caught in her throat and she started to breathe faster than was optimal. She knew she was having a stress reaction, but she couldn't stop it. Her heart rate started to speed up a second later. Remembering a simple anchoring technique, she clenched her hand on top of the open car door and squeezed. But the physical action had no effect.

Suddenly, there were big hands on her face forcing her to look up and meet those odd eyes. "Stop it."

She lifted her own hands and tried to pull his off. Didn't he know that he was making it worse? The pressure had increased a thousand times at the skin-to-skin contact. Heat, sensation, power, everything that was him seeped into her and threatened to short-circuit her already overstretched mind.

"Vaughn, let her go." Sascha's command was a gift. "She can't handle that much sensation."

"Yes, she can." Those cat eyes stared down into hers.

She wanted to fight him, but had no idea how to use her abilities in a nonfatal attack. Starting to feel dizzy, she swayed. Her eyes locked with his. "I'm going to lose consciousness." Starkly aware of the possible danger to her PsyNet shields, she was numb to the physical agony of nerves going haywire.

"No, you're not. If you do, you'll be helpless." Vaughn didn't loosen his hold. "Do you want to be at my mercy?"

She tried to tell him it wasn't a choice she could make.

Her body was shutting down. And then the last neuron flickered and went out.

Swearing, Vaughn caught Faith's body before she fell and hurt herself.

"Damn it! Why didn't you let her go when I said?" Sascha ran to cradle the face of the woman in his arms.

"She's too scared of everything." His beast was driven by instinct and it said that what he was doing was right. "We can't afford to baby her."

Sascha looked like she wanted to argue, but then Lucas stepped up beside her. "He's right. Faith has to learn to deal—if she can't handle touch or normal human interaction, how the hell's she going to learn to handle those visions she says she's been having?"

"You two don't understand. This woman has almost never been touched, much less spent time with people who don't follow the rules of Silence. You know what I was like and I wasn't isolated as she's been." She took her hands off Faith. "Bring her inside. I think she'll be alright in a few minutes—it doesn't read like a seizure."

Vaughn carried Faith into the cabin. Her weight was slight, her whole body built on a small scale. But he'd felt the power of her eyes when they'd looked into his, felt the enormous strength of will inside those fragile bones. She was strong and she needed to find that strength if she was going to survive. The cat knew that as an absolute truth. And sometimes the jaguar understood things far better than the human male.

Once inside, he sat down on the sofa with her in his arms, ignoring Sascha's frown. She narrowed those eyes so like Faith's and yet somehow completely different. He'd never before noticed that cardinal eyes were unique from Psy to Psy, had never been close enough to two of them to compare. But he knew that he wouldn't ever mistake Sascha's eyes for Faith's.

Sascha turned to Lucas and threw up her hands. "You talk to him."

Lucas looked at Vaughn. "He knows what he's doing."

Vaughn wasn't so sure. He just knew that Faith couldn't be allowed to be scared of touch. She *couldn't*. And if there was something slightly inexplicable about his reaction, it was probably because he wasn't Psy.

Sascha cornered Lucas in the small kitchen. "Why is Vaughn acting so irrationally?" she said under her breath, cognizant of the cats' superior sense of hearing.

Her mate smiled and she felt the tug of it in her stomach. The reaction was still new, still powerful. She wondered if it would ever settle down—she had a feeling not, not when she was mated to this male.

The smile changed to reflect his knowledge of her susceptibility to him—pure feline satisfaction. "I can't read minds."

"Lucas." She found a glass and rinsed it out. "I felt nothing off Faith. Nothing."

His body went hunting-quiet. "Like before?"

Sascha didn't like remembering her first brush with the reptilian coldness of a mind that had given off no emotional feedback. The Psy might've buried their emotions, but they were there, a low-level hum most of her race didn't know existed, but which she'd always sensed on a level deeper than consciousness.

However, there were some who literally gave off no emotion . . . because they'd never had any feelings to subjugate—sociopaths given ultimate freedom by Silence. "No," she said quickly. "Not like before."

He glanced out of the kitchen and through to where Vaughn sat holding Faith. "But?"

She walked to stand in the circle of his arms. "It's like

she's encased in a shell, more so than other Psy. Everything's so tightly contained, it isolates her in a way I can barely imagine." His heartbeat was a steady rhythm under her hand, but what brought her a feeling of such safety could well kill Faith.

"This woman has had literally no contact with any race other than her own, and you heard the extent of even that limited contact. We're overloading her senses and the only way she has to cope is by shutting down."

"The seizures—do you think they're a real possibility?"

Sascha took a moment to think. "I don't know for sure. The F-Psy rarely fed data into the PsyNet when I was connected, because in most cases, what they learn has been paid for by someone. But my instincts say she thinks they're real, that she's been taught they're real."

"So she could subconsciously bring one on?"

"Yes." Sascha had once believed she was a cardinal without power—she knew exactly what it was like to live a lie for so long that it became the truth. "Faith has no concept of a life outside of the world in which she was raised. That she's here at all is a testament to the strength inside of her."

"Good. The weak don't survive."

Vaughn felt the woman in his arms stir. Her eyes blinked open almost immediately. "Breathe deep," he instructed the instant she started to freeze up. "If you pass out, we'll have to go through this again."

"Please let me go."

There was no vulnerability in her tone, nothing that gave away her emotional temperature. Then again, she was Psy—she had no feelings. Frowning at the jaguar's demand to continue holding her, he allowed her to sit up on his lap. When she pushed at his arm, he dropped it so she could stand.

She rubbed her hands over her pants. "Where's Sascha?"

"I'm here." Coming out of the kitchen, Sascha handed Faith a glass of water. "Drink."

Faith did so without argument, then put the glass on the table in front of the sofa. Vaughn watched and waited as she looked around for a place to sit. Lucas had already claimed the armchair and now pulled Sascha to sit across his thighs. Faith was left with the option of sitting beside him or in an armchair on the far side of the room. She took the sensible alternative, but tried to put as much distance between them as she could.

"How're you feeling?" Sascha asked.

"Fine. But please tell your pack members not to touch me. I have no capacity to process the stimulation."

Vaughn ran a finger down her cheek. She whipped around to pin him with a look. "I *said* don't touch me."

"When we first met, you'd have threatened to go to pieces with that one touch." He raised an eyebrow. "Now you can deal."

She looked at him. "You're saying you're desensitizing me."

"No, Red. I'm sensitizing you."

Faith looked into those cat eyes and wondered at the intent in them. "I don't understand you."

A curve to his mouth, Vaughn leaned back and slung his arm around the back of the sofa. She realized that if she rested her head against the seat, his fingers would brush her hair. It should've made no difference to her, but she found herself leaning forward as she began to speak. "I need to learn to stop the visions."

"Why do you think we can help you?" Sascha asked.

Faith tried to think past her awareness of the changeling beside her. He might've decided to act civilized, but that could change at any moment—she had to complete her self-appointed task before he went cat on her. "I don't. All I know is what I said before—that you won't turn me in to the Council."

"How long have you been having the visions?"

"About three months. They've been coming on little by little. At first it felt like . . . a heavy weight pressing down on me." It had crushed her until she'd taken to sleeping in her bed and not the monitored chair. "I began waking up with night sweats, my heartbeat racing so fast I should've called the M-Psy, but I didn't." Fingers whispered along her hair and she realized she'd somehow leaned backward without being aware of it.

"Sounds like fear to me," Vaughn said.

"I'm Psy. I don't feel fear." Pulling away, she angled her head to face him.

His focus on her was so intense, she felt stripped bare. "Then what would you call it?"

"A physiological reaction to unknown stress factors."

The slightest hint of a smile played about his lips. "So, what other physiological reactions did you experience?"

She thought he might be laughing at her but had no way of judging the veracity of that conclusion. He was completely unlike any other creature she'd ever come into contact with. "The night sweats deteriorated into what are termed night terrors. I would wake on the verge of screaming, convinced the dark visions had followed me into my waking life."

When she felt Vaughn's fingertips threading through her hair once again, she didn't shift and break the contact. He might be dangerous, but right this second, he seemed to be on her side. And she thought he might be dangerous enough to hold off the visions, unreasonable as that was.

"I don't know what you see normally. Were these different in more than content?" Sascha rested her head on her mate's shoulder, lines of concentration creasing her forehead.

Faith nodded. "Usually, my visions are very focused. Even if they don't start out that way, I can fine-tune them. But these . . . I couldn't do anything. I would compare it to being in a vehicle with someone else at the wheel." That had been the most disturbing part. "They were out of my control, but not chaotic."

Vaughn's hand slid under her hair to cover her nape. She jerked, but didn't move away. He was right—she might not be able to beat back the visions, but she could strengthen her capacity to withstand physical stimulation. "But no more," she said very, very quietly, meeting his gaze.

She was practical enough to realize that she was far from being able to handle everything. For all she knew, her current immunity to the heavy heat of Vaughn's hand was being fueled by adrenaline. When the inevitable crash came, she could seize worse than she might've done if she hadn't pushed herself.

"We'll see," he said as softly, and there was a look in his eyes that she couldn't decipher. Perhaps it was challenge, something she'd read about in the endless books she'd devoured in the aloneness of her cottage. Her reading speed and voracity meant she had an incredible amount of knowledge on a multitude of subjects. But it was knowledge without context. Especially where humans and changelings were concerned.

Choosing the prudent option, she returned her attention to Sascha. "After a few weeks, the dark visions began to get more detailed. I started to see flashes, images in pieces, parts of a jigsaw." Another hobby that kept her sane. Or as sane as any F-Psy ever was. "But it was still out of my control because I couldn't put the pieces together."

Vaughn's thumb rubbed against her skin and she turned her head. "Yes?"

"Why did you wait so long to come to us?"

She was caught by the demand in his voice. That, she recognized. People often demanded things from her. "Because until Marine was murdered, I had no way of knowing whether these visions were real. I thought my mind was disintegrating—it's something that happens to all F-Psy, but generally not until the fifth decade or so of life. I believed my decline was beginning early."

"I've never heard of that," Sascha whispered.

"That's not surprising. The PsyClans don't want to be known as producing defective Psy and by the time we deteriorate, we've accumulated enough wealth to ensure discreet medical care during our decline." She tried not to think about what was coming, tried not to imagine herself being unable to speak in coherent sentences or tell the difference between foresight and reality. But that didn't mean she was ignorant of the inevitability. It was why certain NightStar telepaths had trained in the specialist area of blocking. When F-Psy crashed for the final time, it was the blockers who kept their madness from leaking out into the PsyNet, providing the shields the fractured F-Psy could no longer maintain.

"I think that's a load of bullshit." Vaughn's hand tightened a fraction, but it felt like a full-body hug to her senses. The only thing that kept her from an overload reaction was her concentration on his words. "To what are you referring?"

His touch gentled though she'd made no verbal complaint, that stroking thumb coming to a halt. "They had Sascha convinced she was going mad just because she didn't fit into the mold they'd created for her. Sounds like the same thing."

Faith looked at Sascha. "He doesn't understand."

"What?" Vaughn's tone was more growl than sound.

It was Sascha who answered. "The F-Psy had one of the highest rates of mental illness even before Silence."

Lucas's arms came around his mate in a tight hug. Faith

wondered what Lucas had heard that she hadn't, because from the look on Sascha's face, it seemed to have been exactly what she'd needed. "But highest doesn't translate to all, does it, Sascha darling?"

Faith found her eyes following the movement of Lucas's hand over Sascha's curls. Until Vaughn's thumb whispered over her skin again. She stiffened, caught off guard to find that he'd moved closer. But she couldn't speak, even to tell him to back off. Perhaps she'd exhausted her ability to deal with the amount of new material she was being forced to process.

"Don't believe everything you've been told, Faith."

It was the first time he'd said her name and he made it sound interesting, as if it were more than a useful tag to call her by, made it sound . . . She didn't know to describe it, but she knew it was something she'd never before heard.

"The Psy Council is expert at spinning lies to further their own ends."

She stood without warning and headed for the door, her steps unsteady but determined. "I need to breathe." Walking out into the night, she grabbed the railing around the porch and took several gulps of cold night air.

It was no surprise to feel Vaughn's heat beside her a bare second later. He leaned his back against the railing so he could look at her. When he raised a hand, she shook her head. "Please, don't."

He paused. "You're stronger than this."

"No, I'm not. If I were strong, I would've faced those visions instead of running from them and my sister would still be alive." There, it was out, the truth she'd been hiding from since the moment her father had told her about Marine. "If I were strong, I would've understood what it was that I was seeing." She stared into the darkness of the forest, a darkness that was a gift and not a curse.

"I've seen things since I was a child. Benign, useful things. I see when the market's going to go up or down.

I see if a new invention is going to catch on so businesses can invest money at the outset. I see if a start-up venture has the potential to succeed." Her hands clenched on the wood of the railing and she felt a sense of chaos beating at the back of her mind, a threat from within her own psyche. That was how the madness began—with the inability to control physical reactions. "I don't see death and blood. I don't see murder."

"F-Psy used to." Vaughn's voice was a deep purr that rubbed against her insides in a way that was disturbingly intimate. "They used to see disasters and murders, pain and horror."

She finally looked at him. "No wonder they went mad."

"Only some of them."

But these days, all F-Psy eventually faced that fate. She saw what he was trying to say, but couldn't accept it. Too much. It was far too much. "I need time to assimilate everything."

She expected him to push her as he'd been pushing her since the instant they'd met. But he nodded. "Go on." He jerked his head toward the door. "Sascha's making up a bed for you in one of the rooms."

"Can I ask you a question?"

"Ask."

"Sascha and Lucas—how?" She couldn't fathom how a cardinal Psy could've survived the severance of the Net link, much less entered the changeling world.

Vaughn's face underwent a subtle shift. "Do you see this?" He lifted his right arm and she saw the tattoo on his biceps for the first time. Three jagged slashing lines, they were reminiscent of the markings on Lucas's face. "I'm a sentinel. My loyalty is to Sascha and Lucas. And you might yet be a threat."

She wondered why that caused an odd sensation in her chest. "You really would kill me if necessary."

"Yes." Those cat eyes seemed to glow in the darkness. "So play nice."

"I don't know how to play." She couldn't ever remember doing such a thing. "I've been working since I could form any kind of understandable sentence."

CHAPTER 6

Vaughn's beast scratched at the walls of his mind, wanting a closer sniff of Faith, as she walked past him and into the cabin. He leashed the cat this time. Faith was hanging on by the thinnest of threads. He had no desire to push her over the edge and snap that thread completely.

Because the truth was, he wasn't certain he could kill her without hesitation. And that made him wary. Psy weren't all gentle and empathic like Sascha. Some of them were cold-blooded killers. DarkRiver knew that too well—they'd lost a young female named Kylie to a Psy serial killer less than a year ago and their blood allies, the SnowDancer wolves, had almost lost a female of their own.

Brenna, the SnowDancer who'd been kidnapped and tortured, remained deeply damaged despite everything Sascha and the healers had done to help her. Vaughn could guess why—as one of the hunters who had tracked down and executed the killer, he'd seen the face of the evil that had touched her, knew exactly what kind of atrocities the Psy were capable of committing.

Faith could turn out to be nothing like she seemed. Until they knew for sure, Vaughn had to distrust his reactions around her. While it was true that Psy generally had difficulty manipulating changeling minds, Sascha was proof that nothing was impossible. And notwithstanding the training he'd received from his alpha's mate, he wasn't Psy, while Faith was a cardinal.

Following his quarry into the house, he watched her and Sascha meet in the middle of the living room. His hand rose to rub over the tattoo on his arm—his loyalty to DarkRiver stemmed from an act of the most cruel betrayal and was set in stone.

It was the leopards who'd come to his aid at a time when he'd lost everyone and everything that mattered. And it was Lucas who'd extended the hand of friendship that had brought him back from the savage edge of an all-consuming rage. He'd lay his life down for his alpha and until this moment, nothing and no one had ever threatened to shift the intensity of that focus. That Faith was doing so after only a few hours made him more than suspicious of the reality of his response.

Faith fell asleep seconds after her head hit the pillow, body and mind both worn out. But that didn't stop the visions. Nothing ever stopped them when they were determined to find her.

Darkness brushed her consciousness. Her heartbeat accelerated. She recognized this darkness. It wasn't friendly, wasn't something she wanted to see. But it wanted her to watch. There was a twisted pleasure in it, pleasure she understood because it wasn't her own but generated by the darkness. During these visions, she was the darkness and if she'd felt fear, that fact would've terrified her. But of course she wasn't scared—she was a product of Silence.

It wasn't crushing yet, the darkness. It felt . . . satisfied. Its needs had been fulfilled for the time being and it was relishing the bloody rush. But then it showed her a glimpse of the future. A future she could no more not see than she could stop breathing.

Suffocation.

Torture.

Death.

Unable to bear the ugliness, she tried to draw back. It refused to let her. Her heart beat in a dangerous, jagged rhythm. This was impossible, her practical Psy mind tried to point out. But it was drowned out by the primitive core of her psyche. It screamed because it knew that this *was* possible.

Sometimes, visions didn't let go. Ever. The end result was insanity so deep and true that no more than twisted fragments of the mind remained. Faith clawed at the darkness, but there was nothing to hold on to, nothing to fight her way out of. It was everywhere and nowhere, an enclosing prison she couldn't break. Her racing heart began to go sluggish as her mind concentrated every ounce of energy on finding a way out. Only to slam up against a blank wall.

Touch intruded, a sensory alarm so shocking that it snapped the twining threads of the vision. She woke with a gasp, her eyes clashing with a pair that were not quite human. A ragged breath later, she became aware of hands holding on to her upper arms. *Skin to skin.* Her tank top was soaked with perspiration and, by rights, she should've begun to cascade because of the sensory overload, but she said, "Don't let go." Her voice was a rasp. "Don't let go or I'll fall back in."

Vaughn tightened his hold, worried by the look in Faith's eyes. There was something unfocused about them, as if she wasn't fully awake. "Talk to me, Faith."

She kept breathing those jerky ragged breaths and then, to his surprise, reached out to put her hands flat against his bare chest. Her touch was pure heat when he'd expected coolness. It burned and the jaguar wanted more. "Don't let me fall back in. Please, Vaughn. *Please.*"

He didn't understand what she was so afraid of, but he was a sentinel—he knew how to protect. His senses had lit up in warning minutes ago, though Faith hadn't made a sound. He'd walked into her room on silent feet, expecting her to wake and tell him to get the hell out. Instead, he'd found her barely breathing, her skin sheened in sweat, her hands curled into fists so tight she'd been bleeding from tiny cuts made by her nails.

Now those same instincts had him locking his arms tight around her. Touch unsettled Faith; maybe it would unsettle her enough to bring her back from wherever it was that she'd gone.

Pure black.

He finally realized what it was about her eyes that had worried him—the complete lack of stars. He'd seen Sascha's eyes do that before, but there had been something different about Faith tonight, as if there were a deeper darkness behind the one he could see. He ran a hand up her back and under her hair to close over her nape. The woman he'd met hours earlier would've been shoving him away and threatening to go into seizures. This one was too still, too passive.

"Shall I kiss you, Red?" It was a dare. "Never kissed a Psy before. Might be fun."

Her breath hitched and she shook her head against him like a kitten shaking off wet. *Then* she shoved at his chest. The devil might've made him keep her with him for a second longer, but he was all too aware that her body had had an unexpected effect on his. He was used to his sexuality; what he wasn't used to was it reacting so completely against his wishes. Letting Faith pull free, he watched as she scrambled backward until her back pressed against the headboard. The eyes staring into his were wide and full of stars.

He made his smile a slow tease. "So, you back?"

She nodded, continuing to stare at him as if he were some large wild animal who might see her as dessert. She wasn't far wrong. The cat definitely liked the smell of this Psy and the man found her disturbingly fascinating.

"I've never scared anyone by threatening to kiss them before," he commented, checking her face for any lingering signs of whatever it was that had frightened her badly enough that he'd become safe.

"I don't feel fear."

He tugged at her tank top. "Lost control of your physiological responses again, huh?"

She pulled the damp fabric from his grasp. "Even Psy can't control sweat in sleep."

"You going to be okay?"

Faith didn't want him to go, an illogical reaction. Vaughn couldn't stop the visions if they were determined to come, but some irrational part of her was convinced that if he left, the darkness would return and this time, nothing would make it let go. "Of course."

"You don't look it." He scowled and reached to push her hair off her face. "Do you want to shower?"

His touch made every nerve ending ignite but she held strong. She could handle this. It was what had brought her back from the vision and she'd learn to deal with anything that helped keep the darkness at bay. "Yes. Will I wake Sascha and Lucas?"

"They're not here."

"We're alone?" She suddenly felt vulnerable in a way that was so viscerally female, it was an utterly new sensation.

"You didn't think I'd let our alpha and his mate remain in a spot that a cardinal Psy knew about?" He snorted. "We might've blindfolded you, but Psy have other ways of knowing."

"You thought I'd lead others here."

"It was a possibility."

She didn't know what to say, hadn't expected Sascha to abandon her like this. Though of course, once she thought about it, her supposition had no basis in fact.

"She didn't want to go," Vaughn said, and almost startled her into an overt physical response. "But we weren't going to let her heart put her in danger."

"Her heart?"

"She's an E-Psy."

Faith flicked through a mental file. "There's no such thing as an E designation."

"Have your shower and I'll tell you something else your Council's been hiding from you. It's almost five—you want coffee?"

"Okay." Faith was aware there were peculiar gaps in her knowledge and the taste of coffee was one of them. She knew of it, of course. No one who read as much as she did could miss knowing about it, but she'd never actually drunk it.

Vaughn got up from the bed and her eyes followed the shift of lean muscle and male strength. He was built perfectly in proportion, beautifully constructed. His musculature was well defined and his skin shimmered with a healthy glow that her mind found . . . *interesting*, she thought desperately, when that same mind tried to insert another word.

"Do I pass inspection?"

Her eyes met ones that glowed slightly in the dark and she saw something in them that she now recognized as laughter. Her answer came from a part of her she hadn't known existed. "You appear healthy, but I'd have to dissect you to make an accurate judgment."

To her surprise, his lips curved. "So you can play after all."

She wanted to argue, but he was already walking out. "Wait!" It came out without thought.

He turned. "What's the matter?"

Now that he'd stopped, she couldn't say it. What if he left and the darkness found her again? "The shower—where can I get a towel?"

"Hold on." He stepped out.

By the time he returned, she'd started to breathe faster. He paused the second he got inside the doorway. "I smell fear, Red."

She got off the bed and went to grab the towel. What she couldn't even allow herself to think was that she was going to him because he made her feel safe. "You're imagining things." She tugged at the towel.

He held on to it. "I'm a cat. I don't make mistakes like that. Come on."

Knowing she should argue, but not having the will to do so, she followed as he led her from the bedroom. When he didn't switch on a single light, she realized it was because he could see perfectly well in the dark. Since she couldn't, she reached out with her mind and flicked on the kitchen light as they headed into that room.

He froze. "Telekinesis?"

"A touch." In reality her Tk strength was close to negligible, but she didn't think it smart to admit that.

"Any other 'touches' I should know about?" He gave her a piercing look.

She shrugged. "What are you doing?"

"Starting the coffee before I babysit you." He opened a canister sitting on the counter that ran along the back wall.

It felt like he'd slapped her. "Give me the towel. I don't need babysitting."

Ignoring her, he finished setting up the coffeemaker. "I was teasing, Red. Don't get your fur ruffled." He pointed down the hallway. "Go use that shower and I'll sit outside and wait for you."

She took the towel he held out. "I'm fine." She didn't

know what had driven her to tell that complete untruth. She
never lied—she had no reason to. "And I don't have fur." But
for some bizarre reason, she found herself imagining what it
would be like to stroke that black and gold fur she'd
glimpsed when he'd first stalked her.

"Ask nice and I might let you."

He'd read her mind for the second time. "You're telepathic?"

He nudged her toward the shower. "No, you just can't lie
worth a damn. Everything's in your eyes. Plus I know when
a woman's thinking about stroking me."

"I wasn't thinking about stroking you." She preceded him
down the hallway. "I was imagining your fur."

Heat at her back and a rough whisper against her ear.
"You let me stroke you and I'll let you stroke me—I have a
thing about your skin."

Faith had no idea how to deal with him. So she opened
the bathroom door and stepped inside. "I won't be long."

His eyes lingered over her and she became aware that the
tank top was plastered to her skin, outlining everything
about her, from her full breasts to the curve of her hip. "Take
your time."

Faith wondered why she felt like she'd been marked. He
hadn't touched her and yet . . . he had.

Vaughn heard the shower come on as he leaned against
the wall next to the bathroom. He'd said he'd stay there
while she showered and he would. And it wasn't only because he'd smelled the acrid tang of bone-chilling fear.
Something far more disquieting had been present in that
nightmare-soaked room—a third entity that the cat had recognized as nothing natural, nothing good.

He hadn't been able to define the lingering miasma as either human, changeling, or Psy, but it had clung to Faith like

a second skin, disappearing only in the light of the kitchen. It might be gone now, but Vaughn was far from convinced that he'd seen the last of it. Faith could very well be a psychic carrier of some kind, providing a conduit for the infiltration of DarkRiver.

However, his instincts said otherwise. There had been something malignant about that darkness, something violent and ugly. And while he wasn't sure about his redheaded Psy, his beast scented none of that ugliness in her. Faith smelled warm and female, tempting and inviting.

Whatever it was that was happening, he had the gut feeling that Faith herself was unaware of it. It was even possible that someone else was entering her consciousness through her connection to the hive mind of the PsyNet.

The shower shut off. That was when he realized he'd given Faith nothing with which to replace her sweat-soaked pajamas. He waited for her to figure out the same. She cracked open the door a minute later. "I need new clothing."

He turned and propped himself up with an arm against the wall. "I don't know. I think you'd look good without them."

Night-sky eyes stared at him without blinking. "You're not playing nice."

"You catch on quick, Red." From the gap in the door he could see her holding the towel closed over breasts that appeared surprisingly generous given her small frame. The beast prowled closer to the surface of his mind.

"My name is Faith."

"Hmm." He moved enough to slide a strand of wet silk through his fingers. Right now, her hair was a dark red that reminded him of heart's blood. "Do you have extra clothes in your bag?"

"A shirt and the pants I was wearing earlier." She didn't protest his touch and he wondered if she even realized how far she'd come in mere hours. Something in Faith craved sensation and it was driving her to buck her conditioning under Silence. He was pleased. And it was because he liked touching her. The cat saw no reason to lie about that.

"I'll get you a T-shirt—you can get into your day clothes later in case you decide to go back to sleep." There was spare women's clothing in the cupboards, but he wanted her covered in his scent. And he was animal enough not to care why he wanted that. He just did. "Wait here."

This time, she didn't ask him to stop, but he felt her eyes on him all the way down the hall. She hadn't moved so much as an inch by the time he came back. Whatever it was that she'd seen, it had spooked the hell out of her, spooked her enough to break down her normal shield of cool reserve.

"Here."

"Thank you." She closed the door, leaving him to imagine all sorts of things. He was getting to the part about replacing his T-shirt with him when she walked out.

"I left the towel on the drying rod." She tucked her hair behind her ears.

He saw that his old black T-shirt hit her a bare few inches above the knee, covering way more than he'd expected. "You're short."

"Did you only notice now?"

"What are you, five two?"

"One hundred and fifty-five centimeters to be exact."

That made her a lot shorter than him. Which would make things very interesting in bed. He pushed off the wall, not surprised at the direction of his thoughts, but disturbed by the strength of them. Cats liked sensuous play and Faith was a very enticing female, small but formed just right. And that skin—it made him want to lick her up.

"Why are you looking at me like that?" Faith took a step back and tilted up her head.

No emotion in either her tone or her expression. No scent of desire. But the cat knew full well she found him intriguing.

"Yes, it'll make things very interesting." He could easily

lift her up against a wall and pound into her. Hard. But maybe he'd save that for later—his Psy would probably appreciate a bit less enthusiasm the first few times.

"Vaughn, your eyes are going more jaguar than usual."

He shook his head in a sharp movement and strode down the hallway. "I think the coffee's ready." What the hell was this Psy doing to him? He was known in DarkRiver for being aloof to the point of icy remoteness. Most of the newly mature females gave him a wide berth while they flaunted themselves to every other male, because they knew he wasn't led by his balls. At least not until now.

Faith caught up to him. "Do you have any nutrition I could have?"

"Nutrition?" He scowled. "Do you mean food?"

"I have some nutrition bars in my bag if you don't."

"You're worse than Sascha was." He put his hand on her lower back and urged her toward the kitchen.

She jumped away like a scalded cat. "I told you not to touch me."

He growled very low in his throat. "Minutes ago you were begging me not to let go. Make up your mind, Red." He was aware his voice sounded a touch more jaguar than Faith could probably handle.

"I wasn't completely in control when I woke." She stared at him with wary caution but didn't back away. Then she surprised him even more and took a step closer. "And you know that."

The cat growled again, but it was pleased. This woman might look fragile but she had a spine of pure steel. "Are you sure I'm that logical?"

"No. But you're not an animal either."

He leaned in close until he had her boxed against the wall, his arms on either side of her body. One simple lift and he could have her at his sexual mercy. "That's where you're wrong, baby." He brushed his lips over her ear. "I'm as animal as they come." Before she could say anything, he pushed off and walked into the kitchen.

He heard the ragged gasp of her breath a few seconds later. "Are you really?"

He looked over his shoulder. "What do you think?"

CHAPTER 7

She walked closer. "Your eyes aren't quite . . . human."

Most people never figured that out, believing they were simply an unusual color. "My beast is stronger than most." And had been ever since that week when he'd survived by turning jaguar and staying that way. Because even a baby jaguar had a better chance of survival in the forest than a ten-year-old human boy. But being in cat form for that length of time at such a young age had permanently changed him.

As if reassured by his calmer tone, she took another step forward. "What does that mean?"

He poured some coffee into a cup. "Milk? Sugar?"

"I don't know."

"Here, taste." Lifting the black coffee to her lips, he watched her take a sip.

She closed her eyes and breathed in the scent as she *tasted*. He'd never seen any woman do that with the intensity of Faith, never been so aware of the inherent sensuality in the act.

"Good?"

"Put sugar in it," she ordered, eyes remaining closed.

Vaughn didn't follow orders well, but this was different. This, to him, was a kind of play, though Faith probably didn't think of it that way. Too bad. She was playing with a very interested cat and when that cat got interested in things, it didn't like to be denied. "Here." He let her taste the sweetened coffee.

Once again, she breathed deep and savored the taste. "Milk."

"All ready."

A minute later, she opened her eyes. "The flavors are . . . unusual." She seemed to be searching for words.

"Do you like it?"

"Like? Psy don't feel like or dislike." She shook her head. "But perhaps that's because I've never been given food of such different flavors that I have a basis for comparison. I . . . prefer the coffee with the sugar but not the milk."

He prepared it for her, amused at the way she tried to word things so as not to admit feeling anything even close to emotion. "Here." Leaving her to take a sip, he walked to the fridge and pulled the door open. "You're hungry and so am I. What do you say to bacon and eggs?" He started gathering the ingredients.

"Okay." She was standing right next to him.

Of course he'd heard her move, but he let her be. She was still scared and Vaughn could stroke rather than bite when he wanted to. He put the bread and other things on the counter and closed the fridge. "Come on, Red. Time for a cooking lesson."

She put her coffee cup beside his. "I'm ready."

He ran a knuckle down her cheek and when she jumped, he smiled. "Are you sure?" This close, he saw that while her skin was creamy, it wasn't the pale white of so many redheads, having a rich undertone of gold that only made it more tempting. "What's your history, Faith NightStar? Where do you get that red hair and this skin?"

"The NightStar PsyClan has many redheads—there is a genetic preponderancy of the trait. My skin is courtesy of a number of genes from both my mother and father." She reached for the eggs and held them up. "I'm in need of nutrition."

He showed her what to do with the first egg and then let her try. "So you're all-American?"

"No. My mother was born in the former state of Uzbekistan and moved to America as a child. It is my father who is a NightStar. He is primarily of Anglo-Italian heritage, though his great-grandfather was of Asiatic origin."

"You know the way you Psy mix it up—watch the heat, sugar." He pulled her hand away when it went too close to the heating unit.

She tugged it out of his grasp. "Thank you. I think the eggs are done."

"Uh-huh." He put them on a plate. "If you put the bacon in that container over there, it'll cook without splatter."

"Why do you know about cooking? In the books I read prior to approaching DarkRiver, predatory male changelings were always portrayed as being very dominant and unwilling to learn domestic tasks."

"I never said I liked cooking. But I can do it if the situation demands."

"What were you saying about the Psy?"

"That the way you mix it up would be more impressive if it was actually human-to-human contact. Instead, it's all done on a genetic level. Unless your parents fell wildly in lust and created you in pleasure?" He watched the concentration with which she did such a simple task as cooking and found it strangely arousing. He had the feeling Faith would do *everything* with that same level of concentration.

"You know Psy don't feel lust or pleasure." She pulled off the bacon and put it to the side.

He ran his finger down her cheek again. "If your body feels sensation, then lust is always a possibility."

Lucas watched Sascha pace around the bedroom and enjoyed the view. It wasn't bare skin but it was delectable nonetheless—his practical Psy had fallen madly in love with lacey feminine underthings in the months after dropping out of the Net.

"I can't believe you talked me into leaving Faith with Vaughn." She put her hands on hips barely covered by a pure white slip and glared. "He was behaving completely wild last night."

"We're all wild, Sascha darling." He wondered if she'd put her panties back on. "Come here."

"It's six a.m. We should be heading out to check if Vaughn managed to keep from driving her into complete insanity overnight."

"I thought you liked Vaughn."

"I do, but he's a little too much for Faith to handle—we might as well have left her with a rabid tiger."

"Vaughn would take exception to that." He liked fencing with his mate, enjoyed seeing fire in eyes that had once held only cold Psy focus.

"I'm serious, Lucas." She finally crawled back onto the bed beside him. "I'm worried about Faith."

"Vaughn won't harm her."

"Not purposefully." She put a hand on his chest. "But he doesn't understand exactly what it is that he's dealing with. Changelings think touch is always good, but it isn't, not for someone like Faith. I've been thinking about it and I think she really could break under the strain."

He frowned. "She's that weak?"

"No." Sascha's hand pressed down as she rose to a kneeling position. "But she's lived her entire life in a vacuum. What do you think will happen if you suddenly expose her to the air?"

"Shit." Lucas sat up. "Let's go." He trusted Vaughn implicitly, but Sascha was right—the jaguar had been acting unusually aggressive ever since they'd found Faith. He might unknowingly thrust the redheaded Psy over the edge.

Faith sat in the bedroom dressed in her day clothes. Eating with Vaughn had been an adventure. He hadn't touched her again after she'd threatened to leave midway through the meal, but she knew the promise had ended the minute they'd finished breakfast. If she exited this room, he'd start pushing her again.

The odd thing was, she didn't want to remain in here until Sascha arrived. What Vaughn was doing threatened her sanity, but it also . . . stimulated her. For the first time in her life, she felt alive in more than the mind alone. Her body had always seemed like something that wasn't quite hers, but now it was very definitely a part of her—Vaughn stretched every one of her senses to the extreme.

And he made the darkness go away.

Getting up, she rubbed her palms on her thighs. There was no logical reason to walk out that door, but Faith decided that today, logic wouldn't help her much. She was in changeling territory, predatory changeling territory. They lived by different rules.

He wasn't waiting for her in the hallway as she'd half expected. Neither was he in the living room. Thinking that he might have stepped out, she walked to the porch and sat down in a chair-swing she hadn't noticed the previous night. The motion of the swing was soothing, but the fact that she couldn't see Vaughn left her unable to fully relax.

The scrape of claws on wood.

She sat perfectly still as a large jaguar walked around the corner and prowled over. The eyes that watched her out of that savage, wild face were familiar, but no less dangerous. He walked past her, rubbing the side of his heavy, warm body against her legs.

The sensation was indescribable.

Her mind tumbled as it tried to process the new information. The slide of fur over clothing, the heavy nonhuman heat, the sheer beauty of the creature so close to her. Part of her wanted to reach out and touch, the part that had lived a life inside of walls so thick there had been no other living presence within touching distance. But another part of her wanted to run. Because this predator had very sharp teeth and he hadn't decided whether she was friend or foe.

He turned and rubbed across her legs once again. Her breath caught in her throat, her heart slamming hard against her ribs. And she knew she'd reached overload level. Her mind was about to go critical—the false sense of security that had allowed her to fence with him this morning was gone under the looming reality of a mental cascade. She pulled her feet up onto the swing and wrapped her arms around her knees. Desperately fighting the closing wings of darkness, she heard a low, throaty growl.

She refused to open her eyes, refused to allow any more sensation into her mind. She had to stop hearing, stop feeling, stop seeing. Maybe then she could control the nerves going haywire inside of her. That was when human male hands cupped her face and everything snapped.

Vaughn felt Faith go completely motionless under his touch. A split second later, her body spasmed with such violence that he knew she'd lost control of it. The second time, he barely caught her before she hit her head hard against the back of the swing, but she was already unconscious.

"No," he whispered, voice raw. He *would not* allow the

Council to win and if he left Faith alone and untouched, they would. It had become imperative to him that this Psy became strong enough to make choices other than those mandated for her.

Deciding against taking her inside, he was about to stand when he heard the distant noise of an approaching car. Identifying it from the sound of the eco-engine, he used his considerable speed to go into the house and pull on some clothes. He was outside on the swing with Faith in his arms by the time Lucas and Sascha pulled up. Sascha almost leaped from the vehicle and ran up the steps.

"Oh, God, Vaughn!" Her rapidly darkening eyes moved over Faith's silent body. "How could—"

"I know what I'm doing." Sascha might be an E-Psy, but the jaguar wasn't budging on this one point. The cat knew something she didn't, knew it on the deepest, most primitive level. If anyone had asked Vaughn to explain, he wouldn't have been able to put his certainty into words, but that made it no less strong.

"She's so deeply unconscious that I can't reach her and you think you know what you're doing?" Her words were bullet fast.

"Lucas," Vaughn said quietly.

The alpha's eyes met his. "Are you sure?"

"Yes."

Sascha turned furiously to her mate and when she didn't speak aloud, Vaughn knew she was yelling at Lucas mind-to-mind. Lucas couldn't broadcast speech, but the two had discovered that he could hear her perfectly fine. It made sense given that Lucas's great-great-grandmother had been Psy.

The alpha winced and caught Sascha around the waist to haul her up against his body. "He's a sentinel. He protects. Leave it be, darling."

"He might protect, but that protection doesn't stretch to Faith."

"It does now."

Everyone went silent. "Since when?" Lucas asked.

"Since I decided." ·

"Fine."

Sascha glanced from one male to the other then shook her head in obvious frustration. "Let me see if she's doing any better." Wiggling out of Lucas's grip, she came over. "She's like a butterfly coming out of a cocoon."

He understood, and because she was one of the few beings he respected, he said, "I won't bruise her wings, Sascha darling."

A smile flirted with her lips at the small tease. "What's gotten into you?"

He didn't reply as she put her hands over Faith's body and tried to read her emotional temperature. The truth was, he didn't know the answer. Not withstanding the promise he'd just made, he wasn't sure about Faith. Her story made sense, yet it could very well be a clever facade. The cat didn't think so, but despite its predatory nature, the cat was sometimes innocent in a way the human male could never be.

"She's shut down to a point where I'd compare it to a coma—I don't know when she'll come out of it."

Vaughn cradled Faith against his chest. "She'll be fine in a few minutes."

Sascha rose from her crouch. "How do you know that?"

"Maybe I'm Psy."

She sighed. "Do I smell breakfast?" Without waiting for an answer, she strode inside the house.

Lucas only spoke when she was out of earshot. "I've never questioned your judgment and I won't do it now."

"But?"

"She's not like Sascha, Vaughn. Sascha could already feel before she came to us. Even if Faith's story is completely true, she's as cold as the rest of her race. Don't forget that."

In his arms, he felt her heartbeat, felt the rush of her blood. "She's warmer than you know."

"What happened?"

"I think you and Sascha both need to hear that. Have breakfast and give Faith time to wake up."

Lucas nodded and followed his mate inside. Vaughn felt a strange tension release from his shoulders. He couldn't quite pinpoint the source, but something about the other cat had set him on edge, though Lucas was his friend in the truest sense of the word. They'd never been just alpha and sentinel. The loyalty forged in the dark days of their childhoods went both ways—he trusted Lucas as absolutely as the other male trusted him. But all of a sudden his instincts were reacting as if the other man were a threat.

Frowning, he returned his attention to the woman in his arms. He had a reason for keeping her outside. From what Sascha had told them since she'd become part of DarkRiver, Psy were used to living in boxes and it seemed Faith had been more boxed in than most. But she'd had no problem walking into a forest on her own so maybe a hidden sense in this particular Psy craved the freedom to be found in the wild.

A tiny movement. He ran his hand up and down her arm, fingering the material of her shirt and stroking her back to wakefulness. As her head shifted against his chest, he used his feet to make the swing sway gently back and forth. Her eyelashes lifted and fluttered back down, then lifted again.

"How was your nap, Red?" He lowered the volume of his voice in an effort to keep this conversation private.

She balled up a fist against his chest. "Why are you touching me?" were the first words out of her mouth. They were soft and a little husky.

"Why aren't you seizing again?"

Night-sky eyes blinked and, sitting up, she used both hands

to push her hair off her face. "You're correct. Why am I not having another seizure?"

Surprised, he had no response. Sascha and Lucas came back out at that instant. The look on Sascha's face when she saw Faith, awake and apparently aware, was priceless. Lucas had grabbed a couple of chairs from inside the house and now placed them so they faced Vaughn and Faith. "Sit."

Sascha obeyed, hands full with two plates of food. "You okay?" she asked as Lucas took the bigger plate off her hands.

"I believe so." Faith rubbed her temples. "All my shields are holding against . . ." She paused and seemed to have to force the next words out: "Against the PsyNet." There was something very relieved about that statement, and suddenly Vaughn knew Faith's greatest fear. When she made a move to get off his lap, he had the urge to force her to stay, but that very urge made him let go.

She stood on shaky feet and took a deep breath. "Yes, I think I'm fine. Though the block against talking about the PsyNet is quite strong."

"Tell them about your vision, Red." He'd guessed what she'd seen, but he wanted her to talk about it, confront it.

She covered the small distance to the railing and seemed to focus her attention on the solid green of the trees. "It was another vision of heavy, formless darkness—the beginning. It'll build up until there's a murder to relieve the pressure. At least that's how I think it works. I've never had any contact with a killer before."

"Why do you call it darkness?" Lucas asked.

"I can't see anything in detail. I merely get a sense of *darkness*." It was as if she could find no other word to describe it. "There's evil in the darkness, a malicious intent I understand, though I've never before experienced those things." Her voice held an underlying thread of strain Vaughn could almost taste. "I think it's because I'm somehow actually him for the time I'm having the visions."

"Is any of that normal?" Sascha laid her fork down on her plate.

"No." Faith's back straightened and she finally turned to face them. "I usually see extremely clearly, details down to serial numbers, but it's all very clean. I'm never a participant."

"But not this time." Vaughn didn't like how she'd separated herself from the group when it was obvious she needed to be held.

"No." Her eyes were bleeding to black again and the effect was eerie. "It's like he reaches out and grabs me. I couldn't snap out of the vision until you touched me."

"Come sit here," he ordered, at the end of his patience.

She shook her head. "You won't keep your distance."

"That's exactly what you need."

"Who are you to make that judgment?"

"I saw something in your room this morning. Come here and I'll tell you what."

Her eyes were completely black by this point and full of suspicion. She took a few seconds to think about it before coming and sitting down on the swing . . . as far from him as physically possible. The cat wanted to snarl, but the male knew when to demand and when to let be.

"What did you see?" she asked. "You're not Psy—what could you possibly have seen?"

"There was something around you when you woke. A physical blackness that looked real enough to touch."

"Vaughn, are you sure?" Sascha leaned forward.

"It was like a shadow sticking to her."

Faith had absently begun to propel the swing back and forth. "I don't understand. None of my visions have ever manifested like that and I've been monitored since I was three years old."

"But you've never had these kinds of visions," he pointed out, struck by the delicacy of her profile. She was so easily breakable. He'd never put a bruise on her, but others weren't so careful and the Psy Council was made up of monsters.

"No. That's why I came to you. I need to know how to stop them."

Vaughn glanced up and caught Sascha's pained expression as she answered. "Faith, I'm sorry, but I don't think you can."

Faith's hands tightened on the edge of the seat. "I have to find a way. If I don't, I won't be able to function at acceptable levels."

"You didn't come to us because you wanted the visions to stop." Vaughn waited until she looked at him. "What you want is the ability to control them—so you can see what it is that your mind's trying to show you."

She shook her head. "No. I don't have the capacity to handle the visions. Why would I want them to continue?"

Looking into those ebony eyes, he closed the gap between them. "Because then you'll stop feeling guilty about your sister."

Her body turned to ice and she stared straight ahead. "I'm Psy. I don't feel guilt."

"There was nothing you could've done." He pressed his thigh against hers, forcing her attention back to him. "You were never trained to deal with the kinds of things you're seeing now."

"I shouldn't be seeing them in the first place."

"Why?"

CHAPTER 8

Faith opened her mouth to reply and realized she had no real answer. She'd been taught that because of the Protocol, the visions would always focus on the narrow subject of commerce. But she'd also been taught that predatory changelings were uniformly violent creatures to be avoided at all costs. And she'd been taught that Sascha Duncan was a failed Psy, when the other cardinal's power was a vibrant blaze.

"Faith." Sascha's voice was gentle, her eyes even more so. "Maybe this was what you were always meant to see."

She'd made the logical connections, but found herself hesitating to draw a conclusion. "Why would they lie to me about that?"

"Because there's no money in stopping murder." Lucas's harsh voice cut into the silence.

"No." She brought the swaying motion to an abrupt halt. "No one could condition that out of me."

"They didn't. You're seeing," Vaughn reminded her.

"I'm twenty-four years old. Why would the dark visions come now?"

"Maybe that's the point at which conditioning starts to break down in certain Psy," Sascha murmured. "I'm only two years older."

Faith stared at the other cardinal. "What did they condition out of you?"

"Everything." Sascha leaned into her mate's stroking hand. "They crippled me, told me I wasn't a cardinal. It almost drove me mad."

Madness. The demon that stalked Faith's every waking hour, whispered in her ear, and awaited her at the end of her life. "Is that what you think will happen to me?"

"If you don't embrace your gift, yes."

"It's not a gift. It's a curse." She didn't want to see horror and pain, terror and malevolence, didn't want to *feel*. "It might drive me mad by itself."

"You really think you're that weak, Red?" Vaughn's voice was a husky purr against her ear. "You climbed that fence and walked into changeling territory without pause. We have teeth and claws and you took us on. Compared to that, visions should be easy."

Faith turned and met those amazing wild eyes. "The only thing you could've done was kill me. The visions might leave me one of the walking dead."

"Why are you so scared of them?" Sascha asked.

"I don't feel fear." Faith jerked to her feet. "My PsyClan has always ensured I was taken care of. Why would they want to handicap me in any sense?" She knew, she could reason it out, but she wanted someone else to be the one to vocalize it.

Vaughn shifted and she caught the movement with the corner of her eye. "You know the answer to that."

She should've guessed he'd never let her take the easy way out. "Money." Her PsyClan had sold her out for money. "Why am I the first to . . . break?"

"Maybe you're not." Sascha stood to face her. "Maybe

you're simply the first one who hasn't been found out and silenced."

Faith saw the truth Sascha was too kind to point out. "You mean rehabilitated, don't you?"

"Or perhaps worse, given your value. Any strange disappearances in your family tree?"

"My grandmother was last seen shortly after she gave birth to my father. And five years ago, one of my cousins vanished—Sahara was only sixteen." She let herself think about what that might mean. "You think the Council or the PsyClan might be keeping them captive, working them when they're lucid and letting the dark visions ravage them when they're not?"

"I don't know, Faith. I'm not an F-Psy."

Faith felt Vaughn walk to stand behind her. Somehow that gave her the strength she needed. "I am. And I know that even in the madness, there are moments of clarity. My paternal aunt is held in a care facility—she went conventionally insane during her sixth decade—but she continues to make million-dollar predictions four or five times a year. More than enough to pay for her care." To make her comfortable in her madness.

The last time Faith had seen her aunt, it had been via a communication screen—Carina NightStar could no longer bear any kind of immediate sentient contact. What she'd seen would haunt Faith till the day she died. The icy Gradient 7.5 Psy who'd been one of her trainers, a woman with a record of almost eighty-five percent accuracy, had turned into a creature that no longer looked human. She'd chewed off her own lips and bitten and scratched herself so many times that they'd had to remove most of her fingernails and teeth. Her clothing had been torn, her hair matted. Something strange and *wrong* had skittered behind her eyes.

"But unlike my aunt, the ones who saw the dark visions could never be allowed to speak to the rest of us. It would bring the success of the entire Protocol into question. They'd have to be locked away, caged *before* they fell victim to the mental degradation." Faith began to see the true inhumanity of what it was these changelings were asking her to accept.

"Caged Psy can still forecast. In fact, they'd be the perfect tools—machines no one knew existed, their treatment subject to no laws. And if certain other segments of conditioning were deliberately broken, it would leave them open to everything . . . including visions of plots or rebellions that might come in very useful to those in power."

"Faith," Sascha began.

"I'm sorry." She raised a hand. "I need time to process everything I've learned so far."

"You might not have a lot of time left." Sascha's tone was anything but harsh.

"Will you see me again? I think I can get away in five days or so."

"Of course."

Faith wondered if in those five days she might make some sense out of the pack of lies upon which she'd apparently been raised. What was true and what was false? The changelings might be right in some matters, but who said they were right in everything? Their loyalties were different, their lives controlled by emotion.

Maybe they were wrong. Maybe her own people didn't only see her as a money-making asset. Maybe.

Vaughn escorted Faith to the edge of the trees. "Will you be okay climbing the fence?"

"Yes." She settled her bag carefully on her back. "You'll be here in five days?" Her eyes were looking anywhere but at him.

"I keep my promises, Red." He curved his hand around her nape. "I may even pay you an earlier visit. Wouldn't want to undo all the good we've done."

"Good?"

He rubbed his thumb over her skin. "I like the way you feel under my touch."

"Don't come, Vaughn. If they catch you, they'll hurt you."

His beast heard something it liked in her tone. "I never get caught, baby. If I can infiltrate the SnowDancer den without tipping them off, then this is child's play."

"There are Psy guards, able to scan the area for signs of sentient life."

"These forests are changeling territory—they have to know we're going to keep an eye on them. Don't worry about me. I'm a big boy." But he was delighted by her concern, for that was definitely what he'd sniffed in the air.

"I simply don't want to mess up my next meeting with Sascha. If you're caught, they'll put me under tougher surveillance." Her skin was soft, but her spine as straight as a rod.

He brushed his lips over her cheek. She gasped and moved away. "Go, Red. The guards are at the optimal distance."

She ran quickly to the fence and scaled it with smooth feminine grace. Oh yeah, she'd definitely make things very interesting in bed. And he had every intention of getting her there. The taste of her on his lips was the most intoxicating thing he'd ever felt.

She landed on her feet on the other side and looked back as if searching for him. He allowed his eyes to go night-glow in the forest and knew the instant she spotted him. Then she was gone, hidden behind the fences of the Psy world.

Good thing cats were excellent climbers.

Early the next morning, Faith shored up her shields against the endless mass of the PsyNet and took a step out of her bedroom. As she'd expected, the chime of the incoming call didn't cease. The M-Psy were checking up on her well before her three-day rest period was officially over. If she didn't answer, they'd likely take it as justification to enter her home.

In the past, that knowledge had settled her—if a vision went wrong, they'd be there to pick up the pieces. But today, the lack of privacy, the lack of her ability to live any kind of a real life, made her— She had no word to describe her reaction. No word that didn't imply feeling, the one thing she couldn't embrace.

She pressed the answer key on the touch pad. "Yes?"

The composed face of one of Xi Yun's underlings looked back at her. "You didn't answer our two earlier calls. We wished to ensure you were conscious and rational."

Because F-Psy had a habit of becoming irrational and mad.

Faith realized the M-Psy always subtly pointed that out, never letting her forget the threat looming over her head.

Tell a child something often enough and she starts to believe it.

Sascha's words whispered through her mind and refused to let her return to the isolated, accepting state she'd been in before she'd breached the fence. And run headfirst into the most dangerous predator she could imagine.

"While I accept your need to ensure my safety, I gave notice that I would not be available for three days. That period doesn't end till this evening. Is that so difficult to understand?" Her voice was cold, a knife forged in the fires of isolation. "Or would you like me to have you transferred and replaced with someone who understands my statements?" She'd never threatened any such thing in the past, but the nameless awakening thing inside of her would not be quiet over this latest threat to her independence.

The M-Psy blinked. "My apologies, Foreseer. I will not make this error again."

He'd also log in her unusual behavior and put her down

for a complete physical. Faith turned off the communication console without another word, conscious that she'd shot herself in the foot. The only places where she'd be safe from monitoring now would be in her private areas and even that wasn't certain. It would've been far more logical to have kept her mouth shut.

Or would it?

She stilled and considered her behavior. She was a twenty-four-year-old F-Psy who produced with near perfect accuracy. She was worth billions, not the millions Sascha had guessed at. And she knew that her psychic strength offered her immunity from a lot of things that might otherwise be issues.

Such as being interned at the Center, her mind wiped clean in a process of "rehabilitation."

Put that way, arrogance was almost a given. Merely because they'd subjugated their feelings, it didn't mean that her people were no longer cognizant of distinctions of class, wealth, and power. For the first time, she considered the untapped reservoir of her own political power. Perhaps she even had enough to delete all monitoring of her, aside from when she was in the chair. Maybe not at once, but slowly?

Glancing at the object on which she'd spent so much of her life, she made her decision. Instead of sliding onto it, she returned to her bedroom and lay down on the bed. She was going to use this free time to surf the PsyNet, to look for information she'd never before considered might exist— because her keepers had surrounded her in so much cotton wool that it had become a prison.

They'd gone so far as to warn her against too much exposure to the Net, telling her that her mind was more vulnerable than those of other designations and therefore more easily breached. In response, Faith had built ever stronger firewalls and rarely ventured outside them. But if Sascha Duncan wasn't a flawed Psy, then maybe Faith NightStar wasn't a weak one. Flickers of memory rippled through her mind. Vaughn had touched her, kissed her, had never hidden the intense nature of his personality. But she'd begun to learn how to cope. And if she could handle a jaguar . . .

Taking a deep breath, she closed her eyes and opened her mind to the dark velvet night of the PsyNet. Stars glittered in the darkness, but these flickering lights were alive, the unique minds of millions of psychic beings. The instant she stepped out into the Net, her mobile firewalls rose to protect her surfing psyche. Those without firewalls were vulnerable to sabotage and possible ambush, as cutting off the roaming mind from the physical brain was a sure way to ensure an irreversible coma. Most Psy were fanatical about their firewalls. Faith had gone straight to obsession.

She'd been out a couple of minutes at most, aimlessly letting information filter through her, when she felt something neosentient brush by her. The NetMind. It paused and she felt a second brush, as if it was verifying.

Apparently satisfied by her brain patterns, the NetMind moved on. The pause had been unusual, but Faith could understand it—even the all-seeing NetMind had probably rarely logged one of the F-Psy engaged in an active surf of the data streams.

Around her, the Net buzzed with information and activity. Minds flew smoothly to various destinations, some disappearing without warning as they followed links not visible to Faith's mind. That was normal. The PsyNet was based to some extent on what each Psy already knew—how could she link to a mind, and therefore to a location, for which she had no imprint?

The intensity and unfamiliarity of the flows around her had her moving quietly, keeping her presence low-key. With her cardinal star left behind, she was simply another Psy in the Net. Most cardinals didn't bother to shield their supernova brightness even when they roamed, but Faith preferred to travel incognito. Her complex firewalls did the job of keeping her anonymous. Oddly enough, it was the PsyClan that had first taught the techniques that masked her identity—they'd considered it a precaution against her being taken hostage.

She drifted into a psychic chat room, something she'd never before done. The M-Psy had been very specific about the danger of overload in this completely unpredictable venue.

"I hear they're discussing candidates," a mind threw out into the conversation.

"Took them long enough," another responded.

"Losing a cardinal of Santano's strength has to be worrying some of the weaker members," a third mind said.

Faith might've had no clue as to what they were discussing if she hadn't run across former councilor Santano Enrique's name during her research on Sascha Duncan. Paying more attention, she found an unobtrusive listening point and went mind-quiet.

"None of the Councilors is weak," the first mind retorted. "The only ones who like to think that are the aspirants."

"Any word on the possibilities?"

"I heard the Council's imposed a gag order. Anyone breaking it faces automatic rehabilitation."

"Does anybody actually know what happened to Santano? All that was reported was that he'd died of unknown causes."

"Nobody knows nothing from what I hear."

The same mind that had posed the Santano question now said, "What I'd really like to know is how Sascha Duncan left the Net."

"That's old news—she was weak and couldn't hold the link. Likely her mind was never meant to maintain it in the first place, which is why she survived."

"A tidy answer, but don't you consider it a little too convenient?"

A small silence and then someone said, "Perhaps we should continue this conversation in a more secure venue." The mind blinked out and two of the others followed, probably going to a destination known to all three.

Intrigued by what she'd heard, Faith let herself float through several other rooms, but nobody else was discussing such incendiary matters. However, it was as well that she'd been floating so seemingly without focus, because it became clear toward the end that she had two shadows. She tracked back through her mind and realized they'd been there from the start.

She knew exactly who was responsible for setting them on her. Even in the supposed anonymity of the PsyNet, she was too valuable to be left alone. A kind of cold fury settled in her gut and it was so pure she could feel it burning her. And she didn't care if that sounded like an emotional reaction.

She returned to her mind in as straight a line as possible. The second she was back behind the walls of her psyche, she opened her eyes and considered her next move. Would it betray too much of the changes in her if she demanded privacy? Could she live knowing she'd never be let alone?

No.

Swallowing the things shoving at the walls of her conditioned Silence, she got up, gathered her hair into a sleek roll, and put on one of the flowing dresses she preferred to wear while forecasting. This one was a deep rust brown with spaghetti straps and a hem that skimmed her ankles. Even when the visions refused to let her go, her body at least felt free.

Ready, she walked out into the living room and took her usual position in the chair. Monitoring would've begun the second she entered the living area, but now they'd be sitting up in expectation of a session. Instead, she threw up the strongest blocks she could imagine—she couldn't stop the visions, but she could occasionally contain them for a time—and started reading a book.

By the time she finished it two hours later, she knew they had to be getting impatient. She never used the chair for such mundane things. Then she picked up another book. Ten minutes later, her comm console chimed an incoming call. Using the remote, she flicked on the screen facing the chair.

"Father."

The title was nothing more than a convenient way to refer to him. Anthony Kyriakus was a stranger to her except as the governing force of the PsyClan, no matter that it was half his blood that ran in her veins. "Faith, Medical has informed me of erratic behavior on your part."

Here it came, she thought, the request for a complete mental and physical workup. "Father, would you consider it a breach of your rights as a free citizen to be monitored on the PsyNet?" An ultimately logical question. "Or am I allowed to shadow you wherever you go?"

Anthony's brown eyes remained cool on-screen. "It was for your own protection."

"You didn't answer my question." She picked up her book again. "As it appears I cannot inform myself in private, I thought I should do it in public." The most subtle of threats.

"You've never shown any desire for complete isolation."

Isolation, not privacy. It was becoming crystal clear how they'd been herding her along a certain path her entire life. But he was right—she couldn't show such a drastic change without some explanation. A flicker of memory from the Net gave her inspiration and if it came from the same part of her that showed her the visions, she chose to ignore that. "Perhaps an adult cardinal, one of the rare F designation, might possibly be interested in other opportunities . . . but those opportunities are highly unlikely to be offered to someone with a babysitter."

Understanding filtered so quickly into Anthony's face that she was certain he'd already been thinking along those lines. "It's a dangerous game. Only the strong survive."

"Which is why I can't appear weak."

"Have you heard anything concrete?"

"I'll tell you when it's time." A blatant untruth because the time would never come, no matter what Anthony believed. The Council was hardly going to consider a cloistered foreseer as a possible member. But as far as reasons for privacy went, it was close to perfect.

Something brutal and ugly *shoved* at the walls she'd set up against the visions and she knew she had to get out of here before it erupted and exposed her. Because the business visions were never this powerful, this aggressive. Putting down the book, she swung her legs over the side of the chair. "My answer, Father?"

"Privacy is a citizen's right." He nodded. "But should you need assistance, contact me."

"Of course." She switched off the screen without further good-byes—they were redundant in her situation, something she'd figured out as a child. But at least now she'd be left alone on the Net, a huge step forward. No one could suspect her of anything at this stage—even the information she'd found out about Sascha had come from public bulletin boards. However, her next searches weren't going to be so innocent.

Another push on her mind. She strolled out of the room and forced herself to get water and several nutrition bars from the cooler. The second her hand closed around a bar, Vaughn's mocking smile appeared in the screen of her mind. She could imagine what he'd say to her choice of food and, though it was a dangerous game, she indulged herself and focused on him all the way to her bedroom. Once inside, she put down the food and closed the door.

The next push almost drove her off her feet. She swayed, but remained upright—if she fell, the sensors outside the door might pick it up. Breathing carefully, she somehow got to the bed before collapsing. Sweat dampened her hands and temples—a physiological reaction to unknown stress factors.

Fear.

She was Psy. She should feel no fear. But neither should she be seeing what she was now being forced into seeing. Then the darkness breached the flimsy walls of her defenses and hooked its claws into her mind. Her back arched, her hands clenched, her teeth snapped shut with crushing force, and she was no longer aware of anything but the vision.

CHAPTER 9

It was as if the darkness knew when she was alone and at her most helpless. Like some vicious beast waiting in the shadows for its prey to drop its guard, it crept in through the vision channels and seized control of her senses. And then it—*he*—forced her to watch what would come to pass if he wasn't stopped.

Blood, so much blood on his hands, in his hair, on his skin. The pale fragility of his hand was almost invisible under the rich, dark coating—*wait*. He was older than this, decades more experienced than the slender boy drenched in blood. But it was the same darkness, the same evil. She understood what she was seeing, though this had rarely ever happened to her.

An unexpected expression of the ability of foresight was backsight, the ability to see the past. F-Psy who primarily saw the past were very, very rare. Faith could think of none in the last fifty years. When they did appear, they tended to head into Enforcement. But most active F-Psy usually had one or two flashes of backsight during the year. In her case, she'd always caught innocuous images connected with the future she was trying to glimpse.

Never had she been so covered in blood that she was sticky with it, the iron-rich metallic scent drawn in with every breath. Her eyelashes were crusted with the dried fluid and the blood under her fingernails was so dark it was almost black. The imprint of her footsteps had started to set as the blood on the floor congealed. The knife she'd used was in one hand. When she raised it, the light from a torch glinted off it.

A torch?

Turning, she found herself surrounded by a dozen black-suited men. The vision flash-fractured and the next time she opened her eyes, she was in the confines of a white-on-white room. Bloodlust roared in her veins and she realized she was older, years older. And hungry. So *hungry*. For human prey.

Another violent jerk along the timeline. She was with the dark-suited men once again. They set her free at the start of a maze and she started hunting. The fear she sensed in her prey drew her like a drug. She ran on strong feet, knowing they'd have chosen a suitable sacrifice. They always did.

Her hand clenched on the knife. She spied the vulnerable nape of the girl who'd stumbled onto the hard ground. A smile cracked the anticipation on her face. This would be so much fun.

No!

Faith ripped herself from the vision so violently that she fell to the floor. Curling up into a fetal position, she tried to stifle her whimpers, tried to wipe the taint of blood from her brain. For those long moments she'd become the killer, become the very evil that had taken her sister's life. That was what had brought her back to herself—the knowledge that if she let it continue, she might just feel her own hands slide around her sister's throat.

The bedside comm console chimed. They'd heard her fall

of course. The outside sensors were very sensitive and she'd made a great deal of noise. Forcing herself to get up, she answered without visual. "I tripped on something."

"Are you injured?"

"No. I'm fine. Please don't disturb me till morning." She cut off the communication with that bare statement, aware her vocal mask was about to crack. Her voice wanted to tremble, wanted to cry.

Step two in the inevitable road to F-Psy insanity.

She had to get out of this claustrophobic compound. But she couldn't leave. Not now. Everybody was too aware of her wakefulness—they might even try to contact her again despite her orders. The urge to flee was so strong, it felt as if her skin had been drawn taut over flesh on the verge of explosion.

She couldn't satisfy the urge, couldn't run free, couldn't walk out to safety and toward the night-glow eyes of a predator so lethal that she shouldn't have thought of him in the same breath as the word *safety*. He was out of her reach anyway—she was a prisoner in this place everyone called her home. Would it one day become her tomb?

Shivering at the morbid thought, she crawled back into bed and lay there, staring up at the ceiling, memories of blood and horror her only companions. And though she refused to admit she felt anything, loneliness had a claw grip around her heart.

It hurt.

Faith woke the second someone whispered a breath against her neck. Her heart kicked into high gear. She knew that masculine scent, but its presence here was impossible. Thinking it an illusion of her stressed mind, she opened her eyes and found herself looking into the face of a human jaguar. He was lying alongside her, head propped up one hand.

"What are you doing in my bed?" she asked, too surprised to suppress the question.

"I just wanted to know if I could do it." He'd left his hair undone and it flowed over his shoulders in an amber-gold wave that shone, though the only light came from a small night-lamp.

That tiny lamp usually helped her delineate the line between waking and dreaming, but right now she wasn't certain where she stood. Raising a hand, she touched his hair. Warm strands slid through her fingers. The unexpected shock of sensation had her snatching back her hand. "You're real."

The smallest curving of his lips. "Are you sure?" He brushed a kiss over her mouth.

It was the most fleeting of touches but she felt burned. "You're definitely real." An accusation.

He chuckled, completely unrepentant.

"Don't make any loud sounds," she cautioned. "This room and my bathroom are private but everything else is monitored. Did you—?"

"They don't know I'm here." He looked up at the roof, at the skylight no one should've been able to open. "Psy don't monitor danger from above."

She couldn't figure out how he'd done it, but that didn't surprise her—he was a cat, after all. "Did Sascha send you?"

"Sascha thinks I'll eat you up if given the chance."

"Will you?" She wasn't sure about Vaughn, about the jaguar that prowled in the darkness behind the beauty of his eyes.

A finger trailed down her face and she forced herself not to move. She was strong and she would get past this block. Her fingers tingled with the sensory memory of Vaughn's hair and she wondered what his skin would feel like.

"Come closer and find out." His voice had gone rough, but there was nothing threatening about it. It was almost . . .

She searched the dictionary in her mind and found the answer. "You're trying to coax me." No one had ever before done such a thing. They'd demanded, ordered, asked in pandering terms, but never had anyone coaxed.

He was nearer to her, though she hadn't noticed him move. But he remained atop the sheets while she lay below. Why then could she feel the heat of his body, almost as if he burned hotter than her?

"Maybe."

It took her a second to remember her question. "Why?" Her hands were on top of the sheets, a hairsbreadth from the bare skin of his chest. Her eyes widened. "Are you naked?"

"Unless you have some clothing to give me, yeah." He sounded entirely too comfortable with that fact.

"You can't enter a woman's bedroom naked." That wasn't acceptable behavior in any race.

"I was clothed when I entered . . . in my fur." He was all golden eyes and gleaming skin above her, a male so beautiful that she wondered at his existence in the same world as her. "I can shift back if you'd like."

It was a dare. "Fine." She wasn't going to let him think he could get away with anything he wanted.

"Are you sure you want a jaguar in your room?"

"I think I already have one." But something in her wanted to see the change, the same something that knew Vaughn was beautiful, though she shouldn't have had the capacity to recognize male beauty.

"Don't move, Red."

The world turned into a rainbow-bright shimmer around her. She froze at the utterly unexpected sight. She'd thought the change would be painful for him, hadn't really expected him to do it. But nothing about this spoke of pain, only of awe.

A heartbeat later, the shimmer was gone and she found herself lying next to a jaguar who had very sharp teeth and eyes exactly like those of the man who'd occupied the space moments ago. She swallowed. She was Psy—she felt no fear. But it was practical to be on guard with something this lethal.

The jaguar opened its mouth and growled almost below the range of her hearing.

"Was that a question?" she ventured. "Because I don't speak jaguar." Where had that come from? It was a completely illogical statement—of course she didn't speak jaguar.

The jaguar lowered its head and nuzzled at her throat. Her heart threatened to rip through her skin and to the outside. "I'm stronger than this," she whispered, and forced herself to lift one hand around and over the jaguar's head until her fingers closed on the ruff of his neck. She tugged. He refused to move. She tugged again, harder. A growl that vibrated in her bones.

"Stop it, Vaughn."

Without warning, the fur disappeared from under her hands, the incredible softness shimmering into rainbow-bright sparks that ended with a naked male above her. Her hand was now clenched in amber-gold strands of hair. "So you'll touch the cat, but not the man?"

"I was trying to get you to move." She didn't release his hair, found she couldn't. His scent was everywhere in the air, his skin golden and close enough to touch, his smile pure cat.

"Where would you like me to move, little darling?"

She knew he'd added the "little" on purpose. "Away from me."

"Are you sure?" His smile turned wicked. "If I move, you might see more than you bargained for."

"I know this kind of behavior isn't acceptable among leopards." Technically speaking, she knew no such thing. It merely seemed the sort of thing that ought to be true. "How would you like it if an unknown male came into your sister's bedroom in this manner?"

All amusement was suddenly wiped off his face. He went

still, so completely still that it was as if he were made of stone. The part of her that had been deriving considerable intellectual stimulation from pitching her wit against his went silent, aware she'd awakened something very dangerous.

"Let go of my hair, Faith. And close your eyes. By the time you open them, I'll be gone."

She'd spent the past minutes trying to convince him to leave and now that he'd agreed, she found she didn't want him to go. For the first time, she was with someone who'd come to see her. Just her. Not Faith NightStar the F-Psy, but Faith, the individual apart from her gift.

"I am sorry," she said, hesitant. She knew nothing about changeling interaction, but she understood she'd caused him hurt. It had been part of her training to learn to recognize emotion in order to banish it. That was why she knew. It had nothing to do with the odd sensation in the vicinity of her heart. "If I offended you, I am sorry. I meant to . . . play."

Vaughn was caught completely off guard by that last word. His muscles relaxed without his conscious control. "Changed your mind, Red?"

"I'm not sure." She released her hold on his hair, but then began to stroke through it. "You're nothing I've ever experienced. The rules don't cover situations such as this."

"Rules?"

"The rules of Silence." Her fingers brushed the skin of his shoulders. She withdrew as if she'd been scalded, her hand dropping to lie against the pillow. "Why did my question offend you?"

Vaughn didn't talk about his past with anyone, but he found himself answering Faith—it was almost a compulsion, one neither man nor beast could fight. "My sister died when I was ten years old."

Skye had been so fragile, so weak at seven years of age that she hadn't been able to survive even in jaguar form.

He'd brought her food, given her everything he had, but Skye had given up fighting the instant she'd realized that their parents weren't going to come back for them. It was as if her soul had flown away and nothing he'd done had tempted her to return. She'd stopped eating, stopped drinking, and soon, she'd stopped breathing.

Vaughn had almost died then, too, because Skye had lived in his heart like no one else. She'd followed him around since before she could walk, a constant buzz of activity and energy. He hated his parents with a vengeance, but it wasn't because they'd abandoned him. No, it was because they'd broken Skye's heart.

"I can't understand what she meant to you," Faith said, her voice holding a quiet gentleness he'd never have expected from one of the Psy, "but I can guess. You mourn for her."

"Do you mourn for Marine?"

The quicksilver lights in her eyes dimmed until they were dull echoes against the darkness. "Psy don't mourn. To mourn requires feeling."

"And you don't have any."

"No."

"Are you sure?" Dropping his head, he bit her earlobe with sharp teeth and caught her resulting cry with the palm of his hand.

"What are you doing?" she whispered, pushing away his hand.

"Your body feels, Faith. Your body hungers." He spoke against her ear. "The body and the mind can't be so far apart. Can they?"

She didn't answer. He heard the rapid beat of her heart and knew he'd pushed her too far. But it wasn't far enough. She had to go further, had to understand more. It was imperative. The jaguar knew why, but the man wasn't ready to listen.

"And the answer to your question is that if I'd found a

strange man naked in my sister's bed, I'd have ripped him to shreds." He ran his lips down her neck and tasted the fury of her pulse before lifting his head to look down into her face. "I'll do the same to any other man I find in your bed."

Faith blinked and by the time her lashes lifted up, Vaughn was a shadow sliding out of the skylight. But nothing could erase the scent of him on her sheets, on her skin. The feel of his lips on the suddenly sensitive skin of her neck had her clenching her hands in an effort to find control where there seemed to be none. How could he do this to her? How?

Her strength lay in Silence, in holding her emotions in a stranglehold. If she let go, what other sensations might her jaguar introduce her to? Her brain revolted, insisting on showing her images of her aunt's lipless face and rabid eyes. It was the bluntest of reminders—she had to regain control of her malfunctioning psyche or the visions would take her over as they were even now threatening to do. The logical course would be to go to the M-Psy, admit her conditioning was breaking down, and ask for retraining.

But would they give her what she wanted, or would they use it as an excuse to put her someplace "safe," a location from which she could make predictions without causing them any of the inconvenience she now did by asking for occasional moments of privacy?

It didn't matter what the M-Psy would do, because she wasn't going to go to them. She was going to make a choice where there was no choice; she was going to act in a way that might leave her wide open to the very madness she wanted to escape. That strange, unknown awakening part of her didn't want to stop being fascinated by the jaguar who touched her as if she belonged to him, as if she'd already said yes to his every demand.

Careful, Faith. It was a soundless whisper. *He won't stop when you tell him to.* Because he wasn't Psy, wasn't someone who'd follow her every command, wasn't a man who'd follow *any* commands he didn't want to. And still she wasn't going to keep her distance.

What better proof was there of her accelerating decline?

Vaughn entered his lair deep in the forests to the east of Lucas's aerie and padded up the natural stone steps that led, eventually, to the true entrance. His home was accessed through a warrenlike cave system that acted as his defensive perimeter. His living space was in the central core, brightly lit during the daytime by a clever use of several natural vents and low-tech mirrors.

From above, his lair looked to be nothing but a hill in danger of being taken over by the forest. To date, no one had stumbled upon it either by accident or design. His closest friends alone knew where he lived and how to negotiate the traps in the outer caves. Those who didn't know . . . well, jaguars weren't famous for their kindness.

Reaching the core, he padded through the living room to his bedroom, where he shifted back to human form. Naked, he stretched his arms above his head before walking into the shower, which seemed to be a waterfall cascading from the stone wall. He'd spent hours creating the illusion because his beast wasn't happy in any place that looked too human, too civilized.

But both man and jaguar enjoyed sensation and pleasure. And water. So his home had a waterfall, as well as lush carpets he'd collected year by year on which his paws or feet made no sound. The walls were hung with handmade tapestries finer than those seen in many museums. Not only objects of beauty, they acted to contain the warmth in winter—when he used eco-generators to heat water in the fine tubes that ran throughout his home. That warmth became

particularly useful during those times when he worked
through the night on a piece that required a lot of contact
with cold chisels and hard edges.

His armchairs were comfortable, his bed big enough to
sprawl in, and more than big enough to entertain a lover no
matter how energetic he was feeling. But he'd never once
brought a woman here. However, today, he could imagine
dark red hair against the pillows, creamy limbs against the
thick blanket. Faith would look like an exotic jewel laid on a
bed of the finest black velvet.

A growl rose up in his throat as arousal caught him in a
vicious grip and shook him hard. He could've eased the
physical ache himself, but he didn't want to. He wanted the
Psy he could still smell on his skin. The man advised caution, told him to wait to be certain she wasn't playing with
his mind, wasn't a mole sent in by the Council to cripple
DarkRiver from within, but the cat lived by instinct and it
said Faith was his to take.

For many changelings, the human half would probably
have won. But Vaughn's animal half was stronger than that
of most others. Stepping out of the waterfall, he took a deep
breath. The air should've smelled of the earth and the forest,
but instead held teasing hints of fire and woman.

Pushing his hair out of his eyes, he stood there and considered his next step. Faith had come a long way since their
first meeting. She could bear small touches, hadn't been
made unconscious by his fleeting kiss, had reacted to his
nakedness but in the same way any other woman would've
reacted. He smiled at the memory. Faith wasn't cold, no
matter how much she might try to pretend otherwise.

But all that didn't negate the fact that she was a long way
from accepting the kind of touch the cat craved. He wanted
to lick her from head to toe, with lingering stops in soft feminine places that drew him like a drug. However, the second
he asked more of her than her mind was able to handle, he

might lose her. And that was unacceptable. So, where did that leave him?

"Step by step," he murmured under his breath, body taut with expectation. Faith NightStar was about to be hunted. He had no intention of harming her and every intention of breaking down the sensual walls that separated them. By the time he finished, Faith would be enslaved by her body's hunger, the woman core of her screaming out for him.

It would take patience, but Vaughn was used to stalking prey without break for hours, days . . . weeks.

CHAPTER 10

Faith found herself doing something inexplicable the next day. Instead of spending her time reinforcing shields that were clearly malfunctioning, she kept going over what Vaughn's skin had felt like under her fingertips, so hot, so different from her own. Caught in the memory, she ran her fingers over her upper arm. It was the first time she'd treated her body as a sensual object quite apart from its functionality.

A discreet alarm chimed.

Still disciplined enough to not betray startlement, she terminated the alarm. It was one in the afternoon and well past the time she should've started work. After a quick but thorough review of her shields, which actually proved not to be compromised, she walked out and took a reclining position on the chair. Monitoring functions came online with a hum meant to be inaudible to the human ear, but which she'd always heard with some unknown sense deep within her body.

A few seconds later, the voice of the M-Psy overseeing this session issued from the small communicator built into the arm of the chair. There was no visual because they hadn't wanted her being distracted by another face as a child, and she'd never asked for that to be changed. But she was under no illusion that they couldn't see her.

"All your biological and neurological functions are within the acceptable limits. There has, however, been an increase in your raw psychic potential."

That was a surprise. As a cardinal, she was off the Gradient but apparently, M-Psy could gauge fluctuations in her abilities. "An increase?" She feigned only cool interest. "Is that a sign of mental degradation?"

"On the contrary, it's a sign of health. Such increases have occasionally been noted in high-Gradient minds—we can't measure cardinals past 10.0, but we are able to tell when your abilities shift in either direction," he explained, displaying the truth that everyone, even Psy, liked to talk about what they knew. "We theorize that the mind learns psychic shortcuts over years of constant use, thereby creating extra capacity."

Double-talk, Faith thought. The reason her powers had increased was because the conditioning was falling away. The logical connection was irrefutable. Her vision channels were being forced to encompass more than the narrow field of commerce, thereby becoming wider. The subject matter or palatability of the new visions was irrelevant. That they existed was proof enough of her untapped potential, potential she'd deliberately been taught to suppress.

It made her wonder what else had been stifled. Who might she have been had she not been created in Silence, genetically selected to generate a steady stream of income? What would it have been like to have been born normal, born without fear of certain madness, born woman enough to take Vaughn on?

"Shall we start the session?" the M-Psy asked. "Or would you like to review the new brain scans?"

"I want to do some work first. Initiate random sequence, full list."

A clear panel rose up from behind the chair to curve over her eyes. It stopped half a centimeter from her lashes and clouded to opaque. A split second later, a steady flow of words began to scroll across it at high speed. It was her list of current dormant requests. Foresight could be steered, but not completely controlled, much to many a business's frustration. Faith, however, was a near-certain bet, which was why she had such a high price tag.

Once she'd entered the relevant triggers into her mind, she usually had a vision within a week or two and they could happen anywhere—in the garden as she walked, during sleep, while in a meeting with the M-Psy. However, over the years, it had become apparent that if she put her mind into a receptive frame, the visions could be guided out in a more controlled environment. That particular skill gave her some freedom from being watched twenty-four/seven, but so long as even one vision came outside of this chair, she'd never be accorded total privacy.

Her eye fell on the Tricep symbol among the mass of scrolling data. She kept picking it up again and again in spite of the speed and amount of other information. Her mind had chosen. Closing her eyes, she allowed her breathing to alter. It was the first step in putting herself into the half sleep she personally called suspended animation. While suspended, she existed neither in this world nor on the Net, but somewhere F-Psy alone could go, becoming part of the timestreams of the world.

Then she opened her psychic channels. In truth, she couldn't ever close them, but she could, with concentration, expand them to the nth degree. Part of her brain itself, the channels were inaccessible from the PsyNet—the only things that could come through them were visions. And if there was a part of her that wasn't sure which visions would choose to crawl in, she didn't let those uncertainties filter through to her conscious mind.

The Tricep prediction was child's play. She came out of it with the now-familiar feeling of barely having stretched her mental muscles. As she dictated the details of what she'd seen, it struck her that she if she continued down this path, she'd most certainly go insane—from boredom. Having the M-Psy restart the screen scroll, she gave him two more perfect readings before he called a halt.

"We don't want to strain your mind."

Since the session had utilized a minuscule portion of her considerable powers, Faith could've overruled him, but she didn't. She had other things to do with her time and energy. "I'll be in my private quarters."

"Faith, your monitoring levels have dropped off considerably recently."

Meaning she was no longer spied on every minute of every day. "I've cleared it with my father." A stopgap measure at best. Anthony would soon realize that she wasn't reaching for induction into the Council ranks—then what excuse would she use to escape the stranglehold of surveillance?

Having made it to her bedroom, she peeled off the dress at the same time as ingesting a nutrition bar, then had a quick shower before pulling on cotton pajama bottoms and a singlet top. Ready, she took a classic cross-legged yoga position on the bed and began to calm the rivers of her mind in preparation for entry into the Net.

It wasn't necessary to be in such a state—Psy entered and left the Net at will. The difference was that Faith wasn't used to opening herself up to the massive information archive. Even in her last foray, she'd remained out of the most data-rich, and therefore most chaotic, areas. But she was through with being a perfect conditioned machine; she would not let programmed stress responses imprison her.

So, what other physiological factors did you experience?

Vaughn's amused voice drifted into her mind and threatened to negate the fruits of her meditation. She told herself to forget the scent of his skin, the heavy heat of his jaguar form as he'd brushed past her legs, the sensation of his lips.

"Focus," she muttered, and began to recite the list of companies on the waiting list for a prediction. It took her twenty minutes to complete and her mind was pure calm by the end.

Opening her mind's eye, she stepped out into the biggest and most constantly updated data archive in the world, ready to search for information on the F-Psy, on herself. But today the Net granted her nothing, despite her concentration. Her F designation abilities did pick up something below the surface, but whether it was an echo or a forecast, she had no way of knowing.

Hours later, she finally gave up the fruitless quest and, eschewing another nutrition bar or a cup of soup, curled up under the thin blanket on her bed. Usually when she was so mentally tired, there were no visions, or if there were, she remained unconscious of them. But the darkness hadn't been satisfied the last time it had invaded.

Now, it was going to make her pay.

Vaughn completed his watch on the extended boundary and met up with his replacement, Dorian. The latent male was in human form, as he had no ability to go leopard. That made him no less capable or lethal. He'd never have reached the rank of sentinel otherwise.

Like all of them, Dorian also had an immutable core of loyalty. No sentinel could ever be tempted into betrayal. But being tempted into something else was another matter altogether.

"You know the grid?"

Nodding, Dorian slung a rifle across his back. It was his single visible weapon. "Any problems?"

"Some wolf juveniles are playing at hunting in the east quadrant."

"Can I shoot them?"

"We're friends now." The two packs were, in fact, blood-bonded. But given that Lucas and Hawke, the SnowDancer alpha, had agreed on the bond only a few months ago, it was taking both packs time to adapt. "No using them for target practice."

Dorian's smile was feral. "I promise I'll only shoot to wound."

"I'm sure Lucas and Hawke would appreciate that." Giving the younger sentinel a quick rundown on the other movements in the grid, he changed back to jaguar form and took off.

He should've been going to his own lair to catch up on some sleep—his body had kept him up most of last night. When he had slept, it was to find himself waking from heavy dreams of sensation, more than ready to roll over and sink himself into a very specific female body.

If he'd believed that the hunger could be sated with another, he would've had no trouble finding a willing lover. He might be jaguar to their leopard, but the females in DarkRiver had always considered him a more than satisfactory sexual partner. And they weren't the kind of women who hesitated to let a man know if he wasn't up to scratch.

However, he ran not in the direction of one of those welcoming felines, but toward a Psy who might overload into a seizure at the fury within him. That was unacceptable to either half of his self. He'd marked her and he *would* have her, even if he had to coax her kiss by slow kiss. Cats were good at coaxing. It was only a more sensual aspect of their favorite game—stalking.

The jaguar covered the distance between his watch and her home with the efficient confidence that came from being the most dangerous thing in the forest. But tonight he had no interest in the small creatures that darted into the shadows at the sound of his approach.

Because tonight, he was hunting pleasure.

Faith's instinct was to fight the sucking edges of the darkness, but as she'd learned in the weeks prior to Marine's murder, the more she struggled, the harder it would hold on. So she let it—let him—take her under and bring her into his world.

His darkness churned with faint hints of red. The blood hunger was reawakening far more quickly than she would've guessed—Marine's murder hadn't sated this creature, it had simply whetted the edge of his appetite.

He released her when there was no longer any chance of escape. Now she would watch and see, now she would be his audience and his disciple, for he was a great being and expected others to pay homage. That she was the solitary individual aware of his genius was a source of great anger, which he took out on her by forcing her to bear witness to his every malevolent act. They hadn't yet come to pass, but while in the twisted coils of a vision somehow linked to the killer's mind, they were her reality.

A violent swirl of red sliced her thoughts in half as he shoved into her mind. She lost all sense of self, of being a cardinal named Faith, and became a creature of pain and fear. The darkness pushed her to the raw edge of madness, threatening her with the very emotions she'd been trained not to feel, or to even admit possessing. Her helplessness made the killer laugh. He grabbed her with his teeth, shook her hard.

He wanted her to not only watch, but understand his sick desires. That she didn't, couldn't, enraged him. Surrounded by the vicious thickness of murderous fury, Faith did the sole thing she could to protect herself. She surrendered the civilized thinking part of her mind and retreated into the walled inner core of her psyche, curling up around herself like a child going into the fetal position.

Still, the darkness battered her. He was amused by her inability to deal with him, playing with her as a cat might play with a trapped mouse. He didn't want to kill her. No, what he wanted was to flaunt his power until she stopped resisting and let him rape her mind. Then he'd be free to show her all his desires, every one of his planned future acts, an endless reel of horror.

Too deep inside the most animal heart of her psyche to remember that she wasn't supposed to feel fear, Faith began to struggle with everything in her.

And failed to break out.

Vaughn landed silently on the soft carpet of Faith's bedroom. His feet were bare but his legs covered—he'd cached a pair of jeans in the forest earlier that day, not wanting to scandalize Faith any more than she was already going to be scandalized. Of course, he was still looking forward to seeing the surprise in her eyes when she found him there for the second night in a row.

However, his senses went on red alert the second he took a step toward the bed. Her blanket in a heap on the floor, Faith lay curled into a tight ball, breath shallow and heartbeat sluggish to the cat's keen hearing. The scent of something that shouldn't have been there, something that didn't *belong*, was pungent in the air. When he narrowed his eyes in the semidarkness, he picked out a more extreme blackness around Faith, just as he'd done at the cabin.

Convinced the darkness would grip her tighter if it knew Vaughn was about to intervene, he got onto the bed in si-

lence. His next move was lightning fast. Picking her up, he
crushed her against him, physically blocking the darkness
with the way his body curved over hers. Logic argued it
wouldn't work—whatever was attacking her was doing so
on the psychic plane. But instinct said it would. And instinct
was proven right.

He felt the cold emptiness of sheer evil brush over him as
the darkness was ripped in two by his body. It was unable to
cling to anything in him because he was too different, too
animal. Vaughn allowed a growl to rise up in his throat—his
claws had sliced out the instant after he'd dragged Faith to
safety. Now she lay protected by a human cage and, no
longer able to feed on her, the dark thing withered away.

Vaughn waited until the air was purged of the noxious scent
before he dropped his gaze to Faith. Retracting his claws, he
used one hand to clear the strands of hair off her face. Her skin
was cool, too cool. And her heartbeat was becoming ever
slower, as if she continued to fight with all her strength, unaware she was safe. He wanted to do violence. But instead, he
slid a hand under her nape and kissed her.

Only touch affected Faith deeply enough to break through
the psychic nature of her mind. Most humans would've been
shocked at the animal intensity of his kiss, but he wasn't human. And he wasn't shocked.

Something sizzled along Faith's most intimate inner skin
and, though it wasn't painful, it *demanded*. Fearful that it
was a trick, but incapable of ignoring the flaring pain of
nerve endings snapping to wakefulness, she uncurled from
her protective crouch. And saw energy arcing through her
mind, silver and bright, passionate and unstoppable, a lightning storm that burned away the lingering echoes of malignant darkness.

Her blood began to pump with heat that burned. Around

her, a thousand fires sparked to life. She stood in the center, protected but not shielded from the inferno. These flames wanted to caress, to touch, to stroke.

Unable to take the wild hunger of the storm, to withstand the intensity of the conflagration, she willed herself from the dream and into waking life. But the dream followed her to the outside. Her lips were on fire. Her body exploded with heat. Enfolding her was a stronger flame, skin that seemed to burn with a higher temperature than her own, living heat that lay against her nape, under her thighs, against the cheek she had pressed to a hard muscled surface.

She tried to suck in a breath, but her mouth had already been claimed. Her lashes flicked upward. Night-gold eyes met hers, brutal, savage . . . and safe. Her lips were freed for the second it took her to gasp a breath and then reclaimed. She found that her hand was on his shoulder, holding on, holding him.

Her mind spun with too much sensation, but the alternative was worse. In her not-quite-conscious state, she wasn't sure the darkness wouldn't return if she broke away from this overload. So she embraced it, shifting to wrap her arms around the neck of the dangerous male in her bed, melding her body to his.

If it came to madness, she'd rather drown in heat than be sucked into the sadistic cruelty of darkness. The woman heart of her was aware that his hands were on her back, pressing her to him, and that while those hands were big and powerful, they did no harm. Then even that thought was swept under the shock wave of sensation and she became nothing but flesh, a creature who had no mind and no thoughts. Her eyes closed.

Vaughn sensed Faith's utter surrender. The cat was ready to take what was his, but the man knew this wasn't the kind of submission that would ever satisfy him and it might just scar her. She wasn't giving in to him. She was using him to escape the darkness. Vaughn didn't mind being used by Faith, but he did mind that she wasn't conscious of who it was she clung to.

He broke the kiss and had the pleasure of feeling her nails dig into his skin as she tried to make him return. "Faith."

She pressed closer, her eyes remaining shut.

"Faith." He made his voice a command edged with the roughness of a growl. It wasn't difficult. This aroused, he had trouble controlling the beast. It was something Faith was going to have to learn to deal with, but not today. Today was about keeping her safe. "Open your eyes."

She shook her head, but her hands slipped down from around his neck to curl into fists against his chest.

A slow smile spread over his lips. "I'm not naked." Taking one feminine fist, he pressed it against his jean-covered thigh, then had to bite back a very sexual demand when the fingers of that hand spread and sent sensation straight to his groin.

"Are you real?"

It was a question that made it brutally clear how deep she'd retreated into her mind before he'd pulled her out. Leaning forward, he nipped at the skin of her neck. She jerked and opened her eyes at last.

Silver lightning sparked in their night-sky depths, vivid and wild.

CHAPTER 11

"What?" she asked, when he continued to stare.

"I can see lightning."

"How—?" She shook her head but didn't shift off his lap, and that told him everything he needed to know. "Thank you."

"You're welcome."

She gave him a wary look. "Why are you being so agreeable?"

Because the cat found it amusing to tease her. "I'm always agreeable."

The wariness turned into full-blown disbelief. "You're playing cat games with me."

Surprised by her quick understanding, he shrugged. "I *am* a cat."

"You're right." Then she did something that stunned the hell out of him. Drawing up her body, she took a deep breath and brushed the most fleeting of kisses over his lips. "Thank you. I wouldn't have made it out on my own."

Raw anger wiped out the playfulness. "What the hell

were you doing going alone into that kind of a vision in the first place?"

"You know I can't control them."

Pressing her closer with hands that threatened to go clawed, he stared straight into those lightning-storm eyes. "Then learn."

Faith blinked, not sure how to handle Vaughn in his current mood. But everything she'd learned about predators, about him, told her not to betray her lack of assurance. "I can hardly learn to control something without rules," she pointed out, "and there are none for the F-Psy, none that ensure the visions will only ever come when I want them to come. Yes, I can usually set them off with certain markers, but I can't hold them back for long periods of time."

"Who says?"

"My trainers, the PsyClan, the Council . . ." Understanding dawned. "Why wouldn't they teach me to block the visions if there were a way?"

"What would that control mean for the PsyClan?"

"It would contribute to a considerable rise in income," she said. "I could produce on command—there'd be no chance of my having a vision during sleep or in any other situation where my recall could be compromised, as sometimes happens now. So their not teaching me control, if they know how to accomplish it, makes no sense."

"Faith, why do you live in this house surrounded by sensors?"

She didn't want to answer and the impulse was so against any kind of rational behavior that she knew she couldn't give in to it. "Sometimes the visions are hard on my body and mind. I need to be monitored in case I need assistance."

"And if you could control the visions, then you could contain them until you reached a safe location. There would be no need for you to be caged up here."

Faith slowly drew her hands away from his body. "You

want me to say they don't teach me control because this way I'm dependent on them, my ability at their beck and call. I have no choice but to forecast."

"What I want is for you to use that sensible Psy brain of yours—if they can train your visions to be lucrative and business focused, don't you think they could train you to decide whether or not you wanted to give in to a vision at any particular moment?"

For a member of a race notorious for acting first and thinking later, he made far too much sense. "Be that as it may," she said, instead of confronting his irrefutable logic, "I can't control them now and I absolutely cannot control the dark visions. Neither can I risk betraying the degradation of my conditioning by asking for further training."

"You're a cardinal." Vaughn tipped up her chin until she could no longer avoid meeting that wild gold gaze. "You don't need anyone to hold your hand."

"But I do need someone to hold back the darkness." There was no way she could become proficient enough at control, if control was even possible, soon enough to fight its growing power. "I can't break its grip when it hooks into me."

"Maybe because you've locked away what you need to fight it."

She pushed off his chest and slid down to kneel beside him. "Emotion."

He stretched out onto his back, acting as if this were his territory. She'd read about the way predatory male changelings liked to claim territory, be it land or sexual mates. Flames raced through her, a memory of the earlier lightning storm.

"Fire to fight fire, Red."

The echo of her thoughts might've startled her if she hadn't been concentrating on keeping her eyes from moving over the body lying so carelessly on her bed. Big and dangerous, there was at the same time something ultimately strokable about Vaughn.

"I can't." She shook her head to dispel the strange compulsion. "You don't understand the extent of the madness that infected the F-Psy before the implementation of the Silence Protocol." She'd seen the records, records no one could've doctored. "My own family records show generation upon generation of mad ones."

"How many in a generation?"

She triggered the memory files in her mind. "At least one."

"How many F-Psy in each generation?"

"The NightStar PsyClan has always produced an unusually high number of the F designation. Each generation has had at least one, but sometimes two, F cardinals and around ten lower-Gradient foreseers."

"One in eleven or twelve sounds like pretty good odds compared to what you're facing now."

Certain madness in twenty or thirty years if she was lucky, sentenced to spend the next five or six decades locked in the hell of her fragmented mind. "But the ones who went mad before—they were young. What if I'm the flawed one in this generation? If I break Silence, I'll fall."

"And if you don't break it, you'll spend your life in a cage."

"It's so easy for you to say." She shook her head. "You grew up on the outside, feeling and experiencing everything. You can't begin to imagine what you're asking me to consider."

A big hand flattened on her back, bare inches from the curve of her bottom. "Look at me, Faith."

She turned her body until her toes almost brushed his jeans at the thigh, her eyes on his face. He was nothing tame and she was drawn to that. But she was different. "All my life that I remember, I've lived in this compound. Even the freedom of the PsyNet was almost closed to me by some very delicate conditioning." Conditioning she'd broken on her own, she realized with a warm glow she couldn't fully explain. "I'm changing that. I'm going out into the Net and seeing the information it has to offer."

"None of that involves leaving your safe little cocoon."

It was the blunt response of a man whose animal side clearly saw no reason for lies.

"You think that makes me a coward, that I should go out there and experience the world. What you don't understand is that the world might kill me."

"Then tell me."

She'd known there would be no easy acceptance from this jaguar stretched out on her bed, all gleaming skin and amber-gold hair. "One thing no one can fake is the reaction of my designation when surrounded by a large number of unshielded individuals. All species have a natural shield, though the changeling shield is far tougher, but the upper layer of the mind, the public self, is almost universally unshielded."

"Mine?" His jaw tightened.

She shook her head. "You're fully blocked. That happens with some individuals—an extension of the natural shield. However, in your case I'm guessing Sascha had something to do with it." He didn't answer and she felt some unknown thing inside her shrivel. "Not worthy of your trust, right?"

His fingers pressed lightly on her spine. "Trust is earned."

"I trust you."

"Do you? Or have you been forced into that position?"

There was no answer she could give him, because she didn't know. Moving, she felt his fingers fall off her back, but now her toes were nudging his jean-covered thighs. "The public mind," she began, turning to what was familiar as a means of grounding herself, "throws out a constant bombardment of thought and feeling. All Psy are trained to shield against those random pieces of data, to the extent that most no longer even notice the background chatter. But it's been well documented that F-Psy, no matter how strong their shields, are affected by those thoughts."

"Affected how?" His hand slipped under the thin material of her top to lie against her lower spine.

She felt her stomach twist itself into a tight knot. "You must stop touching me."

"Why?"

"It's too much." Especially on top of the betrayals he was asking her to attribute to her own people, her own family. "Please, Vaughn."

She looked so fragile sitting there, all night-sky eyes and creamy skin. With any other woman, he'd have tugged her down and held her tight. Doing that with Faith, however, might cause her to panic, and right now he didn't want to make her vulnerable in any sense—the darkness could be waiting for a break in her defenses. But neither could he let her run. "Each time I do what you want, I'm helping your PsyClan and the Council imprison you."

"Do you really believe that?"

"Fear of touch is part of how they manipulate you."

The arms she had wrapped around her knees seemed to tighten. "If I ask you to break contact because I'm going to go into a seizure or unconsciousness, you have to do it. That's the only way I'll let you keep getting closer."

Satisfaction was his blood. "So you admit you've been letting me."

She cocked her head with a haughtiness that would've done any cat proud. "I'm a cardinal. We're all born with more than our share of powers—I've spent the time since our initial meeting working out how to use them in offense."

"Tell me."

"No." Enticing in their confident mischief, her eyes were no longer the cold slate he'd seen that first night. "Why should I show someone I don't trust—and who doesn't trust me—my secrets?"

"Ouch." He traced his fingers up and down her delicate spine. "You know how to go for the throat."

"It keeps me alive."

The jaguar didn't like hearing that, didn't like the thought of her needing such weapons, because that implied danger. "You have to leave. Find a way to boost your shields so you can deal on the outside and leave."

Her smile was without any hint of amusement. "I'll die. That's an undeniable fact. The second I drop out of the PsyNet and lose the necessary biofeedback, my mind will shut down. Unless you can do for me whatever it is that Lucas does for Sascha."

"How did you figure that?"

"I'm not stupid, Vaughn. It's clear there's some type of psychic connection between the two of them." She dropped her chin onto hands folded atop her knees. "I can almost touch it, but not quite. It's as if it's something outside the Net but brushes by it."

Every one of his senses went on high alert. If the Psy could pick up the Web that connected the alpha pair to their sentinels, DarkRiver would lose one of its crucial tactical advantages. However, if Faith was unusual, it begged the question why. He had a very good idea of the answer, but the cat never pounced before it was completely certain of success. That was what made him such an efficient hunter.

"And if I were able to bring you out of the Net, do you think you could take me on?" He pressed the pads of his fingers a touch harder against her lower back.

Her spine stiffened. "Don't push me, cat."

It was the first time she'd really clawed at him. Intrigued, he spread his palm and slid it up to the curve of her ribs. Her breasts were so close he was having a hell of a time keeping himself from stroking even higher. "Or what?"

"You don't want to find out."

"Maybe I do." Moving with the animal speed of his kind,

he had her flat on her back with him braced above her before she could reply. Her eyes flashed velvet black and then streaks of silver began to tear jagged lines through the rich darkness. "What the hell—?" That was when he spied the giant wolf in one corner of the room. The clearly rabid creature was crouching down in preparation for attack.

Jaguar instincts took over.

Shoving Faith to the side, he pounced soundlessly toward the wolf . . . and went straight through it. Only his agility saved him from making a racket as he landed hard on the carpet. The awareness of soft feminine laughter, so low that he could barely catch it, the sound rusty and unused, had him narrowing his eyes as he stood. "Very funny." He met the silver-black gaze of the woman sprawled on the bed watching him, dark red hair falling around a face she'd propped up on her hands. He didn't think he'd ever seen a more beautiful sight. Immediately, the sexually hungry cat in him amended that—if she were naked, that would be even better.

"Did you beat the bad puppy?" she asked.

He knew she didn't even realize what was happening. She'd laughed and now she was teasing. Would the change last or would she try to bury it? Not that Vaughn had any intention of letting her choose option two. "Illusions? Don't you need to get into my mind for that?" And his mind was changeling, nearly impossible for a Psy to mess with.

"I'm better than that," Faith said, no hint of arrogance in her tone. "My illusions are concrete in the sense that if a camera had been present in the room, it, too, would've seen the wolf."

He prowled over to her and had the pleasure of watching those amazing lightning-shot eyes flicker and then shiver to a black that was somehow softer than the pure darkness in them after the visions. Going down on his knees beside the bed, he slid his hands under her hair and cupped her face. "You feel like woman." *My woman.*

Dipping his head, he kissed her. It was a chaste kiss from his perspective, a mere taste when he wanted to gorge, but she whimpered and clung to him. For all of five seconds. Then she pulled away. He swore under his breath, the language rough and explicit. This was not going to work if Faith couldn't bear anything more than an innocent kiss— touch was the cornerstone of what he was.

After that week he'd spent in the wild as a child, the only way the DarkRiver leopards had been able to make him respond was by surrounding him in touch. His first month in the pack, he'd slept in cat form, surrounded by other furred bodies. Deprived of touch, he tended to get more and more aggressive, more and more feral, the cat in him rising to the surface until the man was buried deep. Pack usually helped, but these days, he wanted someone else's strokes.

"Vaughn." Faith made her voice very submissive, extremely nonconfrontational. "Vaughn, your claws are out." She could feel them against the skin of her scalp and face and she was terrified enough to admit it. Her reaction came from a primitive self that had existed before Silence, before civilization. All it cared about was survival . . . at any cost.

A shock wave of psychic power would stun the predator holding her prisoner, but might possibly cause permanent damage. She couldn't bear the thought of that. "Don't hurt me, Vaughn." She deliberately used his name again. "I need to feel safe with you." Irrational as it was, she did feel that way even now.

He'd gone cat on her, but those claws were pressed so lightly against her skin they didn't even threaten to bruise, much less cut. However, she knew that control was a fine edge and, right now, the jaguar in Vaughn's eyes was walking the thinnest part of it. "You'll never forgive yourself if you hurt me."

"I would never hurt you." His voice was a guttural sound caught between humanity and the animal within. "Touch me."

About to refuse, she stopped herself. Why was he making that request at this moment? She was smart, she could figure this out. Suppressing her body's instinctive fight-or-flight response, she closed her eyes and forced herself to breathe in a pattern meant to foster mental clarity. The scent of Vaughn rushed into her, wild and earthy, but it somehow had a centering effect on her chaotic thought processes. Why would a changeling demand touch when so out of control? Logic stated it was because he believed it would help reestablish discipline. And if logic was wrong?

"I'm trusting you." Excruciatingly aware of his unsheathed claws, she moved with slow precision and brushed her lips over his. He felt hot, primal, unapologetically male. Her mind started to misfire almost immediately. Tonight had pushed her too far even before Vaughn had gone cat on her. Her brain screamed that she was on the verge of a meltdown. Too bad. She would not let Vaughn down. He'd brought her out of her nightmare—she could do no less for him.

Her teeth accidentally grazed his lower lip and the growl that came from him poured into her mouth. She froze. That was when sharp teeth caught *her* lower lip and bit down in a way that whispered temptation. Something low and deep in her burned and the conflagration of her mind was joined by the shuddering heat of her body.

Her stomach tautened, sweat glimmered over her skin, and somehow her hands were clenched in Vaughn's hair, his scalp under her fingertips. Heat and touch, desire and need, power and fury, it all thrust into her in a brutal wave that tore away her innermost shields. Suddenly the pleasure was pain and the pain edged her vision with ebony.

Vaughn felt it the second Faith broke. Claws long since retracted, he pulled back from the kiss because she seemed unable to do so. "Faith."

Breathing ragged, she opened eyes gone the bad kind of

black. "It's taking me under." The words were a statement of the inevitable.

Rage threatened to shatter his newfound control. "No, it's not." Getting up off the floor, he watched her rearrange herself to lie on her side in the center of the bed. Her eyes tracked his every movement. "Did I help you?"

"Yes." He licked the taste of her off his lips.

"At least I'm strong enough to do that."

"You're strong enough to get past all of it. You've gone from being unable to bear anything to accepting *and* giving a kiss in a very short period." He climbed back onto the bed. And though it went against every one of his instincts, he left enough distance between them so as not to overwhelm her.

"I wish I were strong enough to do more . . . be more." Her voice was a whisper, but the cat was sure he heard an undertone of cold rage. Good.

"You see the future, Faith. That makes you extraordinary."

She moved an inch closer, surprising him. "Don't go until I wake. I'm concerned the dark visions will come again and my shields are currently fragmented."

In other words, she was scared. And if she could feel fear, then she could experience pleasure. "When have I ever given you any indication that I'd leave you even if you asked?"

"Will you wait for me the night after tomorrow? I know I said five days but the visions are accelerating too fast. I think I can work it out so no one will miss me."

"Be careful." Her PsyClan was too powerful not to be connected. One hint of suspicion about the clan's prized asset and the Council would put Faith under complete lockdown from which it'd be far bloodier to extract her. He didn't mind blood, but he did mind that she might be caught in the crossfire. "Sleep, Red. I've got you."

Her eyes closed and soon afterward, he felt the fear coating her fade away. While she slept, he stood watch. Perhaps the Psy would've said he could do her no good on the physical plane when she was a psychic being, but twice now he'd seen and smelled the ugly reality of the menace that had held her captive. Instinct said that if he could keep that darkness from her, he'd keep her safe.

He didn't leave her until dawn broke and her eyes opened.

CHAPTER 12

Faith woke just in time to see Vaughn pulling himself through the skylight. He was so agile, so strong, and so exotic that she couldn't help being fascinated.

"What are you doing to me?" she whispered long after he'd gone.

Last night, she'd fragmented, broken conditioning and *felt*. But it had come at a high cost—her mind had literally stopped as she'd slipped into sleep. And there had been pain, such excruciating pain. She hadn't let Vaughn see the extent of it, somehow knowing that her pain would hurt him. But now she allowed herself to remember the agony, remember the cold emptiness of her mind shutting down section by section.

She'd been reacting to the changelings ever since she'd met them, reacting to Vaughn. Not only had she let them push her into feeling, she'd begun to consider the possibility of breaking Silence. Today she knew differently. The blocks couldn't be so easily bypassed. Yes, she'd somehow skirted the upper levels of prohibition, been able to bear some touch, experience some emotion. But the second she'd tried to go deeper, she'd been punished with vicious swiftness.

It was now starkly clear to her that of course pain had to have been built into the conditioning for it to hold. It was a classic Pavlovian technique—pain for "bad" behavior, rewards for good. As an adult she could reason out the method, but as a child she would've been vulnerable to an extent that was unimaginable.

All they would've had to do was hurt her enough times for "inappropriate" behavior that she shied away from the pain and complied with their demands. It was also certain that the focalized pain wasn't the sole method used to ensure compliance. However, she'd guess it to be one of the major components of the behavior modification section of the Protocol.

Did her knowledge of the underlying basis of conditioning mean she might be able to break it? The harder question was, did she want to? Last night, she'd said she wished to be more than the woman she was. But to become that woman, she'd have to give up everything she'd ever known, turn her back on her whole world. She'd have to abandon her father, her PsyClan, her very people.

And all she'd gain would be a life on the outside with a race so completely unlike her own. She had no idea how to deal with them, a race that considered her an abomination against nature. No, she thought, that wasn't completely fair. Vaughn didn't seem to think her an unfeeling machine. But even he wanted her to change, to not be what she was, to shatter Silence and live a different life.

But giving up her identity as Faith NightStar, Cardinal F-Psy and linchpin asset of the NightStar Group, was no easy choice.

Vaughn catnapped on the high branches of a tree for a few hours before relieving Mercy of her watch. When he

saw her waiting dressed in human form, he realized she
wanted to talk. Shifting, he caught the pants she threw him
and pulled them on. "What is it?"

"Nothing major," she said. "I wanted to know if you
could cover my grid two Fridays from now. I have a late
shindig." Mercy worked for CTX, a communications network funded by DarkRiver and SnowDancer in concert. It
was a good position for a sentinel—work took a backseat to
Pack business and management fully understood. Possibly
because management was made up of wolves and cats.

"No problem."

"How's it going with your latest piece?"

"It's done." He'd already begun a new project. A sculpture in marble of a woman who was passion and heat, temptation and mystery. "If you run into Barker, can you tell him
it's ready for pickup?"

Mercy nodded, her red hair blowing softly in the wind.
The color reminded him of Faith, though his Psy's hair was
darker, more like ripe cherries. "Will do." She waved good-
bye. "Catch you later."

Vaughn decided to run part of the watch in human
form—his speed and strength were more than enough to take
on most intruders. As he moved, he considered his new
piece. He knew it would be stunning, the best he'd ever
done. He also knew he'd never sell it.

The forest zipped past him as he ran, his mind on the
curving lines of a woman with night-sky eyes. But he wasn't
so distracted that he missed the blur of leopard yellow where
there should have been only forest. Backtracking, he followed the scent to find two cubs engaged in a mock battle.
His growl had them splitting apart and staring at him. They
knew they were in big trouble.

"I thought I heard Tamsyn say you were going to spend
today with Sascha." He folded his arms across his chest,
wondering how Tamsyn—DarkRiver's healer and the cubs'

mother—dealt with her double dose of trouble without tearing out her hair. "What are you doing way out here?" Cubs were curious by nature—it wasn't unusual for them to wander off while exploring, and they were safe within DarkRiver lands. But they still needed limits. And the first rule was, no moving more than a mile outside the home they were supposed to be in.

The cubs dropped on their bellies and mewed, trying to charm their way out of this.

"I'm not Sascha or your mother," he told them, though he was amused. These two would make good soldiers when they grew up. They'd also attract women the same way Kit, one of the older juveniles, currently did. "Let's go."

Getting up, they started to pad their way in front of him. Identical twins in human form, Julian and Roman were identical in cat form, too. Only those who knew them very well could distinguish one from the other. Vaughn had always been able to do so, perhaps because his beast was so close to the surface. Herding them back into the safe zone, he crouched down to their level. "You know the rules. They're for your protection and to ensure the women don't go insane." That was no lie. The maternal females were already driven to the brink by some of the stunts the cubs and juveniles pulled. "You want Sascha to go nuts looking for you?"

Small shakes of kittenish heads.

"Then stay in the perimeter." He knew Sascha could track the twins using her psychic gifts, but that didn't alter the rules.

One small clawed paw scratched at his arm. Another joined it on the other side of his body. He chuckled. "No, I'm not that mad. Come on, let's go tell Sascha you're okay." Shifting, he allowed them to playfight with him for a few minutes before he escorted them back to the aerie from which they'd made their escape. Sascha was standing at the foot of the tree.

"I think I'm going to put a leash on you two," she said, sounding very, very sure and very, very Psy. "And didn't I say something about turning you into rats if you misbehaved?"

Both cubs froze.

"What do you think, Vaughn?"

He nodded in agreement. Julian looked at him like he was a traitor and Roman tried to hide behind a tree. Laughing, Sascha picked Roman up by the scruff of his neck and kissed his furry face. Julian ran over and started growling for attention. As she scooped him up, Sascha nodded at Vaughn. "Thanks for finding the Terrible Twosome. I swear, I turn my back for a second and they're gone."

He made a deep, throaty sound to let her know that was alright.

"I'm working with Zara on a revised plan for one of the new houses in the complex," she told him, referring to their outside-Pack design consultant. "Apparently the wolves aren't happy." When he snarled, she smiled. "Yes, I know. Damn wolves. You're as bad as each other, not one of you ready to fully embrace the new treaty."

Julian and Roman wiggled in her arms and she looked down. "Okay, okay. We're going into town to meet Lucas and Nate." At the mention of Nate, their father, the cubs got excited. "I've got clothes for you two little beasties in the car."

As Vaughn was about to turn to leave, Sascha said, "How is she?"

He shook his head. Faith was nowhere near where he needed her to be. And he wasn't comfortable with admitting he needed anyone that deeply.

Faith had just produced a lucrative forecast for FireFly Industries when her comm console chimed. She used her remote to flick it on, but the call was cut off before she could speak. Shrugging, she put it down to an incorrect code and got off the chair. "I'm going for a walk," she said to the M-Psy on this shift. "Tell the patrols not to approach me." It was the same request she made after every time she had a particularly strong forecast. Her Psy senses always seemed to function at a higher level following such visions. She ended up hearing everything around her, including chatter from the guards' supposedly shielded minds.

However, today she felt none of the usual hypersensitivity, was in fact in total control in spite of what had happened the previous night. And she wanted privacy to think about why that might be. Deciding that her simple ankle-length dress would do, she stepped out into the cool afternoon air.

She couldn't see the guards, but knew they were there. Not that they were apparently much good—Vaughn was slipping in and out without problem. And she didn't mind in the least. Last night she'd accepted that she felt fear at the murderous rage of the dark visions. Today, she permitted herself to admit that she liked Vaughn, liked his wildness and even his danger. But any stronger emotion continued to be beyond her reach.

Nobody in the changeling world could understand what it was like to spend a lifetime without emotion and then suddenly be invaded by it on all sides. The darkness had brought menace and evil, psychopathic lust and sadistic need into her life. She might've buckled under the weight had Vaughn not brought pleasure, desire, and playfulness. He wasn't an easy male to deal with, but that was part of what made him so incredibly fascinating. Last night she'd come face-to-face with the animal who lived so close to the surface of his humanity and—

"Faith NightStar."

She stared at the slender, almost delicate brunette who'd appeared from the shadows of a dark-green fir. No one should've been in these grounds but her and her guards. "Who are you?"

A cold smile that did nothing to light up those pale blue eyes. "Interesting. You're so isolated that though you've done considerable work for us, you're unaware of my identity."

Memory flickered at the sound of that voice. "Shoshanna Scott." A member of the Psy Council and its beautiful and photogenic public face.

"I apologize for intruding on your privacy, but I didn't want this conversation recorded."

"You called earlier," Faith said, *knowing* with the sense in her that knew these things. She also knew she was in the presence of someone very dangerous, a woman who might strike without warning and with none of the control of the "animal" she'd faced only hours ago.

"Yes. We were checking the monitoring. It's extensive."

Faith waited for whatever it was that the Council wanted from her. Their requests had always been conveyed through the PsyClan, but perhaps this was a forecast they wanted to keep completely under the radar.

"Your accuracy is impressive, Faith."

"Thank you."

"Shall we walk?"

"If you please." She knew how to speak to the Council— she might've been isolated, but she wasn't stupid. "Was there something you wanted me to try to forecast?" Try, because forecasting didn't work on command. But if Vaughn was right, she might be able to teach her mind to control the timing of the visions that did come. It was a seductive thought.

"I simply wanted to talk to you." Shoshanna linked her hands behind her back, her black-on-black suit making her fingers appear skeletally white. "Do you usually wear this type of clothing?"

Faith knew it wasn't the normal Psy mode of dress. "It

makes it easier for Medical when intervention is necessary."
However, the reality was that she preferred . . . liked, wearing dresses.

"Of course. I've never really spoken to one of the F designation. What's it like to see the future?" Pale blue eyes
bored into hers as they stopped beside a small pond.

"Having never lived any other way, I can't make a comparison," she said, reminding herself to be very careful. One
slip and Shoshanna would know that something wasn't quite
right about this particular F-Psy. "However, it did give me a
purpose at a time when most Psy remain unformed."

"You've been forecasting since you were three?"

"Officially. But my family has records that state I was
making erratic but accurate non-verbal predictions even earlier." She admitted that because she believed Shoshanna already knew her history—Councilors made it their business
to know things about those they wanted to talk to.

"How did passage through the Protocol affect your abilities?"

The Protocol. Silence. A choice made generations ago to
wipe out violence, but that had also succeeded in wiping out
joy, laughter, and love. It had made the Psy an emotionless,
robotic race that excelled in business and technology but
produced no forms of art, no great music, no works of liter-
ature.

"My ability to fine-tune the visions grew apace with my
progress through the Protocol. Instead of needing several
markers to trigger them, I began to need only one or two."
What she didn't say was that as she'd progressed, she'd also
stopped having the dark visions.

The unexpected memory had appeared in a quicksilver
flash. It was as if Shoshanna's prodding had unlocked a secret compartment within her mind, opening her eyes to the
fact that there had been a time in her childhood when she'd

seen darkness. Keeping her expression calm became an exercise in self-restraint.

"Interesting." Shoshanna began to walk once again.

Faith followed in silence. The other woman was beautiful, but she was part of the Council—no one reached that post without having shed blood. Her mind's eye flickered and, for one instant, she could literally see the deep red substance staining the Councilor's hands. The vision was gone as quickly as it had come, but she heeded the warning. Because she'd more than seen blood, she'd had a *knowing*, too.

One day soon, Shoshanna Scott was going to have Faith NightStar's blood on her hands.

Unless she could change the future. That was why F-Psy were so valued—the future they saw wasn't fixed. Businesses could head off a rival if they knew that that rival was about to put out an important invention, or buy up shares in a firm that had been forecast to rise. Faith had never before seen something that had the potential to so directly affect her.

"Are you fulfilled by your work?" Shoshanna's voice was a cool sound that cut through the whispers of the leaves in the wind.

Faith didn't know what Shoshanna wanted so she chose to answer with the truth. "No. It's become too easy. I can forecast share trends in my sleep should I need to. There's no challenge to it." The Protocol may have stripped them of emotion, but it had done nothing to stem their unabating need for mental stimulation. "I'm the best in this hemisphere. The only one in the Southern Hemisphere who occasionally challenges me is Sione from the PsyClan PacificRose."

"Yet you've never applied for entry to a higher position."

Faith began to get an inkling of what this visit was about, but couldn't bring herself to believe it. "As it happens, I have been considering it recently. But since my age would be a barrier, I thought to wait and learn."

"Very efficient." Shoshanna actually sounded impressed by the lie. "No one would think to monitor an F designation cardinal for that kind of shadowing. Learned anything interesting?"

Faith decided on honesty one more time, on the basis that Shoshanna almost certainly already knew. "There are signs of dissent in the PsyNet. The loss of Councilor Santano Enrique in somewhat mysterious circumstances has engendered an unstable level of speculation."

"What do you think we should do to stem the speculation?"

Faith wasn't sure she wanted it stopped—debate and change had to be better for the Net than stagnant obedience. But to say that would be to attract the wrong kind of attention. "I'm sure the Council has thought of a solution far better than anything I could offer."

Once again, Shoshanna smiled that cold Psy smile, something Faith had never adopted. If she felt no amusement or hope, why should she smile?

"Don't worry about offending me, Faith. I want to know what you'd do."

"I'd give the masses an answer. A concrete answer. Nothing stops conjecture as quickly as an irrefutable truth." But what she'd glimpsed in the Net had held murmurs of a deeper dissatisfaction. The Council had already lost ground, important ground. No matter what they said now, some people would remain unconvinced.

Shoshanna stopped and Faith realized they'd circled back to their original meeting spot. "Your view is one I happen to share. Perhaps we can further discuss the subject in the future."

Recognizing the dismissal, Faith nodded. "I look forward

to it, Councilor." Then she turned her back on the woman who'd one day have her blood on her hands and returned to her home with unhurried steps. Good thing Shoshanna wasn't a cat like Vaughn or the erratic beat of her heart might have given her away.

However, one good thing had come out of this encounter—she could lie to her father with a straight face and request privacy for "reasons previously discussed." She did exactly that upon entering the house.

"Have you been contacted?" Anthony asked.

"In a sense," she hedged, beginning to accept that her original lie had never been anything that simple. "I don't believe it's wise to talk of this on the general communications network."

"Of course. Let's meet."

That was the last thing she wanted. "Not yet, Father. Arousing any suspicion at this stage could be detrimental." To her health, certainly. She'd heard of the kinds of things aspirants did to get rid of the competition.

Anthony nodded. "Keep me updated. Next time, use the PsyNet."

"Yes, sir."

That night, the darkness didn't come. But neither did Vaughn. The rational part of Faith told her to use the respite from his constant assault on her Psy shields to tighten and bolster those lines of conditioning at risk of total failure. But that rational part stood no chance against her memories of the night before—bone-crushing terror and the dangerous safety of a jaguar's touch.

The truth was, she'd expected him to be here after the intensity of the previous night, had come to rely on his physical presence—she, a woman used to no one else in her space. And now he wasn't here. Not that it mattered. She was Psy, she told herself as she kicked off her blanket and punched her inexplicably uncomfortable pillow into better shape. She didn't feel anything. Certainly not disappointment and anger.

CHAPTER 13

Having used up all his self-control the night before, Vaughn was waiting for Faith and he wasn't doing it patiently. Though he was in human form, he'd taken to the trees, crouching above the fence to keep a lookout. Her feminine form should've appeared by now.

Five more minutes dragged by. He was considering going in after her when he finally spotted her in the pitch black of the cloud-heavy night. She climbed the fence as easily as she'd done that first time and was nearing his position mere seconds later. He decided to let her go in a little farther before jumping down, so she wouldn't be startled into a scream.

Reaching him, she stopped and looked straight up into the branches. "Vaughn? I hope that's you."

The cat was annoyed she'd discovered him. The man wanted to know why. "Don't make any woman sounds."

Her eyes were cutting as he dropped down to face her, feet bare but everything else covered in jeans and a T-shirt. "I'm hardly likely to do that after taking so much trouble to get here without alerting anyone." Pure, haughty female.

He wanted to bite her. Hard enough to mark. To claim. "How did you know I was up there?"

"I could sense you. It must indicate a previously dormant aspect of my abilities."

"What about other changelings?"

"I don't know. I can't sense anyone else—is there anyone else here?"

He smiled, aware it would make her want to spit. "You know I can't tell you that." Matter of fact, Clay was very close, having come to take over this section of Vaughn's watch. They'd traded off half an hour ago, but the leopard had stuck around to ensure Faith and Vaughn made it out safely. Something feral in Vaughn calmed at Faith's inability to feel the other sentinel. "Never know what you might use the information for."

"What do you want me to do?" she demanded, her tone cold enough to burn. "Write my loyalty in blood?"

"Temper, temper."

"I don't have a temper. Are you planning on standing there all night? I don't have time to waste." Turning, she started stomping her way through the forest.

Vaughn whistled under his breath to signal Clay that everything was okay. A low growl traveled back to him and, to his surprise, it held the faintest tinge of laughter. "Watch it, cat," he muttered, too low for anyone but a changeling to hear. "I'm the only one allowed to be amused by Faith."

Another growl, this one closer, and then silence. Clay was doing his job now. Usually it was the soldiers who patrolled the edges of DarkRiver's considerable home range, with the sentinels concentrating on the alpha pair's defense grid. However, it had been decided that this area needed to be under closer surveillance. Even if Faith proved entirely trustworthy, she wasn't a soldier or a sentinel and could unknowingly lead the enemy to their door.

Vaughn smiled again at the thought of his Psy, a Psy who

was mad as hell but unwilling to admit it. It was clear that her conditioned responses had begun to collapse one by one. He was damn glad. Neither half of him particularly liked spending nights aroused with no relief in sight. He was impatient and more than willing to push her down the right path. The cat saw no reason to play fair when it was obvious she wanted a long, slow taste of him, too.

Catching up, he walked a little behind her, just far enough away to admire the sway of her hips. She was shaped exactly right—though short, she wasn't too thin, her body having more than enough curves to satisfy and tempt. He wanted to watch that pert bottom moving on him. Given their height difference, the best position to enjoy that view would be with him seated and her taking him in, back to his chest. A groan threatened to erupt from his throat.

Faith looked over her shoulder. "Stop it."

"What?" He wondered if her skin was that creamy gold all over, lusciously lickable. Bitable.

"You know what you're doing."

"The question is, how do you?"

"I'm Psy."

"You're an F-Psy, not a telepath."

Her eyes narrowed and he knew she wasn't aware of the giveaway gesture. And while he gloried in it, he'd have to warn her about it before she returned to that prison she called a home. "I'm a woman. We're born with those sensors. So stop it."

"Why?"

"Why?" She gave him an arrogant Psy look. "How would you like it if I thought of you as you're thinking of me and my body?"

He grinned. "You know how I'd like it." Something in her comment made him pause. "Are you saying you can actually see what I see?"

Her cheeks shaded to a dull red and he watched, delighted.

The physical conditioning was starting to erode on a far deeper level than he could've hoped for—Psy did not blush. "Yes. I don't know why when I can't read anything else off you. None of my blocks seem to be working. So restrain yourself."

He pondered that as he took the lead and brought her to the car. The new blindfold was sitting on the passenger seat—a strip of black silk he'd purchased specially for her. Spine stiff enough to snap, Faith put her things in the back-seat before lifting it up. "Make it quick."

He laid the strip against her eyes and moved until his chest pressed against the provocation of her breasts. "I like it slow." He deliberately imagined what it would be like to sexually tease her while she was blindfolded. "At my mercy."

"I told you, I'm not as powerless as you think." They were fighting words, but her voice was husky. Despite her insistence that she was Psy, Faith was no longer fully bound by Silence. That was going to mean trouble. But right now, Vaughn was concerned about pleasure.

"Illusions don't scare me, baby." Taking his time to tie the knot, he let his mind fill with images of her blindfolded and naked, hands braced on the headboard of his bed and legs parted to keep her balance. And then he imagined how he'd stroke that creamy skin, how he'd run his tongue all over, how he'd sink his fingers in the lush flesh of her bottom and hold her in place as he took her.

Electricity zapped his fingers where they touched her skin. "Son of a bitch!" He jerked away with a snarl. "That hurt." But the sharp shock of pain was even now receding from his fingertips.

"You should listen to me next time." Faith slid inside the car without hesitation and pulled the door shut.

Vaughn wondered if he should tell her that what she'd done made her more, not less, attractive to him. Jaguars liked their women tough. Smiling, he rubbed his fingers against his jeans and walked around to take the driver's seat.

Faith said nothing until he'd started up the car. "Did I really hurt you? I've never used the ability against a living being before."

His Psy, the one who didn't feel, was experiencing tinges of remorse. "If you did, I deserved it." He ran a finger down her cheek. "Doesn't mean I'll stop, but I'll be a bit more careful about how I tie you up."

"I should've shocked you harder." She folded her arms across her chest.

He began driving. "Sascha never mentioned that kind of talent. Does it fall under a separate designation?"

"Why should I tell you? You don't tell me your secrets."

"You're hooked up to the Net." An absolute fact. "Anything I tell you could be leaked and you might not even know you were doing it."

"You're right." Her voice had gone very soft. "I'm under constant surveillance and yesterday . . ."

"Yesterday? What happened yesterday?"

He almost heard her mouth snap shut. "I'm not your spy, Vaughn. Get someone else if you want a puppet." The statement was devoid of any emotion that might have made him excuse it, an unwelcome reminder that the woman beside him was a cardinal Psy. One of the enemy.

"You came to us," he grit out. "You came to us because you couldn't trust anyone in your precious world—they would've hung you out to dry. DarkRiver is not a charity for lost Psy." Fur ruffled the wrong way by her words, he accelerated down the road. "Asking you to give us something in return for our help is good business. You understand business, don't you?"

The second the words were out, he knew he should've kept a lid on his temper. He rarely lost it, but when he did, he tended to be brutal. Faith's hurt was all the more painful for being hidden under the brittle armor of Psy Silence, but he could feel it, feel it in the heart of his maleness. "I'm sorry, Red. That was uncalled for."

"Why? You only stated the truth." Her voice was so cold, Vaughn expected to see icicles forming in the air.

Something in him relaxed. He didn't mind Faith's anger—it was the emotionless mask he hated. "Yeah, but that's not why I said it."

"I don't understand." No hint of curiosity, pure Psy calm.

"I said it because you pissed me off." He turned down a leafy lane and glanced over at her sitting so motionless beside him. "We're not above collecting the information you give us—we'd be stupid not to gather as much as possible while you remain in the Net—but we aren't doing it behind your back, so don't accuse us of that."

Faith didn't know how to respond. For twenty-four years, she'd lived in a world that operated on a very different set of principles. Nothing was ever said so bluntly and without any hint of subterfuge. Shoshanna Scott's visit was a vivid example—the Councilor had been all allusions and hints, never quite coming out and saying what it was that she wanted from Faith, though Faith had a very good idea. What she didn't understand was why.

It was almost a compulsion for her to talk about it with Vaughn, but she couldn't. Not yet. If she gave away the Council to the cats, notwithstanding her lack of any definitive knowledge, then she was in a sense giving away her loyalty to the Psy race. And they were *her* race. They understood what she was, what she could do, and the price that she paid. She was respected, more than respected. If Shoshanna's visit was any indication, she might climb even higher, the highest of any in her PsyClan.

If she did as Vaughn wanted and successfully dropped out of the Net, what would she be? Nothing. A broken Psy without race or family. She'd done enough reading to know that her inborn talent wasn't always respected in the human-changeling world. Many scoffed at the idea of foresight. There were some who went so far as to call her entire designation a fraud.

Of course, none of that would mean anything if her abilities continued to spiral into chaos. She had to find a way to exert control over the dark visions, even if she couldn't block them. Vaughn's fingers whispered over her cheek. She was unable to stop her reflexive movement. "Yes?"

"We're here."

As she removed the blindfold, the lingering sensation of his touch threatened to smudge the strength of her recent decision to regain mastery over her own body and mind. She knew it was hazardous to feel anything, that emotions could drive her over the edge, but that did nothing to diminish the temptation to engage with Vaughn on all levels—physical, mental, and emotional. Because she knew that if she succeeded in leashing the dark side of her ability and returned to her normal existence, she'd live the rest of her life without a jaguar who liked to tease in the most sensual of ways, who pushed her to face her fears, and who, quite simply, made her feel alive.

Leaving the blindfold on the dash, she stepped out and closed the door. Vaughn was already on the lighted porch, speaking to Sascha. Faith couldn't see Lucas, but assumed he was nearby—the alpha had appeared extremely protective of his mate. It made her speculate whether the Council had done more than put a simple prohibition over Sascha Duncan.

"Hello, Faith." Sascha smiled and gestured to the chair beside hers.

"Hello." Faith took the seat, but found herself unable to look at Vaughn. He asked too much of her by his mere presence and she didn't know what answers to give him.

"I'll be close by." Vaughn walked off around the corner, and though it was impossible, she thought she felt him change.

"Where's Lucas?" Faith asked, instead of trailing behind him and indulging her need to see him as a jaguar once more. He was beautiful in either form, a lethal blade of a man, and she itched to stroke him. But she could justify it more while he was jaguar, tell herself it wasn't the same as permitting her fingers to trail over the human male's skin. Of course, quite aside from her confusion about which path to choose, she wasn't sure she could touch either man or cat without crumbling.

"My mate had some other business to take care of."

The unexpected declaration wrenched Faith's attention to the woman beside her. "He let you come alone?"

Sascha flicked her plait over her shoulder. "I'm a cardinal of considerable strength. Why does everyone think I need a keeper?"

"I didn't mean any offense."

"None taken." The other woman shook her head. "You're right, DarkRiver males are extremely possessive and protective. But you can't give in to it—you have to learn to take a stand or it'll end in disaster."

Faith found herself intrigued by the chance to learn something about Vaughn's world. "How?"

"Like all predators, the cats are very strong, physically and emotionally. If they don't receive the same kind of, what's the right word . . . feedback, from their mates, they tend to become aggressive in the worst sense of the word." Sascha shrugged. "They try to dominate, but a dominated mate is not what makes them happy. Cats like seeing claws."

Was that what Vaughn had been doing to her? Pushing her to make her show her claws? "Can you tell me the changeling definition of a mate?"

"It's more than marriage, and far, far more than anything the Psy know." Sascha's lips curved. With her hair braided tightly off her face, she was beauty cut in perfect lines. "It's everything I never dared to dream."

Faith wanted to ask so much more, but their time was limited—she had to be back inside the compound before dawn. "The darkness is continuing to hunt me."

"Hunt? An odd word to use."

"But correct in this circumstance. Psychically, it feels as if the darkness searches for and locks on to me."

"It almost sounds like a forced telepathic link, not foresight."

Faith nodded. "Yes, but it's not. I am seeing the future, but the visions are channeled through the murderer, so in actuality, I'm in two timestreams at once. In the mind of the killer as he plans *and* in the future where the actual events take place."

"Go on," the other Psy said after a long pause.

"Once it's—he's—locked on, and maybe there is a component of telepathic interference there," she admitted, "I can't find a way to break away, to end the vision. He decides when to release me."

"But?"

"Vaughn can pull me out. By touch." Memories of his lips on hers merged with the shock she'd felt at having his claws on the tender skin of her face. "There's something else." She wiped her hands on her jeans. "I think I was having fragments of the dark visions as a child, perhaps before I turned three. So young, the memories aren't reliable, but I believe it to be a strong possibility."

"Interesting." Sascha leaned forward, elbows on her knees. "The Protocol may begin from birth, but I've heard it said that it doesn't really 'take' until a certain point of psychological development—which point depends on the individual child."

"I read a similar report a year ago. They're searching for a method to counteract that flaw in the Protocol—the consensus is that it's that period that produces the adult defectives." Even as she said the word, she realized it had been used to define the woman by her side, a Psy who was anything but defective. Another lie. Another break in the wall of her confidence in her own people.

Sascha shook her head. "I don't think it can be fixed. Very young children are far closer to their fundamental animal nature. Nothing short of rewiring the brain itself can alter that."

"That was one of the possible solutions raised in the *Psy-Med Journal*." Even then, months before her mind had begun to go haywire, Faith had found herself intellectually repulsed by the idea. The brain was the single thing that remained sacred among the Psy. To rewire that would equal the erasure of the individual, making the PsyNet a true hive mind.

"I want to not believe you, I want to be surprised and revolted." Sascha forced her heartbeat to lower. After years of hiding everything, the freedom to feel sometimes had her tumbling headfirst into emotion. "But I know the Council too well to believe they'd stop at destroying children's brains in an effort to consolidate their power."

"The procedure hasn't been implemented. It's purely theoretical." The words were crisply factual, but Sascha could feel the other woman's horror, a horror so deep that Faith, caught in the talons of Silence, was unaware of the fury of it.

Sascha understood. In any of the other races, even a theoretical idea like that would've been considered heinous, a fundamental breach of the trust between adult and child. "What's stopping them?"

"They're afraid of damaging potential psychic abilities." Faith's eyes were an impenetrable field of stars. "I can't see how they could possibly neutralize that issue."

Sascha wasn't so sure. "Silence, too, was once a theoretical idea." She'd unearthed a lot of information about her race's history in the past few months and the majority of her research had found success through the most unusual of avenues—human libraries.

Trawling through those libraries dismissed by the Psy as outdated and inefficient, she'd discovered handwritten letters and documents that told of the beginning of Silence. The real beginning. It hadn't been 1979—Enrique had been wrong, his "tribute" of seventy-nine precise cuts on each of his victims, a mistake. And that made her delighted in a sense only her bloodthirsty new family could truly understand.

"I thought it was initiated by the Council in concert with our most noted Psy-Med researchers." Faith's voice drew Sascha back from the grim theater of memory.

"No," she replied. "It was initially raised by a cultlike group named Mercury."

No one had taken them seriously at the time. However, two decades after publishing their idea, Mercury produced their first successful subjects. The test graduates were only teenagers and the conditioning was prone to failure, but they were enough to change things. Mercury stopped being referred to as a cult by the majority and started being spoken of as a think tank.

It took one hundred years for them to morph into a group of visionaries, the saviors of the Psy. "The first pro-Silence Council was dominated by acolytes of Mercury. Two were graduates of their beta version of the Protocol."

"Sascha?"

Startled out of her painful thoughts on the high cost of such absolute Silence, she turned. Faith's hand was outstretched, a touch halted midthought. "You have to be more careful," she said gently. She had no desire to reinforce the straitjacket of Silence, but so long as the other cardinal was in the Net, she had to be hyperaware.

Faith's hand curled into a fist and she tucked it under her thigh. "I'm changing, Sascha. I want to fight it, but the change is happening on a level I can't seem to stop. And I'm not sure that's a good thing."

"Why?"

"I'm an F-Psy, valued and protected among our race. Out here, I'd be nothing."

"That's not true." Sascha attempted to use her empathic gifts to soothe the bruised pain inside of Faith, pain she could feel like a rock on her heart. "If you can learn to utilize and manage your gifts in a different way, you'll be as valued here. Imagine, you could warn of disasters and violence. You could save so many lives."

Faith looked away. She didn't want to see the other side of the ledger, didn't want to consider the deaths on the conscience of every foreseer who'd chosen an easier path. Like her. "Do you have any idea why my normal shields might be failing? These protections are specifically designed to guard F-Psy during visions, but they can't protect me against the darkness. They can't keep me safe."

Only Vaughn could do that, and she wondered why he bothered. If the foreseers hadn't withdrawn into Silence, perhaps his sister, too, would have lived.

CHAPTER 14

"What do you feel during these visions?" Sascha asked, not forcing her to face the issue as Vaughn would've done. "There's no one here but us."

"And a cat with very good hearing." Faith couldn't see him, but she knew he was out there pacing, protecting.

"Actually two," Sascha corrected. "A result of Lucas being overprotective is my guess, though I wouldn't put it past the sentinels to do it on their own." Her laugh was both amused and exasperated.

"Two?" She could bear Vaughn hearing her confession, because no matter what she'd said in the car, she trusted him. But another cat?

"Don't worry. Vaughn would never allow him within hearing range."

Something in the other woman's tone made Faith go still. "What?"

Sascha smiled. "Nothing. So, what do you feel?"

"Rage, pain, malice, fury, bloodlust." She couldn't bring herself to list the sick pleasure felt by the sadistic sexuality of that raping mind. Because during the visions, she *was* him and the pleasure was her own.

It made her want to vomit, to tear out her own mind. No wonder F-Psy had chosen the coward's way out and surrendered to the clean commerce of Silence.

"The worst possible way to snap out of the Protocol." The renegade cardinal's face softened. "I think emotions are the key to why your shields are failing. Psy in the past would probably have fought fire with fire, shoving up blocks powered by the depth of their horror at the acts."

Faith was startled by the echo of Vaughn's earlier comments. "Go on."

"It's speculation on my part, but I know my shields cracked because I was crushing emotion when emotion was my strength."

Faith didn't ask more about Sascha's abilities. Faith *was* linked to the Net. The PsyClan *did* monitor her. On top of that, the Council was now paying her an unusual amount of attention. "But my ability isn't based on emotion."

"I think you're wrong. If emotion wasn't at the heart of foresight, F-Psy would never have seen the things they once did, never have seen murder and disaster. They saw those things because they were people who cared about others, who were driven to try to stop the evil."

Faith couldn't begin to imagine the strength it must've taken to be a foreseer in the time before Silence, to see death and pain in an endless sequence of what could be. "You're saying it's possible that Silence left the section of my mind that has the capacity to see darkness, the emotional center, unprotected. To even accept the existence of such a center would go against the conditioning. Following that logic, I can't shield that which doesn't exist." Leaving her totally exposed to the malicious power of a killer in need of an audience.

"Exactly." Sascha's eyes flashed bright and Faith almost imagined she saw colors. Impossible. "I think that's why

Vaughn can pull you out—his touch awakens that buried center."

Faith's stomach clenched at the mention of the cat who'd somehow become integral to her life. "Even if you're right and I find that area of my brain and reinitiate the protections, it won't stop the visions, just make them easier to escape, correct?"

"Faith." Sascha sighed. "If you continue to try to block your gift as it's been blocked for twenty-four years, you'll destroy yourself from the inside out."

And go insane, Faith finished silently, hands clenching into rigid balls under her thighs. "If I accept these visions, it'll be the same as accepting emotion and I won't be able to hide that for long. I'm too closely watched. The end result will be the same—incarceration in a mental health facility." Another trap with no way out.

"You always have choices. The question is, are you willing to see them?"

Or are you a coward hiding behind the convenient shield of Silence?

Words Sascha would never say, but Vaughn would in a heartbeat. He wasn't gentle like the cardinal bcside her. He was a predator and he went for the throat. And she watched the forest for him until he appeared for her in a flash of gold and black—a jaguar circling her, protecting her, perhaps caging her. She should try to run, try to escape, but of course, there was nowhere to go.

Not when the real threat was inside her own mind.

Vaughn did another sweep of his range and confirmed that the second sentinel in the area, Dorian, was keeping to the outer boundary. Only Vaughn was allowed so close to Faith. Even having Dorian in the same wide range made him want to react with brutal violence. The jaguar suddenly understood the extreme possessiveness that gripped DarkRiver males during the mating dance, understood why some of them turned close to feral.

Because the same violent fury was riding him now.

He roared and everything in the forest went silent. Brooding but ever watchful, he began to once again consider how to seduce the object of his hunger. He wasn't a fool. He knew sex would amp up the electricity between them, not turn it down. But if he didn't have her soon, he might gnaw off a paw.

The cat was frustrated with the man. Take her, it said; pleasure will crush her fear. The man wanted to agree. It would be so easy. Except that it would be a lie. No one raised as Faith had been, in the privacy-less box she called a home, would so quickly be able to adapt to the ferocity of his needs. And a Psy? Impossible.

Sex might actually send her into the very seizures she'd been conditioned to expect.

But she felt him on the psychic level, an intimacy he'd never expected. That she could pick up only his most erotic thoughts delighted him. It gave him the best of both worlds—his privacy and the ability to seduce her without subjecting her to touch, which might send her over the edge.

Sensual hunger beating in every surge of blood, he began to think of Faith and all the ways in which he wanted to take her. The jaguar, being a jaguar, wanted to enter her from behind. A view nothing could match, the man agreed. So much to explore, to stroke, while she lay helpless. His body reminded him of the sharp bite of pain that had been her response to his earlier provocation. Maybe not so helpless, he grinned inside. But this was his fantasy and here she was his—submitting, asking to be touched, to be kissed, to be mounted.

Something "pinged" against his mind.

He went predator-quiet as he tasted the touch. Ever since

Sascha had discovered the Web of Stars that linked the sentinels to their alpha, they'd been experimenting with its tactical uses. Sascha alone had so far been able to send language—to Lucas—but both Vaughn and Clay had proved able to "knock" in a crude sense.

Vaughn could also sense emotion sent by Sascha but he'd never before "heard" anything else. Sascha remained the sole person who could receive everyone, though it looked like Lucas might be able to train his mind to do the same. As a result of their work with the Web, Vaughn had learned that his packmates' mental scents were the same as their physical ones. And he knew what they all tasted like.

Definitely not woman and hunger, need and fear, passion and musk.

The cat wanted to purr. Encouraged, he continued with his erotic fantasies, playing with a woman he'd decided was his. Faith might not agree, but Vaughn had never lost marked prey. Now he imagined curving his hands over her hips, stroking that tempting cream and gold skin, the warmth and woman-softness of her. He'd pet her first, he thought, gentle her as he might a stubborn feline. Then he'd lean down and lick his way to her neck, indulging his desire to taste her skin until he reached the savage beat of her pulse.

Another mental push. Much harder. He took it with an inward growl of pleasure. He wasn't underestimating Faith—a cardinal might not be able to easily manipulate a changeling mind, but she could rip it open and kill him. However, he knew she wouldn't, knew something she wasn't yet ready to accept. The consequence of that truth was that Faith couldn't hurt him.

In his fantasy, he closed his teeth over her pulse. He could maul her very badly, but that he never would, gave her the power. That was something she had yet to learn. As his hand closed over her breast and his fingers found her nipple, he bit down a tiny fraction harder, just enough to mark, to brand.

The next shove at his mind was tinged with desperation. Aware he'd pushed her too far, though it wasn't anywhere near far enough for him, he let her body fade from his mind and forced himself to think thoughts she couldn't see. Not knowing the reason for their connection was probably driving Faith nuts. Good. She needed to experience the unruliness of the wild or she'd never break free of Silence. And she had to smash through those walls. She no longer had a choice.

Lucas arrived to pick up Sascha sometime after two in the morning. Watching the vehicle disappear into the darkness, Faith began waiting for Vaughn. She could feel him inside her where no one should've been able to go, knew he was close by. She was proven right. He walked out of the forest on human feet a split second after the last whisper of sound from the departing car.

He was naked.

Her fingers clenched on the porch support post, her whole body filled with jagged bursts of lightning screaming for escape. It had been her intention to tell him to stop thinking of her with such brazen heat, to stand her ground against this predator who considered her body *his* in a way she barely understood.

But all she could do was watch him walk to her. There was nothing but lethal grace to him, his every move declaring that he was not human, not Psy, not anything civilized. His hair was loose around his shoulders, setting off those wild, not quite human eyes, and his body was pure lithe muscle.

Her own eyes refused to obey her commands and continued to skate down his body when she knew it was a mistake. He'd see it as an invitation. But still she lingered over the fine hair that dusted his chest and reappeared in a darker shade at his navel. That thin line led downward in flagrant challenge—she told herself to look away but it was already too late. He jutted out thick and hard.

A whimper exiting her throat, her hand spasmed around the post. He was magnificent. Never before had she seen a man so unapologetically nude and at ease. Her heart thudded violently enough to hurt. She had to run. She had to watch. Then he was standing a step below her and even then he was taller, stronger, fundamentally, irrevocably male.

Those half-human eyes captured her own. "What do you want?"

"I don't know." The answer was raw, ripped from the secret core of her, the unknown part that had the capacity for both chilling horror and the most exquisite hunger.

"You can touch." His voice was a purr that rolled over her like the softest, most sensual stroke of living fur. "I've touched you—this is your chance to get even."

Touch?

It was a very bad idea. Would in all probability completely fragment her mind and leave her a splintered mess. "I can't."

"Only as far as you want," he coaxed. "I'll give you free rein." Raising his arms, he closed his fingers over the edge of the overhang that protected the porch. "Promise."

Trust a cat? She'd have to be crazy. "I have to go back," she whispered, but her eyes were on the sensual fullness of his lips, her mind awash with echoes of his erotic thoughts.

"Not for a few hours. Plenty of time to play."

Time enough to repair her shields? The ones against the PsyNet were holding, but despite everything she'd learned tonight, she hadn't yet ascertained a method to protect against the darkness *and* remain safe from punishment for having broken Silence. It didn't matter. She was already mad. Because she was going to accept Vaughn's invitation. And she was going to enjoy it. The lightning in her bloodstream was a heated caress, the pulse between her legs an unsettling but exquisite pleasure.

She felt.

Raising the hand not gripping the post, she hesitated, mindful of his animal nature. "Promise?"

He snapped playfully at the fingers hovering so close to his mouth. "Promise."

"Even if I . . ." She didn't know how to say what it was she wanted to say.

"Even if you suck on me and leave me without an orgasm. Even then."

A wave of red fire swept across her vision at the idea of playing with him that way, a way so scandalously intimate she'd never before been able to understand the attraction it held for human and changeling women. What satisfaction could a female get from the act? Now she knew. The thought of having him that much at her mercy, of giving him that much pleasure, was a drug in itself. Maybe too powerful a drug. "I may have an adverse reaction." To anything they tried.

"I'll stop you before you go too far. I won't let you be helpless."

"Too far" was no longer the solid line it had once been. "I have to trust you."

"Yes." No obfuscation, nothing but blunt truth.

Her fingers brushed his lips as he finished speaking and she waited for the rush of fear. Of pain. It came, the conditioned shell of her mind recoiling from the act. Instead of withdrawing, she gave the lightning full rein. It was so extreme, so raw, that it buried the fear and pain under an avalanche of pure sensation. And she was free.

She pressed against his lips and he parted them to allow her to slide a single finger inside. The suction of his mouth went straight through to the pulsing flesh between her legs. "How?" Shaken by the intensity inspired by such a simple act, she began to pull her finger out.

His teeth threatened to bite, but released her after a pain-less graze. "Because it's me."

She wanted to take issue with the arrogance of his re-sponse, but there was something about the look in his eyes, something that felt like truth. Sucking in a jagged breath, she followed her fingers as they whispered hesitantly over his shoulders.

He blazed, as if his body burned for hers, as if he'd keep her warm on the coldest night. Startled by the seduction of the idea, she almost jerked back her hand, but she wanted too much to let go so easily. "I am strong," she said, unaware she'd spoken aloud until Vaughn replied, "Yes, you are."

Her fingers spread through the golden hair on his chest and she felt the beat of his heart under her palm, strong, steady, a little fast. He was as affected by this wild hunger as she was, but he wasn't scared. Because he, too, was wild.

Her own pulse was everywhere. In her head, in her mouth, in her chest, in the heat between her legs, in every inch of her perspiration-damp skin. She knew she was pushing herself and she didn't care. Her mind filled with the earthy scent of Vaughn as she leaned toward him and breathed deep. It was a rush, an addiction she hadn't even been aware of having. Her nipples had tightened long ago, but now they seemed to burn hot, rubbing against her bra as if her breasts had swollen and there was too much pressure.

She had the urge to squeeze her own flesh and ease the ache. Under her palm, Vaughn's pulse kicked hard. She looked up to find his eyes glowing from within, dark knowl-edge in their depths. "Let me," he growled, and it *was* a growl. She should've been afraid of the animal so thinly covered by his human skin, but she was long past doing what she should.

"No." If he touched her, it was all over.

He growled again, low in his throat, but didn't break his word. The muscles of his upper arms stood out in sharp relief as he gripped the roof edge even harder. So much strength and it was at her command. The power was heady, or was that desire turning her blood to fire?

Returning her attention to his body, she finally released the death grip she had on the post and slid both hands down his chest. He made her want to lick her lips. Lick him. Nothing, no one, had ever prompted such hunger in her.

"Do it," he ordered.

She knew what he wanted—the thick length of him was furious with blood. It was her own hunger that surprised. But not enough to stop her. Unconsciously moving closer, she left one hand on his ribs while the other slid down to skim lightly along his erection.

He sucked in a sharp breath, his body thrumming with tension. Captivated, she repeated the movement.

"Don't. Tease."

She barely heard him through the blood fury of pure sensation as she traced the proud evidence of his maleness one more time. His body bucked. And she curled her exploring fingers to hold him.

CHAPTER 15

Faith found herself unable to close her fingers completely around him. How could anything so thick fit in her body? And why was she consumed with the curiosity to find out?

He hadn't said a word since that last barked command, his entire body supple stone that beat for her alone. In her hand he was almost unbearably silky, the skin covering his hardness delicate, surprising her. She hadn't thought her jaguar would be delicate anywhere. That was the last coherent thought she had.

She ran her closed fist up and down his engorged length, indulging the animal inside her, the primal being that knew only hunger, need, and sex. Her breasts hurt so badly that she ached to rip off her clothing and rub herself against his chest, but that would mean releasing him and she didn't want to. All she wanted was to squeeze and stroke over and over. And over again.

"Stop, Faith."

She shook off the unwelcome interruption and thought of the million other things she wanted to do to him. First, she'd place her mouth over the dark gold of his chest and taste the sweat and heat so temptingly close. Maybe she'd even take off her own clothes as a prelude to pasting her body flush against his.

"Baby, stop." A hand knotted in her hair.

She tried to pull away, but he was too strong. Then another big male hand covered the fingers she had around his erection and attempted to ease her off. She reacted by digging the nails of her free hand into his chest while squeezing his erection harder.

His snarl raised every hair on her body. She expected him to bite her. That was fine with her. What she didn't expect was for him to tighten the hand he'd placed over hers, pressing until she thought he'd cause her to hurt him.

"No!" She let go.

He stepped out of reach with jaguar speed, so quick that she had to grab the post to keep herself upright. Her head swam. She found her free hand reaching out for him. "Vaughn." It was nearly a sob. *"Please."*

"Shh." He was behind her before she even saw him move. "Let me ease you down."

"Down?" Need crawled over her skin, pushed at the walls of her mind. But when she would've turned, he used his hands to hold her in place. Struggling with the frenzied rage of a wild thing, she twisted and kicked, her mind having no memory of its offensive capabilities. Right then, she was a wholly physical creature and in that arena, he was far too strong.

"No! No!" Turbulent clouds of anger gathered over the lightning.

Vaughn continued to hold Faith in place with his grip on her upper arms, while ensuring that no other part of his body touched hers. "Put up your walls, baby." The jaguar fought his choice, but a promise was a promise.

"No!"

The word was so violently obstinate, he knew that whatever was driving her wasn't quite sane. "See the forest in front of you?"

A sullen silence. Then, "Yes."

"There are others there who might see us."

"Others?"

"Yes. Do you want others to see me?" He spoke to a part of her she didn't know existed when it was that very part that was exacerbating her hunger.

The answer came without pause. "No."

"Then put up your shields." If she'd been fully aware, she might've challenged him that they could just as easily step inside the cabin. But of course, she wasn't anywhere close to being aware.

Her body shuddered, but she stopped arguing. It took a long time for her to say, "You should stop touching me now. And please put on some clothes."

He didn't push her this time, did exactly as she'd asked. It half killed him to walk away from the promise of what might've been.

It appeared as if the sensual overload had short-circuited some of the other lines of conditioning. An hour after skating on the thin edge of madness, Faith sat on the swing finishing a cup of coffee, Vaughn a larger-than-life presence against the railing across from her. Yet her mind was on someone else.

"My sister's name was Marine." It was a deliberate step into trust. "She was only twenty-two years old, but already integral to the PsyClan's business unit."

Vaughn didn't say a word. Maybe he knew she simply needed his presence, needed to know he'd be there to catch her if she fell. After all he, too, had lost a sister.

"We were less than acquaintances—I saw her maybe once or twice a year, if that. But I used to keep track of her.

I always justified it as staying up to date with the PsyClan as a whole, but that was a lie. I wanted to know my sister." She'd saved every school report, every training log. "She was a cardinal telepath." She glanced up to see if he understood.

His eyes didn't glow, but they pierced the soft black of the night nonetheless. "Extremely powerful."

"Yes." She drank some of the coffee. It warmed her body, but did nothing for the chill inside of her. "Most telepaths are specialized in some way, but Marine was a pure telepath—she could send and receive over distances you can't even imagine." She wanted him to understand the beauty of Marine's exquisite mind.

"Why was that such an asset if you have the PsyNet?"

"It's true that the Net allows us to communicate and meet regardless of our physical location, but it also involves a level of vulnerability. Our minds can be hacked while on the Net. Plus anything said on the Net, even words spoken behind the thickest of mental vaults, becomes in some way a part of the Net. No one may be able to access it, but the data is *there*. 'Pathing cuts out both those factors. No chance of being hacked. No records of any kind."

"Perfect security," Vaughn mused. "Her services must have been in high demand."

"Yes." But she'd taken time out of her busy schedule to train as a blocker for the day when Faith's mind broke.

"Did she look like you?"

Faith shook her head. "Our maternal DNA was different. After my birth, the PsyClan decided not to risk producing another F cardinal. We're valued because we're rare and they didn't want to glut the market." That cold reasoning had been explained to her long ago, no one seeming to consider the psychological impact it might have on a child to realize she was nothing but a product manufactured for a very specific purpose.

"So the M-Psy selected a number of maternal candidates

whose genetic history lacked any foreseers." They'd also chosen highly telepathic women, for the very reason that one day Faith would need a keeper, and her father preferred to retain power in the hands of the immediate family. "It worked. Marine was a Tp cardinal with no hint of F designation abilities. She had skin like . . . like milk coffee, and a mental voice so clear, it had the resonance of a perfectly tuned bell. Her mother was from the Caribbean."

"But she lived with your PsyClan?"

"That was part of the reproduction contract. The maternal side of her family was interested in seeing if they could produce an F-Psy, so my father allowed them to use his genetic material on another female in their line.

"The resulting male offspring has never been considered part of NightStar, as Marine was never considered a member of the Caribbean family." She paused at the look on his face. "You don't understand. Neither do I. I don't think I ever did. If I had, I wouldn't have been so hungry for knowledge of Marine.

"I used to imagine playing with her as a child—before that kind of imagination was conditioned out of me. She was this fantasy and everything I needed in a friend." But never in reality had there been any hint of friendship in their dealings with each other, two perfect Psy with ice water running in their veins. "Now I won't ever have the chance to know her. She's gone." For always.

She stared fixedly at a point past Vaughn's shoulder. When he moved to stand beside her, his hand stroking her unbound hair, she didn't tell him to move away. She needed to know that he'd heard her silent sorrow, that he knew about Marine. Someone had to know, someone had to remember in case Faith didn't make it.

A single tear streaked down her face and it was the first time such a thing had happened in her memory. It was liquid fire across her skin, so hot, so pure. "She was killed to satisfy bloodlust, her life snuffed out because the darkness was hungry for pain and torture. *And I was too weak to stop it.*" She uncurled the fingers of one hand and rubbed it across her heart, trying to ease the guilt that had twisted a knot inside of her.

"You didn't have the skills." Vaughn's voice was so consciously gentle it hurt.

"Didn't I? Or maybe I didn't want to see what the visions were trying to tell me, was too much of a coward."

"The guilt won't ever go away," he told her with changeling frankness, "but you can stop it from being so corrosive."

"How?"

"By doing something that balances the scales, by saving someone else's daughter or sister." The sharp blade of knowledge cut every word.

She looked up into his face, unsurprised to find his eyes gone utterly cat. "Will you tell me about her?" Already she knew this jaguar walked alone. But she wanted him to trust her this much at least.

His hand stilled on her hair. "My sister starved to death because I was too young and weak to find enough food to keep her alive. And I miss her every day of my life."

Faith reached out in an effort to give comfort, the first time she'd done so. The hand she put on his thigh was tentative, but it held so much and, though he said nothing to acknowledge the act, he began to stroke her hair again.

"What was her name?"

"Skye." His voice dropped until it was more growl than human. "Our parents abandoned us in predator territory with nothing but the clothes on our backs."

"But they were changelings."

"Being animal is no guarantee against evil." Vaughn's thigh turned rock-hard under her hand. "My parents weren't evil, but they were caught up in it—I have to think that to keep myself sane."

She stayed silent, trying to give him what he'd given her.

"My parents were very young and unmarried when they had me—most jaguars don't follow human customs. Skye was born three years later. When she was two and a half, they joined a new church and got married. Soon afterward, they gave up their worldly possessions and we began living in a commune." His voice was hard. "That wouldn't have mattered if I hadn't begun to notice the way some of the 'elders' looked at Skye. She was a baby and they wanted to put their hands on her."

Faith couldn't imagine anything so horrendous. "You protected her."

"I got her killed." Vaughn had lived with that knowledge for over two decades. "I was always with her—I refused to allow them near. I was labeled a problem child and my parents had to discipline me according to their new religion." Hours of beatings, of isolation, of being told he was "full of sin."

It had terrified him that they'd get to Skye while he was locked up, but his parents must not have been completely lost because they'd always kept Skye close while he was being punished. "When it became clear that I wasn't going to relent and that I'd taught the other kids to be wary of the elders, too, they began a campaign to get rid of us. They told our parents to prove their devotion to their new God by giving up the 'fruits of sin,' the children they'd borne out of wedlock."

"How could . . . ?" Faith shook her head in bewilderment and he realized how hard he'd clenched his hand in her hair.

Softening his grip, he smoothed the silken mass. "It took a long time for my parents to buckle under." But by the end of it, his mother hadn't been able to look at him without seeing sin and his father had stopped hearing anything Skye had to say. "When they put us in the car and told us we weren't coming back, we were so happy." He could remember every glittering facet of the hope that had gripped his ten-year-old heart. Because despite everything, he'd still been a child.

"Instead, they took us deep into the forest and left us there." That was when they'd spouted the evil they'd been indoctrinated with. Skye had cried and tried to run after them, but they'd been full-grown jaguars and she'd been a baby. Following, Vaughn had waited until she was too exhausted to run anymore and then he'd found them a place to hide.

"Oh, Vaughn."

"She died in my arms five days later." His heart had broken so completely that day he hadn't been sure it would ever recover. "I buried her in a cave." Where it would never rain and she'd never be cold again. "Afterward, I decided to keep walking. I wanted to get to my parents so I could kill them."

"How did you get out?" Her voice was soft, passing no judgment on his need for retribution.

"I didn't. I collapsed two days later." But even exhausted, broken, and lost, he'd been caught in the claws of the most vicious kind of anger. "What I didn't know was that I'd inadvertently walked into DarkRiver territory." If only their parents had left them a little less deep in the forest, Skye, too, would've survived.

"A sentinel found me within hours. Once I could talk, they asked me what had happened and were ready to go for blood on my behalf. But it wasn't necessary. My parents were dead by then."

He felt Faith's shock in the sudden jerk of her head. "What?"

"My mother tried to come back for us." Knowing that gave him some sense of peace, some sense of there being a better God. "My father was determined to stop her. Two adult jaguars fighting in animal form can do a lot of damage—he killed her, then committed suicide."

Faith stood and his hand dropped from her hair. "I'm sorry." Inching closer, she touched his cheek in a caress that lasted a mere second.

However, he knew exactly how much it had to have cost

her after her earlier meltdown. "It was better that way. If they'd lived, I would've been the one to kill them." And that might've destroyed him beyond any hope of redemption. "DarkRiver tipped off Enforcement about the cult, and it was raided and shut down. Because the victims included humans who opposed death, they were incarcerated rather than subjected to changeling law." Blood for blood, flesh for flesh, *life for life*. The judgment had left him with nothing on which to focus his anger, his rage.

He could've gone very bad, but DarkRiver hadn't let him.

"How did you survive?" Faith asked, hugging her arms around herself. "How? That much pain? How, Vaughn? How can you be so strong?"

"Sometimes rage can be a good thing. It keeps you going when nothing else remains." He met those night-sky eyes, so eerie, so beautiful. "Be angry, Faith. Use the need for vengeance as your shield against the darkness while you hunt it down."

"What if I don't have that in me? What if I'm too weak?"

"What if you do?" he countered. "What if you only have to open the door?"

Faith made it back to the compound in the nick of time. The comm console chimed as she exited her room early the next morning. It was Anthony again.

"Father."

"Faith, I have some information for you."

"I understand." She turned off the screen and returned to her room. Locking herself in, she leaned against the wall, closed her eyes, and opened a door on the psychic plane. Anthony's roaming consciousness was waiting for her as she stepped out. Like her, he preferred to travel incognito, his true strength masked by patterns of ordinariness.

"Follow me."

They were behind the walls of a NightStar vault less than a minute later in real time. Most people who wanted privacy in the Net tended to use a simple room that could be created instantaneously. Of course, the security status of that room depended on the strength of the Psy involved in its creation.

In contrast, the NightStar clan could afford to maintain a number of permanent vaults on the Net, sustaining them with a constant trickle of power from most of its members. All the vaults were impenetrable as far as hacking was concerned, but Faith wondered if the NetMind was able to enter them at will. And if it could, did the Council then have a way to retrieve the data it collected?

"I have allies in the Council ranks," Anthony told her. "People close to the Councilors."

"What have you learned?"

"You're one of the favored candidates for replacing Councilor Enrique."

"Who are the others?" Faith kept her mental self calm. She couldn't afford to let her physical mind's disrupted state bleed over to this roaming self. Her father was far too strong a Psy not to detect the anomaly.

"It appears that the name of an M-Psy was also put forward, but the Council is concentrating on you and a Tk named Kaleb Krychek."

"I've heard his name mentioned in relation to several events within the Council."

"Correct. Kaleb has climbed extremely high in the ranks at a very young age—he's about to turn twenty-seven. He's highly competent at reading and initiating power plays."

"While I have no experience with such strategic games."

"You have an advantage he lacks."

"I'm an F-Psy." And the Council enjoyed being in a position of power. Her skills would increase that power by several magnitudes.

"I've prepared a file on Kaleb." He showed her the point

in the vault where it was stored and she downloaded the information into her roaming mind. "He's dangerous and has certainly killed, notwithstanding the lack of evidence."

"I'll take care to ensure I don't become the victim of an unexpected accident."

"It's not clear which of the Councilors are backing you and which favor Kaleb, so don't let your guard down around any of them."

"They're not Psy I'd ever let my guard down around."

"Who approached you?"

"Shoshanna Scott."

"What was your impression?"

"That she hadn't made any firm judgments." Except for the blood on her hands. Faith crushed that thought as soon as it awakened. It could not be allowed to color her Net presence. "I'm assuming I'll be contacted by the others in due course."

"If you need to speak to me at any stage, don't worry about formalities. 'Path."

She nodded, cognizant it was a privilege. Anthony might be her father, but only a select few had the right to initiate telepathic contact with him. "Of course. Thank you for the file. I'll study it carefully." She meant that. Her mind might be starting to spin out of control, but it wasn't yet gone and neither was she. Maybe she could still salvage her sanity and her life as a Psy, the only life she knew how to live.

What she refused to think about was the inevitable consequence of achieving that goal—never again being able to experience the exquisite agony of emotions that pleasured as well as hurt . . . never again tangling with a jaguar.

CHAPTER 16

After spending all day on the sculpture of Faith, Vaughn met up with the other sentinels and their alpha pair late that night to work on shielding. The location was a glade close to Lucas's lair, not far from a small river that bisected the area and turned the air damp. Tamsyn, their healer, was also present.

Sascha ran them through the drills over and over, merciless in her drive to make them invulnerable to Psy attack, only calling a halt when they started to snarl at each other. "Given your psychic blindness, you're doing far better than I expected. You're actually learning to shield on a level beyond the normal changeling defenses."

"Which are pretty damn strong." Nate threw an arm around Tamsyn's shoulders. His mate smiled and laced her fingers through his hand.

"Yes." Sascha nodded. "Soon you'll be close to invincible."

"We already are, Sascha darling," Dorian said from where he was sitting with his back against a tree.

Sascha walked over to the blond sentinel and tugged him

to his feet for a quick hug. Dorian was no longer the open wound he'd been straight after his sister Kylie's murder at the hands of serial killer—and former Councilor—Santano Enrique, but he remained badly damaged. The violent loss had done nothing to affect his abilities as a sentinel, but they were Pack. And Pack didn't look the other way when one of their own was hurting.

Dorian's needs made him no less respected in a pack where touch-hunger was accepted and fed. Sascha's empathy in particular seemed to reach the latent male far deeper than anyone else. Now, she leaned her back against his chest, his arms around her waist, and closed her eyes. "Let me check the Web to see if any of these changes are manifesting there."

She opened her eyes a second later and looked straight across to where Vaughn crouched. But she didn't say anything of what he knew she wanted to say. "Everything looks good."

"Then school's out?" Dorian asked. "Anybody got detention?"

"Go before I change my mind." Sascha kissed him on the cheek, laughing at his attempt to steal a more intimate kiss. "Vaughn, could you stay? I want to talk to you about something."

Mercy made a sound of doom. "In trouble with Teach, cat. Didn't do your mental exercises, did you?"

"He's been distracted," Clay murmured, a shadow almost invisible in the darkness.

"It speaks!" Mercy threw up her hands into the air. "How many words does that make for today. Ten?" She was still kidding the silent sentinel as she walked with him and Dorian out of the training area.

Tamsyn hugged Sascha good-bye. "I think my sons are in love with you. You should hear what they're like when they get home—Sascha said· this and Sascha said that." The healer shook her head. "Lucas had better watch out."

Wrapping an arm around Tamsyn's waist, Lucas dropped a kiss on her hair. "Tell your damn brats to leave her alone."

"Lucas!" Sascha sounded shocked.

Tamsyn laughed. "Don't take him seriously. He took my adorable brats out for a run yesterday with Kit and some of the others."

"Sorry, I'm not completely used to the way you interact."

Coming around to hug his mate from behind, Lucas began nibbling on her neck.

"Don't worry, honey." The healer smiled at Sascha's attempts to make Lucas behave. "You've only been cat for a few months. Give it time."

Nate took Tamsyn's hand. "We'd better go pick up Roman and Julian before Lysa decides she's no longer our friend."

Lucas waited until Tammy and Nate were out of earshot before saying, "Why don't we head home to talk? It won't take long if we run."

"What about me?" Sascha asked, looking from one to the other. Honestly, they kept forgetting she couldn't go furry.

Lucas gave her his back. "Hop on, darling." His smile was this side of sinful, reminding her of the very first time he'd offered her a ride.

Later. It was a mind-to-mind warning that turned into a promise.

Seconds later she was on his back and they were running. She trusted him absolutely, even at this breakneck pace. The changelings could *move* in either form. Holding on to the muscular body of her panther, she considered what she'd learned tonight. Only one thing was certain—Vaughn's life was about to become very, very complicated.

A cold rush of wind across her face. The low rumble of Lucas's growl as he warned away something in their path. The rich scents of the forest. It all dragged her firmly into the physical. Glorying in her freedom to indulge, she threw herself into the experience as only a former inmate of Silence could.

But the exhilarating ride was over too soon and they were at the lair. Leaving her alone with Vaughn, Lucas went to grab some drinks. Sascha glanced at the male lounging against the window ledge across from her. "Vaughn."

"I know." The jaguar folded his arms across his chest, his tattoo hidden by the gray sweatshirt he was wearing over his jeans.

Lucas walked back into the room. "Catch." He threw a beer to Vaughn and handed her a bottle of cranberry juice—alcohol had an odd effect on Psy minds.

She waited until both men had taken long drafts from the dark green bottles. "I saw something in the Web."

Lucas wrapped one arm around her neck and began to play with the end of her braid. "What?"

"Maybe Vaughn should be the one to explain." She felt uncomfortable. "I didn't mean to breach your privacy. I'm really sorry."

The jaguar threw the half-empty bottle from hand to hand. "I knew you'd see the bond."

"With Faith?" Lucas stopped tugging at her braid. "Why didn't you tell us you'd mated?"

"Because Faith doesn't know." Vaughn thrust a hand through his hair, his frustration evident. "She's not ready."

"You can't ignore a mate," Lucas pointed out. "The bond has a way of showing itself at unexpected moments."

"She's feeling trapped as it is—how do you think this is going to look to her?" Vaughn rocked back on his heels. "Could other Psy detect the bond?"

Sascha took a moment to think about it. "They shouldn't. The mating bond is changeling in nature, completely separate from the PsyNet. But"—she paused—"Faith is linked to both. I don't know how that's going to affect things. You need to tell her."

"It might make her run. She's had enough as it is."

Sascha knew he was right. Vaughn was the sentinel Sascha had always been the most wary of—there was something dangerously primal about him. His animal roamed very close to the skin. She couldn't imagine how Faith was going to deal with such an aggressive male. The F-Psy was new at emotion, at feeling anything. To ask her to embrace not only a male like Vaughn, but also the extreme devotion implied by the mating bond, might be to ask for far too much.

But as Lucas had already stressed, the bond couldn't be ignored. "She might surprise you," Sascha said. "She's seeing some horrific things without any training in how to deal with them, but she hasn't crashed. I think Faith is tougher than even she knows."

Vaughn's body was a tight wall of muscle as he faced them. "How do we get her out of the Net? Will the Web be able to support both of you at the same time?"

Sascha bit her lower lip. "I think there's enough biofeedback." Feedback no Psy could live without, the reason why dropping out of the PsyNet usually equaled suicide. "Two Psy minds should, in theory, augment the multiplication effect."

"Should?" Lucas shifted around to scowl at her.

Vaughn watched Sascha scowl back. "It's pure guesswork. DarkRiver's Web isn't supposed to exist in the first place. I don't know how it'll work, but we have to try. There's no other choice."

Lucas turned to him. "Shit, Vaughn. You had to go and mate with another damn Psy." Dragging his mate closer, he bit her lightly on the neck. "Okay, so we have to utilize the Web. We'll figure out the rest later."

"It could kill all four of us if we get it wrong and there's not enough feedback," Vaughn said, fists clenched.

"Then I'll just have to blood-oath some new sentinels if that's what it takes to strengthen the Web." Lucas's promise held the determination of a friendship forged in the darkest of fires. "But first, we need to get Faith out. Any ideas?"

"Use the disc?" Sascha was referring to the incriminating recording they'd created when they'd taken down the serial killer who'd butchered Kylie and mind-raped the Snow-Dancer, Brenna.

Vaughn wanted to grab at the idea, but he was a sentinel, sworn to protect DarkRiver. "The reasons why we didn't originally release the recording still apply. We can't take the risk of the Council feeling backed into a corner." An animal in that position had nothing to lose by trying to go for the kill.

"He's right," Lucas said. "They can't know how many more times we might blackmail them."

"Talk to me, Sascha." Vaughn folded his arms and tried to contain the urge to simply take what he wanted and damn the consequences. "Is there anything else you can think of?"

"Faith's isolated lifestyle is one thing in our favor." Sascha leaned against Lucas's side. "People know her name, but very few have actually seen her. Her dropping out won't cause as big a ripple as my defection did. But on the other hand, losing her will rob the Council of millions."

"How?"

"Taxes in the most basic sense," Sascha answered. "F-Psy create enormous amounts of money and it flows up. I know from my mother that in certain cases, the Council uses fore-seers to increase its wealth in a much more direct fashion. They get the service free or at a generous discount."

"Let me guess," Vaughn interrupted, enraged at the idea of his mate doing anything to assist that group of cold-blooded monsters. "Nobody wants to piss off the big, bad Council by asking for payment."

Sascha nodded. "People who get paid have a habit of disappearing and leaving their money to the Council."

"So they'll fight hard to keep her. They can't pretend she's defective like they did with Sascha." Lucas's facial markings stood out in sharp relief as anger pulled his skin taut. "And she's a cardinal, too. Those eyes mean she can't be hidden effectively."

"No one's going to be hiding Faith." Vaughn knew his voice had dropped several octaves, but he was beyond caring.

"What about Faith?" Sascha asked softly.

"What about her?" Vaughn put the now empty bottle on the window ledge.

"Have you asked her whether she wants to leave the Net?"

"She's my mate." Of course she'd leave the Net. "I'll try to give her some time to get used to the idea, but in the end, she has no choice."

"I think she does."

Vaughn's beast prowled to the surface of his self. "How?" Mating was a compulsion with changelings. Even the most independent females, the ones who fought the hardest, found it difficult to spend long periods apart from the males who were meant to be their mates.

"She's not changeling, so it doesn't affect her the same way it does you, not unless she opens herself up to it like I did with Lucas. It might be uncomfortable for her, but she can probably block you."

"Are you sure?" Vaughn's claws were so close to his human skin that he felt the hard prick of the tips waiting to break through.

"No. She's different from me. Being an empath meant I couldn't ignore what I felt for Lucas. I don't know if Faith is as bound to you."

"So I could be mated to someone who could choose not to be my mate?" A nightmare idea. Mating was a one-shot deal. The link usually involved a conscious decision at some point by the female, which made Vaughn and Faith's bond very unusual. But no matter how it had come into being, once made, even death couldn't break it. No one mated twice. They might find a lover, but the hole in them would never be fixed. *Never.* "I need to run."

But though he ran himself to exhaustion, his beast could find no comfort in an act that had always before meant freedom. Because he was chained, tied on the deepest level to a woman who just might destroy him.

Faith missed her jaguar, missed him badly enough to stumble in her act of normality.

She was strolling the grounds in the cool light of morning and considering how to arrange another night escape when she started to think of Vaughn, of his presence, and yes, his touch. So deep was she in her thoughts that she nearly walked into a guard. That wasn't the problem. It was the fact that her nerves were poised to jump in alarm.

Catching the reaction the barest instant before it could become action, she inclined her head. "My apologies. I wasn't concentrating on where I was going."

"The fault was mine." The guard gave a short nod and continued on his rounds.

She forced herself to walk in the opposite direction, her heart a drumbeat in her veins. Careful, she told herself. One slip was all it would take. Deciding to try to distract herself with something less incendiary, she took a seat on a small garden bench and opened up the mental file Anthony had given her.

Kaleb Krychek had led an interesting life. An unexpected Tk cardinal born of two low-Gradient Tp-Psy, he'd been raised almost like her, having spent his entire childhood in a training facility. Her father had managed to dig out that one of young Kaleb's instructors had been none other than Santano Enrique. She didn't know why Enrique had disappeared, but that piece of history could prove a weapon should she ever need it.

Kaleb had been conscripted into the Council ranks almost immediately after his successful graduation from the Protocol. His climb up the ladder had been phenomenal, even more so because he was a cardinal—most cardinals, while they worked for the Council, were too cerebral to bother with politics and power.

Faith turned another page in the file and found herself looking at a list of missing persons. At least ten high-ranking members of the Council substructure had disappeared under mysterious circumstances and, in every instance, it was Kaleb who had benefited. However, nothing had ever been traced to him—a fact that would only make him more appealing to the lethal beings who were the current Council.

Faith was a babe in the woods in comparison. Which begged the question of why she was even a candidate. She was about to dig deeper into Kaleb's file when she felt it. The push of darkness. "No." It seemed obscene that after three days of psychic peace, the evil should hunt her down in bright daylight.

Her first instinct was to fight, to stop a recurrence of the last malicious invasion. But she was through with running. If she could tangle with a jaguar and come out alive, then she could deal with this ugliest facet of her own abilities. Releasing a withheld breath, she let him take her under and exhibit his triumphs. She saw through his eyes, forced herself to watch that which had not yet come to pass. It was changeable, mutable. One day soon, he'd stalk the target of his fantasies, stalk and plan. Faith studied every aspect of his intended victim and tried to figure out who she was, where she was, and, most important, *when* she was.

Her suit was black, her shirt white, her skin a hue rare among the Psy after generations of intermingling—a pure white that held faint undertones of palest blue. But the expressionless cold of her face made it indisputable that she was, in fact, a member of Faith's race. The unknown Psy's hair was a white-blonde that went with her skin and her eyes were a vivid blue. She looked nothing like Marine.

But, her mind insisted on whispering, the killer hadn't felt the same with Marine. The visions involving her sister had focused on the death itself and the killer's emotions during it, while this new victim was going to be stalked, watched, savored. Yes, it had been a rush for him to take Marine's life, but he'd experienced none of this extreme anticipation. Perhaps if he had, she might've understood in time . . . might've saved Marine from the agony of having her breath choked out of her.

She shook off the leaden chains of guilt, chains that might cost another life, and followed her earlier line of thought. Newly awakened instinct said that the key to everything lay in answering the question of why Marine and this new target inspired such disparate reactions in the perpetrator.

Even as she wrestled with that question, the darkness faded away from her consciousness. The killer had been placated by her acquiescence, but that was an unreliable effect. He could as easily decide to rape her mind the next time. However, she couldn't think about that possibility right now. Because someone was watching her. And that someone raised every hair on her body.

Opening her eyes, she found herself looking up at Nikita Duncan, Councilor and one of the most dangerous women in the Net. The poison of her mind was reputedly more lethal than the deadliest biological virus. And she'd found Faith in the grip of a dark vision.

Faith stood and brushed down the back of her dress. "Councilor Duncan."

"I apologize if I disturbed you." Nikita's almond-shaped eyes were disquietingly focused. "I thought your visions took place in monitored surroundings."

Faith shook her head and told a half-truth. "Sometimes I inadvertently activate a trigger while considering how to

best approach a project, or my mind simply finds these surroundings more conducive to a particular vision."

"I see. Well, I suppose you're not far from the guards, so
there's no cause for alarm."

And no real privacy. "No." She met Nikita's eyes. "What
can I do for you today, Councilor?"

The last thing Vaughn expected to see when he leaped
over the fences and tracked Faith's scent to a hidden part
of the property was his mate deep in conversation with
Nikita Duncan. Mindful that Sascha's mother was a powerful telepath, he allowed the beast to rise to the surface of his
mind—if she did notice him, she might not recognize him as
a changeling. He also kept considerable distance between
them. But he could still hear every word they spoke. And
what he heard made him want to shred the tree branch under
his claws.

"You're not stupid, Faith. You have to know why I'm
here."

"Of course. However, I'm at a loss to know the reason behind the nomination." Faith's voice was as cold and efficient
as a scalpel, utterly different from how she sounded when
speaking to Vaughn. It shook him to realize she was that
good an actress, made him question which persona was real
and which a fraud.

"There are things you won't know until you've been
accepted."

"I understand the need for the Council to keep things
confidential, but to be perfectly honest, I see no advantage
I have over other possible aspirants."

Nikita's ruler-straight black hair shifted around a face
that looked nothing like her daughter's. "Who would you put
on that list of aspirants? I'm curious to see how much of a
finger you have on the pulse of the Net."

"If you don't mind, Councilor, I'll keep my thoughts to myself." Faith glanced in Vaughn's direction and he waited for her to reach out to him with her mind, but she didn't. Disappointed despite his anger, he continued to watch. And listen. "There are certain names it's better not to speak of in advance."

"True." Nikita was silent for a few seconds. "Your monitoring is extensive."

Faith said nothing and he realized it was because Nikita had made a statement, not asked a question. It was the cold logic of the Psy in operation. And Faith hadn't missed a beat.

"How do you know anything if you're wrapped in cotton wool?" Nikita asked.

"The PsyNet."

"I was given the impression that F-Psy rarely frequent the Net."

"Some of us do." There was knowledge in her tone and the predator in Vaughn appreciated that. She couldn't afford to appear weak in front of Nikita, a woman so without heart that she had cut off her daughter as easily as another woman might throw out the garbage.

"Good. Before I go, you should know that certain Councilors are not in favor of your nomination." Nikita glanced at her timepiece. "Expect a summons within the next week."

Vaughn kept to his hidden position until Nikita's scent was inside the car waiting at the gate. Then he tracked his treacherous human prey to another isolated section of the compound. Faith's eyes widened when he landed in front of her in jaguar form but she didn't back away. "Vaughn. I thought I saw you."

He knew she was lying. She hadn't seen him. She'd felt him. That she didn't want to admit that truth only added fuel to the fire of his anger. Butting at her with his head until she got the message and sat down on the ground, he went behind the gnarled trunk of a nearby tree to shift.

Part of him wanted to shock her with his nakedness, but there was too much anger riding him right now—he didn't want to taint her awakening sexuality with the bloodred of fury. It was as well that he'd utilized the jaguar's instincts soon after meeting Faith and cached several articles of clothing nearby. Having already retrieved a pair of pants, he slid them on before making his way back to her.

She was waiting with her arms wrapped around her knees, watching for him in the exact direction from which he came, though he hadn't made a sound. "Vaughn, the guards—"

"—make enough noise to wake a garrison, not to mention that they stink to Psy heaven." He crouched down in front of her, but didn't touch. He didn't trust himself enough.

"What?"

"Never mind. What the hell was Sascha's mother doing here?"

Those night-sky eyes, which had been edging toward wariness, hardened. "You have no right to talk to me like that. If you're planning on intimidating me into whatever it is you came for, you can go crawl in some dark hole and stay there!"

CHAPTER 17

The jaguar was impressed by Faith's claws. If he hadn't been so sure of her betrayal, his temper might have thawed, soothed by her open emotionality. But that wasn't going to happen today. "Nikita Duncan is Council, our enemy. What were you doing consorting with her?" He understood what he'd heard, but he wanted to know if Faith would tell him the truth.

Her mouth thinned. "This is the second visit I've had from a Councilor. Shoshanna Scott was the first."

"That doesn't answer my question." Anger was a fine tremor over his skin, his muscles held in savage check. He'd never physically hurt her, but damn he was mad.

"If you'd listen instead of just threatening to go jaguar on me, I'd tell you. Do you realize your eyes have gone completely cat?" She shook her head. "Nikita was here for the same reason as Shoshanna. I've been nominated to fill Santano Enrique's position on the Council."

Vaughn curled his hands into fists so tight, his bones

protested. "Enrique was a piece of Psy garbage. And you want to take his place?"

Faith jerked at the verbal slap. "What do you know about Councilor Enrique?"

"Ask your fucking precious Council." Eyes no longer even partially human, he stared at her, daring her to continue.

Lines of conditioning already stretched to the limit by her earlier vision snapped with an audible mental sound. She was angry. Really, truly angry. Angry enough not to care about maintaining the appearance of Psy normality. The only thing driving her to keep her voice to a harsh whisper was her awareness of the guards.

"Yes," she hissed. "They are my fucking precious Council, the leaders of my race. How would you feel if I asked you to cut Lucas's throat simply because he didn't behave according to the rules I said were the right ones?"

"Lucas doesn't hide murderers from his own people."

"Neither does the Council." It was an instinctive reaction. The Psy were her people for better or for worse. She refused to withdraw her loyalty so easily.

"Bullshit." Vaughn leaned forward and, in spite of how infuriated he'd made her, she hoped for his touch. But he kept his hands to himself. "The killer you see in your visions is Psy and there are lots of others exactly like him."

She shook her head. "Serial killers are always human or changeling."

"Why the hell would you be having visions about races you've never come into any real contact with?" He was the one who shook his head this time, a violent movement reminiscent of the jaguar, not the man. "Christ, baby, listen to yourself—this bastard is supposed to be a vision, but he holds you prisoner. No human or changeling would have that ability."

The endearment was rough, almost a growl, and it broke

her. Because he was making too much sense. "It can't be true. Silence ended violence."

"Yeah, and your sister's still alive."

She slapped him. Hard. The second it was done, her whole body began to tremble. "I'm sorry. I'm sorry." She stared at the white mark on his face, now filling with blood. "Oh, God." This was her ultimate nightmare come to life. "I thought my inner protections were holding, but I must've been wrong—I must be close to a total psychic and mental breakdown." Insanity by any other name.

"Shit." He cupped her face, his hands gentle. "There's nothing wrong with you. I went way over the line. You had a right to do more than slap me."

She put her hands over his. "I'm sorry. I'm sorry," she repeated, frantically attempting to locate the fissures in her mind and coming up blank. "I've never hit anyone. I didn't even know I could—why did I hit you?"

"Because Marine was your sister and I had no right to use that loss against you." He dropped his head until their foreheads touched. "I'm the one who should be apologizing. Don't look like that, Red. If you were a cat, you'd probably have gone for my face with your claws."

She shook her head at the savage image. "That can't be true."

"We're not human," he said slowly. "We play by different rules and we're never going to act civilized when in the grip of passion, good or bad. That's when the animal is at its strongest, most powerful."

Faith wondered if she was imagining the underlying warning . . . the underlying invitation. "But I'm not changeling. I don't hit people."

"Human women have been slapping men for being bastards for centuries. You were doing what comes naturally."

"Not for a Psy."

"Faith, Silence isn't normal. It's an imposition. What you are without it is normal." His head snapped up. "Someone's heading this way."

She felt the brush of a guard's mind hit her peripheral shields. "Go," she whispered. "Go!" Her fear for him was greater than any other emotion.

"Tell me something first—are you going to accept the offer?"

She knew what he wanted her to say, but she couldn't lie to him. "I don't know."

"Decide. You can't live in both worlds."

Then he was gone, a blur within the treetops. Rising, she headed toward the house and away from the approaching guard. She was afraid of what her eyes might reveal. Because for the first time in her life, the night sky within was starting to show something other than the endless Silence of a perfect cardinal; it was starting to show vulnerability.

She could still pass for normal, could still live in her world, but she was changing. That change had to be either embraced without reservation or irrevocably erased from her psyche. There was no middle ground. If she became Council, she couldn't expect the changelings to remain her friends, couldn't expect Vaughn to visit her, hold her, awaken her.

She had to choose.

Vaughn completed his watch rotation without speaking to a single packmate, then took off into the purple glow of day turning to night. He ran for hours, heading deeper and deeper into the Sierra Nevada, territory that had once belonged solely to the wolves. The chill mountain air ruffled his fur in a way that usually gave him the greatest of pleasure. But not tonight.

Tonight, the human half was very much in charge and it was beyond furious. He'd mated to a woman who might reject him and walk away. Forever. It made him want to shake her until she came to her senses and accepted the bond between them. How could she not see it? Yet she didn't.

Powered by a chaotic mix of anger and pain, he ran so far that he left everything known behind. Only then did he take to the trees and find a perch from which to watch the night moods of the forest and think. But thinking wasn't what he ended up doing, his emotions too violent for anything that rational. So he tried to wrap himself in the aloneness of the night, tried to teach himself the sound of silence, the sound he'd be living with if Faith renounced their bond.

It took him bare seconds to realize he'd been mistaken. He wasn't alone, the scent of Pack was strong in the panther who'd tracked him. Lucas didn't make a sound as he padded to a spot on another branch of the same tree as Vaughn. Neither did he make any move to instigate a conversation, and when Vaughn took off again, he ran beside him.

It was hours later by the time Vaughn led them back to his home and they shifted. Uncaring of their nakedness, they sat atop the small hill that the cave was buried under and watched the edge of a brilliant dawn lighten the sky.

"Where's Sascha?" Vaughn asked.

"She and Tammy stayed over at the SnowDancer den after working with Brenna."

At the mention of the SnowDancer female who'd been violated by Enrique, Vaughn's simmering anger exploded into full-blown fury. "You trusted her to the wolves?"

"Yeah. Hawke never breaks his word." Lucas grinned. "And the damn wolf knows Clay and Nate will tear him to shreds if he so much as lays a finger on either of our women. They're up there, too."

"So much for trust."

"Trust takes time."

And while the economic partnership between DarkRiver and the SnowDancers had held for almost a decade, the blood alliance between the two packs was only months old. "Why did you track me?"

"Thought you might want to talk."

"Why?" Vaughn disappeared on long runs nearly every week, the jaguar seeking solitude.

"Sascha. She said something before heading up to the SnowDancers."

"What?"

"Her powers are developing in an unexpected way. Either that or it's the influence of the Web." The leopard male crossed his arms over his knees and clasped the wrist of one hand with the other. "She didn't feel anything from you the whole day and she got worried."

"She got worried because she *didn't* feel anything?"

"She says she's constantly aware of the presence of everyone in the Web, a hum that lets her know you're alive. But yesterday you shut down so violently she thought something might've happened to you."

Vaughn didn't particularly like the idea of being shadowed. "I want her to teach me how to block her."

"Yeah, she figured. She's been working on something for everyone."

"Good."

"So, you hurt?"

"No." Nothing physical.

"Want to talk?"

"About as much as I want a lobotomy."

"Then how about we go one-on-one?"

Vaughn decided that pounding Lucas into a pulp sounded like an excellent way to work out his frustration and anger. "Fine."

They changed back into animal form and went at it. Lucas might be his alpha, but tonight they were simply friends. And Vaughn was a jaguar. They were generally bigger than leopards—he was no exception. However, Lucas was faster, a result of being born the pack's Hunter, charged with the responsibility of executing former packmates who'd gone violently rogue. Put together, it meant they were evenly matched in most situations, but today Vaughn was full of so much anger that he was lethal, a savage hail of teeth and claws and dangerously powerful jaws.

When they finally called it quits, both were bruised and a little bloody. Lucas wiped a red streak from his chest. "Sascha's going to be pissed. Maybe it'll heal before she sees it." It wasn't a vain hope. Most surface cuts and scratches healed relatively fast on changelings.

"You're gonna have a black eye."

"Fuck." Lucas touched the eye. "That's not going to heal before tonight."

"Yeah, well, you almost took off my hand." He flexed his wrist, raw from the grip Lucas had had on his paw.

"Had to keep you from clawing off my ear. I don't think my mate would've been too impressed with a one-eared panther." Lucas began to grin.

Vaughn scowled. "What?"

"Faith'll teach you."

Dropping his head between raised knees, he blew out a rough breath. "Faith—" He couldn't say it, couldn't betray her even to Lucas. She was his mate. That loyalty came before everything else. Until she walked away, until she broke the bond, he'd honor it with everything in him.

Lucas gripped his shoulder. "She'll tear you up worse than any animal, make you feel as if your heart's being cut into a thousand pieces, but she'll also heal you in a way no one else will ever be able to do."

If she came to him.

For the first time in over twenty-four years, Faith was absolutely lost. Her life had been circumscribed since birth.

She'd never really had a choice. But now she had to make one that would change the course of her entire future. The problem was, she didn't know how to make that choice.

So she spent the morning uploading a backlog of vision triggers into her mind, and the afternoon spitting out prediction after prediction until Xi Yun intervened. "You can't sustain this level of activity."

Showed what he knew. "Thank you for stopping me. I forgot." What had once been truth had become nothing more than a useful excuse.

"It's my job." A small pause. "I'm sending a meal plan to your kitchen computer. Your bioreadings are showing low amounts of certain minerals."

"Acknowledged." Ending the communication, she went into the kitchen and took her time sipping the prescribed soup and chewing the meal bars.

But it was still only four in the afternoon when she finished. Restless, she went into her bedroom and opted to occupy her mind with the data flows of the Net. It was procrastination, but she decided she was allowed—no one should have to deal with as many shocks as she'd had to in the preceding days. Given room to breathe, maybe her subconscious would discern an answer on its own. In the meantime, she'd put her conscious mind to decoding the puzzle of the Council's sudden interest in her. And they weren't the only ones she had to be wary of.

Kaleb Krychek could prove a very dangerous adversary if he decided she posed a real threat to his promotion. She wanted to see whether she could learn anything further about him—likely a futile task given his skills, but it was better than obsessing over a jaguar who wasn't there to confuse, challenge, and infuriate her.

Who might never be there again.

The PsyNet was the same star-studded darkness—bright, brilliant, and beautiful. Vaughn didn't understand what it was that he was asking her to give up. This sprawling net of minds was full of such energy, such mental capacity, such strength. The cardinals blazed supernova bright, while the lowest Gradients were mere glows, but every single mind contributed to bringing light into the black isolation of total individuality. The PsyNet was the greatest gift of her race, the greatest art they'd ever create. If she dropped out of the Net, she'd lose the light, be alone as she'd never before been alone.

The Council's possible offer was a chance to immerse herself even deeper into the Net, to become one of the caretakers of this magnificent creation. And Vaughn? Wasn't he something amazing, too, something she'd never imagined she'd be allowed to touch? He assuaged the loneliness inside of her by his very presence, giving her an intimacy, a closeness the Net could never provide. If only she could have them both.

But she must choose.

Mentally shaking her head to dislodge the question for which she had no answer, she took herself to one of the main data conduits. Though information could be accessed from anywhere in the Net, most of the raw data was shunted through these points and, as such, was in its purest form.

Eschewing a search that might send up red flags, she set her mind to copy files that responded to certain keywords and then simply let the continuous uploads flow through her. Her act was nothing unusual, so she didn't bother to check if anyone was following her.

When nothing met her specifications after almost an hour, she left the stream in favor of surfing the Net, sieving the random data through preset filters. The process wasn't as haphazard as it sounded for a very straightforward reason: the Net was anchored in the minds of millions of psychic beings and was therefore itself ordered by the principles of psychic energy. No one had managed to completely explain those principles to date, but all Psy knew that if you looked for something with enough focus and for long enough, the Net would start to throw you cookie crumbs of relevant data.

As it did for Faith.

A few whispers reached her. As she'd told her jaguar, something spoken within the Net never left the Net, though words spoken behind vaults and shields were locked into place and degraded in secret. Unshielded whispers, too, would eventually degrade, but until they did, they were part of the biggest living information system in the world.

Kaleb Krychek has been seen with Nikita Duncan.

The Council has a short list.

. . . possibly an F-Psy . . .

Enrique was Tk-Psy, too.

She was surprised by the whispers—the Council was skilled at ensuring a data blackout when necessary. Logically that meant they had to have leaked the short list. A test? Set Kaleb against Faith and wait to see which one walked out alive? She wouldn't put it past the Council to employ such barbaric tactics under the guise of efficiency, but it made no sense in this situation.

If they'd wanted pure lethal strength combined with cold Psy practicality, then Kaleb was, without a doubt, the correct candidate. He'd proven that over and over. Which could mean the leak was a warning to Kaleb that this time, something else was part of the equation. If it was, it was a worthless one. Faith knew nothing would ever keep Kaleb from taking her down if he decided she needed to be neutralized.

Something brushed her mind and it was so familiar she barely gave it a thought. But seconds after the NetMind had passed, she found herself turning to look for it, though of course, it couldn't be seen. It just was. Something in its fleeting touch had stimulated the section of her mind that housed the vision channels. The knowing was vague, less a vision than a premonition that the NetMind was going to be important to her life.

After another few moments of trying to refine the thought, she gave up and dropped back into her body, her psychic energy exhausted by the chaos in her mind. It was tempting to try to avoid sleep as a way to escape the darkness, but she fought that voice with inarguable logic—the visions would come whether she was awake or asleep. In that, she had no choice.

As she had no real choice in the decision to stay or leave the Net.

But two hours later, the touch that woke her wasn't of evil, but of something far more dangerous. "You came back."

His finger trailed down her cheek. "You have bruises under your eyes—I should've let you sleep."

"No. We need to talk."

He broke the skin-to-skin contact and rose fluidly to sit on the bed. Following, she sat up to face him. "I've been thinking about what you want, about the choice you want me to make, but the fact is I have to live in this world. If I cut the Net link, I die."

"You once asked me if I could do for you what Lucas does for Sascha. The answer is yes."

Every certainty shattered. "How?"

"Make your choice and then ask. I can't risk trusting you with that information while you're hooked up to the Net."

"Because of Sascha." An emotion she recognized as jealousy dug its claws into Faith.

"Because of every Psy who might one day need the knowledge."

. "You're asking me to make a decision about my whole future, my life, based on your belief that you can get me out. What if you're wrong?"

"I'm not wrong." His words held the assurance of a predatory male used to having his way.

"How do you know?"

He touched her again, a quick, shocking graze of his lips against hers. "Because you're already out—the only thing you have to do is open your eyes and see."

"Vaughn." It was a whisper that held her need, her frustration, her desperation.

"Always." His breath was hot on the shell of her ear.

She shook her head in reproach. "Not if I choose to continue living the life I'm good at living."

Something twisted in those not quite human eyes. "Even then, Faith. Even then. If you call for me, I'll come."

And it would break him apart, destroy his sense of honor and loyalty . . . because he'd be sleeping with the enemy. But she had to make him see why this was such a difficult choice for her. "These are my people, my version of Pack, and I'm tied to them by so many bonds. They may not love me in the sense DarkRiver loves you, but my PsyClan needs me.

"If I leave, a hundred jobs directly connected to me will go, from the guards to the M-Psy. But it's the ripple effects that'll really devastate. Money will stop flowing into the Psy-Clan. Schools won't be affordable, research will be stopped, children will be pulled from mental enrichment programs when it might be those very programs that allow some of us to fight Silence."

"You're talking about loyalty." His voice was uncharacteristically toneless, but she could feel the coiled intensity of his beast as if it were a third being between them.

"Maybe it's not your kind of loyalty, but it is loyalty."

"You're right," he said, surprising her. "But, baby, loyalty has to be earned and honored. Your PsyClan will one day lock you up in a mental institution and call it care."

She knew he hadn't said that to be cruel. Her jaguar was merely using every weapon in his arsenal. "Maybe they won't," she said, silently pleading with him to lie to her, to make this easy. "If you and Sascha are right, then I won't go insane if I embrace my true abilities, if I accept that the darkness will come for me at times."

He shook his head. "What happens the first time you see a vision of murder and realize you're part of the body that's going to authorize it?"

A shadowy realization took form in her mind, but faded away before she could grasp it. "Why would the Council—?"

"Sascha calls them anchors. Apparently your PsyNet needs them, but for some reason they're the ones most likely to fall victim to one of the lesser-known side effects of Silence—murderous sociopathy."

"You're saying the Council feeds their need to kill." Her heart was a rock crushing her chest from the inside out.

"We know they do." His eyes had gone night-glow, beautiful and wild.

She didn't doubt him—Vaughn was too much animal to lie. "Why?" Why would they continue to support the Protocol if it had proven so fundamentally flawed?

"Because they can." A cruelly honest answer.

And one she couldn't hide from. The Council had been the Psy race's absolute law for over a hundred years. Before Silence, rebellion and dispute had apparently spouted freely in the Net, keeping their rulers in check. Now no one dared to speak and no one kept watch. "Say you're right about everything. Can you imagine how much good I could do from the inside? I could work for the freedom of my race from a position of real power."

"And if you cut free, you might sow the seeds of a revolution so your people, your pack, could fight for themselves."

"They'll never let me go."

"No one could stop me from getting you out if you said yes." *Say it,* his eyes urged, *say yes.*

Faith fought the need inside of her that wanted to obey, a hungry, desperate, painful thing. "I need to think. Just let me think."

"Alone, Red?"

She hated that the darkness had reduced her to this, to a cowering creature afraid to close her own eyes. "Yes." *No more,* she thought, furious. *No more.*

"Always, Faith. Always."

She watched him leave via the skylight. He remained in human form, but was no less graceful, no less magnificent. The play of muscle under his skin was pure beauty, enticing, coaxing, seducing. Her fingers uncurled without her conscious knowledge and she reached for him.

But he was already gone.

CHAPTER 18

Faith had barely gotten dressed the next day when she felt a polite but firm telepathic page. Her eyes widened. The touch was unfamiliar and only one group of individuals had the right to contact anyone they wished in this manner. *This is Faith NightStar.*

Your presence is requested in the Council chambers. Authentication documents have been sent to your personal inbox.

Yes, sir. She knew the mind was male and guessed it to be Marshall Hyde, the most senior member of the Council.

You will be escorted there. The telepathic link terminated.

The first thing she did was check her inbox—she wouldn't put it past Krychek to use such tactics to ambush her. But there it was, the unforgeable reality of the Council seal. Cheeks blazing alternately hot and cold, she told the M-Psy not to disturb her under any circumstances and tried to calm her disordered thought processes. Nothing of her confusion could be allowed to leak through. Nothing.

Choosing a chair near the curtained window as her seat, she took a deep breath and entered the PsyNet without her cloak of anonymity. Today, she had to blaze cardinal bright, a silent statement of strength. Two minds were waiting for her. If she'd been in her body, the hairs on the back of her neck might've risen in primeval warning, there was something so intrinsically disturbing about them. As they led her link by link toward the dark core at the center of the Net, she considered whether she might be in the presence of two of the Arrow Squad.

Though their existence or nonexistence had never been confirmed, rumors of the unit had turned up repeatedly in the research materials she'd unearthed in her quest to understand the Council's interest in her. Faced with two highly martial minds, neither of whom had identified themselves with anything other than a high-level Council imprint, she came to the reluctant conclusion that the Arrow Squad wasn't merely an idle rumor.

The idea of a secret squad, one allegedly used to permanently silence the Council's critics, among other things, hardly inspired confidence. But none of that could show in the mental face she presented to the Council, so she buried her musings on the irrelevant matter. The guards led her through the first two checkpoints in the central core, then handed her over to a second pair, who took her even deeper. But when the door to the final vault opened, she alone walked in.

The door shut behind her.

She was locked in with the blazing minds of the six most powerful and deadly beings in the PsyNet. Nikita Duncan with her mental viruses. Ming LeBon, famed for his skill at mental combat. Tatiana Rika-Smythe, rumored to have the rare ability to disrupt the deepest shields. She was the one Faith was most wary of, because if the speculation were true, Tatiana could disrupt first-level shields without the victim's awareness.

Which was why Faith was shielded four times over. Perhaps it was an overreaction, but she didn't want anyone learning her secrets . . . Vaughn's secrets. In addition to the layering, she'd learned an unusual and highly effective way to make certain her shields never settled into a static pattern, and were therefore nearly impossible to predict and unravel. Sascha had taught it to her that night on the porch—before Faith had broken conditioning on the most intimate level.

"Faith."

"Yes, sir." She answered Marshall without pause, having kept her other thoughts in a hidden segment of her mind. While with the Council, she couldn't afford to be anything but absolutely on guard.

"You're aware by now that we're considering you for Council membership." Marshall's mind was a blade, sharp enough to make others bleed.

"Yes, sir." If Vaughn was right, then the Psy Council protected murderers to protect Silence. Maybe they'd appreciate her warnings, appreciate stopping the murders before they made waves in the Net. And then? Vaughn's accusations of murder by official sanction rang in her brain. Those she might not be able to stop, those she might choose not to stop, because it was the will of the Council.

Her will.

Could she become that inhuman? The slow creep of horror rolled through her veins, tiny claws that ripped and caused biting pain. She didn't want to think of her people that way, didn't want to be part of a race that would condone such a thing.

"What are your thoughts on the matter?" Ming LeBon, the Council member who never appeared in any news broadcasts or had his name linked to any high-profile events, a frighteningly dangerous power behind the civilized public facade presented by Henry and Shoshanna Scott.

"I'm young," she answered. "That may be seen as a vulnerability by certain sectors of the populace." And she wasn't equipped with the ruthless ability to kill. The thought of stealing a life, of not only accepting but sanctioning the sick evil of the darkness, nauseated her.

Yet she understood that Vaughn had killed and would do so again in defense of his people, perhaps even in defense of her. But that didn't fill her with revulsion. Maybe because there was a difference between the brutal but honest law of the wild, and cool, clear-eyed murder to increase the power of the very people most apt to misuse it.

"That's true. However, your shields are extremely strong. You appear to have the capability to withstand attack." Tatiana's comment seemed a substantiation of the rumors. Faith hadn't felt a thing, but her shields had evidently been tested and deemed adequate. It made her want to shiver—how many people had had their minds picked clean by Tatiana without ever perceiving the violation?

"Your foresight skills will also come in very useful," Marshall added.

No.

She would not lend her mind to the furtherance of goals meant to keep her people in bondage to a Silence that was false. In that one second, her decision was made. That was when she realized that no other option had ever been truly viable—only her fear of going out into the unknown had made it seem that way.

Now all she had to do was survive the Council.

"While I'm flattered at being considered a candidate, I'm not ready to die." Not when she'd just learned to live. "I'm well aware that Kaleb Krychek is one of the other candidates. He's had years in the Council ranks to perfect his skills." The ability to get rid of competition chief among them.

"I have no wish to be made a target when he's the Psy you really want. I'm not arrogant enough to believe that I could best him should he decide to guarantee his promotion by removing me from the equation."

"So you admit you're weak." Shoshanna, who'd never

been anything but an enemy. Faith's core mind whispered a knowing down the bond that linked it to her roaming self—the blood had spread on Shoshanna's hands. The future remained unchanged.

Admitting weakness to the Council was never a good idea. "I'm saying that if you want me to consider joining you, I won't do so until I've come to . . . an understanding with Mr. Krychek." Let them think she meant to take Kaleb out. Of course, if Shoshanna was backing Kaleb, then he'd be apprised of what she'd said seconds after she left this room, if not sooner.

Survival was going to become a dicey thing if she wasn't careful. "What I won't agree to is being used by the Council as a pawn to test Kaleb's strength. Find another target to pin the bull's-eye on."

Her stomach was a knot and her muscles ached, but she'd walked out alive. Faith knew she had very little time. Either Kaleb would get impatient and decide to push his own agenda or the Council would figure out what Faith was doing behind their backs. And what she was doing was hunting a murderer.

She refused to leave Marine's killer free to take another life. Whoever he was, he was too strong, too mentally powerful. She had to pinpoint him before he figured out a way to circumvent her new protections, protections that held faint, dangerous tendrils of emotion. He might not have tortured her again with his fantasies of death, but it wasn't for lack of trying—his darkness had been scratching at her mind for two days, wanting to show her what he would do.

Tonight, she was going to let him in.

But first she wanted to gather as much useful data as possible. Not for herself, but for the changelings, the only people who'd ever treated her as anything other than a highly profitable machine. "Vaughn." Her jaguar's name was a talisman. Fur brushed over her hands, lips pressed against her neck, the sensations so real that she wrapped them around her like a protective cloak as she closed her eyes and stepped out into the starry field of the PsyNet.

Minds bright and weak flickered around her, a thousand points of beauty and grace. Once again, she made no effort to hide herself, to pretend to be anything but what she was—a born cardinal, her star bright enough to burn. While no one seemed to trail her, she wasn't stupid enough to think that the PsyClan wasn't attempting to track her in some fashion.

She'd made a plan to deal with that, prewarned by the same sense that had told her to be on the Net tonight. It had to be tonight. She didn't know why, but hoped it was because the murderer was going to make a mistake. For now, she was out here to do the simplest of things—to listen to the pulse of the Net, to hear the voices the Council couldn't hear because they were too hushed, too secret.

But something didn't make sense to her. It was often said that the NetMind had been trained to flag any conversations that might be of interest to the Council. So why wasn't the Council cognizant of the brewing dissent, the embers of rebellion? And it was clear that they weren't aware of it. Because if they had been, those voices would've been mercilessly Silenced, rehabilitated until they had barely enough neurons for simple tasks like eating and washing.

Spurred by thoughts of the Rehabilitation Center, she put her plan to attain privacy into action, streaking through time and space to a far-off sector of the Net. At the same time, she raised the firewalls that ensured her anonymity. To any watchers, it would appear as if she'd popped out of existence. A very simple way to evade trackers, but she'd never been to this public link, having recorded its imprint unobtrusively during her last foray, so maybe they didn't have a way to trace her.

Arriving at the link, she circled around it to merge into the local data flows. There was nothing particularly interesting in the information, composed as it was of regional news and other bulletins, so she spun out of the flow and breezed through to a public chat room. The participants were discussing propulsion theory. She stayed anyway. That way, if she hadn't been successful in shaking off her shadows, and did find what she was seeking, it wouldn't look odd if she hung around, given the other things she'd listened to.

After all, she was an F-Psy. They were meant to be a little weird.

Propulsion theory was followed by a chat area devoted to the newest yoga master in the Net. Effective as it was in teaching Psy to focus their minds to laser sharpness, yoga was considered a highly useful exercise. Faith, however, had begun to form a different opinion as to why Psy gravitated toward what had once been an ancient spiritual discipline and it had nothing to do with focus. Maybe they were simply trying to find something to fill the void inside of them.

From yoga, she found herself in a newsroom full of talk about how the groundbreaking DarkRiver/SnowDancer-Duncan deal was already paying huge dividends. Faith didn't know the full details of the deal but was aware it had to do with a housing development geared toward changelings. Though it was a Duncan family project, they'd contracted out the design and construction to DarkRiver on the theory that only changelings understood the needs and wants of their own race. The SnowDancer wolves had apparently supplied the land—through DarkRiver—making the project a partnership, the first of its kind.

Now she heard that the entire development had sold out before the first house went on the market. And orders were piling up. Several minds suggested that such partnerships should be tried out in Europe with some of the more civilized changeling groups. On the heels of that came the logical rebuttal that the leopards and wolves were hardly civilized, which seemed to be the reason for their success.

She filed away the data—DarkRiver would appreciate knowing that Sascha's defection hadn't cut off the possibility of future trade. On the contrary, it seemed as if the changelings' negotiating power had actually risen. Psy might not be allowed to talk to the Duncan renegade, but doing business with her pack was a different matter entirely. Something the Council had been smart enough not to attempt to stop.

When the talk progressed to other matters, she listened for a few more minutes before leaving. Two hours later, she was starting to think that the knowing had been a mirage bought on by her own need to assuage her guilt. But in the next split second, she caught the edge of a conversation in a small room half-hidden behind another. Given its location, it was clear that those inside had come seeking the room.

"—lost two members in the past three months. That's not statistically explicable."

"I thought both were ruled accidental."

"The bodies were never recovered. We have only Enforcement's word that they were accidents."

"We all know who holds Enforcement's strings."

More than interested, Faith remained on the farthest edge, trying not to draw attention to herself.

"I heard the Sharma-Loeb family group lost a female two years ago in similarly unexplained circumstances."

"Since we last discussed this, I've been tracking other disappearances. There's too many to be rationalized away, no matter how you look at it."

"Any suggestions as to what it could be?"

"There are rumors that certain components of the training aren't functioning."

Clever, Faith thought. The Psy had deliberately not used the words *Silence* or *Protocol*, both of which would likely have alerted the NetMind to the potentially rebellious talk. However, the very fact that this conversation was taking place in the public space of the Net was a sign in itself. Either the Council had become lax in its policing or the populace was getting more confident.

Several of the leading minds in the conversation suddenly winked out, probably heading to a safer location. But whether they'd ever be safe from the NetMind was another question altogether—a sentience that was the Net, trying to hide from it was like trying to hide from air.

But then, her mind asked again, why did the Council not seem up to date with the level of dissent? It certainly wasn't huge but neither was it safe to ignore. Or . . . ! A revolutionary idea exploded into her mind. Deciding she had nothing to lose, she shot back out into the Net and continued her seemingly aimless stroll, coming across another whisper of rebellion in the process.

But those stirrings of disaffection were no longer enough to hold her attention. Even the futile search for information on Marine's killer had taken a backseat to a new compulsion born out of a knowing that veered on the edge of being a vision.

She wanted to talk to the NetMind.

However, she had no idea how to achieve contact. It wasn't sentience as they knew it. It was something other, something unique, the only one of its kind. It might not speak, might not think, might not do anything as she did. She didn't even know how to find it. It was everywhere and it was nowhere.

Since it had already brushed past her several times since she'd entered the Net, she decided to head out to a quiet area, near the least interesting data flows, and wait for its next pass. In doing so, she was ignoring the voices of logic and reason— a certain jaguar had taught her that logic wasn't always right. Sometimes, you had to go with instinct, even long-buried and rusty instinct.

The brush when it came was so subtle and familiar that

she almost missed it. Catching the trailing edge of the pass, she sent out a narrow thought aimed at a restricted area around her entire consciousness. *Hello?*

No response.

Can you hear me?

She had no idea if it was even present or whether she was talking to herself. She assumed it was visible on some psychic level or had a permanent core the Council could access, but if that was so, it was a well-guarded secret. Seemingly alone in this particular sector, she decided to take a wild chance. If the NetMind was young and unformed, it might be normal. And if it wasn't, then the Council would come for her.

I am not weak, she told herself.

No, you're not, Red. Vaughn's voice was a husky whisper in her ear.

If they come for me, I'll fight and I'll get out. I have a jaguar to tame.

With that thought in mind, with Vaughn in her heart, she laid her life on the line.

Please. A single word, but one that shimmered with persuasion, joy, and hope. The emotions were awkward from lack of use. But in this barren place, they were the solitary hints of gentleness.

Something swept across her mind a microsecond later. She tasted the texture and found it unlike anything she'd ever before touched . . . or was it? Vaughn's image blazed into her mind and she felt the wildness in his eyes, the teasing in his voice, the pleasure in his touch. He was alive as this sentience was alive.

???

CHAPTER 19

She almost stopped breathing. Very carefully, she narrowed the already constricted ring of thought. *My name is Faith. What's yours?*

???

It didn't seem to understand speech, but had reacted to emotion. Biting her lip in the physical world, she took a deep breath and sent out an image of her as she was, dark red hair, less than average height, eyes of a cardinal. She was nothing extraordinary, but she was unique and so was the NetMind. Would it understand her message?

A long silence and she thought she'd lost it, but then she was hit by an avalanche of images, an endless fury that threatened to crush her mind. She staggered against the overload on the psychic plane, and on the physical, her hands clutched at a head that threatened to explode.

Stop! Images of endings, feelings of pain.

Sudden halt. Another brush. Silence.

Slow. Accompanied by forgiveness, happiness at the contact, pictures that conveyed the need for less speed.

Another silence, as if it was thinking or had been scared. Wanting to reassure it, she awakened one of her most cherished memories—the way Vaughn had stroked her hair when she'd spoken of Marine. She tried to put the unbearable tenderness of that caress in the next thought she sent out.

A slower rush of images answered her. Fast even for a Psy, but bearable. It was obvious that the NetMind thought much faster than she did, calculated much more quickly, much more easily, but it was also clearly young. It needed instructions and, even more, it needed care. Understanding its hunger as perhaps only a cardinal F-Psy could, she let it show her whatever it wanted, what mattered to it. A child's secrets.

They were not images per se, more like broken pieces of thought. Pieces of what it knew, snapshots of what it had seen, hints of mystery. It was testing her. She couldn't blame its wariness if the Council had indeed tried to enchain it. With that realization went her final fragile illusions about the leaders of her people, because after scant seconds of contact, she knew that the NetMind was a truly sentient being. As such, it should've been accorded respect and the freedom to develop without interference or manipulation. But then again, the Council didn't even accord those things to its own people.

She wanted to ask the NetMind why it had chosen to speak to her, but could think of no image to represent the question. Finally she sent out an image of her conversing with someone, but her partner was a blur. The answer came back at whiplash speed and she saw what the NetMind saw itself as—the PsyNet given form. It had mimicked the image she'd sent of herself, but colored it in starlit night. She got the sense that in spite of the feminine shape, it was in no way male or female. But it was beautiful and she attempted to say so.

In reply, it sent her a second self-portrait. But this one was eerily different. Not one, but two women stood side by side. The second was without starlight, such pure black that she was shadows within shadows. Faith was still trying to grasp the image when the NetMind sent her a snapshot of dark stars zeroing in on her position.

Faith didn't stop to think. She jumped to another remote anchor point, acting on instinct, instinct that screamed these dark stars were nothing friendly. Either Kaleb Krychek had hired others to do his dirty work or the Council had discovered the NetMind was in contact with an unauthorized individual. She'd have banked on the latter possibility—Krychek wasn't known for frontal attack.

???

It had found her again. When she remained silent, it sent her images of the dark stars becoming lost in the echoes of a false trail. A false trail the NetMind had laid in split seconds. Because it was everywhere.

Relief was a cool wind in her mind. Faith sent it a bouquet in thanks and, like the child it reminded her of, it multiplied the images a hundredfold and gave them back to her. She wanted to laugh, so she sent it copies of those feelings that Vaughn inspired when he teased. It responded by showing her a safe path home, one that would skirt the searchers and set off no alarms.

Her conclusions about it shifted again—while it might be childlike in some senses, it was an endless, ageless intelligence in others. Sending it a rose in thanks, she headed home via the links it had given her the imprints for.

She slipped into her core self like water melting into water, her inner mind recognizing and accepting her roaming self. She was safe, but that safety was precarious at best. Her firewalls might be impregnable, but if survival of the target weren't an issue, a massive burst of open power could kill her in minutes.

Vaughn had spent the night pounding out his frustration on a new sculpture—he couldn't stand to work on the one of

Faith. But despite his sleepless night, his skin crawled with
energy in the midmorning sun. The cat didn't like being in
the same territory as the wolves, even if they were hemmed
in by nothing but earth and sky.

"Nice suit." Hawke, the SnowDancer alpha and the one
who'd called the morning meeting.

"What's so urgent?" Lucas scowled. "I have a meeting at
Duncan HQ."

"Sascha going with you?" The wolf said Sascha's name
as he always did, as if he had some intimate claim on her.

"It's a good thing she likes you." Lucas's skin pulled taut
over the markings that scored the right side of his face. "Hell
yes, she's coming with me. I'm not letting that ice-cold bitch
Nikita ignore her. And my mate knows their secrets." An em-
phasis on *my*. After years of distance, Vaughn now understood the urge to claim, to mark, to brand.

"Indigo found something you should know about."
Hawke jerked his head at his lieutenant.

The tall female with blue-black hair and cool white skin
was beautiful. She was also lethal. Vaughn had seen her take
down males twice her size without batting an eye. The cat's
claws pricked at his skin.

"I ran into a lynx while out on patrol." She stepped up beside her alpha in a smooth movement that told him her skills
were as sharp as ever.

"No clearance?" Vaughn frowned. The rules about entry
into predatory packs' territories were explicit—if you wanted
to visit, you asked permission. Otherwise, in most cases, you
were signing on for a quick death. Harsh, but necessary. Without those rules, territorial wars would've destroyed them long
ago.

"Yeah. But that's not the fun part." Indigo's jaw was a
tight line. "He was out of his mind on Jax."

The mind-altering substance was the Psy poison of
choice. "What the hell was a changeling doing on Jax?" Its

effect on the Psy was well known—not only did the addictive substance eventually destroy their capacity for speech and rational thought, it stripped them of the very abilities that made them Psy. What did that say about their race?

"He was too out of it to tell me." Indigo's namesake eyes narrowed in fury. "The Psy have to be behind this—they invented the stuff. The fucking Council's trying to poison us since they can't risk an open attack."

"Lynx part of a group?" Lucas asked, his voice having dropped into leopard range.

"I couldn't track any particular scent and they're known to be happier in small family groups." She glanced at her alpha and, at his nod, continued. "He was messed up, and not like the Psy get on Jax. When I found him, he was in human form but his hand was a paw and he had random patches of fur over his body."

Vaughn didn't understand the problem. "He was changing?"

"No. He was stuck midshift. Babbled enough that I was able to figure out he hadn't been able to shift properly since a few days after he first took the damn stuff."

It was a horrifying thought. To be unable to be the animal was akin to losing one's soul. "Where is he?" Vaughn felt pity for the creature. That was what made him changeling rather than pure, savage beast.

"Dead." A flat response. "I didn't do it, though. I couldn't. It would've been like kicking an injured pup. I was herding him back to our healer when he went into convulsions. His body snapped into the change then back out several times. When it was over, he was dead and . . . messed up." Her voice held traces of shock, unexpected in a woman reputed to be made of ice-fired steel. "Human, lynx, skin inside out and bones in the wrong places. Christ, I've never seen anything like that."

"The body?" Lucas looked at Hawke.

"At the den. We want Tamsyn to come out and have a look at it with Lara and the other healers."

"I'll send Nate and Tammy over as soon as we've finished talking."

"We can pick them up in the car," Hawke offered, a certain look in those pale blue eyes that were the same shade in either form.

Lucas snorted. "Would you trust your mate to one of us?"

"That'll never come up." Hawke's tone was very final—as if he *knew* he'd never have a mate. If that was true, no wonder the alpha was terminally pissed.

"Here."

Vaughn caught the image slide Indigo threw across and took a look. His stomach revolted. "Fuck." He handed it to Lucas. "Let's get this out—both the fact that someone's peddling this stuff to the weaker changelings and the effect it has. That should stop anyone who wants to give it a taste."

"I say we send copies of the pictures," Indigo suggested. "Once you see those, even the idea of Jax will give you hives."

Hawke watched Lucas study the slide. "We have to move soon. I don't want to chance someone else being sucked in."

Lucas nodded. Vaughn was in complete agreement. Being at the top of the food chain came with responsibilities. When under attack, it was the predators the other changelings looked up to. And in California, SnowDancer and DarkRiver were it.

"Cian can coordinate the info spread with that old wolf of a librarian in your pack." Lucas returned the slide.

"Dalton." Indigo put it back into her pocket without looking. "He's good at this sort of stuff. I'll get him to contact Cian."

They were about to break up when Lucas asked, "How're the Laurens?" He was referring to the family of Psy defectors who'd found unlikely sanctuary with the wolves. The

Council believed the Laurens dead, which gave the wolves a strategic advantage. But not enough to balance out the aggravation, if Hawke's scowl was anything to go by.

"Your mate's roped Judd into helping her with Brenna and you can imagine how popular that was with Andrew and Riley. He so much as blinks wrong around their baby sister and they'll slice him up—except the crazy Psy doesn't seem to give a shit about anything, which might be the only thing keeping him alive." The alpha folded his arms. "And yeah, Walker's trying to train the kids to do something with their shields so they don't accidentally give away the game."

Which left out Sienna Lauren. The teenager was probably the cause of Hawke's scowl. The alpha confirmed Vaughn's guess a second later.

"Sienna's so damn much trouble, I'm starting to think the brat's a she-wolf in bloody disguise."

"You're too easy on her." Indigo's words didn't go with the spark of amusement in her eyes.

Hawke let out a low growl. "You think it's so funny, I'm putting you in charge of training her in self-defense. She fights like a housecat, all hiss and no bite."

Indigo paled and that was one thing Vaughn had never expected to see. "How long?"

"As long as it takes." Smile satisfied, Hawke returned his attention to Lucas and Vaughn. "We'll keep an eye out for your people. Give Sascha darling a kiss from me."

The wolf barely avoided having his throat torn out by Lucas's claws.

Vaughn shadowed Lucas back to the site of the joint Psy-changeling housing development, close to where Hawke had called the meeting. His alpha, his friend, paused at the edge and took a slow breath. "It hurts Sascha to see Nikita. It damn near tears her up."

"I know." Vaughn understood exactly what it did to a child to watch her mother walk away.

"It'll be better once there's another Psy in DarkRiver. The Laurens are different. They're locked into their own familial Net. Another mind in the Web is what she needs."

Vaughn fisted his hands. "I can't force Faith."

"What about persuasion?" Putting his own hands into his pockets, Lucas rocked back on his heels.

"I'm not in enough control." The blunt truth.

"Trust yourself. You can't hurt her."

"The cat's getting desperate." Desperate enough that Vaughn could feel claws constantly pressing against his flesh, a mere thought away. How the hell could he trust himself with Faith's delicate skin?

"Then feed it," Lucas finally said. "We aren't Psy and Faith has to accept that before she makes any choice. Show her what you are."

"I've hardly been gentle with her so far."

"But you haven't demanded what you need either. I can feel your tension and it's already affecting the younger males in the pack." Another blunt truth—as sensitive as they were to scents in either form, Vaughn's unceasing sexual need was probably rubbing the juveniles raw. "Take her or find a cat to scratch the itch."

He bristled. "Would you fuck around on Sascha?"

"Exactly." Lucas shook his head. "You can't live without her. Do you even want to try?"

Hell no! And that quickly, he knew what he had to do. "Can you deal without me for a day or two?" The cat had had enough. It was taking over.

Lucas's attention shifted to the car gliding to a quiet halt on the other side of the site. "Good hunting. I'm going to go kiss my own woman."

Vaughn melted back into the forest, his beast stirring in anticipation of the most important hunt of his life. He was through playing by Faith's rules. The jaguar was loose and it was hungry. A roar came from his throat, rough and dangerous. Faith NightStar was about to come face-to-face with a predator determined to possess her.

No compromises. No mercy.

Faith completed the forecast for BlueZ Industries, Semtech, and Lillane Contracting, then turned off the trigger panel. "I'm going to walk the grounds."

"Understood."

Only when she was outside and hidden by several large trees did she take a deep breath and rub her hands down the front of her jeans. She'd put them on instead of her usual dress in response to an early morning vision.

A jaguar was coming for her.

The vision had been a warning: *choose*. But she'd already made her decision, already accepted his claim. After today she'd never again return to this house, her safe place, her familiar place. Though she'd failed in her quest to track down Marine's killer—he hadn't bitten at her open mind last night, or this morning—she had to leave the PsyNet. Vengeance would still be hers. She *knew*.

Returning to the house, she did three more predictions before lunch. "Are you sure you feel no stress?" Xi Yun asked after the third.

"I think I've pushed myself far enough today." She'd need her strength to handle the predator heading in her direction.

"I can request a medical team attend you."

"That's not necessary. Given the increase in my raw psychic potential, I was trying to see how far my powers had come."

"Yes, of course. You should've told me in advance. I'll forward you the details of the scans. It appears your mind is regulating your body more efficiently during the forecasts. No stress lines at all."

"Excellent." An idea came to life. "I'll probably sleep deeply after this morning's exertion, so please ensure I'm not disturbed for at least twelve hours after I retire."

"Noted."

"Thank you."

Aware she was being scrutinized for any erratic behavior as a result of nonexistent stress, she forced herself to follow her normal routines. Going into the kitchenette area, she poured and consumed a glass of the high-energy drink that carried most of the vitamins and minerals she needed, then ate two energy bars with slow deliberation. Next, she downloaded the promised medical scans onto her personal organizer and took a seat in the lounge area to go over them.

She had every intention of taking the data with her when she defected. It would likely be her last chance to access scans this detailed, and they were invaluable for an F-Psy, charting as they did every area of the brain. Including those sections most vulnerable to mental degradation. Because no matter what happened, she was an F-Psy and with that came a higher risk of insanity. It always had.

It was only after two hours that she stretched and walked into her bedroom, her eyes continuing to scan the files. Dropping the facade the second she was inside, she quickly packed her backpack with the few things she didn't want to leave behind. There wasn't much—her organizer, a holo-shot of Marine downloaded from the PsyClan's database, and one of her father. He'd consider her a traitor after tonight, but for all his coldness, he'd been the single constant in her life and she'd miss him. Finally, she threw in a change of clothes and that was it. A sad commentary on the life she'd lived to date.

Walking back out into the living area, she was surprised

to hear the chime of an incoming call. "Yes?" she answered on audio.

"Your father wishes to speak to you."

"I'll turn on the screen."

"There's no need—he's at the gates."

Her hand dropped away from the screen-activation key, mouth suddenly the driest of deserts. "I'll meet him in the grounds." It hadn't been what she'd planned to say but, once again, the *knowing* had come to the fore.

Ending the call, she exited the house and started down the path that eventually led to the gate. Anthony only ever paid her a personal visit when he wanted to talk about confidential business and being outside was the easiest way to ensure privacy. She could think of two reasons for his surprise appearance today. It might be as simple as a request for a particularly sensitive forecast, but it could also be about a far more treacherous subject—her possible nomination to the Council.

Then there he was, striding toward her. A tall male with skin two or three shades darker than hers and black hair silvered at the temples. In his black suit, white shirt, and dark blue tie, he looked every inch the perfect Psy. What would he do if he discovered her planned defection?

Stop her. By any means necessary.

"Father."

"Walk with me, Faith." He turned off the main path to one that snaked deeper into the grounds. "I've heard some disturbing news."

A chill wind swept through her body in spite of the early afternoon sunshine. "Kaleb Krychek?"

To her relief, he nodded. "There are rumors he's decided to give the Council no alternative choice."

"Nothing we didn't expect."

"I want you to retire from the race."

"Father?" She turned to face him, pure surprise rooting her to the spot.

Anthony halted beside her. "You weren't trained in offensive maneuvers. Kaleb has had years of practice."

"I know that, but—"

"You're too valuable to chance being damaged."

So, her monetary profitability outweighed her father's ambition. "I understand. Business is business. But what if I wish to pursue the offer?"

"The PsyClan will assist you, of course. However, think carefully, Faith. As a cardinal foreseer, you already have considerable political power should you choose to wield it."

"I'm completely isolated."

"That can change if you want it to."

She spoke without thinking. "Can it?"

Anthony looked at her for several long moments. She wondered whether he suspected something. Then he said, "I've already lost one daughter. It's enough. I'll do everything in my power to keep you safe."

She wanted to read emotion, care, love, into his statement, but knew it'd be a self-deluding lie. "Did your sources give a time frame for any attack? Or the type of offensive?" Forcing herself to think past the needs of the lonely child inside of her, she started walking again.

"Within the next two days. As for type, Krychek is known for using the PsyNet. It's suspected he has an undocumented subset of powers beneath his Tk abilities that allow him to attack without detection."

"Do you think it's something similar to Nikita Duncan's talent?"

"Mental viruses?" Anthony seemed to consider that idea. "No. It's something else. The end result of his particular skills being utilized are unique and extremely disturbing."

"I thought his targets had a tendency to disappear?"

"They do. But I've discovered that it's not Krychek who

does the disappearing. It's the individual family groups—
they don't want to be associated with his victims."

"What results could cause such a radical reaction?" She
wanted to gather as much information as she could on the man
almost certain to become the newest member of the Council.
Information was power and she was through with being powerless.

"Are you sure you want to know?"

"Of course."

"Nikita's targets either die or become incapacitated to the
extent that they can't care for themselves—similar effects to
certain kinds of accidental brain damage. Unfortunate for
the individual but nothing organic or genetic, nothing that
reflects on the extended family group."

It was very unlike her father to dance around a subject.
"Why is Krychek different?"

"His targets go clinically insane."

CHAPTER 20

Faith was very, very glad she'd fallen a step behind Anthony, because at that moment, she couldn't have hidden her terror. "Insane?"

"As far as anyone has been able to determine, his targets begin to exhibit highly erratic behavior approximately two days after infection. By the fifth day, they're no longer sane in any sense, though the actual psych diagnosis varies from individual to individual."

She shoved down her panic and horror and attempted a semblance of calm. "That makes the decision considerably easier—I have no desire to go insane before my time. Perhaps you should inform the Council as the head of the household. It may prove unhealthy for me to venture out into the PsyNet. At least until Krychek knows I'm out of the running."

"I'll do it en route to the city."

They turned to make their way back. "Thank-you." Faith ached for even the smallest indication of care, something Anthony would never be able to give her. But he was her father. How could she not hunger for his approval if nothing else?

"Faith."

"Yes, Father?"

"Be careful. Krychek may attempt to get to you some other way. Don't trust anyone until I've ensured he knows you've conceded the race."

Since she trusted no one who was connected to the Net, that wasn't going to be a problem. "What if he decides to eliminate me anyway? I might become a rival in the future."

"I've thought of a way to counter that possibility. I'll make it known that you're being put under lockdown because of aberrant mental patterns."

A cage. Her father was going to put her in a cage. Faith told herself not to care but she did. And it hurt. "How long will I have to maintain this fiction? I assume it means I have to stay out of the PsyNet?"

"I'd suggest a year. Krychek needs to forget you were ever a threat."

A year cut off from the only freedom she'd ever known. "Isn't that extreme?" No matter what else he'd done, she'd always believed that Anthony had tried to keep her safe. But this . . . this was an attempt to put her in chains and disguise it as protection.

"It's a question of your life. One year isn't much in the greater scheme of things."

A year was everything if you had decades of madness to look forward to. Though if she left the PsyNet, perhaps Vaughn could somehow heal the broken pieces in her mind. Even as she thought that, she knew it to be an impossible dream. But no matter—she'd still have more years of sanity than she would have under lockdown, a lockdown she suspected would never be reversed, reasons being found to keep her isolated and performing like the machine they'd almost turned her into.

"I'll accede to three months. Let's reconsider the situation after that." She couldn't give in, not when her recent behavior had made Anthony expect more from her.

"Agreed. Stay out of the Net."

"Yes." In a day, perhaps even in as little as a few hours, she'd be gone from the PsyNet forever. And if Vaughn didn't catch her as she fell, she'd be gone from this world as well. She wondered if her jaguar knew the extremity of her trust in him.

"Good-bye, Faith."

"Good-bye, Father."

Faith forced herself to return to the house, though she was half-afraid she'd never be allowed out again. The door closed behind her with a soft snick that felt as loud as a deadbolt. Taking a deep breath, she thrust her incipient panic into a tiny box in her psyche and walked to the communication console.

Xi Yun responded to her page in seconds. "What can I do for you, Faith?"

"Could you send me some of the earlier reports of my mental processes during visions? I'd like to compare them against the current scans." Not now, but one day.

"How far back would you like to go?"

She paused. The organizer could handle a massive amount of data, but even it couldn't cope with twenty-four years. "To my sixteenth birthday." The age at which her abilities had become relatively stable.

"That's the period I would've recommended," Xi Yun said. "Prior to that, you continued to be somewhat erratic."

Sixteen was the unofficial end of conditioning, the two years till eighteen a safeguard against any "mistakes." Had Silence helped her discipline her foresight, or had it stunted her mind until it produced patterns deemed acceptable instead of erratic? The memory reminded her of something else. "How is Juniper doing?"

"Well for an eight-year-old. Her skills fall short of what yours were at that age, but in comparison to others in her age bracket, she's advancing through the Protocol at considerable speed."

Meaning that the young Gradient 8.2 foreseer was becoming a machine faster than others. "Would I be able to see her records as well? I'm considering offering her some training." A perfectly legitimate thing for a cardinal to do for a younger member of the family.

Such help was especially important in the restricted field of foresight and for that abandonment, too, Faith felt guilt. But she had every intention of trying to find a way to help Juniper and others like her from the outside.

"I'll clear it with her guardian, but I don't anticipate a problem. You're the foreseer they study during training."

"When can you have everything to me?" It was a few minutes past four now.

"Within the hour."

More than enough time to download the files before Vaughn hunted her down.

Vaughn neared the fence around Faith's compound hours later than he'd intended. He'd been halfway to her when an alert had gone out over the Web—Sascha sending emotion for Dorian. Changing direction, he'd responded, aware that the others were all tied up. Because he couldn't hear words over the Web, he'd had to go to the nearest packmate's house and call for the location, another small delay.

When he'd arrived at the site, it was to find Dorian up to his neck in angry male juveniles. The sentinel had had them under control, but it was clear he'd had to bust a few heads to do so. Kit was bleeding from a split lip and Cory looked like he had a broken jaw. Several of the others wore bruises and everyone but Dorian was naked—a sure indicator that they'd been in leopard form.

"What happened?" he asked, shifting from jaguar to man.

Dorian thrust a hand through his hair. "Kit here decided to romance Nicki and Cory thought he had exclusive rights."

"This is about a girl?" Vaughn couldn't believe that, not with the way juvenile females were known to put their freedom above anything and anyone else.

"What it's about is these two boneheads using the excuse to call out their 'packs' on each other to settle who's more alpha." Dorian caught Vaughn's eye. Both of them knew it was Kit who had the smell of a future alpha. The kid was just faster, harder to hurt, and more aggressive than the others. But until he'd proven his alpha status, he was simply another juvenile.

"Kit." Vaughn dragged him up by the scruff of his neck. "What the hell is this about your own pack?"

The boy wiped blood from his mouth with the back of his hand. "It's just a bunch of us who are friends."

Vaughn didn't speak, didn't break eye contact.

The kid shrugged, but the anger remained in his eyes. That was why young alphas needed careful guidance, and if they stepped out of line, harsh discipline. They could go bad very easily. "So what if we call ourselves a pack?" His hands fisted into balls. "It means nothing."

"Cory?" Vaughn looked to the lanky kid propped up against a tree. "You think the same?"

The boy spit out blood. "Yeah."

Dorian slapped down a couple of others who tried to rise in renewed rage. "Stay the hell down or I swear I'll break all of your jaws."

Nobody protested. Dorian might be latent, but he was also a sentinel—he could snap these kids in two without thinking.

Vaughn returned his attention to Kit. No matter what

Cory thought, it was Kit the juveniles looked up to. "If you're the alpha of your pack, you won't mind me challenging you for authority."

Some of the arrogance seeped out of Kit's eyes. "What?"

"You want to lead your own pack? Fine. But if you're the alpha of another pack, you give up your right to be part of DarkRiver." Harsh but true. "We have no treaties with you, which means you're in violation of Law. I have the right to kill you for trespass."

Kit wiped away another trickle of blood. "We don't want to separate from DarkRiver." He was beginning to look a little green around the gills.

"There is only one *Pack*. And none of you is alpha." Vaughn made sure he met the eyes of every juvenile in the clearing. Several heads dropped. "If and when you can challenge Lucas for the title, I'll respect you. Until then, you're a bunch of whiny brats who've fucked up the defense grid by pulling two sentinels from their duties."

Wounded pride showed on the face of more than one boy, but predictably, it was Kit who spoke. "We didn't ask for interference."

Vaughn actually liked the kid for his spine, but not enough to cut him any slack. Not after what he'd glimpsed in his quick reconnaissance before entering the scene. He glanced at Dorian. The younger sentinel dragged an unconscious juvenile out from behind a tree and dropped him at Kit's feet. "You did this."

The injured male had had his chest sliced open. If he'd been human, he'd have been dead by now. And that was before you added in the head wound. "Were you going to be able to stop without Dorian's 'interference'?" Vaughn made his question a whip.

Kit swallowed. "Oh, shit. Oh, man—I didn't realize—is Jase going to be okay?" Suddenly he was a child again, no trace of the alpha he'd one day become.

Vaughn let go of the boy.

Dorian was the one who answered. "Tamsyn's on her way back from the wolf den. Can you get Jase to her without killing him in the process?"

Kit nodded. "Yeah."

"I'll help you." Cory stood, one hand on his jaw.

The two boys looked at each other and then at the sentinels. "We can deal with it from here."

"You no longer have the right to my trust," Dorian responded, tone flat.

Vaughn saw the effect it had on Kit—the kid worshipped the blond sentinel, looking up to him like an older brother. But to his credit, he only nodded. "We'll get him to Tammy's, I swear."

"I want every single one of you in the Pack Circle tomorrow. The women can decide your punishment," Vaughn ordered, and it was no kindness. Leopard females were merciless about breaches of Pack law, because they knew that without Law, their children would start to die one by one at each other's hands.

Pack was One.

That was the ultimate rule.

Cleaning up the mess the juveniles had made, including tracking down and notifying Jase's roaming parents as well as the maternal females in charge of discipline, swallowed up several hours. It was almost five by the time he reached Faith's compound and he was feeling so violently possessive that he probably shouldn't have gone to her. But no way in hell was he waiting any longer.

He was about to scale a tree from which he intended to jump the outer fence when he smelled his prey on the perimeter of the compound. Surprised, he flattened down into a cautious stance. Her scent came nearer, until he could hear the flutter of her heartbeat, the sound of her breath. She stopped inches from him and when he appeared out of the tree shadows, she nodded. "I'm ready."

Her unexpected surrender calmed the beast, but only a fraction. He led her farther into the woods and toward one of his caches before moving out of her sight to shift into human form and pull on a pair of jeans—this was not a time to push Faith any more than she'd already pushed herself. Yet when he returned to her, her face went immediately wary.

"Your eyes are more cat than man."

"I know."

She walked to him. "I'm coming home with you."

"For how long?" He was keeping her. That was nonnegotiable. He just wanted to know how much persuasion it would take.

Her hand rose to lie over his heartbeat. A tentative touch that made the cat snarl for more. "For always."

It was the one answer he hadn't expected, but instinct told him what to do. Closing his fingers over her hand, he raised it to his mouth and kissed her fingertips. Her pulse shuddered, but she didn't pull away. The cat was pleased. Dropping that slender hand, he turned his back to her. "Jump on."

A beat of hesitation and then her hands were on his shoulders. He slid his palms up the back of her thighs and felt her fear, her confusion, her need. But when he pushed upward, she wrapped her legs around his waist and held on.

Exhilaration lacing his bloodstream, Vaughn ran through a forest slowly fading from day brightness—night fell quicker under the canopy. Faith's weight, even given her small pack and the long distance, was nothing. The jaguar gloried in having her in his territory, in his world, though he knew they still had to extract her safely from the Net. But that could be done anytime she was ready. First, he needed to claim her on a much more primal level.

He took her deep into DarkRiver territory and then even

deeper into his own, not stopping until she was in the bedroom of his lair, the only woman he'd ever brought there. Lowering her to her feet, he let her stretch and explore, able to wait now that she was in his home.

Her face tried to maintain that cool Psy look, but wonder broke through in sporadic patches. "Your home is amazing. Like we're part of the forest."

He let out a jagged breath. "Do you want me to shower?"

She froze, eyes flicking to the waterfall behind him. "What?"

"The run made me sweaty." The falling night had been cold, the wind crisp, but a fine layer of perspiration covered his skin.

"Oh." The answer was soft, breathy. "No, that's okay."

He watched her mouth as she spoke, surprised to realize he'd closed the distance between them without being aware of it. Raising his hand, he rubbed a finger over her lips. "I want to eat you up."

Even as her eyes widened, the beast began to haze his brain with unforgiving sexual need. He *wanted*. And he was through with waiting. Faith was his mate. It was his right to take her. He'd angled his head to claim a savage kiss when out of nowhere, something else kicked in—the protective instincts that would never allow him to harm her. And if he took her now, he might even break her.

Shaken into civilized thought by that unforgiving truth, he forced himself to do the hardest thing he'd ever done. He took a step back. "I might hurt you if we do this." He was too much on edge, too hungry, too damn strong to chance a loss of control while in the grip of passion.

He watched her swallow and the cat wanted to lick at her neck, to hold her pulse in its mouth and feel the power of her heartbeat. It was about sex, not pain. The thought of abusing her was abhorrent to him, but he was afraid of caving in to the violent need of the beast and losing his capacity for rational thought. And when he rose from the animal hunger, he might find that his claws had permanently marred Faith's skin, that he'd bitten and cut. The possibility terrified him as nothing else had ever terrified him.

"Vaughn," she said, "it's okay. I know you won't hurt me. It's my conditioning and the impact it might have that we have to worry about."

"I could rip you to pieces if the cat takes over. I won't think I'm hurting you, but I will be." His voice held the thickness of a growl—his beast might have saved his life as a child, but the payment it demanded was being a greater part of his consciousness. "I want you too much, so much that I might damage you without meaning to."

Faith didn't move any closer. Instead, she stood watching him, studying him with those night-sky eyes that seemed to shimmer in the dim light of this cavern he called home, which seemed to soothe her. It had surprised him when he'd picked up the signs of relaxation, but now he was glad. At least she could feel safe in this place. *His* place. He'd never steal that feeling from her by using it as a trap to maul her.

"The longer we wait," she said, her voice that of the most practical Psy, but her eyes holding the first flicker of lightning, "the worse it's going to get. It's become clear to me that you need touch and I haven't been giving it to you."

He knew that. "If I'm not tied down, I can't trust myself." It was an offhand comment that hid his very real frustration. To be close enough to touch, but be barred from doing so, caused excruciating pain.

"Then let's tie you down."

Cat and man both went absolutely motionless. "What?"

Her cheeks held the faintest hints of pink. "Maybe it would help me, too, if I knew I could walk away at any time. The backlash from the conditioning might not be as bad."

"Tie me down?" he asked again.

"It was only a suggestion. I'm sorry if I offended you."

He scowled. "I'm not offended. But I don't want to be powerless to defend you if something happens."

"Your reflexes are much faster than those of any other creature I've ever seen. I'll put a knife or knives within reach. You could grab them and cut the bindings free if necessary."

"I tell you I'm dangerous and you want to put knives near me?"

"Vaughn, you're scared you'll hurt me because you want me so much." Psy logic combined with enticing hints of feminine temper. "Unless you've been hiding something, using knives on me is hardly likely to arouse you."

She was right. He wasn't afraid of harming her on purpose, but doing so in the midst of claiming her, tasting her, sliding into the tight sheath of her body.

"Stop that," she whispered, "if you're not going to . . . play."

He caught the use of the changeling word, caught the rich musk of female desire. And remembered that he wouldn't be helpless to seduce her even if he was tied down. Moving to the side of the room, he pulled out an old shirt from a trunk and used his claws to slice the material into strips. "I'm in your hands, Red." Claws retracted, he passed her the strips.

She blushed, eyes tracking him as he placed several weapons in easily reachable positions around the bed. "Tie my legs down, too," she ordered, blindingly aware of the ways he could harm her with the strong muscles that made him one of the predators.

Eyes wide, she nodded. "Vaughn?"

"Yeah?"

"If I can't finish this, will it hurt you?"

"Hell, yeah. But my balls turning blue won't kill me. So don't worry about it. When you can't handle it, get up and get the hell out. If I look like I've gone cat, lock the door behind you and take the car. Hyperspeed." He showed her the keys. "Car's in the left cavern as you enter. Do you remember the way out? You have to follow it without deviation or you'll set off the defenses."

Oddly, there was no fear in her scent. "My memory's highly trained. Don't worry about me being caught in a trap."

He had a sudden thought. "Did you see this in a vision?"

"N-no!" Her Psy facade cracked. "I've never seen anything this pleasurable." Night-sky eyes went to his hands as he pulled off his jeans and threw them aside. Her intense focus made his already painful erection pound in echo with his heartbeat.

"How do you know it'll be pleasurable?" He got on the bed and lay down.

Breath a whisper, she came closer and tied one wrist to the headboard. The cat growled but didn't try to make him wrench free.

"Because just looking at you gives me the most extreme pleasure I've ever felt."

"Christ, baby, tie me up before you start talking like that." He wasn't joking. He knew his beast, knew its limits, knew its demands.

She went to the other side of the bed to tie up his free hand before coming to his feet. The jaguar didn't think this was okay anymore—claws pricked at his inner skin and a roar pushed at his throat. Forcing the beast to back down, he spread his legs to help her. But he knew there would come a point when he'd lose the battle with the cat. "The doors are closed," he told her, voice very low. "If you have to run, don't give me any warning and don't stop to get dressed. Just go!"

Faith stood at the end of the bed and met his eyes. "Why do I trust you more than you trust yourself?"

"You don't know the beast. Do what I tell you."

"Vaughn, I can fight back."

"Yeah, but can you kill? Because as far as I know, that's the only way you have to incapacitate me."

"You won't hurt me. But"—she held up her hand when he would've spoken—"I promise I'll do everything you've asked if you go cat on me. Promise."

He nodded, satisfied that she'd keep her word. Then he watched her as a cat watches prey. Except this time, he couldn't pounce. He wondered what she'd do, whether she'd torment him. The thought wasn't unpleasant—a little tormenting in bed could be very interesting. The one thing he didn't allow himself to think was that she'd complete the act and accept him into her body.

She crawled onto the bed to sit on her knees beside him. "May I touch you?" Such a polite question, but there was an inferno in her eyes. A Psy not sure she could fully break conditioning. And yet gutsy enough to try. Was it any wonder she was his mate?

"Anywhere." He wished he could kiss her. Unable to gratify the wish, he indulged himself with thoughts of how the softness of her lips would feel against his. The tart sweetness of her mouth was a remembered sensation that tightened his already impossibly taut body.

Lightning-shot eyes met his. "I like your kiss, too."

He loved being able to arouse her with his most erotic thoughts. "Then come here."

"Vaughn, should I drop out of the Net before— What if my shields collapse?"

"You can drop out the second your shields fail. I'll catch you." He'd already caught her, but she wasn't ready to accept the depth of their connection.

"Then I'll wait until it becomes unavoidable," she whispered, "I have things to do."

He smiled, using sex to banish the taint of sadness. "Yes, you do. Kiss me."

"I think that's an excellent idea." She braced her hands palms down beside his head and placed her mouth over his. It was an utterly feminine kiss, gentle and exploratory, not ravaging but coaxing. To his shock, Vaughn found he enjoyed being coaxed. The cat settled, too, pleased. It liked being petted and this was the most intimate kind of petting.

When her tongue whispered across his lips, he opened his mouth and allowed her to taste him as he tasted her. He could feel her knee against his side, but she remained out of reach, her breasts not pressing against his chest where he wanted them. He imagined her kissing him naked, her body pasted along his, a sizzlingly intimate meeting of mouths that might short-circuit all of her nerves.

Gasping into the kiss, she broke it. Her eyes were filled with white lightning, her lips moist from his kiss, her skin flushed with a soft glow that signaled arousal. He took pleasure in the markers though he didn't need them—the scent of her acted like a drug to his senses. Breathing deep, he fed the hunger, stoked the fire, and waited.

CHAPTER 21

Faith's whole body felt tight, as if her skin had been stretched too thin and was close to bursting. She wanted to rub herself up against the beauty of the male in front of her. He was a stunningly sensual creature, an invitation to every one of her starved senses. Her conditioning warned that too much sensation after a lifetime of numbness could cause the most brutal kind of mental cascade, but she wasn't listening.

Licking her tongue over her lips, she put one hand flat on his chest. A shudder shook his powerful frame. Startled, she looked up to find his eyes closed. He was making no effort to hide his pleasure in her caresses and his unflinching surrender gave her the confidence she'd lacked to this point.

Removing her hand, she ignored the low growl that came from his throat and put her hands to the bottom of her T-shirt. The growl cut off. His intense focus was a physical touch as she lifted the soft material over her head and threw it to the floor. Her bra might've been practical white cotton, but the look in Vaughn's eyes made her feel as if she were encased in something designed to bring a male the most exquisite pleasure.

He jerked at the bindings without warning. "I want a taste. Come here."

Wondering at his meaning, she leaned over, her lips brushing his as they spoke. It was deliberate on her part—she liked kisses with Vaughn. "What do you want to taste?"

He caught her lower lip between his teeth in a playful bite and she shivered. "Your pretty breasts."

"I'm still wearing my bra."

"Take it off." It was a demand.

Faith's reaction to his attempt to exert dominance in bed surprised her. There was no fear and more than a frisson of sexual pleasure, a dramatic contrast to her negative response to his attempts to dominate her in other situations.

It was an interesting dichotomy and if she'd been thinking with the cerebral discipline of her race, she might've explored it further. But the fact was, she was thinking with her body. And she was coping. More than coping. She was *enjoying*. Much more of her conditioning had failed than she'd initially estimated. She didn't care.

Sitting back up, she reached behind her to unhook the bra and slide it down her arms and off her fingertips. Knowing that Vaughn couldn't touch her, couldn't push her, gave her courage, but it also increased the heat. There was something highly erotic about what they were doing and Faith knew it had to do with trust and intimate secrets. Vaughn would never let anyone else tie him down as she'd done.

He growled again and this time she could hear the difference. The deep rumble wasn't a threat but a demand. Flicking aside the discarded bra, she straddled him, blindingly aware of the pulsing length of his erection. If she slid back a bare few inches, she'd be able to rub over him with the hot, swollen flesh between her legs.

Mercy.

The temptation was intense but she remained rational enough to know she couldn't overload her senses that quickly. She hadn't reached her limit. It was simply a question of speed.

Letting her hair cascade around them, she leaned down, but kept her breasts out of reach of his mouth. She had no idea why she was teasing him like this, hadn't even known she had the ability to tease, yet she was certain it was bringing him pleasure. Her jaguar might demand, but not having his demands fulfilled at once didn't anger him. It only heightened the sensations.

Not really caring how she knew that, she used her finger to trace his mouth and when he threatened to bite, she acquiesced to him, taking that wandering finger into his mouth. He sucked so hard she thought she could feel it in her womb.

The sensation was rich, heady, and had an unexpected effect. "My breasts hurt." Such a private complaint.

He allowed her to withdraw her finger. "Come here."

More than willing to oblige him this time, she watched as his mouth closed over her nipple. Her mind blanked at the instant of contact and then restarted in a shock wave of desire. She clawed the sheets beside his shoulders but didn't move away. Because she was desperate for more, her addiction to Vaughn was growing with alarming speed.

A scream locked in her throat as he switched his attention to her neglected nipple. When he tugged with careful teeth, she bent even closer, her hair a dark red curtain that focused the intimacy to an excruciating pitch. Silver shot through her mind. Sanity broke piece by piece. She didn't care.

Shifting focus, Vaughn let go of her nipple to scrape his teeth along the vulnerable underside of her breast. Her heart seemed to stop beating.

Giving an incoherent cry, she jerked down his body in a ragged movement. She might've kept going had Vaughn's roar not split the soft darkness into two. Her entire body froze. That was when she realized her jean-clad form was rubbing over the head of his erection. Vaughn jerked at the restraints, the veins on his arms and shoulders pumped with blood. And she became conscious of the fact that he could break the bindings with his strength alone.

But there was no danger, not yet. Heart still not back in the right rhythm, she slid farther down, freeing the hot, hard length of his arousal. He didn't care for that. "Get back." It was a snapped command in a voice coated with the thick animal sexuality of the changeling he was.

Shaking her head, she used her hand to claim him as she'd done at the cottage. His body bucked upward, powerful muscle and gleaming flesh.

"You're so hot," she whispered, breath coming in pants, "so silky." She loved touching him.

He growled and it was very close to the edge. "Enough."

"No." She wasn't going to let go until she was finished— if the conditioned pain crippled her, this chance might never come again. And there were lots of things she wanted to do to this magnificent male at her mercy.

"It'll feel better if you take off the jeans."

She blinked, surprised to see that she'd changed position so she could grind the ache between her legs against one muscular thigh. Her hand tightened on him.

His breath hissed out. "Off," he ordered. "Take those damn jeans off!"

"But to do that I'd have to stop," she muttered.

Vaughn's eyes went even more cat, if that was possible. "Imagine how good it'll feel."

Explicit images crashed into her mind, scenes of her naked and wild above him as she ground her moist heat in slow circles against his thigh. The images were so rich in detail, so sexual, she could almost smell the scent of her need. Then she realized that the musky scent was real. It was her. And it appeared to be driving Vaughn over the edge.

His nostrils flared. "Those jeans are coming off right now if I have to tear them off." Claws sliced through his skin but he didn't try to break the bindings.

Something still sane in her said that this was dangerous, that too much skin-to-skin contact could trigger a catastrophic mental backlash, but she was in no mood to listen. If she'd stopped thinking, then so had Vaughn, neither cognizant of the one huge risk they'd forgotten to speak about.

"Do it!"

Releasing the silky hot flesh in her grasp, she rose to stand above him and shimmied out of her jeans and panties. She caught Vaughn's expression as she threw the clothing aside—he was pure starving male, a very hungry jaguar. His eyes lingered over her breasts before dropping to the curls at the apex of her thighs. And she knew.

He wanted to devour her.

But she was in charge of this intimate game and she wanted him first. Going back down onto her knees, she fisted her hand around him again. His whole body became solid muscle as he waited to see what she'd do. She wasn't sure herself. So much contact, so much sensation, so much *need* had smashed into her mind that she was no longer sure of anything.

"But you're mine to play with." It was a stubborn, possessive declaration.

The thick heat of him pulsed in her hand as a roar erupted from his throat. She was fascinated by his untamed fury, overwhelmed by the answering wildness in her, wildness that had been contained for a lifetime and now wanted to tear loose.

She ran her nails down his chest. Hard.

His hands jerked at the bindings and the eyes that looked back at her were on the wrong side of feral. "More."

Awash in uncensored images of what he wanted, she

dipped her head to his neck and bit the skin above his pulse. This time she was gentle, teasing, taking, tasting. His body pushed up and hers pressed down. Shocking heat, raw pleasure. Whimpering, she rubbed her damp need against him to the point where both of them were so out of control, thought was something they'd done in another lifetime.

Neither of them spoke as she sat up and used her hand to guide him inside her. He was thick. She should've gone slow, but she'd moved way beyond doing what she should. The biting pain of a sudden sharp tear inside her didn't snap her out of the passion-darkness. It was far too late for that. She'd been conquered by the most primal core of her self.

Mind cascading around her, she began to ride him. He bucked and slammed into her despite his bonds as she slid downward over the near painful thickness of him. Screaming, she did it again. And again. And again.

Until lightning was all she was and her mind ceased to exist.

Faith was surrounded by fire. Rough, yet deliciously smooth, the contrasting textures enticed her to open her eyes. Gleaming skin lay under her cheek and her fingers were stroking through dark-gold chest hair as if petting a great big cat. The last word opened the floodbanks of memory and she woke fully with a gasp.

"Shh." One of Vaughn's hands stroked down her spine while the other pushed damp hair off her forehead.

"You're free." The bindings were shreds on the headboard.

"Hmm." He moved so she was half under him and he could kiss the line of her neck.

"I survived." She was remembering that explosion in her mind, when everything she was and everything she'd ever been had seemed to be wiped out.

His teeth scraped her skin and she shivered. Lightning

danced along her bloodstream, nerve endings already sensitized to the extreme.

"You taste good, Red."

Her body was loose, her limbs heavy and sated. "Vaughn. I felt too much." Yet she was still here, still functioning. She checked her shields. To her shock, the ones against the PsyNet were holding strong, as if anchored by a source outside of her overloaded mind. Impossible.

All her other shields were gone.

She clenched her fingers, only then realizing she'd sunk them into Vaughn's hair. "My shields."

"Mmm." He was licking at her pulse, quick flicks that tugged at something low in her, something rich and dark and hungry. So hungry.

"The ones that help me hold out the world, they're gone." Burned out.

"Rebuild them. Later." Moving down her body, he ran his teeth over the upper slopes of her breasts.

Swallowing, she tried to think. She was safe against other Psy. There was no one out here but Vaughn. And he'd already been everywhere inside of her, gone so deep that she wasn't sure she'd ever be able to push him out, or that she'd even want to. One large hand stroked down her side and lingered in the hollow where waist flared into hip.

She found herself holding her breath in anticipation, her mind emptying of thoughts of shields and protection. She was a novice at emotion caught in the claws of the most powerful of them—so much so that she failed to check the vision channels for damage.

Vaughn nuzzled between her breasts and made his way down her tensed stomach, dropping kisses on every inch of exposed skin until he reached the curls at the apex of her thighs. One hand closing over her thigh, he dropped a kiss on those curls. Her back arched. "Not yet."

He finally looked up. Those cat eyes were sated, golden

and pleasured. "Why?" It wasn't a demand, but as close to a purr as she'd ever heard a human being sound.

"I need to calm down a little." She tugged at his hair and to her surprise, he came without argument, kissing his way back up her body. A body that had been well used and was already aching for more. It was her mind that wasn't ready.

When he was braced over her once more, she ran her hand down his jaw and found herself unable to stop nuzzling at his throat, dropping kisses on his pulse. "Why can't I stop touching you? I might've broken conditioning, but I'm still Psy." Still from a race where touch was infrequent and cold. "I shouldn't be so needy for touch."

"You're hungry." He ran one hand up to close over her breast in a gesture that screamed possessiveness. "You've been starving for decades."

"But . . ." She licked salt from the skin of his shoulder and curved a leg over his waist.

"The shield holding you back burned out."

How did he know that? Not that it mattered to her. "Does that mean I'm mad?" Right this moment, she didn't care.

"No. It means you're free."

"Mmm." Pulling herself up using his shoulders, she drew his head down in a kiss that was so luscious, she melted. He was all slow heat and seduction against her mouth while his hand gently massaged her breast.

When his thumb rubbed over her nipple, she moaned into the kiss, but this time it wasn't lightning that flickered through her bloodstream but a thicker, richer vein of fire. It spread with languorous ease and she was filled with it before she could even think to fight. Pleasurably overwhelmed, she wrapped her arms around him and curved her other leg over his back.

When he slipped inside of her again, it felt like perfection. He moved in a slow, sensual rhythm, a sated predator giving his woman everything she wanted. The hand on her

breast slid down her body to cup her buttocks and hold her at
the tiniest angle, but one that let him touch things in her that
turned the slow-moving river of lava into a boiling inferno.
But still it didn't overwhelm.

She rode the waves of pleasure that lapped at her as he
rode her, his lips on her mouth, his tongue dancing with
hers. And when he finally pushed her over, she didn't crash.
Instead the heavy fire inside of her turned into a shimmering
mass of sensation. Rich and lush and addictive, it took her
under and she went with a smile.

Faith let the spray of the waterfall that was Vaughn's shower
wash over her, hardly able to stand upright. Not that she had
to. A certain changeling was more than ready to help.

He nipped at her neck. "Stop thinking."

"Too late." She turned in his arms and wrapped her own
around his torso. He was so beautiful, so deliciously male
that it kept surprising her. Her self-restraint where he was
concerned was close to zero. But in spite of her lack of impulse control, her mind remained sane.

"I think we're clean enough." His hands were big and
warm on her skin. "Come on."

She followed him out onto the drying platform and let
him rub her down with a huge fluffy towel. "Silk sheets and
plush towels," she said with a sigh, unaccustomed to such
hedonistic pleasures. "You like comfort."

"I'm a cat. Soft silky things make me purr." He nipped at
the vulnerable skin of her thigh and smiled at her shudder.
"Sometimes, though, they make me want to bite." Rising from
his kneeling position to tuck the towel around her body, he
caught her rusty attempt at a smile.

"What?" One eyebrow rose.

She shook her head. "You're a pussycat."

Nothing could have prepared her for the blush that

streaked across his cheekbones. Grabbing a towel, he began to dry himself, but the full-bodied grin across his face was so gorgeous and rare that she stared. "Yeah, well, you sucked all the meanness right out of me."

She found her own smile growing wider, an unfamiliar action that was suddenly natural. "How long will this transformation last?"

"Until I get hungry for you again." He wrapped the towel around his hips. "Which could be anytime soon."

His delectably slow kiss was welcome. "You're insatiable."

"Just for you." He tapped his finger on her nose and the gesture was so silly, so tender, so unbelievably heartbreaking.

"Why don't you smile more?" She liked his smile, liked seeing such uncomplicated happiness on his face.

"Never had much to smile about."

Looking into that smile, Faith gave up her last hazy dream of somehow returning to the only world she'd ever known. "I'm never going back."

The smile faded and something darker whispered into his eyes, something wild and savagely possessive. "Good. Because I wasn't planning on letting you go."

She laughed and it was the first time in her life she hadn't been afraid. Silence had numbed her, but what she finally understood was that it was a numbness caused by fear. Her race was so afraid of their own talents, their own unique minds, they'd crippled themselves. But she was no longer in bondage.

Throwing her arms around Vaughn's neck, she let him pick her up and spin her around in a circle. They'd talk about his stubbornness, his liking for getting his own way, but not now. Not in this perfect moment.

Perhaps her newfound happiness was why she made the mistake, why she forgot that there were things hunting her that didn't live on the PsyNet, things that had direct access to her mind. She went to sleep in Vaughn's arms, but woke to find herself in the grip of malignant darkness. She knew she could move, could alert Vaughn, and he'd probably be able to bring her out of it.

But with the fire of Vaughn's chest pressed to her back, she knew where she was, *when* she was. Her shields against the visions might've burned out, but her emotions were wide awake. And though those emotional muscles were unfamiliar, she was confident she could use them if the need arose—they were as natural a part of her as Silence had been unnatural. It would be hard, but not impossible to break out of this vision.

Decision made, she let the vision sweep her under in an ebony wave of malevolence, let it swirl around her, let it show her.

Vaughn knew Faith was having a vision. Beneath closed eyelids, he could see her eyes flickering in rapid movements that were not those of deep sleep. He'd awakened when the cat had sensed a change in the rhythm of her heart rate. Now her scent, too, changed.

There was something not quite right about it, a sick miasma that made it seem as if she'd been infected by something vile. The beast raged to tear her from the grip of the vision, but Vaughn forced himself to think. Maybe Faith didn't want it to stop—he'd thought she'd been awake and aware when it started. Able to make a choice.

He never wanted to stifle her gift as Silence had, but fighting the beast was hard, especially when the man had the same protective instincts. The urge to shake her awake intensified when he glimpsed the hovering edges of a physical darkness above her. It couldn't get in, but circled like a vulture just waiting for a vulnerable spot.

Growling low in his throat, he held Faith closer. But iron-

ically the sight also calmed him—it hadn't fully clawed into
Faith, which meant she could break out on her own. If he
made the decision for her, he might steal from her a chance
to avenge her sister's death. And the need for vengeance was
something both parts of his self understood.

"I'm here," he whispered in her ear. Then he settled down
to keep watch over her and hold back the darkness. It didn't
matter that a psychic phenomenon should have had no physical form. He knew it existed, he saw it. And he would not let
it touch Faith.

Even in the depths of the vision, Faith was aware of
Vaughn beside her, a wall of pure fire between her and the
ugly menace that awaited. That was unusual enough to have
broken her concentration had she not already made the decision to complete this. The darkness would never again steal
a life.

Even if Faith had to end his.

The vision began to change from the unclear mix of emotion that had first roiled around her, the curtains of darkness
parting to once again show her the face of the woman he
meant to kill. The scene was clean—part of the stalk, not the
kill—which left her free to concentrate on details that might
identify the target rather than battling her own fear responses. By the time the vision faded, she thought she had
what she needed. She was about to pull out when she felt a
tug that signaled more was to come.

Calm from the lack of brutality in the opening scenes, she
let the next phase roll over her. Blood dripped down pale
green walls, soaked into the slightly darker carpet, splattered
the comm console. A charnel house she could smell—hints
of putrid death hidden in the iron-rich taint of blood. Revolted, she could do nothing as he walked farther into the
room, placing his feet in the dark red liquid that had once run

in a living being's veins. The blood in the bathroom had had nothing to soak into. His feet slapped into it with a splash.

Her mind shuddered under the overload. The carnage, the smell, the sporadic flashes of backsight that had her hearing screams of such terror that her bones chilled, it all smashed into her with the force of a truck going a hundred miles an hour. That was when she realized she *hadn't* survived the sexual heat with Vaughn.

The earlier cascade had fractured her mind on the deepest level. It had no ability to withstand the fury of this blood-soaked vision. She felt herself start to cascade again but this time, it was nothing survivable—the Cassandra Spiral. A silent scream tore free from her psyche. The Cassandra Spiral was the worst grade of cascade, turning victims into mute vegetables without reason or sentience.

No one survived without rapid M-Psy intervention.

But there were no M-Psy here and she was drowning, sinking so fast that soon she wouldn't be able to breathe. The blood was creeping up her body, coating her feet, her legs. . . .

CHAPTER 22

No!

It was a shout from a section of her mind she'd never before seen. Stubborn and rebellious, it slapped her back to her senses and told her to pull out. Now! If she didn't, the Council, the M-Psy, the PsyClan, they all won.

The violence worked. Her mind's eye watering with the strength of the emotional slap, she shook off her panic and began to find reason again. She refused to let them win, refused to have Vaughn feel that he'd taken a weak woman as his lover, someone who'd constantly need rescue.

Layered in determination born out of a lifetime of withheld rage, she threw a solid psychic block across the cascade. The Cassandra Spiral wasn't so easily escaped. It shoved at the block with such force that the wall bulged outward. But it didn't break—she had an excruciatingly small window before the avalanche hit. Not allowing herself to focus on that, she began to repair the cracks that had led to the cascade in the first place.

The work was hard.

Very, very hard.

Her mind felt as if it was caught in a vise. Only her unpolished, ungovernable emotional reaction, her fury at the darkness, and her hunger for vengeance kept her going. That and the need she had to make Vaughn proud of her, to be a woman worthy of a jaguar. Without that wild cauldron of emotional fire, she would've been crippled as she had been for so many years, dependent on others to pull her out.

However, none of her previous cascades—triggered by strong business visions—had ever been this severe. Never had she even touched the periphery of a Cassandra Spiral. A trial by fire, it threatened to engulf her in flames of poison, but Faith had no intention of being burned.

She worked with single-minded determination, and as each fracture healed, the psychic block bulged a little less. Oddly, it was her training for commercial forecasts that came to her aid at a critical moment, when exhaustion was starting to dull her mental muscles and she was in danger of making a fatal error. She fell back on the trick of locking her neurons into certain repeating patterns, a step by mechanical step use of her mind that required no conscious thought.

Leaving that pattern to repair the "easy" fractures, she focused her thinking self on fixing the almost invisible breaks in her innermost core. The next time she looked up, it was after she'd successfully rebuilt the core. The surface of her mind was peaceful, the darkness banished, the cascade subjugated. Tired but triumphant, she took a step back from the psychic plane and opened her eyes. She discovered herself cradled tight against Vaughn, the arms wrapped around her front pure immovable muscle.

"You were in trouble." A rough accusation. "I could smell it."

She tilted her head to look up at him. "I got myself out."

His eyes were jaguar, but he wasn't completely gone. "I knew you could." Shifting to lie flat on his back, he curved

one hand over her bottom as she rearranged herself to lean
up against his chest.

"Why didn't you break it?"

"You knew what you were doing."

Vaughn, she realized, would never let her shortchange
herself. He'd always demand that she be all the woman she
could be, even if that woman promised to make life more
difficult for him. A stark contrast to the people she'd called
family for so long.

Heart aching in an inexplicable way, she ran her palm
over a jaw roughened by stubble. "Vaughn, when my mind
was pure quiet at the end, I saw something." Something so
impossible that she wasn't quite ready to believe. And yet . . .

"What?" His hand smoothed up her spine and little sliv-
ers of lightning danced through her bloodstream, sparked in
her mind.

"Another bond." She slid her hand down to lie against his
shoulder. "Technically similar to the PsyNet link, but different in every other way. It's wild. Like you." Though she was
no changeling to scent things, that bond had held Vaughn's
mental scent, a scent as familiar to her as her own, though she
had no recollection of ever being in his mind. "What is it?"

"It ties you to me. Forever," he said, his tone absolute.
"You're my mate."

"Mate," she whispered, considering everything she knew
about changeling society, which wasn't much. "Like Sascha
and Lucas?"

"Yes."

She could barely breathe. "Really?"

"Yes. It's done. You can't get out." His fingers tightened
on her hip.

"Get out?" She wanted to laugh, but couldn't find enough
air to make the sound. "Vaughn, I was scared I was imagining it because I wanted it so much."

His fingers relaxed. "Good."

"How does it work?"

"I don't know. It's the first time for me, too."

"Oh." That strange ache inside of her intensified.

"But I do know it'll keep you alive after you drop out of the PsyNet."

"One changeling mind can't give a Psy brain the feedback it needs. Experiments have proven that conclusively." She shook her head, nails digging into his skin. "I won't kill you to keep myself alive."

"Trust me?"

She did, so much. "Always."

"Then don't worry about it."

"You can't provide the necessary biofeedback," she insisted. "It's psychically impossible."

He kissed her. "Trust, Red. Trust doesn't have any logic or sense."

"I trust you with my life." Placing a kiss on the hard angle of his jaw, she raised her lashes to meet his eyes. "But I'm not sure I trust you with yours." Because she knew how protective the cat was, how possessive.

A slow smile curved over his lips. "Oh, no, Red. I'm planning on living a long, long time now that I've got me a mate who'll satisfy my every need." His fingers lingered on the swell of her buttocks, that wicked smile accompanied by images of—

"Not on my knees," she said, more to tease than anything.

"What if I licked you into submission?" His fingers dipped to stroke lower, hotter places. "Would you go down on your knees then?"

"Perhaps." She felt her breathing start to alter. "You're trying to distract me from the point."

"No, Red. I'm trying to make you see." He stopped teasing her with his fingers. "If I die because of the feedback, then so will you. I'm not letting that happen." Grim determination in every word.

"The protections are holding. I could stay linked and download more data."

"Don't be scared of letting go."

She drew circles on his chest. "The PsyNet is so beautiful, so alive."

"But it's time for you to cut away from it. You know that."

"Yes." The second she was found missing, NightStar guards would be sent to locate her on the psychic plane and haul her back in. Whatever it took. That was if the Council didn't decide to do the job itself—she hadn't forgotten those cloaked martial minds.

Arrows.

Assassins.

In her case, they'd probably attempt containment. But she'd rather die than be incarcerated.

"I've got you." A calloused hand pushed strands of hair off her face to cup her cheek.

The unexpected tenderness wrenched at the heart of her, and deep within her mind, she saw the bond pulse. But then it stopped. A frown forming before she could Silence it, she looked inward. "I can't experience the bond in its entirety until I cut the Net link."

"I thought you were unconsciously jamming it." He scowled. "Unless . . . Usually, both sides have to deliberately accept the bond for it to come into complete effect. I thought we'd skipped that stage."

"I'm not doing anything. I didn't even know it could be." She paused. "It must be an automatic mental process. It makes sense that only one deep link can be functional at a time. Otherwise, the risk of overload would become unacceptable. But the mating bond is functioning to a certain extent." She could see the images he sent. He could feel when she was in psychic trouble.

Vaughn kissed her hard on the mouth. She gasped and stared.

"You can analyze the bond all you like. After you're out." A demand. "I don't like you being open to Council attack."

"Vaughn." She felt things for him she couldn't even have imagined feeling mere weeks ago. "My sister."

"Do you think you have a real chance of finding the killer through the Net?"

She took her time to answer, to order her thoughts. "The visions are the single link and they come through the channels of my mind. I haven't found anything on the Net."

"Then do it now, Faith. Before they realize you've come over to the side of the damn troublemaking animals."

A small laugh bubbled out of her. It was over before it began, but it had been spontaneous and it had been very real. "Hold me."

"Anytime."

Laying her head on his chest, she took a deep breath and closed her eyes. Pain squeezed her heart. It was almost a compulsion to step out into the PsyNet for one last look at the magnificent world that was about to be lost to her. But she couldn't. Too much was at stake. The mating bond tied Vaughn to her—if she were ambushed or erased, who knew how it would affect him? And he was more important to her than anything. She did, however, regret that she wouldn't have a chance to say good-bye to the one entity within the Net that wasn't broken, wasn't twisted. It was her hope that the NetMind would understand what she'd done and why.

Drawing in the scent of her mate, she went deep, deep inside herself, past every shield and block, past reason and cognition to the primitive nucleus—because the link to the PsyNet was powered by instinct and made at the instant of birth, the one thing about her race that wasn't controlled or manipulated.

And there it was, in the absolute and utter center.

She'd thought she'd linger over this, but she couldn't. It

hurt too much. Saying a soft good-bye, she reached out and sliced through it in a single fatal stroke.

Everything ended.

For one microsecond, she was the only thing in the universe, the only light in the darkness, the only living being in memory. Nerve endings screamed in agony and she felt her physical body jerk in hard spasms that threatened to tear muscle from bone. Life couldn't exist in a vacuum and she was—

But someone was holding her safe.

Someone else breathed.

Someone else lived.

Someone else blazed bright in the utter black of nothing.

She came awake with a gasp as her mind shoved through the lone avenue left to it—the bond to Vaughn. A flood of color, an overwhelming rush of scent and sound, fur under her fingertips and the sharp claws of animal passion, it all thrust into her heart and began to dig.

Then someone kissed her.

And that someone was *hers* in a way no one else would ever be. She comprehended that he was the fury and the passion, the male heat and the rich earth. She even knew his name. *"Vaughn."*

The soft whisper into his mouth kick-started Vaughn's heart with a vicious jolt. He'd never been as terrified as he'd been the moment he'd felt Faith just stop.

No heartbeat.

No breath.

No life.

It had been less than a second, but he'd almost died. Then had come the avalanche of loneliness crashing into him with the violence of a freight train going downhill at full speed. It had nearly torn out his heart. "I'm here, baby. I'm here." Kissing her again and again, he fed his need for her down the bond, letting her know that she wasn't alone, that she'd never be alone again.

Murmuring wordlessly, she wrapped her arms and legs around him in a desperate movement. Her kiss was that of a woman trying to convince herself of his existence. He let her take what she wanted, would've given his life had she asked for it. But what she wanted was his passion, his hunger, his heat.

So he gave her that, moving his hands to caress every inch of her creamy skin, branding her with his touch and his kiss. She wouldn't unclasp her body from his. Not willing to break the contact either, he found a way to love her as she was, sliding his hands under her bottom to position her above his erection, his skin stretched so tight that the pleasure was exquisite pain.

He meant to go gently, but she wouldn't wait, pushing down hard and taking him into her body like the most perfectly crafted glove. He held her tight and flipped them over, her body lush and welcoming under his. Bracing himself above her with one arm, he used the other to grasp her hip.

"Faith." It was a warning she responded to by dragging her nails down his back and biting hard on his shoulder.

Growling low in his throat, he thrust into her. Deep. And again.

She was liquid fire in his bloodstream, sheer woman heat, and when her closed eyes flashed open, he saw jagged sparks of white lightning.

Faith lay in Vaughn's arms and listened to his heartbeat. Real, true, steady, it anchored her. But despite that and the fact that it was close to dawn, her mind continued to race. She had to see the new world in which she lived. Unlike for the changeling who was the most important being in her life, the mental plane was as much a reality for her as the earth and the sky, the trees and the forest.

She'd rather know now whether that plane was barren, and she'd do it while Vaughn was asleep. She didn't ever want to hurt him by intimating that it wounded her to not be part of the PsyNet, cut off from a facet of her existence that was central to her identity as a Psy.

Closing her eyes on one plane, she opened them on another. But she couldn't step out, couldn't bear to face the endless darkness.

"Open your eyes, Faith. Look at the Web of Stars."

How had he known what she was doing? He wasn't Psy. But he was her mate. "The Web of Stars?" she asked, standing poised on the doorstep of her mind. His answer was a kiss placed carefully on the pulse at the curve of her neck.

Finding strength from the power of that simple caress, she took the next step and looked. There were no stars on black velvet, no isolated lights burning like blades, no black spaces. Her breath rushed out of her. Not because this place was barren, but because it wasn't. There was color everywhere, multicolored sparkles that flickered rainbow-bright and teased the eye with quicksilver speed.

Heart thudding, she looked past the stunning beauty that threatened to hold her spellbound and found Vaughn's mind. He was cardinal bright but hot and golden, wild and passionate. A fragile-seeming gold thread linked her to him, but she knew it to be unbreakable. When she looked further, she saw that he was linked to a central mind by another thread, but that thread was different from the bond that tied the two of them together.

Her Psy mind was at home here. It somehow understood that the other bond could be broken. That it wasn't, was its strength. More minds linked out from the core. Not many, but enough to sustain her without draining anyone. More than enough. These minds sparked with so much energy, it was as if each was more than it seemed. Tears falling inside her most secret heart, she searched for the source of those brilliant, beautiful sparks that she, a child raised in the dark, had never imagined might exist.

She found it shielded below the central mind, as if the unique sentience that created such beauty needed more protection than others. Perhaps it did. Even with a single glance, she knew that this mind was incredibly gentle, that it would never do any harm, never kill.

Astonished by the explosion of color and life in her new psychic world, a world that for all its small size would never bore, never grow stagnant, she withdrew and opened her eyes in the physical world. "The colors. It's Sascha, isn't it?"

"I can't see what you see, Red," Vaughn pointed out. "But she's an empath."

"I don't know what that is." But she had a lifetime in which to find out. "Vaughn, how can this Web exist? The other minds I saw except for Sascha were changeling." And Psy knowledge said that changelings didn't have the capacity to maintain psychic links. Of any kind.

He nuzzled at her before kissing her again. She wasn't averse to him indulging himself. Not when she remained shell-shocked from the Net separation.

"It has to do with the blood oath the sentinels take. We don't know how it works—we'd forgotten it even existed."

Vaughn had never been this content. It was as if a missing part of him had come home, a part that he'd been functioning without but, now that he'd found it, the loss of which he'd never survive. Faith was inside of him, held in the core of his animal heart, protected with every ounce of strength he had. If she saw their bond on the level of the mind, he saw the physical reality of it, the strength and the purity.

She ran a hand through his hair and he purred against her, asking for more. She complied, understanding him without words. It was part of the bond, but it was also because she wanted to know, wanted to please him. And that gave him more pleasure than anything else.

Yet a sadness lingered in her and he knew why. "You're thinking about Marine."

"We have to stop him."

"I'll call Pack."

"Pack?"

"You're one of us. They'll want to help."

"Even a Psy?"

"You're my Psy now."

His possessiveness was welcome, but it set off a less joyful thought. "The Council isn't going to let me go without a fight."

"Leave that to me. You think about how to catch this killer and I'll work out a way to keep you safe."

"Alright." Trusting Vaughn was easy. He'd never made a promise he didn't keep.

Faith wasn't surprised when Vaughn drove them to the now familiar wooden cabin for the meeting with his pack-mates. She had a feeling her jaguar didn't like too many people in his home territory. Exiting the car, she straightened her spine and began closing the distance to the porch. She didn't want to look weak in front of these people who mattered to the man who meant everything to her.

However, it wasn't only Sascha and her mate waiting for them, but also a stranger dressed in black.

"This is Judd Lauren," Sascha said, from her chair beside Lucas's.

Faith nodded, conscious of the sudden rise in Vaughn's aggressiveness. Lucas didn't look too happy either. The truly peculiar thing was that the silent stranger triggered her internal alarms as well. She couldn't reason why. What she did know was that for all his icy masculine beauty, he was deadly. But then so were the two changelings.

Aware she was being rude, but unwilling to let it go, she continued to stare at him where he leaned against the outer wall of the cabin. "I've seen you before."

"No." His expression betrayed nothing, not even by the flicker of an eyelash.

No one was that controlled. No one but a Psy. But of course Judd wasn't one of her race. "No," she agreed. "But I've seen others like you." He inspired the same primal fear response as those cloaked guards who'd escorted her to the candidacy meeting.

Judd was hardly likely to be one of the almost mythical Arrows, but he made her very uneasy. And if that wasn't enough, another male who set off her defenses appeared that second from around the corner of the house. He prowled to lean against the railing a small distance from the others, his green eyes watching her with the unblinking stare of a predator sizing up prey. She was extremely glad Vaughn was beside her.

Lucas jerked his head at the new arrival. "Clay, I thought you were bringing Tammy."

"Cubs. Rosebushes. Thorns," came the truncated reply.

Everyone but her seemed to understand. Sascha shook her head, a small smile on her lips. "Are they okay?"

Clay nodded.

Feeling out of the loop, she leaned her back against Vaughn's chest. White fire licked up her fingertips where they touched his jeans. He seemed to freeze and then reawaken, his hand never ceasing its soothing strokes down her arm. "You all know why we're here."

"To locate the man who murdered Faith's sister," Sascha said. "But I thought you didn't know enough."

"Red?"

"At first," she began, "all I saw was her, the intended

victim—very pale skin, white-blonde hair, blue eyes. Unusual looks for a Psy, but not a practical way to track her." She forced herself to go back into the evil of the visions. "Then I started to get more—"

"Because he's stalking her?" Sascha interrupted.

"At the time, it was because he *was going* to stalk her."

Everyone went silent as they digested the reality of her life. Lucas was the first to shake himself out of it. "How far gone is he?"

"In the final stages. The visions I'm seeing now are of blood." Vaughn's arms came around her though she'd betrayed nothing by either gesture or tone—being unemotionally Psy was a form of protection against these predators, not all of whom were in her corner. "We have to stop him at the kidnapping because I know the location and I even know the time."

"How?" It was the dark-skinned male called Clay.

She had to force herself not to press closer into Vaughn. "There were time markers in the last series of images, things that let me place a vision in the correct time frame. Some markers are hard to spot, like seasonal changes or the color of the sky, but these were unmistakable."

No one spoke so she continued, grounding herself in the muscled heat of the body surrounding hers. The embrace was a silent statement of his loyalty, she knew that much. "I saw a datebook open on her desk as well as the face of an electronic clock. Both the same." Time markers didn't get much clearer than that.

Then she revealed something she'd told Vaughn in the car after unraveling all the other markers. "We have one day." Too close for comfort, far too close. "If we don't get him . . . it's likely we won't save her. He feels"—she searched for the right words—"full, full of anticipation, of need. He doesn't keep and torture his victims, either. While stalking his intended victim excites him, his biggest thrill comes from the actual kill." Like when he'd killed Marine. Once again, her heart clenched and now she knew what to call it: a mixture of pain and grief, sorrow and loss.

"Where?" Judd asked, his voice utterly toneless.

"You're Psy." She was suddenly positive beyond any reasonable doubt. "Only Sascha is supposed to be outside the Net."

He didn't answer her implied question. "Where?"

She decided to ask Vaughn later. "The small private university that went up a few years ago on the edge of Napa. It specializes in viticulture."

"Most students and staff are human or changeling," Lucas pointed out. "What would a Psy be doing there? They're not much into organic assets."

"I think she's some kind of technician. Don't wineries have sophisticated temperature monitoring and cooling systems?"

"It could be that." Vaughn's hands dropped to rest on her hips—an act of male ownership, one she didn't have any desire to fight. "Not that it matters if she's going to be there on that date and at that time. We'll pick him off before he gets to her."

"Why are we cleaning up a Psy mess again?" Clay's deep voice. "Faith's not in any danger. The killer and possible victim are both Psy. Shouldn't the Council be taking care of this?"

"Clay!" Sascha looked shocked. "We're speaking about a woman's life."

"I'm not saying we forget about it, just that we let those responsible tidy it up."

"And what if they don't?" Faith asked softly, staring into that harshly masculine face that was so without mercy. Clay was different from Vaughn, no matter that Vaughn's animal roamed nearer to the skin. There was something very dark in the leopard, something that walked a fine line between good and evil.

She had a knowing almost on top of that thought—Clay's time was coming. One day soon he'd have to decide which side of that line he wanted to be on. "What if she simply disappears like the others I heard about on the Net? Will you be able to sleep at night, your conscience clear?" Because he wasn't quite gone yet, was still on the good side of the line. By a bare fraction.

Clay raised an eyebrow. "So we take this guy out. Great. What about the next and the next and the next?"

Faith didn't know where her answer came from. "Some futures we can't see, some lives we can't save, but this one we can. Let's discuss the rest later."

"There's a bigger problem." Lucas rocked back in his chair, propping his feet up on the railing. "If neither victim nor killer is changeling, it falls within Enforcement jurisdiction. We don't have the right to enforce Law."

Faith had forgotten that. "We could let the authorities know."

"Same as telling the Council." Clay snorted. "Unless you're ready to hand over the whole fucking mess to your psychopathic race?"

Vaughn went utterly still around her. "Watch it, cat."

Faith didn't understand all of what was going on, but she could read the aggression in the air. She shifted to wrap an arm around Vaughn's waist. He didn't take his eyes off Clay.

After a tense moment, the other male gave a slow nod. "I was out of line." A pause. "She reminds me of someone."

Faith worked through the statement, startled at the belated realization that Vaughn had turned hostile toward Clay because of his rudeness to her. Warmth spread in her secret heart. But notwithstanding that, she didn't want to be the cause of Vaughn fighting with his pack.

"About Enforcement," she said, sliding her hand under his T-shirt to lie palm down on his back. Her cat responded to the stroking, looking away from Clay at last.

"I know a couple of cops we can trust," Clay replied, surprising her. "If they make the arrest, it'll be legal."

"And the killer will be out by nightfall, sprung by the Council. He'll disappear into the Net, never to be seen again." Sascha's voice was grim. "They'll either kill him to ensure no one learns of the breakdown in the Protocol, or if he's one of theirs gone rogue, attempt to reinstate control."

Lucas dropped his feet to the porch and leaned over to kiss his mate. Softening, she curled her fingers around his biceps, but Lucas's eyes were narrowed when he turned back to them. "Sascha's right. We saw what happened last time."

Anger was suddenly alive in the air. Faith happened to be looking at Sascha and saw the other cardinal breathe deeply several times, eyes going the pure black of a Psy expending large amounts of power. The anger level dropped.

"I can take care of him." Judd sounded like he was talking about the weather. "Even from a distance."

Faith's stomach curdled. "No. We can't commit one murder to stop another." She'd thought to do precisely that, but that had been in the red-hot heat of anger. She was no stone-cold killer.

"You have a better idea?" Judd asked, something very much like insolence in his otherwise icy tone.

"Back off," Vaughn said, in a very quiet voice. She could hear a difference from his reaction to Clay—he was dangerous this time, where before he'd been issuing a warning. "You're here because you helped save Sascha's life, but that only goes so far."

The other male's smile was humorless. "It doesn't go far at all."

Faith was a babe at understanding emotion, but it seemed to her that the Psy *wanted* a physical fight. What could possibly inspire that kind of death wish? Even if Judd was an Arrow, Vaughn was a jaguar.

"Wait, I do have an idea."

Everyone looked at her.

"Incapacitate him." She stared at Judd. "Tie his mind up in mental ropes he'll never be able to break."

"What makes you think I can do that?" Judd stared back, daring her.

"If Arrows exist, then you were an Arrow." She heard Sascha gasp. "A telepathic Arrow is likely to be trained in all sorts of things."

He didn't deny either her accusation or her guess about his Tp status. "It'll send him insane. Imagine never being able to act out any of your impulses—he'll function, but only on a very basic level."

Faith felt fury arc through her. "Then that will be his life sentence." At least he'd have a life to live, unlike Marine and the other women he'd killed. And there had definitely been others. His appetite was too certain, his tastes too set.

"Will you have to hack the PsyNet to do what Faith's suggesting?" Lucas asked. "Will they be able to track it back to you?"

"No, I can do it telepathically, but it's a specialized skill. They'll deduce that they have an unknown renegade, but they already know that." He didn't explain why. "However, it'll involve getting through his protective walls."

"How hard will that be?"

"He has to have considerable power given what Sascha's told me about his effect on Faith, but he's going to be in the grip of the killing instinct. Anyone affected by strong emotion becomes vulnerable. He's going to be no exception." He looked at Faith, unblinking, eerily focused. "If you distract him at a critical moment, it'll ensure I get through."

Vaughn's growl was almost too low for Psy hearing, but she felt it in her bones. "She's not going anywhere near the son of a bitch."

"Vaughn, listen—"

"No way in hell, Red. Forget about it."

"It needn't be physical," she said. "I could just brush up against him telepathically. He'd recognize my mental scent."

"Because he's somehow able to connect to you through the visions?" Sascha clearly remembered their earlier conversation.

"Yes. I see the future, but I see it through the lens of his mind," she explained for the sake of the others. "It's as if we experience the visions together. . . ." Her mouth fell open. "An F-Psy. He must be one of my designation." The implications were staggering.

"Maybe," Judd broke in. "But before we get into that, are you sure you can identify him?"

"Yes. Don't worry that you'll be incapacitating an innocent man."

"I'm Psy. Worry is a changeling emotion."

She wondered which one of them he was trying to convince, because the truth was, Judd was no longer Psy. He'd ceased to exist in the PsyNet, probably been written off as dead. And now he lived in a different world. "I'll know. I've seen his face."

All sound ceased.

CHAPTER 23

Judd picked up the logical disconnect in milliseconds. "You just said the visions are from his point of view."

"They are."

"Then how, Red?" Though there was no anger in Vaughn's voice, she knew he had to be asking himself why she hadn't told him earlier.

"I didn't want to see," she whispered, so low it wasn't even sound.

One of his arms rose to wrap around her shoulders from the front and she knew he'd heard. "Never alone."

It was a promise, one she armored herself in, but it still took every ounce of Psy skill she had to keep her voice from breaking as she relived the horror. "I saw his reflection." A reflection cast in blood, a ruby-red mirror in the charnel house of that last vision.

"Then there's no question—Faith has to be present," Judd said.

"She might be present, but she's not going to stick out her neck and attract his attention." Vaughn's arm was pure steel around her shoulders, not the least bit hurtful, but also not the least bit movable.

"Vaughn." She kept her voice low, but guessed that Clay and Lucas could hear nonetheless. "I think we should go for a walk."

He released her from his hold and took her hand. "This won't take long," he told the others, but didn't say anything else until he'd brought them to a stop several meters into the woods. "I'm not letting you put yourself in danger."

"There's very little danger, almost none, in telepathy."

"Yeah, well, maybe this guy falls into the 'almost.' He's different—he was able to trap you into the visions."

"Perhaps," she agreed. "But that doesn't change anything."

He didn't reply, the jaguar very much apparent in his eyes.

So she spoke to the animal. "You once asked me about guilt. I said I didn't feel any. That was a lie." She forced herself to break another wall of Silence—to do and feel was easy compared to putting those things in words. "The guilt walks beside me from morning till night, from instant to instant. I'm an F-Psy, but I couldn't save my own sister's life. That makes me a failure."

"You had no way of knowing what it was you were seeing," he grit out.

"Logic doesn't work here, Vaughn! You know that more than anyone." She pushed him, asked him to remember the guilt he felt for Skye's death though he'd been a child himself.

He curved his hand around her neck. "There will come a time when I won't bend, won't be reasonable, won't act human."

She'd realized that in the first few seconds after meeting him. "But that particular point hasn't been reached."

"I want you with me at all times. The second anything goes wrong, you get out. I don't care if you have to turn his brains to jelly. *Get out*."

"I have no intention of permitting him close enough to hurt me. I'll be a shadow and then I'll be gone."

The cat clawed at the walls of Vaughn's mind as they worked out the details with the others. "There's something else," he said, after they'd agreed on a simple plan.

"The Council." Sascha leaned forward. "They have to know she's defected by now. They'll come after her with every weapon they have. As an F-Psy, she knows far too much."

The animal in Vaughn wanted to eliminate the threat and take care of them once and for all—Psy with crushed skulls couldn't harm his mate—but the man knew it wasn't so simple. Currently the Council had six heads, but it was a multi-limbed monster. Taking out one head would cause two or three more to sprout in its place. The only way it could ever be totally destroyed was for it to be torn out by its very roots. And the only people who could invoke a change that deep were the Psy themselves.

Faith rested her body against his side. "There may be something that will stay their hand."

The beast calmed at the gentle heat of her. "You have an idea?"

"Less an idea than a knowing." Her voice was suddenly heavy with grief. "It's always bothered me why Marine was murdered. He has this sick excitement leading up to the kill he's planning to make tomorrow, but there was nothing like that with Marine. He didn't stalk her. The buildup was in how clearly I saw the end result—loss of breath eventually metamorphosing into total suffocation."

Her strength impressed him to animal pride. Shifting his hold, he leaned against the railing and pulled her into the cradle formed by his spread legs. She came without complaint, putting her own hands over the ones he'd draped around her hips.

"Could she have been a chance kill, taken because the opportunity was there?" Judd Lauren's voice made the jaguar want to snarl—the cat didn't understand the fine distinction between enemy and uncertain ally.

"No, there was no sense of him being rushed or unprepared."

Vaughn hated to hear the pain in her voice, but knew time alone would heal those wounds. Though they'd never disappear, they'd turn into scars and that was okay, because those scars made them stronger.

Sascha tapped her foot. "What did your sister do?"

"She was a cardinal telepath. A communications specialist for the PsyClan."

"While I was in the Net, I heard rumors that your PsyClan did a considerable amount of sub-rosa work for the Council."

Faith's fingernails dug into his skin. "And if she was 'pathing for them, then she knew everything that was being sent and received, knew every secret, every detail of every plan."

"A liability if she decided not to play the game." After all, Marine NightStar had been his mate's sister and Faith was too intelligent, too independent, too human, to have ever made a good Council cipher.

Faith suddenly gave a violent shake of her head. "This isn't getting us anywhere. A knowing doesn't usually give me details—we'll have to wait and see if we can scan the killer's mind. Even if the Council comes after me, it won't be before we incapacitate him."

Clay crossed his arms across his chest. "How do you know?"

"I *know*." Her voice was haunted and very, very certain. "We have that much time. The answer will come to us tomorrow."

"And if it doesn't?" Sascha asked quietly.

"Then at least Marine will have been avenged." The

bone-deep fury in her found an echo in the heart of the jaguar. "I want him to pay for what he did."

The males looked to each other and understanding passed in a current. Three predatory changelings and a Psy who might be a trained assassin, they found nothing wrong with Faith's rage. It was real, it was true, and it would be satisfied.

"He will." Vaughn spoke for all of them. "Even if I have to crush his skull myself."

"**Vaughn.**" Faith stood beside her mate as he worked on a sculpture. Dressed in nothing but a pair of faded blue jeans, he was pure muscle and heat, amber-gold hair tied carelessly into a queue.

"What is it, Red?" He put down his tools to run his knuckles over her skin. The touch was tender, the look in his eyes anything but.

"Why are you doing this now?" She smoothed her hand over one marble curve. "Come to bed. We both need to mentally prepare for tomorrow."

"I'm not Psy, baby." His voice dropped. "I don't need to calm my mind."

She suddenly understood. "I'm ready."

"Go to sleep." He picked up what looked like a chisel. "I'll be there soon."

She took it from him and put it back on the workbench. "You're afraid of hurting me." Such a thing was wrong between mates, she knew that without having to be taught. "You're scared I'll cascade like I did yesterday."

"What we did yesterday was perfection, but you're not ready for another round. And I don't have gentleness in me right now." Rough, harsh, blunt.

She put her hand on the golden skin of his chest. "You're never going to be truly gentle."

He flinched.

"I didn't mean it like that. I like your wildness, your passion, your demands." She swallowed at the molten heat in his eyes. "You make me feel alive."

"I can sense the way you hurt when your mind breaks."

"But I get stronger with every loving." Something she was now starting to understand. "If you try to contain yourself, you'll shortchange both of us. I need to satisfy you in the same way you need to touch me."

"I won't be tied down this time, and what I demand from you, you might not be ready to give. I'm in no mood to play."

Because, she realized, he was in the grip of a possessive protectiveness that left no room for half measures. She could feel the dark red of his hunger through the mating bond, feel his passion, his wildness. "Show me," she whispered, pushing aside her own fears. If the Council did come for her tomorrow, she wanted to look at them with the confidence of a woman who'd broken every rule of Silence and done so in the most unquestionable way. "I won't cascade." A vow. To both of them.

The T-shirt she'd meant to sleep in floated in shreds to her feet—Vaughn's claws had moved so fast she hadn't even had time to take a breath. Heart in her throat, she watched him retract those razor-sharp weapons, excruciatingly aware that he hadn't left a scratch on her. Eyes locked with hers, he slid his hands down her back and under the waistband of her panties to cup her bottom.

She gasped as her breasts rubbed against his chest, full and aching. When her panties disintegrated off her body, she barely felt it, so stunned was she at the pure sensuality that spread across Vaughn's features. He'd been scared of physically harming her yesterday. Today he was in full control of his strength . . . but not of his hunger. Notwithstanding her confident talk, she wasn't positive she could handle his demands.

He smoothed one hand to the front of her body and the

roughness of his skin rasping over her navel had her holding her breath. The tips of his fingers touched her curls. She clenched her hands on his shoulders.

"So soft," he murmured, and drove his fingers through the curls to cup her intimately.

Her scream reverberated off the stone walls.

When he rubbed the heel of that possessive hand against her, she rubbed back, starving for a sensation she'd never thought would be so exquisite. He liked that, a very male smile curving over those sensual lips. "More," he demanded. "Give me more."

She rose on tiptoe and his tormenting hand followed, spearing through her softness to capture her most sensitive flesh in a hold that threatened madness of a new kind. Pressing her thighs together, she dug her nails into his shoulders and tried to reach his lips, but he wouldn't cooperate. So she bit at his chest, scratched lines down his back.

"Cat," he said, and it was a pleased statement as he squeezed his fingers and rocked a shudder through her body. "I'm going to take you like I dreamed about."

Images of her bent over in the most submissive of positions, her bottom shamelessly upturned and her thighs spread in welcome. She didn't fight the erotic onslaught, luxuriating in the psychic seduction. "You have to—"

Sliding two fingers inside of her without warning, he palmed her breast with his free hand, a rough brand that set fire to her skin. "I have to what?"

"H-have to get me there first," she challenged, unable to stop her hips from plunging up and down on the hard intrusion of his fingers.

He chuckled and spread those invading fingers just enough to intensify the pleasure. "You should know never to dare a cat."

"Meow," she teased, even as she felt her body begin to gather itself for a storm.

"Come for me," he demanded. "I want to taste your surrender." His fingers moved in a faster rhythm, stroking her so intimately that she had no defense.

The pleasure swept her under and it was lighting and fury, heat and hunger. But it wasn't a cascade, the overload shooting down the mating bond to the wild heart of a jaguar more than able to handle the influx of sensation. When she came down from the rush, it was to find herself held against him as he withdrew his fingers from her body. The musky scent of her filled the air, rich, heady, and ultimately female. And though his erection was a hard flame between them, she somehow knew that her surrender had only increased his sensual patience.

Lazy, sated, she didn't protest as he carried her from the workshop to the bed and stroked her onto her hands and knees. She arched into his touch, enjoying the feel of him running his hands down her back, over her buttocks and down the insides of her thighs. Spreading her for him. When he pushed down between her shoulder blades, she remembered his erotic fantasies and, bending her arms at the elbows, she lowered her head to the sheets and tilted up her bottom.

Her mind was pure lightning by this stage, but she refused to give up. Instead, every time the pleasure threatened to sweep her under, she gripped tight to the mating bond.

"Good girl," Vaughn murmured, one hand on her buttock. "I think I know what you're doing. I can feel you holding on to me deep inside."

That he was pleased wasn't even a question—she heard it in the indulgent sensuality of his tone. Not really considering the consequences of success, she sent an erotic request down the bond simply to see if she could.

His hand squeezed. "Baby, I can't see an image, but I think you just read my mind."

That was the only warning she got before he ravaged her with his mouth, pure demand and rough heat. She screamed at the first touch and orgasmed at the second. Ten minutes later, she was shuddering almost continuously, her body held up by Vaughn's hands on her hips. The man was relentless. But still she didn't cascade, her mind soaking up the sensations like a starved thing.

"Hold on." A dark whisper, a breath of air across exquisitely sensitive flesh.

She whimpered . . . and he used his teeth to capture the engorged flesh of her clitoris. A wave of black crashed into her. The pleasure was so acute, so piercingly sensual that she sobbed as she shattered, clutching at the bond with desperation armored in sheer need.

That was when he took her.

Hot, hard, dominant, nothing that came before could compare to this claiming. She felt branded on a level that went beyond sex and heat, claimed, owned.

Both ways. It was a thought from her mind to his, a feeling that required no words to be understood.

"Oh, yeah, baby. I'm yours." Hot breaths against her neck as he bent to kiss her pulse before rising up, tightening his grip on her hips, and riding her to ecstasy.

Even then, she didn't cascade, didn't go mad . . . didn't break.

Only hours later, Faith stood beside Vaughn's tense form as they waited in the courtyard of the private university where she'd placed the target. She couldn't see the others through the mirrored lenses of her sunglasses, but knew they were there, silent shadows to ensure justice was done.

Anticipation simmered in her blood, veins filled with the most physical energy she'd ever felt, Vaughn's wildness mixing with her own on a level beyond telepathy. She was becoming a tiny bit jaguar with each contact and that was fine with her. Claws were sometimes necessary. Today, those claws were helping her withstand the impact of so many unshielded minds within receiving distance.

Looking at the gently leafy campus, at the students walking alone or in groups, Faith felt her resolve harden into granite. If they failed, an innocent woman would lose her life, this campus would be forever tainted by a darkness no amount of soap or water could wash away, and Marine's ghost would find no peace.

So they would not fail.

"We'll get him." Vaughn's voice was husky in her ear.

"How do you always know what's on my mind?" she asked. "I wasn't sending you anything." They'd spent some time after last night's tumultuous loving working out that while Vaughn couldn't hear her words, he could read the emotions she sent with unerring accuracy.

"There are other ways of knowing and I'm going to have fun introducing you to all of them." A thread of steel underlay his teasing words. The jaguar wasn't in charge right now, but it was very, very close to the surface. Because she might be in danger.

"Vaughn, I'm not weak. I can protect myself." She wouldn't die on him as his sister had, but neither would she hurt him by referring openly to an event that had scarred him so violently. However, she could try to address those scars in an oblique way. "I didn't cascade yesterday and once I would've believed that impossible. My strength is increasing day by day." Perhaps being Psy hadn't taught her about emotion, but it had taught her about strategy. That skill could be put to use for good as well as evil, couldn't it? "Vaughn?" she said, when he didn't respond.

"Yeah?"

"Not everything about the Psy is bad, is it?" It caused a tearing pain inside of her to think that everyone she'd ever known, that her father, her sister, had been nothing good.

"Hell, no. You're not."

"I'm not talking about individuals. The Psy as a race have done some good, haven't they?"

"They were once the most amazing people on this planet." His response was a surprise. "Take your gift. Without it, civilization might've been destroyed a thousand times over."

"That was before. What about now?"

"They create more jobs than their own race can ever fulfill, employ millions of humans and even some changelings."

"But all at low-level positions."

"Sometimes that position is the only thing that stands between a life and starvation. And changelings aren't any different in that sense—high-level jobs in our businesses are always held by Pack."

"But," she said, "it isn't so much, is it?" She saw the truth in spite of his uncharacteristic gentleness. "Changelings have kept the Earth beautiful and pollution free, and it's mostly humans who've hung its walls with art and filled its corners with music. What's the Psy legacy—endless steel towers of pure function, businesses that deal in emotionless currency . . . and Silence?"

The knowing that came to her was unexpected and as clear as the bright light of morning. "If we don't change, the Psy race will one day be forgotten." And that would be a tragedy. No one who'd seen the beauty of the PsyNet, the potential in it, the stunning energy of life even in Silence, could doubt that.

"Then change the future, Faith. Change the Psy."

An extraordinary task for a renegade from the Net. "Will you be with me?"

"I can't believe you asked that question," he mock-growled, throwing an arm around her neck and dragging her to him. "Of course I'll be with you, and so will the rest of the pack. We're family."

"Family." A bittersweet word. "Always?"

He bit the side of her neck. "Beyond always."

"He's coming." The words fell out of her mouth without conscious thought.

Vaughn drew back from her and gave a very low growl that she didn't actually *hear*, but which made every hair on her body stand up in attention.

"What—?"

"It's a signal," he whispered, pretending to nibble on her earlobe. From the way she'd seen women looking at him ever since they'd entered the campus, she was probably the focus of considerable feminine envy. Something primitive in her was pleased by that, by the fact that this wild and magnificent creature was hers. He wasn't, and never would be, tame, but he was willing to play nice for her sake. And no one else's.

"Can you feel him?" The quiet question broke into her thoughts. She was shocked at how distracted she'd become from something so important. Vaughn did things to her she couldn't control.

"The knowing works with my ability. It's a kind of vision on a very deep psychic plane. I'm not telepathically connected to him." That horror only happened during actual visions.

"Then how are you going to find him?"

"I'm going to send out my telepathic senses. I'm a Gradient 6 telepath." Very powerful, though nowhere near where she estimated Judd to be. "If I brush up against other Psy, I'll withdraw before they can get a lock on me." She didn't mention that some of those minds could track her very, very quickly.

"But if I touch him, I'll attempt to pinpoint a physical location. It doesn't really matter if I can't—Judd can take the mental signature from my mind and use his stronger Tp abilities to zero in on the killer's position."

"I don't like that damn Psy being in your mind."

"Neither do I." Faith didn't think Judd was out to harm her, but he was an unknown, a rebel Arrow with undetermined loyalties. "It'll be a surface link, a simple data transfer."

"If he tries anything, use the bond."

Her heart skipped a beat at the welcome reminder that she'd never be alone again. "I will. I'm going to begin the search now." She 'pathed the same message to Judd.

I can see you. The masculine voice was so clear, her suspicions about Judd's status on the Gradient solidified into certainty. The man might not have the night-sky eyes, but he had to be near cardinal strong. *If you keep the scan radius small, I can pinpoint him almost immediately after you.*

Faith whispered the suggestion to Vaughn. "We'll have to change position and go out farther into the open as I scan. But it'll give us an unmistakable target when we do find him. Judd won't have to enter my mind, either."

Vaughn's answer was nothing she could've predicted. "Faith, this is your world. What option do you think will work best?"

"You won't try to overrule me?"

"Only if your choice puts you in unnecessary danger." The cat was in his voice, low and husky. "I can't protect your mind, but I sure as hell will keep your body safe."

She figured that was as good as it was going to get with her jaguar. "Then let's do it. If I start to feel we're getting too close and I can't find him, we'll stop. I don't want to paint a bull's-eye on myself." For the first time in twenty-four years, she was truly alive, and she had no intention of changing that.

CHAPTER 24

"If this works like I think it will," she said, "the second he feels me, he'll try to connect and that should give Judd the opportunity he needs."

"I can smell Judd. Tell him to make sure he's well hidden. He doesn't fit into this campus."

"And you do?" She relayed the message.

"I'm the rough type the good girl always falls for," he said, displaying a rare vein of humor. "That Psy just looks like he's here to take someone out."

Shaking her head, she sent out the first seeking touch. "Nothing."

Vaughn silently picked out a spot closer to the building that housed the intended victim and she repeated the scan. "Nothing."

Two more attempts produced the same frustrating result. Emotion definitely had a downside—an emotionless Psy would've continued scanning with mechanical precision until they achieved success. "Nothing, nothing, nothing!"

"I don't want you any nearer the prey. If you know what he looks like, he might have seen you, too."

"I hadn't considered that, but if he is an F-Psy, that may be a possibility."

"Whatever else he is, he's also a coward," Vaughn spit out. "They're always dangerous when cornered."

She agreed. Certain telepathic abilities could cause massive damage when used offensively. Judd was the perfect example. "Let me try one more sweep. I know he's here." Taking a deep breath, she spread out her senses. *This one's for you, Marine.*

And there he was.

The darkness recognized her, too. Homing in on her position with frightening speed, it scrabbled for purchase into her mind. Gut instinct came to her aid—she snapped her entire psychic self into a tiny ball, burying it deep within the bond with Vaughn. Changeling wildness locked around her and the talons of darkness slipped away without finding purchase.

It had taken mere milliseconds, but when she opened her eyes, she felt as if she'd run a marathon. Vaughn's body was so tense next to her that she knew he'd sensed the danger. "He's a telepath with attacking capabilities. Foresight might be a secondary talent."

She could see him now. He was standing a few easy meters from her, a tall male with Silent discipline stamped onto his handsome features. In his black suit and white shirt, he was just another anonymous Psy as he swept the area in an effort to find her. "Why doesn't he look like a monster?"

"They never do." Vaughn's claws pricked at her skin through her clothing.

Panic a knot in her throat, she closed her hand over his. "You can't go for him. Enforcement would love to get their hands on you."

"You're my mate."

She knew it was killing him to not be the one to ensure her vengeance. "I need you alive and with me. Vaughn, please. *Please.*"

"Tell the damn Psy." A growled command.

She did and shot by the killer's mind once more in a move calculated to break his concentration. It worked— Judd located him. Dropping his head into his hands all of a sudden, the killer began to whimper. But he wasn't yet incapacitated. There was too much intelligence in those black eyes as they searched the area for the source of attack. She wondered why Judd was holding back.

Then the Tp-Psy materialized to stand beside her. "Be sure," he said. "This is irreversible."

About to give an answer powered by fury, she forced herself to think, to consider the fact that this was a life. Going back over that last contact, she added them to the ones before. And came to a startling realization. "Something's wrong."

"Do I pull out?" No judgment, no worry; Judd Lauren was so cold he made her want to shiver.

"It *is* him, but . . . Vaughn, remember what you said about seeing darkness around me?"

"Not something I could ever forget." A voice walking the finest edge of rage.

She leaned more heavily against him, afraid the cat would take control and overrule his decision not to rip the man to pieces in plain sight. "Well, that used to coat him, too. In the visions when I was him, it was a cloak around us." It was why she'd instinctively called him the darkness. "But now it's gone. I can't see into his mind, but I know it's gone."

"Do we move on him, Faith?" Judd asked. "I've only got one shot at this—he's starting to recover and fight back."

She looked at the target again, this man who'd become so much a part of her life but was a stranger. Once more, what chilled her most was his ordinariness. It was too dangerous to try to enter his mind, so she had no idea what had driven him to murder. It was even possible that he'd been the pawn of a greater evil and was now purged, free like her. To order his death might be to kill an innocent.

She found herself frozen and in that instant, she saw the blood that would be spilled if he did not die. The darkness might've been sloughed off, but he remained a nightmare. "Yes. Go."

And that quickly, vengeance was hers.

Three hours later, she found herself sitting inside the alpha pair's aerie surrounded by Sascha and several changelings—Vaughn, Clay, Lucas, and a blond sentinel who'd been introduced to her as Dorian. There was something angry in Dorian's blue eyes when he looked at her, a cold rage she couldn't understand, not when he hadn't participated in the hunt. A changeling word. A changeling punishment. Delivered by a Psy mind. That Psy had disappeared afterward and she was glad. She owed him for what he'd done, but Judd had a tendency to push Vaughn the wrong way.

Everyone else was considering how to keep her safe, but she was thinking about that morning's events. She'd ordered the destruction of a mind, a decision that should've filled her with guilt. But though she felt sorrow, she also felt a sense of rightness. Marine could now rest in peace, safe in the knowledge that no other woman would die at the hands of the darkness.

Vaughn walked over from where he'd been standing talking to Clay. "Up."

"What?"

Scowling, he simply lifted her up off the large cushion on which she sat and settled back down with her in his lap. She curled into his warmth, conscious of the others sitting or standing mere steps away, but not caring. Cats lived by different rules and she was adapting.

"Sometimes," Vaughn said, "blood has to be spilled."

She could still hear the raw anger in his voice and it worried her. "But I can't not think about it. That would make me a monster, too."

He just held her as she made her peace with what she'd done. Some time later, she was about to join in the conversation going on around her when she felt a prod at her mind. Instead of reacting with a defensive strike, her ability took over and opened a telepathic channel.

Hundreds of images of flowers waterfalled through that narrow band.

"Oh." Faith's hand clenched on Vaughn's upper arm.

Her cat was instantly on the alert. "What is it?"

"Shh." She closed her eyes and tried to figure out a way to send her reply without affecting the others, but couldn't. "Everyone who can receive Tp thoughts, ignore this." Then she shot back a single flower, layering it with sheer joy and excitement.

A complicated set of images answered her.

Deciphering the message, she endeavored to tune her mind to the right frequency, one so unusual, she knew no other sentience that used it. "Sascha, can you see this?" She sent out a test image.

"No."

But the NetMind had seen. It sent her another flower. Smiling at having worked out how to broadcast to it without telling everyone her thoughts, she considered the best way to ask her next question.

An image of the PsyNet, with a bridge connecting it to her.

The image came back devoid of the bridge.

Frowning, she sent confusion.

The PsyNet. Her. A night sky–colored glow passing from one to the other.

"Of course. You don't need a bridge," she whispered. "Because this is what you were born to do." Trusting her instincts and putting more than her own life on the line, she showed it a snapshot of the Web of Stars.

What came back made her gasp aloud.

She understood. She told it so. It gave her back sunshine. Happiness. But then it followed with rain. Sadness. Images of the PsyNet with rivers of unrelieved darkness running through it, places where it could not go. In the darkness, she saw nothing alive. Death ruled.

She sent it a teardrop to wash the darkness away.

In response, it sent her images that made no sense . . . until she realized they were the memories of a child, but one who was more ancient than she could imagine—pictures of the PsyNet as it once was, rainbow-hued and alive. Then it showed her something else, something that stunned her into silence.

Barely able to think, she answered its good-bye sunshine with a flower, and opened her eyes. Vaughn was holding her, but he was relaxed.

"I felt something touch you." He frowned. "It wasn't bad. Like a cub isn't bad. But different."

"The NetMind." Her answer set off a cacophony of questions from the others.

"How—?"

"—a leak?"

"—Council?"

"Is it—?"

"Quiet!" Vaughn cut them off with a roar. "Go on, Red."

She laughed and, to everyone's surprise, kissed him on the lips. "I love you."

His growl vibrated along her nerve endings, the most intimate of caresses. "Hell of a time to tell me."

The tension diffused from everyone but her jaguar—she felt his continuing anger through the direct connection of the mating bond. She wanted to soothe, to stroke, but for that she needed privacy and right now, the others were waiting for her to speak. "I'm assuming everyone here knows about the NetMind?"

"I tried to explain it," Sascha said, "but I think you're the expert. You speak to it in images?"

"Yes. It looks like we've managed to work out a number of pictures that translate as the same every time—sunshine is happiness, rain is sadness."

"It feels?" Sascha whispered.

"Yes." And that signaled a precious hope.

"How can it contact you if you're not in the Net?" Lucas asked from his position against the window ledge.

"It's a sentience that finds it natural to live in networks of minds," she said, bursting to share what she'd learned. "If there is a network, it can travel to that place."

"The Web of Stars." Sascha walked to stand in her mate's embrace, back to his chest. "I've never felt it there."

"I'm saying this wrong." Faith tried to order her thoughts. "It won't come into a different network, perhaps not unless it's invited—I think I did that by thinking of it after I dropped out of the PsyNet—because each network has its own NetMind."

Everyone went completely silent.

"It seems as if each time a network—a web—forms, it sows the seeds for the creation of a new sentience. The Net-Mind in the Web of Stars is a baby, a mere thought. Do you know of any other webs?"

Lucas narrowed his eyes. "Tell us what you saw first."

Able to read changeling aggression to some extent, she knew it wasn't a display of distrust, but an unwillingness to color her perception. Her Psy mind appreciated that. "I saw several small networks, but it showed me one other in particular made up of five Psy minds. And if our NetMind is a baby, theirs hasn't even been born."

"Christ. It's the Laurens." Lucas's statement shook her—she hadn't known that Judd was part of a group. A family. And yet he'd chanced helping her. "Does this make us vulnerable to the Psy?"

"No. The NetMind is no longer bound by the Council, though they don't know it."

"What? How?" Sascha tugged her plait from Lucas. He just lifted it back up and dropped a kiss on the curve of her neck.

Faith watched Sascha melt and understood. These predators were impossible to resist when they played nice. "In our terms, it's a teenager now," she answered. "It can think beyond what it's been told, understand the bigger picture." Sadness flowed into her. Vaughn's nuzzled kiss was a welcome burst of sensation, of hope. "It showed me evil in the Net, badness that's infecting everything. If that evil isn't stopped, it'll kill the Net itself."

"A rot." Sascha voice went heavy with sorrow that sank into every person in the room.

The sentinel named Dorian walked over to pull her into his arms. Lucas allowed the embrace though Faith had expected him to react with possessive violence. Another facet of her new family, one that would take time to become accustomed to. Such open affection was disconcerting to a mind fresh out of Silent bondage.

"Anything else?" Clay asked.

She nodded. "I think the killer was possessed." Everyone looked at her in blatant disbelief. "Maybe I should think about it a bit more."

Vaughn kissed her forehead. "Possessed, Red?"

"Do you think the mental degradation's taken root?" It was an attempt to make a joke out of her greatest fear. She might have cut free from the Net, but she was still an F-Psy, her mind more fragile than others.

"I think you're beautiful for a crazy woman." His hungry

kiss brought the lightning to life, but when they separated, the others' expressions hadn't changed.

"The NetMind showed me something the first time we spoke." She explained the images. "I think the starry woman represents the good side and the one empty of stars, the bad."

"What about the Web of Stars?" Sascha asked from within Dorian's embrace.

Faith wriggled to a more upright position. "It's a single entity. Same with the LaurenNet."

Vaughn wrapped his arms around her neck and pulled her back against his chest. The wall of fire was a sweet benediction. "So what makes the Psy NetMind different?"

"Emotion." Sascha's eyes had gone pure black.

Lucas reached out to tug at her plait and Dorian released her to her mate. "Talk to me, Sascha darling." He ran his finger down her cheek.

"The Psy have cut off emotion, tried to suppress it into nonexistence. So if the NetMinds are created when a net is created, then the basic material is provided by the net in question."

Faith saw where Sascha was going. "Our Web is fed by everything—love, hate, fear, joy."

"So is the Laurens', probably because of the children." Sascha tangled her fingers with Lucas's. "The PsyNet, however, is fed mostly by emotionless Silence."

"But the NetMind is good. It feels joy." She was convinced of that.

"Yes, but the aim of Silence was to wipe out violence. The core of the conditioning says that any kind of darkness is bad. It must be contained, caged, kept *separate* from everything else."

"And that's become amplified in the twin NetMinds." Faith suddenly understood what the empath had seen at once. "A DarkMind for everything negative while the NetMind is pure goodness. It's so vulnerable."

"I'm not so sure about that," Sascha said. "If it's aware of the DarkMind, then perhaps it's aware of everything its other half knows. You did say it's fooled the Council."

"Yes." Some of Faith's concern faded. "But even if the twins function as a team, their separation has to have a consequence."

Sascha's eyes met hers and there was such grief in them. "Until the DarkMind and the NetMind are merged again, the Psy will continue to produce the most vicious serial killers on the planet."

"Killers without an ounce of mercy." Faith thought about what she'd seen. "The DarkMind is using them to give itself a voice. Maybe it can't speak like the NetMind can, because it's been Silenced, but it can communicate with its acts of violence."

"A child screaming its existence." Sascha's words gave emotional force to the cold facts.

The image chilled Faith. So much death, so much rage, all because of a child's need for acceptance. "Until Silence ends, the only thing we can do is try to stop the manifestations of darkness."

"Killers." Vaughn's beast prowled in the energy of his skin.

"Yes."

"Why does it speak to you?" Sascha asked, after a small silence.

"Maybe because I speak to it and I'm a Psy who has emotion. I think it needs that contact, needs to know that such Psy are possible."

Sascha's sadness softened into hope. "Can I speak to it, do you think?"

"It adores what you are." Faith felt her own lips tilt upward in the faintest of smiles. "I think I might even be jealous."

"Why?"

"How do you think you escaped detection in the Net as

a child, before you were old enough to hide your rainbow mind?"

"The difference didn't appear until I was a teenager."

"No, Sascha. It was always there. Think about it—our basic abilities are something we're born with." Faith shook her head. "It showed me a thousand hidden minds exactly like yours, protected by something other than their own shields."

The look on Sascha's face was priceless. "The NetMind knows about us?"

Us. The E-Psy. The designation Faith had barely begun to understand because they'd been slated for deletion from the Net. But they'd survived. Because, Faith now comprehended, they *had* to exist. If they didn't, the Psy would cease to be human, cease to be sentient. All sentient races had a conscience. Take that away and what you were left with was something horrifying.

"Yes. It's been protecting you for decades, ever since it started to understand what Silence was doing to you. Maybe that's when it started to think on its own. I don't know. All I know is that we're dealing with a life form that has a heart and that heart is made up of a thousand E-Psy. The NetMind will never be evil so long as those minds exist. In contrast, its twin will be absolute evil."

"Your NetMind might be good, but it's not the only one who knows where you are," Clay reminded them.

The conversation turned once again to the question of how to protect her from the Council. Someone brought up a recording—one that apparently showed the confession of a Psy killer.

Clay shook his head. "We play that card, we have to be prepared for war."

"None of our reasons for not going public with it have changed," Lucas added. "Let's save it for a last-case scenario. Vaughn?"

Vaughn grunted and it was agreement.

"They won't stop hunting her." Dorian spoke for the first time, his voice so coldly angry that she wanted to hide from it. "Murder is what they're good at."

"Anybody dares touch her, I'll eviscerate them." Vaughn's words held the calm confidence of a beast that knew it was the most dangerous of predators.

"Well, there is that," Sascha said. "If she keeps her mind heavily shielded, they'll have to get close to attack her. DarkRiver can take care of them before they reach her."

"How long can I live like that?" Faith shook her head, frustrated that her earlier knowing had faded into mist. "There must be some way to keep them from making an example out of me."

Vaughn's hand was on her nape, a possessive grasp. "They'll never get that close, Red."

She believed him.

"We have a walk-through at the site with Nikita tomorrow," Lucas said into the pensive silence. "Let's see if they're open to a deal—Faith's too valuable for them to do something stupid and risk getting her killed."

The meeting ended soon afterward.

Vaughn had driven to the meeting as far as he was able, then run the rest of the way with Faith riding his back. But as their feet touched the ground after leaving the aerie, she asked to be put down.

"Let's walk awhile." Her eyes were more black than he was used to.

"I'm at your command, Red." Taking her hand, he led her through the trees until they hit a pathway almost completely hidden from sight.

"What do you see?" she asked him. "I could have never located this path."

So he showed her the marks, the clawed parts of certain

trees, the subtle positioning of rocks that appeared randomly strewn. "It's a code, a way of speaking to each other that doesn't rely on words or on telepathy. We can read these signs in either human or cat form."

She traced a pair of claw lines with utter gentleness. "A language the Psy don't even know exists."

"My Psy does."

She let him lead her deeper into the forest. "Lucas is right; if the Council comes for me, it won't be to kill me."

"You're worth too much alive." His gut burned. She was so much more than a moneymaking machine. She was a woman of spirit and courage with a gift that had the power to change the course of the future itself.

"I didn't say anything to the others, but I don't think Nikita is going to agree to a deal. There's nothing to deal with. We don't have proof that Marine's murder was a setup."

"Like Lucas said, it's a last-case scenario, but we do have Enrique's confession on record." He told her about the former Councilor's crimes and his punishment. Vaughn had been there that night, had taken vengeance on Lucas's behalf because his alpha had been locked in an attempt to save his mate's life. "He gave us everything." Before they'd ripped him into a thousand bloody shreds.

Face pale, Faith squeezed his arm with her free hand. "You agreed with them that you couldn't use that."

"We won't. Not unless we have no other choice."

"No, Vaughn! Not ever. If you back the Council into a corner, they *will* come at you with everything they've got. And they'll kill your most vulnerable, the children, first."

His vows as a sentinel slammed up against his unspoken vows to her. "You're my mate." A loyalty that overshadowed any other.

"That's why I'm asking you to never use that recording on my behalf." Stopping, she looked up into his eyes. "I need to know that I didn't bring death into this new family. I need to know I'm something good."

"You're everything good." He enfolded her in his arms. "Don't worry. We have the capacity to take them on—we had to devise a countermeasure after Sascha's defection. The cubs will be safe." Exposing them to danger had never been a possibility.

"But how many adults will die in the fight?"

"You're Pack." And Pack stood together. He'd bled for them and they'd do the same for him.

"I can't have their blood on my conscience." She hugged him hard. "Promise me you'll never use that recording in a fight for me. Not even as a last-case scenario."

"And if I don't?"

CHAPTER 25

"Then I'll turn myself in to the Council." An intractable expression clouded her face. "I'll do it the first chance I get."

He knew she was stubborn enough to go through with the decision. "You've left me no choice." And the beast was angry at that, at her. But what enraged him most was having his hands tied. Judd had taken out the killer. Lucas and Sascha were meeting Nikita. He could do seemingly nothing to protect the one person he *needed* to protect. "Get on." He didn't want to speak any longer.

Faith didn't argue, letting him hoist her onto his back and then holding on as he raced through the forest, an animal on two legs, a jaguar caught tight in the grip of a trap that had no acceptable way out. Tonight he saw nothing of the beauty around him, felt no exhilaration, no joy. He was furious at everything and everyone. The Fates, the Psy who was his mate, and mostly, himself.

Ignoring the waves of tenderness coming down the mating bond, he poured himself into the forest and let the beast take over. Though he remained human in shape, his mind, his heart, his soul became jaguar. And the cat didn't allow human foolishness to color its thinking. It just was.

Vaughn didn't know how long he ran in that semishift state, but they were close to the car when his keen hearing picked up something very odd. He came to a complete stop. Faith clutched at him and he knew she was about to speak.

"Shh." He kept the sound extremely low.

But she'd heard. The second he released his grip on her legs, she slid down with utter quietness, allowing him to ease her down using his strength. Once there, she remained motionless. He scanned the surrounding area with his animal senses and felt every one of his instincts flare in warning.

Glancing over Faith's head, he looked back the way they'd come. The perfect tree stood almost directly in his line of sight. He turned his back to her and she jumped on. Moving with the catlike silence that was second nature to him, he retraced his steps to the large sequoia and began to climb, using his claws to dig into the wood. Faith held on tight and didn't say a word as he went ever higher. He was proud of her.

When he spotted what he was looking for, he shifted position so she could get off and sit down in the hiding place formed by the intersection of several branches. Only then did she whisper, "What did you hear?"

He made sure she'd be invisible from the ground. "Something that doesn't belong." Leaning in, he kissed her. His way. Hard, savage, and raw. "Don't leave this tree until I or one of the pack return for you. And don't try to telepath Sascha or use any other Psy sense."

The stars in her eyes were blotted out by blackness in an eyeblink. "They've come for me."

"Nobody will touch you." That wasn't even an option. "Do exactly what I told you. They might be able to track you if you try anything Psy." He wasn't Psy, but he was a soldier—he knew about strategy and drawing out a target.

"Let me help," she whispered.

"I'll tell you if I need you." He watched understanding spread across her face. The mating bond wasn't Psy, therefore the others wouldn't be able to intercept it.

"Be safe and come back to me."

He had every intention of doing that, but first, he had to get rid of some vermin. Going back down the tree took almost no time. He touched the ground with silent feet and started to determine and categorize what his senses were telling him. There was definitely more than one Psy out there.

That they'd gotten this far into DarkRiver territory without alerting anyone told him they were good. Very good. Vaughn had no intention of underestimating their skills. He also knew he had to get them before they realized he was hunting. Otherwise, they'd smash his mind with a blast of pure power.

Stripping off the jeans, he cached them a small way up the tree and went jaguar. The Psy might be good, but this was Vaughn's territory and in this territory, his paws were silent, his senses even keener, his savagery unparalleled. These Psy had broken the first rule when they'd come into an area off-limits to anyone but cats and wolves. They'd broken the second by lying in ambush for his mate.

The first was a mistake. The second, unforgivable.

Vaughn walked a ways on the ground before taking to the trees. His sense of smell was not as strong as his sight, but it was far better than an ordinary human's, sufficient to tell him that there was a Psy to the left of his position and within meters. He padded along a branch until he was directly on top of the male. Dressed in black, his face camouflaged with paint, the Psy lay flat on the ground, one eye pressed to the scope of what looked like a Series III Ramrod.

An illegal rifle meant for hunting big cats.

Vaughn didn't give the Psy any warning. He couldn't be allowed to send a telepathic signal to his team members, though the communications link clipped to his ear probably indicated they were maintaining mind-silence. *They didn't want to tip off Faith.* In that case, they were likely not scanning the area telepathically either, relying on their physical senses alone. Mistake number three—never go into a predator's territory thinking to beat him at his own game.

Slamming down on the male's back, Vaughn crushed his skull between powerful jaws before the Psy ever knew he'd been marked as prey. He'd broken the would-be assassin's back, and in all likelihood killed him, with the jump, but no one could rise after his brain had been caved in as this Psy's was.

One down.

Pain shot through the mating bond. He froze. Faith had experienced his kill. It had disturbed her. He waited to see what she'd do. And realized the pain was for him—for having to do this for her. The jaguar had no time for such foolishness. Of course he'd do this for her—she was his mate.

He took to the trees again, knowing she was with him now. That was good. She should see the other side of his nature, know that he wasn't human, wasn't civilized. Then he silenced that thinking part and became the predator again. West of the first Psy, he found the second. This one had a small gun in his hand. Not a weapon meant to kill, but to subdue. For Faith.

This Psy was more wary, scrutinizing the area around him with the trained eyes of a scout, looking up into the trees with every sweep. He knew what hunted him. But jaguars were patient—Vaughn simply waited until the male was scanning a different section, then dispatched him with the same efficient technique he'd used on the first male.

Two down.

The third was northwest of the second Psy. He saw their tactic at once. A half circle with his vehicle as the center point. Likely six armed Psy mercenaries. Now two were dead and the positions of the other four had become obvious. Mistake number four. He'd never have placed his men in such a predictable pattern. But, of course, the Psy thought of changelings as animals too stupid to reason.

Mistake number five.

Assassin number three was gone in a minute. Four followed. Five actually saw Vaughn coming and fired off a shot, but that was as far as he got. However, he'd warned number six. Instead of launching a psychic attack, the last Psy took off, zigzagging through the forest on an evasive path that would've eluded most humans. Unfortunately for him, Vaughn wasn't human. He could've let the Psy think he was getting away, could've tortured him by playing with him, but that wasn't who he was.

He stayed in the shadows as he ran down the sixth assassin, knowing the Psy couldn't attack him if he didn't know where he was. Changeling minds were tough. Psy had to aim and focus to destroy them—a diffuse hit would never penetrate his natural shields. In the end, taking the man out was almost an anticlimax. The Psy had no idea what hit him. One second he was running, the next he was dead.

The jaguar flipped him over onto his back and Vaughn shifted into human form to search the body for evidence of further plans. He found something in the left pants pocket. A small, flat, closed pad that he immediately identified as a long-distance remote. Flipping it open, he checked the computronic readout.

The car was rigged to blow.

If they hadn't been able to capture Faith, they'd had orders to destroy her. He growled. It was a good thing these men were already dead. Shifting again, he took the pad in his mouth and ran back to Faith. There was blood on his fur, which would translate to his skin when he changed forms. That couldn't be helped. But he was human and dressed in his jeans by the time he came to her.

"Are you alright?" Her eyes flicked over every inch of him. "You're bleeding!"

"It's not mine." He watched her expression for signs of disgust.

Instead, it was only relief that showed. "I got the sense that one of them got off a blast."

"He missed. Come on." He brought her down from the tree.

Her face remained white, strain lines at the corners of her mouth. "You had to kill for me."

"It's what mates do." He kissed her for several long minutes, grounding his beast in the feminine scent of her. By the time he drew away to pull the pad from his pocket, there was a healthy flush to her cheeks. "See this?"

She took the pad. "It looks like a remote of some kind." She placed it in the center of her palm, her curiosity apparently cutting through the residual shock. "Exceptionally compact and nothing that's on the market at this time. I'd say it's a prototype from Exogenesis Labs—they had me do some work last year."

"It's to blow up the car."

Her head jerked up. "They wanted you dead."

Suddenly, he knew she was right. Faith was too important to kill. "*Wanted* is the operative word. I assumed you could talk to Sascha—can you?"

"I'm not sure about 'pathing, but if the Web works the same way as the Net, I can try to do it that way."

"Tell her to give Lucas a message: We need a cleanup crew. Five cats to our location."

"How will they know where to come?"

"They know the general area where I left the car and they'll track us the rest of the way by smell."

Nodding, she closed her eyes. "Okay, I'm trying a telepathic page. She's not that far and I know her . . . there you go. She's receiving me." Silence for a few beats. "Lucas says they're on their way. One extra man to take me back to the aerie."

"Fine."

She opened her eyes. "Why do I have to go back?" Stubborn, her forehead furrowed with lines.

"Because you can't drag one of these bodies where it needs to go."

She swallowed but didn't admit defeat. "And where would that be?"

"Nikita Duncan has the bad luck to live closest to us."

"I see." She looked at her feet and then back up at him. "You felt no guilt at killing those men."

He waited, able to see her working something out in her head. Though he'd never admit it aloud, he was a little worried. She'd seen him at his most brutal. Now he waited for her reaction.

"And yet, it was clean. You didn't taunt them and you didn't get pleasure from it."

"I will when I take down animal prey." He wasn't going to lie.

"I think I can deal with that because it's natural." Ignoring the blood, she wrapped her arms around his waist, her fingers delicate points of heat where they brushed his skin. "I won't say I wasn't shocked by the way you dispatched the assassins so quickly, but I wasn't repulsed or horrified. This is who you are. And I love you."

The simple declaration brought him figuratively to his knees. Enclosing her in his arms, he let the tension seep out of him. This was who he was. And she loved him. It was all he'd ever wanted.

Faith followed Dorian along the path back to the alpha pair's lair, glancing over her shoulder to try to catch a last glimpse of Vaughn. But he was already gone, a blur in the forest. Five leopards and one jaguar. So much power. So much fury. For her.

"I could run with you," Dorian offered after ten minutes. "I'm latent, but I have the strength of a changeling."

"I'm sorry." Faith made her tone very polite, conscious that Dorian didn't like her. "I don't know what latent means in your world."

"I can't shift into leopard form." Said without any hint of self-pity.

She looked at him. With his sky-blue eyes and blond hair, he looked more like a college student than the merciless predator he was. "Thank you, but no. I'm not comfortable being that close to anyone but Vaughn."

He nodded and they kept going. She thought over his words, wondered if that was why he had such anger in his eyes. But that anger was directed at her and she'd had nothing to do with his latency. After almost half an hour of silence, she decided that the only way to know was to ask. He was family now.

"Why don't you like me?"

He didn't answer for several long minutes. "I don't know you, so I have no reason to dislike you as a person."

It didn't take her long. "My ability. That's it, isn't it? You think I could've prevented something."

"Not you. Foreseers as a whole."

"You're right. Maybe we could have." That they hadn't, was a tragedy. "But I don't think foreseers ever saw everything. If they had, then nobody would've ever been murdered, no great disaster would've ever killed millions." It was something she'd been thinking over. "So maybe we could've prevented whatever it was that happened to you, but maybe we couldn't."

"At least you could've tried if you'd been on the outside."

"Yes." That was an irrefutable truth. "Yes."

He didn't say another word for five more minutes. She

spent the time thinking over her own statement. It was what she believed, but it was also a guess. She didn't know what past F-Psy had seen. Those records had been purged from the PsyNet, lost in the mysteries of time.

The knowing, when it came, was quiet, silent, like the male beside her. *Dorian.* Broken, shattered Dorian would one day be whole. And in a way not even he could imagine. She saw him clearly in her mind's eye, a beautiful leopard with dark facial markings and, in this form, eyes more green than blue.

The knowing drifted away and she wondered whether to share it with him. It hadn't been a true vision as such, had told her no specifics. But he'd been older. Not old, but at least two or three years older than he was now. What if she told him and then the future changed because of some act of his or another's? A false hope. She made the hard decision to keep the knowing to herself. Sometimes, Silence was the right choice. It was only when it wasn't a choice that it turned into a cage.

"I heard you lost your sister."

She'd gotten so used to his quietness that she was surprised into a soft gasp. "Marine. Her name was Marine."

"My sister's name was Kylie."

Their eyes met and she understood. He'd try to forgive her for being what she was, if she'd try to never let another sister die. "Yes."

Vaughn returned to Faith about three hours before dawn. From the coffee on the table and the alert expressions on their faces, he could see that neither she nor Sascha had slept. When he appeared, Faith stood and came to him. Nobody said a word as he took her hand and they exited the lair for the second time that night, leaving Lucas with his mate.

They covered the distance to the car in silence. It had been cleaned of explosives by Dorian, but Vaughn did another check before opening the passenger door for Faith. The cat continued to monitor the area for threats—he wouldn't breathe easy until they were back in his personal territory.

The drive took almost another hour, but neither of them was in any mood for sleep at the end of it. Faith didn't ask any questions, didn't demand any answers, just watched as he showered, then stripped and joined him under the flow of water. He felt her worry.

"It was done without any problems," he told her. "They never knew we were there."

"Nikita Duncan's residence?"

"And a few others connected to the Council at the highest levels." He'd had to fight the urge to go in and crush some more Psy skulls when he'd made his delivery.

"I could feel that you weren't hurt or in danger."

"Good." He wanted her to get used to the bond, had no problem with her utilizing it to see if he was okay. That's what mates did. He couldn't see the bond as she did, but he could feel it in a way that had no explanation—if she were ever hurt or in trouble, he'd know.

She went quiet again. He walked them out of the shower and dried them both. When he carried her to the bed, she didn't protest. And when he claimed her in the most physical way, she gave him her surrender. Afterward, they lay intertwined, watching dawn infiltrate the room on slender beams of light.

Faith moved to rest with her cheek against his chest, her hand over his heart. And then she cried. He stroked her hair and her back, not knowing how else to comfort her. But what he did know was that these hot, wet raindrops had nothing to do with him. He enclosed her in his arms and the jaguar spoke to her in rough, wordless murmurs.

Several long minutes later, she took a shuddering breath. "They came after me as if I were an animal to be tracked down and bagged."

He clenched his fist in her hair, but didn't interrupt.

"I thought—perhaps my father—of course not, he's Psy. He wanted his investment back. It didn't matter to him to find out the choices I'd made, that killing you would kill me, too."

"I'm not that easy to take out, Red."

"It's stupid, but I feel betrayed by Father, though he was never truly a father to me. How could he have allowed them to come after me like that?"

Vaughn had no answers to soothe that hurt. So he just held her, held her and told her that her worth to him was beyond any price. After a while, she slept. Secure in his home, a home no Psy could enter without setting off a hundred booby traps, he, too, went into the twilight.

Faith woke at nine. Her body didn't want to sleep in, despite having been deprived of rest. Her cat, on the other hand, complained when she moved and told her to lie still. Able to smile this morning, though the smile was a little fragile, she settled back against him, listened to the sound of the waterfall, and took in the sunlight pouring in through the ingenuity of Vaughn's vent designs.

The light swept through carefully placed pieces of colored glass to lay mosaic patterns on the carpets. Her Psy mind found them intricately beautiful. So organized but different with every minute, changing as the light changed. She was admiring them from the bed when the wall-mounted communication console chimed. Knowing there was no way Vaughn was going to budge, she wiggled out from under his arm and walked over to answer it. They really had to get something for the bedside, she thought, answering with audio only.

The voice that returned her greeting was so unexpected, she didn't reply for ten complete seconds. In those ten seconds, Vaughn was fully awake and by her side. She let him make the rest of the decisions. Because for her, the person on the other side of the communications hookup was akin to a ghost.

CHAPTER 26

Less than four hours later, Faith walked into a meeting room at DarkRiver's business headquarters, Vaughn by her side. Located near the bustle of Chinatown, the building was both central and heavily protected, not only by changeling strength but also by the human ability to blend in—thus hearing things most Psy thought secret. In turn, the people of the area looked to DarkRiver for reciprocal protection against gangs.

However, Faith's mind wasn't on security right then. She was, in fact, incapable of any rational thought. But she reacted almost automatically, years of training kicking in. "Hello, Father."

Anthony NightStar rose to his feet, but didn't approach her. "Hello, Faith."

Faith didn't know what to feel. She'd readied herself for being cut off from the Psy, contact with her forbidden under Council mandate.

Anthony's eyes flicked to Vaughn's silent presence. "Privacy may be in order."

She felt Vaughn bristle, but he let her answer for herself. "Vaughn is my mate. He's welcome to my secrets."

Anthony didn't press the issue, which wasn't surprising. Her father was an eminently logical man and had quickly understood that this issue was nonnegotiable. "Then let's talk."

She took a seat across the table from him and put a hand on Vaughn's arm in unspoken request. He acquiesced, sitting down to her right instead of standing like a jaguar just waiting for an excuse to pounce.

"Your defection has affected every aspect of the Psy-Clan."

"I know." Her choice had been the right one, but the far-reaching consequences continued to haunt her. "How much did the clan lose?" How many jobs had been affected? How many lives?

"Not as much as we would have had we not taken pre-emptive action."

She frowned and saw Anthony's eyes focus on the betraying gesture. "I thought Juniper wasn't yet forecasting with high accuracy."

Anthony shook his head. "She isn't. She's eight years old and nowhere near as skilled as you were at the same age."

Vaughn spoke for the first time. "She's a child. Let her be one."

"Our worlds are different, Mr. D'Angelo," Anthony responded, though he hadn't been told Vaughn's last name. "To let Juniper be a child as you suggest would leave her abilities untrained and unshielded, open to exploitation." He raised a hand to forestall comment. "Yes, the PsyClan will use her talents as we used Faith's, but we'll also undertake to ensure her welfare. In the past, before the PsyClans came into being, some F-Psy were kept captive by others of all races for personal gain."

"Father," Faith interrupted, "if not Juniper, then who?"

"You."

Vaughn's entire body went hunting-quiet beside her. She was glad. She knew the power of the PsyClan and exactly how far it would go to get its way.

"She's no longer yours." A human voice but a jaguar's lethal challenge.

"No. But her ability exists whether she's in the Net or not." Anthony didn't flinch. "She can be subcontracted to do the work for NightStar."

Faith had to catch her mouth from falling open. "But the Council—surely they've prohibited contact with me?"

"They tried." Anthony moved his attention from Vaughn to her. "However, NightStar is no Council puppet."

Vaughn leaned forward. "You told them to stick their prohibition where the sun don't shine." A faint note of respect had entered his tone.

"Crude, but correct. They are our Council, not our absolute rulers. And the pursuit of commerce is inviolate. Cutting off access to Faith would've affected thousands of businesses and none of those businesses was going to sit by and let that happen."

Faith's mind was spinning. "You want me to provide forecasts for NightStar's clients, with you as the go-between?"

"Yes. The PsyClan can afford to be seen working openly with you. The combined power of the businesses backing us, added to our strength as a family group, protects us from the Council."

That made sense. NightStar's history of producing F-Psy had earned it many allies. It knew a lot of secrets. And it never told. No matter who asked.

"The Council's already tried to kidnap me once." She would not ask the question that tormented her. *Had her father known?*

"That's been taken care of. In more ways than one. I have my doubts about their operatives ever being able to reach you"—he glanced at Vaughn, then back at her—"but if they do and anything happens to you, every business with an unfulfilled forecast will stop its tax payments."

"How many?" Vaughn asked, when she remained silent.

"Faith's waiting list currently exceeds a thousand. The Council's reach is vast, but even it can't police that many renegades, especially when they include most of our major corporations. Like I said, business is inviolate."

"How sure are you of that?" Vaughn pushed.

"If the Council harms her—as she will inevitably be harmed in any attempt to capture her—it'll be seen as a violation of the basic law that rules our race: no interference with family groups or business. That will not be tolerated. All the Councilors have been informed of that by the corporations associated with their own family groups."

"You won't stop the Council from 'rehabilitating' your own, but you'll draw the line at business interference?" Vaughn shook his head. "Hell of a list of priorities."

"But good for Faith in this case."

"I'm forecasting different things now," she said quietly.

Anthony nodded. "Understood. We're asking you to provide regular business ones as well, unless you can't access those abilities any longer."

"So the rich can prosper?" Vaughn asked, but she didn't hear any animosity. It was almost as if he were trying to get a feel for her father as he would another animal.

"You're a predator, Mr. D'Angelo, at the top of the food chain. In the business world, the same rules apply."

"Survival of the fittest." Vaughn turned and ran his hand down her hair in a public caress that was as tender as it was possessive. "So, Red, what's the verdict?"

"I can provide the forecasts without problem, but I need time to think," she said past the lump in her throat. How could he do this to her without even trying? "But one thing I do know is that if I do this, I expect far more by way of profits than I was previously getting." She was happy to be in a situation where she could strengthen the financial position of her new family. Money was power the Psy understood.

But she also wanted the money for a far more subversive plan. Barely an inkling at present, it was an idea that could change the Psy from within. An idea that might save those like her cousin Sahara, people who'd disappeared into the mystery of the Net, but might still be alive. Caged. Brutalized for their abilities.

"You are my daughter. I expected nothing less." If Anthony hadn't been Psy, she'd have said he was proud.

"And if Faith accepts, she won't be going anywhere," Vaughn added. "All attempts at visions will be undertaken in DarkRiver territory."

"No records, no monitors." She was through with being violated.

"Your safety?"

Vaughn leaned forward. "Leave that to me."

Anthony took a moment to consider that before nodding. "Take care of her. She's invaluable."

"Actually, to the PsyClan and to you, my worth is quantifiable." Faith smiled, but it was colored by sadness not joy. Then Vaughn's hand slipped under her hair to curve over her neck and the heavy warmth was a reassurance that to someone at least, she truly was invaluable.

"Not as my daughter."

She was disappointed. "Father, don't try such psychological tricks on me—they are beneath you. If you cared that much about your children, you would've hunted down Marine's killer and you would've learned the name of your Caribbean son."

"I don't understand your reference to your sister's murder. She was an unfortunate victim of the human and changeling appetite for violence."

Faith saw that he truly had no knowledge of the facts, but

she couldn't speak of that pain. It was too raw, too fresh. Vaughn spoke for her. "It was one of the Psy. Probably one of your Council's pet killers. What we haven't been able to figure out is why she might've been targeted when she was in the inner circle."

"I see." Anthony's voice remained toneless, but what he said next was nothing expected. "As for your other question—his name is Tanique Gray. He turns twenty-two in three months. Though not an F designation as his mother hoped for, he has a Gradient 9 ability in psychometrics, the first Ps-Psy born into our line in centuries.

"I've seen him twice a year since his birth, per the clause I inserted into the reproduction contract. He has your bone structure, but of course, it is Marine whom he favors most."

Faith wanted to believe it was nothing more than a clever ploy to win her heart and make her malleable to his requests, but somehow knew it wasn't. "Why?" Why go against Psy Protocol, against everything he'd ever taught her?

"Loyalty is not guaranteed by birth. You were such a perfect Psy."

And he'd believed she might see his choices as flaws.

Without giving her a chance to answer, he stood. "Never forget that half your genetic material came from me. Perhaps even the part that gave you your conscience."

Picking up the organizer on the table, he turned to business again. "I'll await your decision—try not to take too long. If you're not going to accept, the clan needs to take other measures to forestall further loss, and you need to find another way to keep yourself safe from the Council in the long term."

Faith watched him walk to the door. "Wait!" Getting up, she made her way to him and then, for the first time in her adult life, she touched her father, hugging him quickly. He didn't return the gesture, but neither did he push her away. When she let him go, she searched his face and found the same blank slate she'd always seen. "Don't you want to break free?"

It seemed as if he wouldn't answer, but then he said, "If all the strong ones leave, then the Council will be completely without limits. I am precisely where I need to be."

"To do what?" Vaughn asked from behind her.

Anthony looked over her head to the jaguar who was her life. "That, Mr. D'Angelo, is not something you've earned the right to know." He left without another word, escorted out by Clay, who'd been standing watch outside the door.

"Your father is a very interesting man."

Faith turned. "Why do you say that?"

"Psy are hard to judge, but what I can say is that your father doesn't give off the stink most Psy do."

"Me?"

"You smell like my kind of sugar, Red." He grinned at her blush. "I want to lick you up from head to toe."

"We were talking about my father." She scowled, but there was lightning in her bloodstream.

"Your father doesn't stink. You and Sascha don't either." He scowled. "Come to think of it, neither does that damn Psy."

She didn't have to ask him to clarify. There was only one Psy who seemed to make him react so badly. "And?"

Scowl fading, he ran his fingers down her spine. "I have very little evidence to back it up, but I think the bad scent is a marker of complete immersion in Silence. Those who have some conscience left, some spark, some ability to break conditioning, don't smell."

She thought that over and whispered a single, shocking word, "Rebellion?"

"From within? It wouldn't surprise me—your Council's created the perfect environment for it. History paints them as a strong body, but one that had checks and balances. These days they're crossing line after line. Maybe they've crossed too far for some of their own."

"It'll take a long time even if it is happening." Though the commercial world had stayed its hand in regard to Faith, the Council wasn't something to be taken down without taking down Silence. And as Vaughn had pointed out, there were thousands, millions, who were completely conditioned and would die that way.

"It's a start."

She nodded, feeling hope for her people, her race. "Maybe that was why Marine died. Because she was somehow part of a rebellion and they found out." If that was true, then her sister's death hadn't been senseless. Her life had been lost in a battle no one knew was taking place. And she would honor that.

"I want to do the forecasts. As well as generating income for DarkRiver, it'll let me use skills I've spent a lifetime developing. More importantly, it'll allow me to keep in touch with Father." She looked to see how he was taking the news.

"I'm not going to stop you, Red. You're out of the Net. That's what matters."

"Maybe I can help change things from the outside as Father works on the inside." She believed in Anthony, this father she'd never known. Now she had the time and the opportunity. Without monitors, he might begin to trust her and they could speak about many things, perhaps even whispers of rebellion.

Two weeks later, Faith was glad to be alive and with Vaughn. Glad? That didn't begin to describe her utter and complete joy, her feeling of belonging, her delight in being with him. But . . . "I don't know how to be in this world," she whispered in the sultry darkness of their bed.

He turned to lie on his side, one arm under his head, the other stroking her hip almost absently. "I know, Red." He dropped a kiss on her nose, the gesture bringing a smile to her face. Only with her was he so tender. "I know what it's like to not quite fit. But you're strong. You'll find a way."

She hadn't expected him to say that, to lay the responsibility for her happiness in her own hands. "I've developed the ability to venture out sometimes, but I don't think I can ever live in a populated area."

"Baby, do I look like a city slicker to you?"

Her laugh was startled out of her. "Right. So that isn't going to be a problem?"

"No." The hand on her hip curved over her buttock and slid back.

Her heart kicked against her ribs. "But I want to be able to go into the city for longer periods if necessary. I want to have those shields. I'm working with Sascha and Tamsyn on them." The DarkRiver healer was psychic in a way that neither Psy had ever encountered. She understood the concepts of the Psy, but was not Psy, was utterly changeling, her ability to heal coming from the heart and soul.

Faith was a little intimidated by Tamsyn's strength, but like Sascha, the other woman exuded warmth and kindness. In contrast, Faith knew she appeared cold and standoffish. The leopards didn't offer her the same affection they gave each other, though she'd come to a point where she could bear some touch from others. "I don't know how to be with your pack. I don't think they like me."

"They don't know you," Vaughn said. "Liking comes with knowing. Trust comes with loyalty."

"But you're all so warm. I try, but sometimes . . ."

"Red, the pack puts up with Clay. In comparison, you're a barrel of laughs."

She hit his chest with a closed fist. "Be serious."

"I am. DarkRiver has its loners, its quiet ones. They're liked as much as any other member—I'm living proof. Give them your loyalty, give them your heart, and they'll treasure it."

"Promise?"

"Promise."

She finally slept. Because Vaughn kept his promises.

At that same instant, a door slammed shut in the dark heart of the PsyNet.

"The situation with Faith NightStar needs to be addressed," Shoshanna said the second the Council was pronounced in session.

"We might have been able to pacify the NightStar Group if you hadn't taken unilateral action," Nikita retorted. "Anthony NightStar holds a substantial amount of power and he's decided to obstruct us."

"How certain is that?" Henry asked.

"The man was a Council candidate soon after my ascension." Marshall's statement was news to Nikita, but she had no doubts as to its veracity. "He turned it down, not because he didn't have the strength, but because he preferred running the NightStar Group. Anthony doesn't like bowing down to anyone."

"If he was a candidate, then he's aware of the realities of Council. Surely he can be talked around," Henry insisted.

"No, he can't." Male, cold, cutting, Kaleb Krychek was the newest member of the Council. "The Scotts' move against his daughter without his prior authorization put him into a situation where his power was questioned. He's reasserting it and will continue to do so. We've lost any goodwill we might've had with the NightStar Group."

A silence as everyone considered the implications of that.

Tatiana was the first to speak. "That is indeed unfortunate. NightStar is one of the leading families. As well as the favors they've done us, the income they control with their various alliances gives us a large portion of our tax revenue."

"Is it possible to remove Anthony NightStar from the equation?"

"Not without attracting the unwelcome attention of several other top-tier families." Nikita usually preferred the clean approach, but it would only cause more problems at this point. "I'm sure everyone understands why we don't want any additional scrutiny right now. We've had two recent incidents." First Enrique and then the Gradient 9 telepath who'd escaped his handlers before being found near a college campus in Napa, his mind permanently compromised.

"Would you care to explain yourself, Shoshanna." Marshall's words weren't a question.

"Someone had to make a move. We should've acted against Faith the second she dropped out of the Net. There was no reason to wait."

"There was every reason." Nikita closed her mental file on the NightStar Group. "She was deep in DarkRiver territory when she cut the link. Have you forgotten that piece of Enrique you got on your pillow only months ago?" The leopards and wolves had announced the former Councilor's death by sending flesh and blood souvenirs to the rest of them.

"If they were going to use what they know, they would've done so by now," was Shoshanna's answer.

"Or they could be sitting on it until it provides the biggest impact." Kaleb sounded nothing like a newcomer, the very reason he was Council. "They were right in this case—they had no need to tip their hand. None of us can argue that their point wasn't made."

"They might've taken out six men, but they won't be able to destroy a squadron," Henry responded. "We go in full force, pull her out, and destroy anyone who attempts a retrieval."

"Dental imprinting showed that a single cat executed all

six soldiers." Ming broke his silence. "It was confirmed by three different M-Psy. Only one had fired a weapon. We were unable to check for the use of offensive psychic weapons—their brains were too badly crushed."

CHAPTER 27

"**It seems that** Henry's assertion is incorrect," Kaleb stated. "They could conceivably take out a squadron."

"Faith NightStar isn't worth the loss of so many highly trained men, especially as she's agreed to provide her services through her family group." Ming's glacial mental voice again. "These men are worth millions, both in terms of their training and the work they do for us. Added to the income we'll lose if the businesses implement their tax strike, it's an easy equation."

"We can't allow the changelings to keep getting the better of us." Shoshanna clearly had no intention of conceding defeat. "How does it look if we lose two Psy within months and the most recent was a candidate? The populace is starting to talk."

Kaleb cut into the small pause. "We say she ran when it became clear I had no intention of leaving a rival alive."

"Perfect," Nikita agreed. "F-Psy are known to be mentally weak. A few well-placed rumors will shred her credibility."

"We need to know how the leopards are keeping the two women alive," Tatiana said. "I've heard of no unexplained changeling deaths since Sascha's defection and if she were feeding off them, there would've been at least two by now."

Nikita conceded the other Councilor had a point. "They must have discovered a way to skirt the biofeedback issue."

"I don't think it's that big a problem." Marshall's razor-blade mind. "If they had a foolproof method, we'd have lost more than two."

"I'll put some of our people on it nonetheless," Tatiana said in response. "If we break the connection keeping Sascha and Faith alive, we wipe the issue off the slate."

No one was in opposition.

"Then it's agreed, we don't move on Faith NightStar," Kaleb stated with Tk arrogance, turning against the very Councilor who'd supported his initial nomination. "Any member who moves unilaterally will face eviction from their post."

"You have no right to make that call." Shoshanna's psychic presence was icy with control.

"But we do as a unit. You and Henry appear to be the only ones who disagree; therefore you're in the minority." Marshall, the voice of experience, a Councilor who'd survived many others.

"He's correct." Tatiana. "Faith NightStar cannot be touched."

"I agree." Nikita added her vote.

"Then we have no choice. We concede to the majority." Shoshanna spoke for both Scotts and if there was something a fraction eerie in the way she and her husband moved as one to leave the Council chambers, the Councilors were not close enough to their instinctive core to understand.

"We need to increase security for Councilor Duncan," Kaleb said to the remaining minds.

"There is no need." Nikita had no desire to be seen as weak by any member of this Council. Especially not the newest recruit.

"Then this session is closed."

Several weeks and a hundred new experiences later, Faith found herself sitting in on a meeting at the aerie. As a member of the Web of Stars and Vaughn's mate, she'd gained entrance into a very tightly knit group.

"So, what's next? Nate, you had something." Lucas looked to the oldest sentinel.

"I've got a couple of contenders to take over from me when I step down."

"Which isn't going to be for a while." It was an order from the alpha.

Nate grinned. "Don't worry, I'm not in any hurry. I have a few more years left in me."

"More than a few, darling." Tamsyn blew him a kiss from the cushion beside him.

"But I wanted to put the names forward and see what you thought. The first is Jamie. He's one of the best soldiers we've got and he's proven himself." Nate paused and when no one spoke, he continued, "Then there's Desiree. Girl's got a mind like a razor blade and a tongue as sharp, but she's good and she's loyal."

Something flickered in Faith's consciousness, a quiet limb stretching awake. Curious, she followed it. And when it showed her pain and death, she didn't flinch.

"Any other possibles?" Lucas asked.

"We've got a few who've got some growing to do," Tamsyn muttered. "I swear the juveniles are giving me gray hairs."

"How's Jase?" Dorian asked, and his voice was a distorted rumble in Faith's mind.

"Healed. Until the next . . ." Tamsyn's voice faded.

Faith gripped her cup tighter, attempting to understand what it was that she was seeing. There was pain, things breaking, such terrible loss, but it wasn't yet set in stone, it wasn't yet done. It was a foretelling and it had nothing to do with business. "Seven children are going to die."

Vaughn went motionless as those words left his mate's mouth. He brushed back her hair so he could see her face—eyes closed, lines of concentration carving sharp grooves in creamy skin. "Faith?"

"Seven children. Not cats. Wolves. Seven wolf children." She was in his arms, but her gift had taken her somewhere, some*when* else. "A part of a tunnel is going to collapse. To-night. Or early tomorrow morning."

Everyone was listening. Sascha had already passed Lucas his phone. Vaughn stroked Faith's back, relieved at the pulse of love that came down the mating bond. She was traveling to places he couldn't go, but she knew how to come home. "Where, baby? Which part of the tunnels?"

Her eyes scrunched as if she were squinting to make something out. "There's a painting on the stone of a wolf pup sleeping under a tree. Oh, there's another one creeping up on it through the bushes and a third on the branches."

"Jesus," Clay whispered. "It's the nursery where the lit-tlest ones are."

Vaughn, too, remembered the nursery. When DarkRiver had first infiltrated the SnowDancer den to leave their mes-sage, "Don't hurt us and we won't hurt you," they'd made sure to place their scent near the nursery, to show that they'd been close to the wolves' most vulnerable and done no harm. There was no greater indication of friendly intent.

Vaughn watched Lucas punch in the SnowDancer alpha's code. The conversation was short, but Hawke apparently took the warning seriously. Lucas was hanging up when Faith shook her head and blinked awake.

"You okay, Red?"

"Yes. I'm fine." She pushed her hand up under his T-shirt to lie against his skin. The jaguar was delighted to be her anchor.

Leaning down, he kissed her, bringing her completely home. "No cascade?"

"No. The new shields are working." Her face grew pensive. "Why the wolves? I don't know them."

"We're bonded to the SnowDancers," Vaughn said, realizing he hadn't explained that aspect of the pack to her. "The blood pact was physically completed soon after Sascha joined us, though we were business allies long before that."

"Oh. I—"

Lucas's phone beeped.

The alpha checked the readout and flipped it open. "Hawke?" A pause. "Pups safe?"

Vaughn could hear the other end of the conversation, but waited until Lucas had hung up to tell Faith. "Hawke said they found a huge crack in one of the walls supporting that area, hidden behind some wall hangings. They're shoring it up as we speak." He nuzzled her neck. "He also said thank you for the warning."

"What about the last part?" Lucas raised an eyebrow.

Vaughn growled. "That wolf likes living dangerously."

"What did he say?" Faith asked, intrigued by the smile on Sascha's face. The other Psy looked like she already knew what Hawke might've said.

"Nothing." Vaughn bit lightly at the shell of her ear, the gesture so possessive that she could feel color attempting to fill her skin. It was at times like this that Psy training came in very useful.

"Tell me." She scratched her nails on the skin of his chest. "What did he say?"

"The damn wolf asked if our F-Psy was pretty. And bloody Lucas said yes." He sounded less human with every word. "So Hawke said he'd kiss your pretty mouth in thanks the next time he saw you."

Everyone except Vaughn was grinning. Even Clay had a small smile on his face. After her initial wariness and in spite of the knowing she'd had about him, Faith had discovered she liked the intense sentinel. She'd invited him to dinner a week ago and, much to Vaughn's surprise, he'd come. And he'd touched her. A slight brush of knuckles against her cheek, it had told her she was accepted. Was Pack.

"Well, he can't," Faith said, not hesitant in front of these cats who lived and loved with wild fury. "Because I only want to be kissed by you."

"Yeah?"

"Yeah."

"I think I like the wolf if he makes you say things like that."

Laughing, she let him kiss her, allowing it because Vaughn needed her to allow it. He was more openly possessive and dominant than the other males she'd seen with their mates. But that was fine with her. She could bear being thought of as utterly his.

"I **used** to worry that the dark side of my ability was evil, a materialization of the twinning of the Net," she said to Vaughn as they sat outside near their home. Stars peeked through the thick canopy and the denizens of the forest went about their business, safe in the knowledge that the resident predator was otherwise occupied. "But now I know that though what it shows me can be either good or bad, it in itself isn't evil."

Vaughn, sitting behind her with his arms and legs cradling her, rested his chin on her hair but didn't interrupt. Her cat knew how to listen. It was getting him to talk that was sometimes a problem.

"I haven't come to terms with it completely, but I'm starting to understand what it is I was meant to see, what anyone with my ability is meant to see."

"Your gift, Faith. It's a precious gift."

"Yes." She smiled, liking the word. "What I feel like right now—I'd compare it to waking from a dream and seeing the real world. It's a beautiful place, but it also has darkness. If you try to eradicate that darkness, you also destroy the light." Pain for the future of her people tightened her heart.

"There's hope. Your NetMind is fighting back."

She had to believe that. "And others, too, are starting to wake from the dream." A dream of Silence. "It might take years for the ripples to chase across the Net, but they're there now." Putting her hand on his bare arms, she anchored herself in touch, the very thing that had once threatened to shatter her. "I'm so glad I found you."

His chuckle was a rumble that vibrated in her bones. "Sorry, Red. But I found you first."

"No, you didn't." She scowled—he liked getting his own way far too much. "I walked out into the forest."

"Yeah, but I was waiting for you to walk out." He nuzzled the side of her neck. "I was drawn to your place like an addiction. If you hadn't walked out when you had, I would've come looking."

Her eyes went wide. "Some things can't be changed." It was a thought that might've scared her once.

"What?"

"The future isn't always mutable." And what did that mean? "I've never before considered that. The ramifications are enormous. What is, what isn't changeable—who chooses? What sets some things in stone and others in clay?" Excitement whispered through her. Finally she was in charge of her gift, able to chase things that fired up her imagination.

"Some things are meant to be." Vaughn bit her neck, forcefully bringing her attention back to him. "You were never going to be anyone's but mine."

"You're very possessive." She tilted her head to meet his gaze. "So am I."

The jaguar in his eyes was pleased. "I like your claws."

She stretched to brush her lips over his unshaven jaw. "Do you think you can teach me to purr?"

"Baby, you purr every time I stroke you into orgasm."

Lightning swept over her and everything seemed to become sharper, more in focus. She pushed away and rearranged her body until she straddled him. Face-to-face. It was fast becoming her favorite position, though she did have to bargain with Vaughn for it—her changeling's preferred mode of sex was far more raw. Her flesh heated at the memory of his driving thrusts as she put her hands on his shoulders and leaned in to kiss him. But the expression on his face made her pause. "What?"

"I love watching the lightning in your eyes."

She smiled. It seemed right that her eyes now reflected her mind.

???

"Is it talking to you again?" Vaughn asked, having learned to read the shift in their bond that signaled a visit.

She nodded. "It's curious about you."

"What does it want to know?"

"Everything. It's thirsty for life, for hope, for sunshine." She spread her fingers over his skin. "Like me. Make me purr, Vaughn."

"Inside or outside?"

Her eyes went wide and she looked up at the night sky, a blanket of beauty and darkness, light and shadow, black and white, as it should be. "Here."

"What about your curious friend?" He slid his hands under her shirt.

Sensation skittered along her nerve endings. "It's gone." The NetMind came and went throughout the day, touching her mind as a child would touch its mother's, looking for reassurance that she was still there. It would be back. And it would teach her more about itself, learn more about her and their world.

"Good. I don't like an audience." His hands came up to close over her unfettered breasts. "You're mine to see, to touch, to pleasure." His fingers squeezed her nipples.

She knew she should protest his possessiveness, but the thing was, she liked her jaguar like this in bed. She liked being his. Liked belonging to a male who'd never let her go, never give her up, Council be damned.

Those fingers were driving her mad and when his mouth followed, she fell into insanity. But what sweet insanity it was.

In the Web of Stars, a hundred rainbow sparks crept into Faith's mind without her conscious knowledge. These were the sparks born of an empath, the single functioning empath in the world, the only one who'd escaped the torture of Silence. It was the lack of working empaths in the PsyNet that had sentenced the F-Psy to certain madness. Yes, to be born a foreseer was to be born with a higher chance of madness, but before Silence, it had been a tiny percentage of the minority who succumbed, not the majority.

The Council didn't understand that in its attempt to purge the E designation from the Net, it had also destroyed the F designation and so many others. Because everything was connected. Everything had a purpose.

The PsyNet was no longer fully functional.

But the Web of Stars was. It was different from the PsyNet and always would be. Because this Web had rainbows and sunshine, emotion and heart, predatory hunger and utter loyalty. Now those sparks healed the broken pieces of Faith and she never even knew that she'd been fractured.

Turn the page for a preview of
the next paranormal romance
by Nalini Singh

Caressed by Ice

Now available from
Berkley Sensation!

A fist crashed into Judd's cheekbone. Focused on eliminating his opponent from the field, he barely noticed the impact, his own fist already swinging out. Tai tried to evade the blow at the last second but it was too late—the young wolf's jaw slammed together with a thick sound that spoke of damage on the inside.

But he wasn't down.

Baring teeth stained red from a cut on his top lip, he rushed at Judd, clearly aiming to use his heavier build as a battering ram to smash his adversary into the hard stone wall. Instead it was Tai who ended up with his back slammed against the stone, his mouth falling open as air whooshed out of his lungs in an uncontrollable blast.

Judd gripped the other male by the throat. "Killing you would mean nothing to me," he said, tightening his hold until Tai had to be having trouble breathing. "Would you like to die?" His tone was calm, his breathing modulated. It was a state of being that had nothing to do with feeling, because unlike the changeling across from him, Judd Lauren did not feel.

Tai's lips shaped into a curse but all that materialized was an incomprehensible wheezing sound. To a casual observer it would have seemed that Judd had gained the advantage, but he didn't make the mistake of lowering his guard—so long as Tai hadn't conceded defeat, he remained dangerous. The other male proved that a second later by slicing upward with hands turned to claws.

Those sharp talons cut through leather-synth and flesh without effort but Judd didn't give the boy a chance to cause him any real injury. Pressing down on a very specific pressure point in Tai's neck, he slammed his erstwhile opponent into unconsciousness. Only when the changeling was completely out did he release his hold. Tai slumped down into a seated position, head hanging over his chest.

"You're not supposed to use Psy powers," a husky female voice said from the doorway.

He had no need to turn to identify her but did so anyway. Extraordinary eyes in a fine-boned face topped by a choppily cut cap of blonde hair. Those eyes had been normal and that hair hadn't been short before Brenna had been abducted. By a killer. By a Psy.

"I don't need to use my abilities to deal with little boys."

Brenna walked to stand beside him, her head just reaching his breastbone. He'd never realized how small she was until he'd seen her after the rescue. Lying in that bed, barely breathing, her energy had been contracted into a ball so tight that he hadn't been sure she was still alive. But her size meant nothing. Brenna Shane Kincaid, he had learned, had a will of pure, undiluted iron.

"That's the fourth time this week you've been in a fight." Her hand rose and he had to stop himself from jerking away. Touch was a changeling thing—the wolves indulged in it constantly and without thought. For a Psy it was an alien concept, something that could ultimately foster a dangerous loss of control. But Brenna had been broken by an evil spawned of his own race. If she needed touch, so be it.

Faint imprints of heat on his cheek. "You'll have a bruise. Come on, let me put something on it."

"Why aren't you with Sascha?" Another renegade Psy, but a healer not a killer. Judd was the one who had blood on his hands. "I thought you had a session with her."

Those stroking fingers slid to linger on his jaw before dropping off completely. Her lashes lifted. And revealed the change that had taken hold five days after her rescue. Eyes that had once been dark brown were now a mix he'd never seen on any sentient being, human, changeling, or Psy. Brenna's pupils were pure black but surrounding those dots of night were bursts of arctic blue, vivid and spiking. They jagged out into the dark brown of the iris, giving her eyes a shattered look.

"It's over," she said.

"What is?" He heard Tai moan but ignored it. The boy was no threat—the only reason Judd had allowed him to land any of his punches was because he understood the way wolf society worked. Being beaten in a fight was bad, but not as bad as being beaten without putting up a solid resistance.

Tai's feelings made no difference to Judd. He had no intention of assimilating into the changeling world. But his niece and nephew, Marlee and Toby, also had to survive in the network of underground tunnels that was the SnowDancer den, and his enemies might become theirs. So he hadn't humiliated the boy by ending the fight before it began.

"Is he going to be alright?" Brenna asked when Tai moaned a second time.

"Give him a minute or two."

Glancing back at him, she sucked in a breath. "You're bleeding!"

He stepped away before she could touch his shredded

forearms. "It's nothing serious." And it wasn't. As a child he had been subjected to the most excruciating pain and then been taught to block it. A good Psy felt nothing. A good Arrow felt even less.

It made it so much easier to kill people.

"Tai went clawed." Brenna's face was furious as she glared down at the male slumped against the wall. "Wait till Hawke hears—"

"He won't hear. Because you won't tell him." Judd didn't need protecting. If Hawke had known what Judd truly was, what he had done, what he had *become*, the SnowDancer alpha would have taken him out at their first meeting. "Explain your comment about Sascha"

Brenna scowled but didn't press him about the scratches on his arm. "No more healing sessions. I'm done."

He knew how badly she'd been brutalized. "You have to continue."

"No." A short, sharp, and very final word. "I don't want anyone in my head again. *Ever.* Sascha can't get in anyway."

"That makes no sense." Sascha had the rare gift of being able to speak as easily to changeling minds as to Psy. "You don't have the capacity to block her."

"I do now—something's changed."

Tai coughed to full wakefulness and they both turned to watch him as he used the wall to drag himself upright. Blinking several times after getting vertical, he lifted a hand to touch his cheek. "Christ, my face feels like a truck ran into it."

Brenna's eyes narrowed. "What the hell did you think you were doing?"

"I—"

"Save it. Why did you come after Judd?"

"Brenna, this is none of your concern." Judd could feel blood drying on his skin, the cells already clotting. "Tai and I have come to an understanding." He looked the other male in the eye.

Tai's jaw set but he nodded. "We're square."

And their relative status in the pack's hierarchy had been clarified beyond any shadow of a doubt—if Judd's rank hadn't already been higher, he would now be dominant to the wolf.

Shoving a hand through his hair, Tai turned to Brenna. "Can I talk to you about—"

"No." She cut him off with a wave of her hand. "I don't want to go with you to your college dance. You're too young and too idiotic."

Tai swallowed. "How did you know what I was going to say?"

"Maybe I'm Psy." A dark answer. "That's the rumor going around, isn't it?"

Streaks of red appeared on Tai's cheekbones. "I told them they were talking shit."

This was the first that Judd had heard of the clearly malicious attempt to cause Brenna emotional pain, and it was the last thing he would have predicted. The wolves might make vicious enemies but they were also fiercely protective of their own, and had closed ranks around Brenna soon as she'd been rescued.

He looked at Tai. "I think you should go."

The young wolf didn't argue, sliding past them as quickly as his legs would carry him.

"Do you know what makes it worse?" Brenna's question shifted his attention from the boy's retreating footsteps.

"What?"

"It's true." She turned the full power of that shattered blue-brown gaze on him. "I'm different. I see things with these damn eyes he gave me. Terrible things."

"They're simply echoes of what happened to you." A powerful sociopath had ripped open her mind, raped her on the most intimate of levels. That the experience had left her with psychic scars was unsurprising.

"That's what Sascha said. But the deaths I see—"

A scream ripped the moment into two.

They were both running before it ended. A hundred feet down a second tunnel, they were joined by Indigo and a couple of others. As they turned a corner, Andrew came tearing around and clamped his hand on Brenna's upper arm, jerking his sister to a halt and raising his free hand at the same time. Everyone stopped.

"Indigo—there's a body." Andrew snapped out the words like bullets. "North East tunnel number six, alcove forty."

Brenna wrenched out of her brother's hold the second he finished and took off without any warning. Having caught the unhidden blaze of her anger before she'd quickly masked it, Judd was the first to move after her. Indigo and a furious Andrew followed at his back. Most Psy would have been overtaken by now but he was different, a difference that had predestined his life in the PsyNet.

Brenna was a streak in front of him, moving with impressive speed for someone who had been confined to a bed only months ago. She'd almost reached the number six tunnel when he caught up. "Stop," he ordered, his breath not as ragged as it should have been. "You don't need to see this."

"Yes, I do," said on a gasping breath.

Putting on a burst of speed, Andrew grabbed her from the back, linking his arms around her waist to lift her off her feet. "Bren, calm down."

Indigo raced past, a flash of long legs, dark hair streaming behind her.

In Andrew's grip, Brenna began to twist furiously enough to cause herself harm. Judd couldn't allow that "She'll calm down if you set her free."

Brenna jerked to a stop, chest heaving and eyes surprised. Andrew wasn't so silent. "I'll take care of my sister, *Psy*." The last word was a curse.

"What, by locking me up?" Brenna asked in a razor-sharp

tone. "I'm never going to be put in a box again, Drew, and I swear if you try, I'll claw my hands bloody getting out." It was a mercilessly graphic image, especially for anyone who had seen the condition she'd been in after they had first found her.

Behind her, Andrew paled, but his jaw remained set. "This is what's best for you."

"Perhaps it's not," Judd said, meeting Andrew's angry eyes without flinching. The SnowDancer soldier blamed all Psy for his sister's pain, and Judd could guess at the line of emotion-driven logic that had led him to that conclusion. But those same emotions also blinded him. "She can't spend the rest of her life in chains."

"What the fuck would you know about anything?" Andrew snarled. "You don't even care about your own!"

"He knows a hell of a lot more than you!"

"Bren." Andrew's voice was a warning.

"Shut up, Drew. I'm not a baby anymore." Her voice held echoes of darker things, of evil witnessed and innocence lost. "Did you ever stop to wonder what Judd did for me during the healing? Did you ever bother to find out what it cost him? No, of course not, because you know everything." She took a jerky breath. "Well, guess what, you know nothing! You haven't been where I've been. You haven't even been close. *Let. Me. Go.*" The words were no longer enraged but calm. Normal for a Psy. *Not* for a wolf changeling. Especially not for Brenna. Judd's senses went on high alert.

Andrew shook his head. "I don't care what the hell you say, little sister, you don't need to see that."

"Then I'm sorry, Drew." Brenna slashed her claws across his arms a split-second later, shocking her brother into letting her go. She was moving almost before her feet hit the ground.

"Jesus," Andrew whispered, staring after her. "I can't believe . . ." He looked down at his bloody forearms. "Brenna never hurts *anyone*."

"She's not the Brenna you know anymore," Judd told the other male. "What Enrique did to her altered her on a fundamental level, in ways she herself doesn't understand." He took off after Brenna before Andrew could reply—he had to be beside her to deflect the fallout from this death. What he couldn't understand was why she was so determined to see it.

He caught up with her as she raced past a startled guard and into the small room off tunnel number six. She came to such a sudden halt that he almost slammed into her. Following her gaze, he saw the sprawled body of an unknown SnowDancer male on the floor. The victim's face and naked body bore considerable bruising, the skin splotched different colors by the damage. But Judd knew that that wasn't what held Brenna frozen.

It was the cuts.

The changeling had been sliced very carefully with a knife, none of the cuts fatal but the last. That one had severed the carotid artery. Which meant there was something wrong with this scene. "Where's the blood?" he asked Indigo, who was crouching on the other side of the body, a couple of her soldiers beside her.

The lieutenant scowled at seeing Brenna in the room but answered. "It's not a fresh kill. He was dumped here."

"Out of the way room." One of the soldiers, a lanky male named Deiter, spoke up. "Easy to get to without being spotted if you know what you're doing."

Brenna sucked in a breath but didn't speak.

Indigo's scowl grew. "Get her the hell out of here."

Judd wasn't much good at following orders but he agreed with this one. "Let's go," he said to the woman standing just in front of him.

"I saw this." A faint whisper.

Indigo stood, an odd look on her face. "What?"

Brenna began to tremble. "I saw this." The same reedy whisper. "I saw this." Louder. "I saw this!" A scream.

Judd had spent enough time with her to know that she would hate having lost control in front of everyone. She was a very proud wolf. So he did the only thing he could to slice through her hysteria. He moved to block her view of the body and then he used her emotions against her. It was a weapon the Psy had honed to perfection. "You're making a fool of yourself."

The icy-cold words hit Brenna like a slap. *"Excuse me?"* She dropped the hand she'd raised to push him aside.

"Look behind you."

She remained stubbornly still. Hell would freeze over before she followed an order from him.

"Half the den is sniffing around," he told her. Pitiless. Psy. "Listening to you break down."

"I am not breaking down." She flushed at the realization of so many eyes on her. "Get out of my way." She didn't want to look at the body anymore—a body that had been mutilated with the same eerie precision Enrique had used on his victims—but pride wouldn't let her back down.

"You're being irrational." Judd didn't move. "This place is obviously having a negative impact on your emotional stability. Step back out." It was a definite order, his tone so close to alpha it set her teeth on edge.

"And if I don't?" She gladly embraced the anger he'd awakened—it gave her a new focus, a way to escape the nightmare memories triggered by this room.

Cool Psy eyes met hers, the male arrogance in them breathtaking. "Then I'll pick you up and move you myself."

At the response, exhilaration burst to life in her bloodstream, chasing away the last acrid tang of fear. Months of frustration, of watching her independence being buried under a wall of protection, of being told what was best for her, of having her rationality questioned at every turn, all that and more snowballed into this single instant. "Try it." A dare.

He stepped forward and her fingertips tingled, claws threatening to release. Oh yeah, she was definitely ready to tangle with Judd Lauren, man of ice and the most beautiful male creature she had ever seen.

Nalini Singh is passionate about writing. Though she's traveled as far afield as the deserts of China and the temples of Japan, it is the journey of the imagination that fascinates her the most. She's beyond delighted to be able to follow her dream as a writer.

Nalini lives and works in beautiful New Zealand. For contact details and to find out more about the Psy-Changeling series, please visit her website at www.nalinisingh.com.

Penguin Group (USA) Online

What will you be reading tomorrow?

Tom Clancy, Patricia Cornwell, W.E.B. Griffin,
Nora Roberts, William Gibson, Robin Cook,
Brian Jacques, Catherine Coulter, Stephen King,
Dean Koontz, Ken Follett, Clive Cussler,
Eric Jerome Dickey, John Sandford,
Terry McMillan, Sue Monk Kidd, Amy Tan,
John Berendt…

You'll find them all at
penguin.com

*Read excerpts and newsletters,
find tour schedules and reading group guides,
and enter contests.*

Subscribe to Penguin Group (USA) newsletters
and get an exclusive inside look
at exciting new titles and the authors you love
long before everyone else does.

PENGUIN GROUP (USA)
us.penguingroup.com

M224G1107